About

Cat Schield lives in M...
opiniated Burmese cat...
Winner of the Roma...
Golden Heart® for seri...
she's not writing sexy, romantic stories for Mills & Boon Desire, she can be found sailing with friends on the St. Croix River or in more exotic locales like the Caribbean and Europe. You can find out more about her books at www.catschield.net

Cathy Williams is a great believer in the power of perseverance as she had never written anything before her writing career, and from the starting point of zero has now fulfilled her ambition to pursue this most enjoyable of careers. She would encourage any would-be writer to have faith and go for it! She derives inspiration from the tropical island of Trinidad and from the peaceful countryside of middle England. Cathy lives in Warwickshire her family.

Caitlin Crews discovered her first romance novel at the age of twelve and has since began her life-long love affair with romance novels, many of which she insists on keeping near her at all times. She currently lives in California, with her animator/comic book artist husband and their menagerie of ridiculous animals.

Dangerous Liaisons

December 2020
Desire

January 2021
Propositions

February 2021
Seduction

March 2021
Innocence

April 2021
Passion

May 2021
Secrets

Dangerous Liaisons:
Desire

CAT SCHIELD
CATHY WILLIAMS
CAITLIN CREWS

MILLS & BOON

All rights reserved including the right of reproduction in whole or in part in any form. This edition is published by arrangement with Harlequin Books S.A.

This is a work of fiction. Names, characters, places, locations and incidents are purely fictional and bear no relationship to any real life individuals, living or dead, or to any actual places, business establishments, locations, events or incidents. Any resemblance is entirely coincidental.

This book is sold subject to the condition that it shall not, by way of trade or otherwise, be lent, resold, hired out or otherwise circulated without the prior consent of the publisher in any form of binding or cover other than that in which it is published and without a similar condition including this condition being imposed on the subsequent purchaser.

® and TM are trademarks owned and used by the trademark owner and/or its licensee. Trademarks marked with ® are registered with the United Kingdom Patent Office and/or the Office for Harmonisation in the Internal Market and in other countries.

First Published in Great Britain 2020
By Mills & Boon, an imprint of HarperCollins*Publishers*
1 London Bridge Street, London, SE1 9GF

DANGEROUS LIAISONS: DESIRE © 2020 Harlequin Books S.A.

Unfinished Business © 2012 Catherine Schield
His Temporary Mistress © 2014 Cathy Williams
Not Just the Boss's Plaything © 2013 Caitlin Crews

ISBN: 978-0-263-29882-6

MIX
Paper from
responsible sources
FSC C007454

This book is produced from independently certified FSC™ paper to ensure responsible forest management.

For more information visit: www.harpercollins.co.uk/green

Printed and bound in Spain
by CPI, Barcelona

UNFINISHED BUSINESS

CAT SCHIELD

For my parents. Your love and support have helped me follow my dreams.

One

"You." The word came out as an unfriendly accusation.
"Hello, Max."

Rachel Lansing had been bracing herself for this meeting all day, and now that it had arrived, it was so much worse than she'd imagined. Her heart stopped as the gunmetal gray of Max Case's gaze slammed into her with all the delicacy of a sledgehammer.

She dug her fingernails into her palm as his broad shoulders loomed closer, blocking her view of the tastefully decorated lobby with its soothing navy-and-olive walls and stunning original art.

Was it her imagination or did Max seem bigger, more commanding than the creative lover that haunted her memories? Or maybe his presence overwhelmed her because in a charcoal business suit and silver tie, he was less approachable than the naked fantasy man that frequented her dreams.

Only the public nature of this reunion enabled her to

subdue the flight impulse in her muscles. She rose from the comfortable couch in the reception area at a deliberate, unhurried pace. Keeping her body relaxed and her expression professional required a Herculean effort while her pulse jittered and her knees shook.

Pull yourself together. He won't appreciate you melting into a puddle at his feet.

"Thank you for seeing me." She stuck out her hand in a bid to restore her professional standing and wasn't disappointed when Max ignored it. Her sweaty palm would betray her nerves to him.

When he remained mute, Rachel plowed into the tense silence. "How great that Andrea had her baby. And two weeks early. Sabrina told me she had a boy. I brought her this." She raised her left hand to show him the pink and blue bag dangling from her fingers. She'd bought the gift for his assistant weeks ago and was disappointed she wouldn't get to see Andrea's expression when she opened it.

"What are you doing here?"

"I was supposed to meet with Andrea."

"You're with the employment agency?"

She whipped out a business card and extended it across the three feet that separated them. "I own it." She made no attempt to disguise her pride at what she'd accomplished.

He rubbed his thumb over the lettering on the business card before glancing down. "Rachel...Lansing?"

"My maiden name." She wasn't sure why she felt compelled to share this tidbit with him. It wasn't going to change how he felt about her now, was it?

"You're divorced?"

She nodded. "Four years."

"And now you run an employment agency here in Houston?"

She'd come a long way from the girl who was barely able

to support herself and her sister on the tips she made waitressing in a beach restaurant in Gulf Shores, Alabama. And yet, how far had she come when no matter how well her business did, she never felt financially secure?

"I like the freedom of running my own business," she said, pushing aside the worry that drove her day and night. "It's small, but growing."

And it would grow faster once she moved into larger offices and hired more staff. She had the space all picked out. A prime location that wouldn't have lasted on the market more than a few days. She'd signed the lease yesterday, gambling that the commission she'd get from placing a temporary assistant with Case Consolidated Holdings would give her the final amount she needed to move. Maybe then she could stop living day to day and start planning for the future. However, now that she'd run into Max, that fee seemed in jeopardy, and just to be safe, she'd better back out of the lease.

If only Devon had been able to come here in her stead. A skilled employment specialist, he was her right hand. Unfortunately, his mother had gone to the hospital yesterday with severe abdominal pain and had been rushed into surgery to remove her gall bladder. Rachel had told Devon to stay with his mother as long as she needed him. For Rachel, family always came first.

"How many assistants have you placed here?" Max's piercing stare didn't waver from her face as he slid her business card into his breast pocket. The effect of so much icy heat coming to bear on her was starting to unravel her composure.

"Five." She dropped her hand into her jacket pocket to keep from plucking at her collar, lapel or buttons and betraying her disquiet. "Missy was the first. Sebastian's assistant."

"That was your doing?"

Rachel blinked at the soft menace in his voice. Did Max have something against Missy? She'd been with Case Consolidated Holdings for four years and had worked out great. In fact, it was that placement that had jump-started her business.

"I heard she recently got promoted to communications director." And married Max's brother, Sebastian. Surely that proved how good Rachel was at her job.

"That means you've been in Houston four years?" The question rumbled out of Max like a guard-dog growl.

Anxiety spiked. "About that."

"Why here?"

When she'd left him in the Alabama beach town, he'd never wanted to see her again. Was he wondering if it was fate or determined stalking on her part that she'd shown up at Case Consolidated Holdings?

"I moved here because of my sister. She went to the University of Houston and has friends here. It made sense for us to settle in Houston after she graduated."

Inferring that Rachel hadn't had friends where she'd lived before. Curiosity fired in Max's eyes. The intensity of it seared her nerve endings. Five years had passed since she'd last seen him and her physical response to his proximity hadn't dimmed one bit.

"I have three clients in this building," she told him, her tone firming as she reclaimed her confidence. She'd been dealing with executives for over ten years and knew exactly how to handle them. "The fact that I've placed five assistants here and we've never run across each other should tell you that my interest in your company is purely professional."

He surveyed her like a cop in search of the truth. "Let's talk."

"I thought that's what we were doing." She bit the inside of her lip as the smart-ass remark popped out.

Once upon a time he'd liked her cheeky banter. She doubted he'd say the same thing today. Five years was a long time to stay mad at someone, but if anyone could manage, it would be Max Case.

"In my office."

Pivoting on his heel, he strode away from her down the hallway that led into the bowels of Case Consolidated Holdings. He didn't look back to see if she was following. He expected obedience. He'd always been bossy that way. Telling her where to put her hands, how to move her hips, the areas of his body that needed her attention.

Her skin flushed. Desire found a warm and welcoming home inside her. She couldn't move. What was she doing? Her memories of those four days with Max belonged in the tomb with all her girlish hopes and dreams. Her moratorium on men and sex remained in full force. Indulging in lusty thoughts of Max was the height of stupidity if she hoped to cultivate a professional relationship with him.

Max disappeared around a corner. This was her chance to run. She should make some excuse. Send Devon to do the interview tomorrow.

No. Rachel squared her shoulders. She could do this. She had to do this. Her future required this placement fee.

Five years ago, she'd learned a hard lesson about running from her problems. These days, she faced all difficulties head-on. Lansing Employment Agency needed this commission. She would do a fabulous job for Max, collect her money and treat herself to a bottle of champagne and a long bubble bath the day the agency moved into its bigger, better office. It all started with this meeting.

Rachel forced her feet to move. Step by step she gathered courage. For four years she'd been scraping and clawing her way upward. Convincing Max that Lansing was the agency for him was just one more hurdle, and by the time she reached the enormous office bearing Max's name, she had her chin set at a determined angle and her eyes focused on the prize.

"Did you get lost?" he asked as she crossed the threshold.

A long time ago.

"I stopped at Sabrina's desk and asked her to send the baby gift to Andrea."

Rachel glanced around Max's office, curious about the businessman. During their four days together, she'd learned about his family and his love of fast cars, but he'd refused to talk about work. In fact, until she'd met Sebastian four years ago, and noticed the family resemblance, she didn't know he was Max Case of Case Consolidated Holdings.

The walls bore photos of Max leaning against a series of racecars, helmet beneath his arm, a confident grin on his face. Her heart jumped in appreciation of how handsome he looked in his one-piece navy-and-gray racing suit, lean hips and broad shoulders emphasized by the stylish cut. A bookshelf held a few trophies, and books on muscle cars.

"You cut your hair." Max shut the door, blocking her escape.

She searched his expression, but he'd shut all emotion behind an impassive mask. His eyes were the blank stone walls of a fortress. Nevertheless, his personal comment aroused a tickle of awareness.

"Never liked it long." Her ex-husband had, however.

A softening of his lips looked suspiciously like the beginnings of a smile. Did he recognize her attempt to camouflage herself? Shapeless gray pantsuit, short hair, no jewelry of any kind, a sensible watch, flat shoes, minimal makeup. Dull as dirt to look at, but confident and authoritative about her business. She'd never been any man's fantasy. Too tall for most boys. Too flat-chested and skinny for the rest, the best she'd been able to hope for from her male classmates in high school was best friend or buddy. She'd grown up playing soccer, basketball and baseball with the guys.

Which is why it continued to blow her mind that a man

like Maxwell Case, who could have any woman he wanted, had wanted her once upon a time.

An enormous cherry desk dominated a position in front of the windows. The piece seemed too clunky for Max. Rachel pictured him behind an aerodynamic glass and chrome desk loaded down with the latest computer gadgets.

Instead of leading the way toward his desk, Max settled on the couch that occupied one wall of his office. With a flick of his hand, he indicated a flanking chair. Disliking the informality of the setting, Rachel perched on the very edge of the seat. Her briefcase on her lap acted as both a shield and a reminder that this was a business meeting.

"I need an executive assistant here first thing tomorrow."

Rachel hadn't been prepared for Andrea to have her baby two weeks early. She had no one available that was skilled enough to fill in starting in the morning. "I have the perfect person for you, but she can't start until Monday."

"That won't do."

With her commission slipping away, panic crept into her voice. "It's only two days. Surely you can make it without an assistant until Monday."

"With Andrea gone today, I'm already behind. We're up to our necks in next year's budgets. I need someone who can get up to speed swiftly. Someone with world-class organizational skills." His focus sharpened on her. "Someone like you. You're exactly what I need."

Her gut clenched at the flare of something white hot in his eyes.

A matching blaze roared to life inside her. Five years ago, that similar fire had charred her self-protective instincts and reduced her sensible nature to ash. She'd flung herself headlong into his arms without considering the repercussions.

The last time she'd lost herself that way, he'd ended up hating her. Meeting his gaze, she realized that his anger hadn't been blunted by the passing years. Time hadn't healed. It had honed his resentment into a razor-sharp tool for revenge.

Rachel braced herself against the earthquake of panic that threatened her peaceful little world and set her jaw. "You can't have me."

Her declaration hung in the air.
But he could have her...
As his assistant.
In any of the dozens of ways he'd had her before.
His choice. Not hers.
Energy zipped between them, fascinating and unsettling. The scent of her perfume aroused memories. Reminded him how sharp and sweet the desire was between them.

"Are you really ready to risk disappointing a client?"

"No." A rosy flush dusted her high cheekbones. Had she picked up on his thoughts? "But I can't abandon my business to be your assistant."

"Hire someone to fill in for you." He bared his teeth in an unfriendly grin. "Even you can see the irony in that."

For the last few minutes, cracks had been developing in her professionalism. "You're being unreasonable."

"Of course I am. I'll call someone else." The telltale widening of her eyes was gone so fast he nearly missed it. This is where he challenged her reputation for providing excellent customer service to test how badly she wanted his business. "I'm sure another agency would have what I need."

"Lansing Employment has what you need," she countered, the words muddy because she spoke through clenched teeth.

He held silent while she tried to stare him down. Every instinct told him to send her on her way as he would any other supplier who couldn't provide him with exactly what he wanted.

But they had unfinished business. At some point in the last five minutes he'd decided he needed closure. Four days with her hadn't been enough time for the passion to burn out. Much to his dismay, he still wanted her. But for how long was anyone's guess. From past experience he knew his interest rarely lasted more than two months.

And when he grew tired of her, he would end things on his terms. On his schedule.

"Fine." She glared at him. "I'll fill in for two days."

"Wonderful."

She stood, ready to stalk out of the office, but something held her in place. Her eyes were troubled as they settled on him. "Why are you doing this?"

"Doing what?"

"Demanding that I act as your assistant until I can find a replacement."

"You're here. It's expedient."

His current workload was crushing him. His managers had finalized their forecasts and forwarded next year's budget numbers a week ago. With the economy slow to recover, controlling spending and increasing sales was more important than ever. Case Consolidated Holdings owned over a dozen companies, each one with very different markets and operations. It was an organizational challenge to collect and analyze data from the various sources given that each entity operated in a completely unique environment with it's own set of parameters and strategic plans.

Andrea knew the businesses as well as he did. Losing her now threw off his entire schedule.

"Are you sure that's all it is?" Rachel demanded.

Max stopped worrying about deadlines and reminded himself that his desperate staffing situation was only half the reason he'd insisted Rachel fill in for a few days. "What else could it be?"

"Payback for how things ended between us?"

"It's business." That she was suspicious of his motives added spice to the game.

"So, you're not still angry?" she persisted.

Yes. He was still angry.

"After five years?" He shook his head.

"Are you sure?"

"Are you challenging whether or not I know my own mind?"

His irritation had little effect on her. "Five years ago, you made it very clear you never wanted to see me again."

"That's because you never told me you were married." He kept his tone smooth, but it wasn't enough to mask his dangerous mood. "Despite my telling you how I felt about infidelity. How it nearly destroyed my parents' marriage. You involved me in an extramarital affair without my knowledge."

"I'd left my husband."

He breathed deep to ease the sudden ache in his chest. "Yet when he showed up, you went back to him fast enough."

"Things were complicated."

"I didn't see complications. I saw lies."

"I was going through some tough times. Meeting you let me forget my troubles for a while."

"You used me."

She tipped her head and regarded him through her long lashes. "We used each other."

Max's gaze roamed over her. She wasn't the most beautiful woman he'd ever met. Her nose was too narrow. Her chin a bit too sharp. She hid her broad forehead with bangs. Boyishly slim, her body lacked the feminine curves he usually appreciated in a woman. But there was something lush about the fullness of her lips. And he'd adored nibbling his way down her long, graceful neck.

He wasn't surprised to be struck by a blast of lust so intense, it hurt. From the first, the chemistry between them had been hot and all consuming. The instant he recognized her in the lobby, he knew that hadn't changed.

For a second, doubts crept in. Would spending time with her open old wounds? The last time they'd parted, he'd been out of sorts for months. Of course, he'd been in a different place then. Full of optimism about love and marriage despite the painful lessons about infidelity he'd learned from his father's actions.

Thanks to Rachel, his heart was no longer open for business.

"What time should I be here tomorrow morning?"

"Eight."

She headed for the door and he let his gaze slide over her utilitarian gray suit. One word kept rolling over and over in his mind. Divorced.

Fair game.

She hesitated in the doorway, her back to him, face in profile. Her quiet, determined voice floated toward him over her shoulder. "Two days. No more."

Without a backward glance, she vanished from view. Sexy as hell. She'd always had an aura of the untouchable about her. As if no matter how many times he slid inside her, or how tight he wrapped her in his arms, she would never truly be his.

For a man accustomed to having any woman he wanted, that elusive quality intrigued him the way nothing else would have. He couldn't get enough of her. They'd been together for four days. He'd been insatiable. But no matter how much pleasure he gave her, no matter how many times she came apart in his arms, not once did he come close to capturing her soul.

It wasn't until she left him and went back to her husband that he'd understood why.

Her soul wasn't hers to give. It belonged to the man she'd pledged her life and love to.

Rage catapulted Max from his chair. He crossed to his door and slammed it shut, not caring what the office thought of his fit of temper. His hand shook as he braced it against the wall.

Damn her for showing up like this.

And damn the part of him that was delighted she had.

Two

Rachel hurried through the plate glass doors of Lansing Employment Agency and nodded to her receptionist as she passed. She didn't stop to chat as was her habit, but went straight to her office and collapsed into her chair. It wasn't until she'd deleted half her inbox that she realized she hadn't read any of the emails. Sagging forward, she rested her arms on the desk and her forehead on her arms. Reaction was setting in. She was frustratingly close to tears.

"That bad, huh?" a male voice asked from the hallway.

Rachel nodded without looking up. "It's worse than bad."

"Oh, you poor thing. Tell Devon all about it."

With a great effort, Rachel straightened and looked at the man who sat down across from her. In a stylish gray suit with lavender shirt and expensive purple tie, he dressed to be noticed. Only the dark circles beneath his eyes gave any hint of his sleepless night.

"How's your mother?"

"She's doing fine. My sister just arrived from Austin and is staying at the hospital with her." Devon leaned back in his chair and crossed one leg over the other. "How'd it go at Case Consolidated Holdings?"

"Worse than I'd hoped."

"Damn. They didn't hire us?"

"They hired us." Rachel's eyes burned dry and hot. As she blinked to restore moisture, it occurred to her that she'd cried a river of tears over Max five years ago. Maybe she'd used up her quota.

"Then what's the problem?"

"Max Case needs an assistant immediately."

"But we don't have anyone available."

Rachel grimaced. "That's why I'm filling in until we do."

"You?" The gap between Devon's front teeth flashed as a startled laugh escaped him.

No one knew what had happened between her and Max in Gulf Shores. She figured if she kept it to herself, no one could criticize her for running away from her farce of a marriage and jumping into bed with a virtual stranger, and those amazing four days could remain untarnished in her memory. But she'd been wrong to start something with Max before she'd legally ended her marriage. And she'd paid the price.

"I was the expedient choice." The word tasted bitter on her tongue. Why had it bothered her that she was merely a convenient business solution to Max? Had she really hoped he might still want her after she'd kept quiet about her marital status, and let him betray his vow never to get caught up in an affair?

Those days in Max's arms had been magical. She hadn't felt that safe since her father died. It was as if she and Max existed in a bubble of perfect happiness. Insulated from the world's harsh reality.

Heaven.

Until Brody showed up with his threats and dragged her back to Mississippi.

"I hope you told him no."

"Not exactly."

"Then what exactly?" Her second in command frowned as if just now grasping the situation.

"It's not like he left me any choice. I signed the lease for the new offices. We need this placement fee to move into them."

"You agreed?"

"He backed me against a wall." She leaned back in her chair, remembering too late that the ancient mechanism was broken. She threw her weight forward before the cursed thing tipped her ass over teakettle.

Devon oversaw her antics with troubled eyes. "I still don't understand why he wants you personally. There are a dozen agencies that he could call."

She hesitated. As much as she liked Devon, she wasn't comfortable talking about her past. Five years ago, she'd been a very different person. Explaining how she knew Max meant she had to own up to the mistakes she'd made. Mistakes that haunted her.

"Once upon a time we knew each other," she said.

"Knew..." Devon's focus sharpened. "As in business associates? Friends?" His eyes narrowed. "You dated?"

As much as she hated talking about her past screwups, she decided to put her cards on the table. She owed Devon the truth. He'd been with her since the beginning and had labored as hard as she had to grow the agency. In fact, she was planning on making him a partner when they moved into the new offices.

If they moved.

"Not dated, exactly." She played with her pen, spinning it in circles on her desk.

"You slept with him."

"Yes."

Rachel shifted her attention from the silver blur and caught Devon's stunned expression. He looked so thunderstruck she was torn between laughter and outrage.

"Don't look so surprised. I wasn't always the uptight businesswoman I am now. There was a time when I was young and romantic." And foolish.

"When?"

"A long weekend five years ago."

Devon's lips twitched.

"What?" she demanded.

"It's just that Max is well-known for the volume of women he dates. I'm a little surprised he remembered you."

"He probably wouldn't have," she muttered. The truth hit closer to her insecurities than she wanted to admit. The thought had often crossed her mind that she'd had a pretty brief interlude with Max. Since moving to Houston, she'd learned a lot about the man who'd swept her off her feet in a big way. She'd often wondered how she'd feel if she ran into him and he looked right through her without recognition. "Except he was pretty angry with me at the time."

"Why?"

"Because I didn't tell him I was married."

Now Devon really goggled at her. "We've worked together four years and this is the first I've heard about that."

Rachel rubbed her right thumb across the ring finger of her left hand. Even after four years, she recalled the touch of the gold band against her skin and remembered how wrong she'd been to ignore her instincts. She wouldn't make that mistake again.

"It's part of my past that I'd prefer not to talk about." And in five more years, she'd be completely free. At least financially. She'd live with the emotional scars for the rest of her life.

"Not even if I tell you I'll expire from curiosity if you don't dish?"

"Not even," Rachel said with a chuckle. She loved Devon's flare for the dramatic. Having him around was good for her. Kept her from taking herself, or her problems, too seriously. She'd done that all too often in the past and turned molehills into mountains.

"Do you think Max is trying to start up with you again?"

From one unwelcome topic to another. "Hardly."

"I don't know." Devon shot her an odd look, half surprised, half crafty. "Demanding you act as his assistant, even for a couple days, seems a little odd for a businessman with Max's no-nonsense reputation."

Rachel exhaled. "Well, there's not much I can do at the moment. He's set on having me there." She grimaced. "Besides, you'll do great without me. Lansing Employment Agency wouldn't be anywhere near profitable without all your hard work."

"Yes, yes, I'm wonderful but the success has been all yours. I've just been along for the ride."

And what a ride it had been. When she'd first started the agency, she'd been waitressing on the weekends to make rent and put food on the table.

Today, providing things went right with Case Consolidated Holdings, they'd be moving into larger downtown Houston offices. That's why she was willing to do whatever Max wanted of her to stay on his good side.

"I just hope you know what you're doing," Devon said, getting to his feet.

"I know exactly what I'm doing." Her stomach gave a funny little flip as she said the words. Rachel shoved the sensation away. She was a professional. She would not allow her emotions to get all tangled up in Max again. The first time had left her with a battered heart. Letting it happen again might lead to serious breakage.

"You're a first-rate bastard, you know that?"

Max Case looked away from the photo on his computer screen and smirked at his best friend. "I've been called that before."

It was late Friday morning. He'd spent the last day and a half alternating between admiration for Rachel's keen business mind and annoyance that he couldn't stop imagining her writhing beneath him on his couch.

"I've been after Sikes to sell me that car for five years," Jason Sinclair grumbled, his gaze riveted on the image of Max standing beside a yellow convertible. "And you just swoop in and steal it out from under me?"

"I didn't swoop, and I didn't steal. I offered the guy a good price. He went for it."

"How much?"

Max shook his head. He wasn't about to tell Jason the truth. In fact, he wasn't exactly sure what had prompted him to offer the sum. He only knew that Bob Sikes had driven the rare muscle car off the lot in 1971 and wasn't about to let it go without some major convincing. The Cuda 426 Hemi convertible was one of only seven made. At the time, convertibles were too expensive, too heavy and too slow to interest the true racing enthusiasts. Thus, with fewer produced, they'd become extremely rare.

And now, Max owned one of the rarest of the rare.

"Are you ready to get your ass kicked in tomorrow's race?" He meant for the question to distract his friend.

"You sound awfully confident for a man who lost last weekend." Jason continued to frown over the loss of the Cuda. "A win that put me ahead of you in points."

"For now."

Max and Jason had been racing competitively since they were old enough to drive. They were evenly matched in determination, skill, and financing, so on any given weekend, the win could go either way.

For the last two years, Max had beaten Jason in points over the course of the season. Like the street racers of old, Jason and Max competed for cars. The guy with fewer points at the end of the season forfeited his ride. But Max knew coming in second bothered his best friend more than the forfeit of his racecar two years straight.

Jason adopted a confident pose. "If you think you're going to have the most points again this year, you're wrong."

Before Max could answer, Rachel appeared in his office doorway. Despite her severe navy pantsuit and plain white blouse, his pulse behaved as if she wore a provocative cocktail dress and a come-hither smile.

"Excuse me, Max. I didn't realize you had company."

He waved Rachel in. "Did you get those numbers I needed?"

She took one step into the room and stopped. "I updated the report." She glanced in Jason's direction. "I also scheduled an interview for you at two this afternoon and emailed you the candidate's resume. Maureen has a background in finance and business analysis. I think you'll find she's a perfect fit."

"We'll see."

Her lips thinned. "Yes, you will."

Amusement rippled through him as she tossed her head and exited his office. Did she have any idea that annoyance gave her stride a sexy swing?

"Hell."

Max noticed Jason was also staring after Rachel. "What?"

"That was Rachel Lansing. What is she doing here?"

"Working as my assistant."

"Have you lost your mind?"

Probably. But Jason didn't know about his affair with Rachel. No one did. Those four days had been too short and too intense. The end too painful for him to share. And after badmouthing his father's infidelity for years, how could he admit to family and friends that he'd had an affair with a married woman and not be viewed as a hypocrite?

"What are you talking about?"

"Lansing is a matchmaker."

"A what?" Max searched his best friend's serious expression for some sign that Jason was joking around.

"Lansing Employment Agency is a matchmaking service."

"You're kidding, right?" He was deeply concerned that his friend might not be.

Jason glared at him. "Don't look at me like that. You have no idea what you're dealing with."

Rubbing his eyes, Max sighed. "Right now I'm dealing with a lunatic." Confusion and amusement jockeyed for dominance. He'd never seen his best friend exhibit such over-the-top behavior.

"It's not funny."

A gust of laughter escaped him. "Sit in my chair for a minute, and I think you'll see it's really funny."

"My dad used Lansing last year." Jason's eyebrows arched. "He married his executive assistant six months later."

"Your dad was a widower for fifteen years. I'm a little surprised he didn't remarry a lot sooner. Besides, Claire is a knockout."

"You're missing the point. They're all knockouts."

"So," Max drawled. "It's a conspiracy?"

"Yes." The thirty-two-year-old CFO stopped looking wild-eyed and his attention settled laser-sharp on Max. Jason's chest lifted as he pulled in an enormous breath. "You think I'm crazy?"

"Certifiable."

"I know of five other guys that have hired their assistants from Lansing and ended up marrying them. I know two more guys that met their future wives at work. Wives that got their jobs thanks to the Lansing Employment Agency. Including your brother." Jason's lips thinned. "Still think I'm nuts?"

"How did you find all this out?"

Jason shrugged. "Do you really need to ask? After Dad started looking all gooey-eyed at Claire, I did a little research on the agency."

"What did you find?"

"A spotless reputation. And one hell of a track record."

"For what?"

"For turning executive assistants into wives."

"Don't you think that eight marriages out of hundreds of placements is a little insignificant?"

"It's more worrisome when you take into consideration the ratio of single executives with single assistants to married executives with married assistants."

"You lost me."

"The bulk of the executives are already married, so when you look at the numbers in that way…"

"The ratio looks worse."

Jason flung his hands forward in a that's-what-I'm-talking-about gesture, before sinking back with a relieved smile. "Exactly."

Max was still having a hard time swallowing the notion of Rachel as a matchmaker. "Well, you don't need to worry about me. Where Cupid's arrows are concerned, I'm wearing Kevlar."

Jason pointed a finger at him. "You can't be sure of that."

"On the contrary, I'm very sure."

"I'm not really feeling convinced," the CFO said. "Maybe you'd care to make things more interesting."

Max buzzed with the same adrenaline that filled him at the start of every race. "What'd you have in mind?"

"Your '71 Cuda."

"Double my punishment, double your fun?" Max snorted. "I lose my freedom and the rarest car in my collection?" Suddenly, he wasn't feeling much like laughing. "What sort of best friend are you?"

"The kind that has your best interests at heart. I figure you might not fight to stay single for the sake of your sanity, but you'll do whatever it takes to keep that car."

Interesting logic. Max couldn't fault Jason's reasoning. "And what are you putting on the table in case you lose?"

Now it was Jason's turn to frown. "You want my '69 Corvette?" He shook his head. "I just got it."

And Max was looking forward to taking it away. "What are you worried about?"

"Fine. You've got a deal." Jason got to his feet and extended his hand across Max's wide cherry desk. When you've met the girl of your dreams and gotten married, I'm going to miss you, buddy. But at least I'll have the '71 Cuda to remember you by."

Rachel sat at her desk outside Max's office and tried to concentrate as her nerves sang a chorus of warnings. For the last two days, he'd been professional, making no further references to their past. But his gaze on her at odd moments held a particular intensity that promised he wasn't done with her. Not by a long shot.

Despite his assurances otherwise, she suspected that his motives for strong-arming her into becoming his temporary assistant were personal. She wouldn't put it past him to lure her into bed, enjoy his fill, and then walk away in the same fashion he believed she'd walked away from him. And that wasn't her paranoia talking. Max wasn't someone who forgave easily or at all in the case of his youngest brother, Nathan, and their father.

From what she'd gathered from her sources inside Case Consolidated Holdings, ever since Nathan had blown into town almost a year earlier, tension amongst the Case brothers had risen. She'd learned from Max five years ago that there was bad blood between the older Case brothers and their illegitimate brother that went way back. According to Andrea, however, things had recently gotten better between Sebastian and Nathan.

If Max couldn't let go of the past where his family was concerned, he would certainly never forgive a woman he barely knew.

Shoving personal concerns aside, Rachel concentrated on something she could control. Max had a trip scheduled next week. The hotel arrangements and flight had been made some time ago, but she needed to arrange for a rental car, to work on a PowerPoint presentation and fix a hundred problems that hadn't even come up yet.

The phone rang. Anxiety gripped her at the familiar number lighting up the screen. "Tell me everything's running smoothly," she said into the receiver.

"You sound edgy." Devon's amusement came through loud and clear. "Is Max on your case?"

While Devon laughed at his joke, Rachel signed on to the computer using Andrea's ID and password. At the moment, Max was interviewing a candidate for his temporary executive assistant. If all went well, Rachel wouldn't need to contact the IT department for her own computer access. She scanned the assistant's contacts, searching for the phone number of the restaurant downstairs. Apparently, Max had his lunches catered in most days. Andrea's contacts gave Rachel a pretty good sense of Max's activities.

Restaurants. Florists. Even a couple jewelry stores. He enjoyed entertaining women. Clicking one particular restaurant Rachel had been dying to try except that it was way beyond her means, she saw the manager's name, the particular table Max preferred, even the wine he enjoyed.

The man was a player. She hadn't seen that about him during those days on the beach, although she'd figured it out since coming to Houston. Max didn't know it, but she'd seen him in action during her early days in the big city.

Rachel stretched a barricade of caution tape around her heart. If Max wanted to start something with her with the express purpose of payback, she'd better be wary.

"...doing?"

Devon had been talking the whole time her mind had been wandering. Whoops.

"I'm sorry, Devon. I wasn't listening. What did you ask?"

"How is it going with Maureen?"

"She just went in ten minutes ago. Max kept her waiting for half an hour."

"I know that tone. Stop worrying. She's perfect. Max won't find anything wrong with her skills or her references."

"I hope not."

And she didn't have long to wait to find out. Five minutes after she'd hung up with Devon, Maureen exited Max's office. Unsure whether to be delighted or concerned at the shortness of the interview, Rachel stood as the assistant candidate headed her way.

"How'd it go?"

The beautiful redhead's mouth drooped. "He didn't seem to like me."

"Max is very hard to read. I'm sure he found your qualifications and your experience exactly what he requested."

Rachel kept her expression cheery. "I'll go have a chat with him now and give you a call later."

"Thanks."

As soon as Maureen disappeared around the corner, Rachel headed into Max's office. "Isn't Maureen great? She has a BA in business and five years of experience in a brokerage house. She's great with numbers—"

"Not a self-starter."

How had he come to that conclusion after a fifteen-minute interview? "That's not what I heard from her references."

"She's not going to work out. I need someone who takes initiative. Find me someone else."

Rachel hid her clenched hands behind her back and concentrated on keeping her shoulders relaxed and tension from her face as her mind worked furiously on an alternative candidate. "I'll set up someone for you to interview on Monday."

"Single?"

His question came out of left field and caught her completely off guard. "By law we don't discuss anyone's marital status."

"But they'd be wearing wedding rings. You'd know if they were single or married."

"I could guess..." She floundered. What did he want? Someone single he could hit on? That didn't seem right. Max might be a player, but he wouldn't be unprofessional at work. Seeing he awaited the answer to his earlier question, she heaved a sigh. "She's single. Does that matter?"

"Your agency has a certain reputation." He didn't make that sound like a compliment.

"For providing the best."

"For matchmaking."

Rachel wasn't sure if she'd heard him right. "Matchmaking? Are you out of your mind?" The words erupted before she considered how they might sound. Taking a calming breath, she moderated her tone. "I run an employment agency."

He nodded. "And how many of your clients have married the assistants you've sent them?"

What the hell sort of question was that? "I don't know."

"Eight, including Sebastian and Missy."

Rachel didn't know what to make of his accusation. Is that why he sounded so annoyed earlier? He thought... She didn't quite know what he thought. A matchmaking service? Was he insane?

"Don't look so surprised," he muttered.

"But I am. How did you know that?"

"A friend of mine has done a fair amount of research on your little enterprise." He sneered the last word, leaving no doubt about his opinion of her or her company.

Rachel inched forward on the sofa as she wavered between staying and disputing his claims and walking out the door. Fortunately, her business sense kicked in and kept her from acting impulsively.

"I assure you I'm not in the business of matchmaking." She straightened her spine and leveled a hard look at him. "My agency is strictly professional. If my ability to find the perfect match between executive and assistant means that they're compatible in other ways, then that's coincidence." Serendipity. She grimaced. If word got out that something unprofessional was happening between her clients and her employees, she was finished. "If you're worried about finding yourself in a similar predicament, I'll only send you married assistants."

She recognized her mistake the second the words were out of her mouth. Annoyance tightened his lips and hardened his eyes to tempered steel.

Once upon a time she'd been married, and he'd fallen for her. Well, maybe fallen for her was pushing it a little. They'd enjoyed a spectacular four days together and he'd been interested in pursuing her beyond the weekend.

"Or really old and ugly assistants," she finished lamely.

One eyebrow twitched upward to meet the lock of wavy brown hair that had fallen onto his forehead.

Rachel's professionalism came close to crumpling beneath the weight of his enormous sex appeal. Fortunately, the grim set of his mouth reminded her that they hadn't parted on the best of terms. He wouldn't appreciate the feminine sigh bottled up in her chest.

"I'll arrange some candidates for you to interview on Monday," she said, her heart sinking as she realized she was now stuck acting as Max's assistant for the indefinite future.

Three

Monday came and went and Max was no closer to liking any of the candidates she'd arranged for him to interview. By the time Rachel pulled into her driveway at six-thirty, she was half-starved and looking forward to her sister's famous chili. It was Hailey's night to cook, thank heavens, or they'd be eating around midnight.

She entered the house through the kitchen door and sniffed the air in search of the spicy odors that signaled Rachel was going to need three glasses of milk to get through the meal. No pot bubbled on the stove. No jalapeño cornbread cooled on a rack. Rachel's stomach growled in disappointment. No pile of dirty dishes awaited her attention in the sink. Why hadn't Hailey started dinner?

"I'm home," she called, stripping off her suit coat and setting her briefcase just inside the door. "I'm sorry I'm late. The new boss is a workaholic. Did you…"

Her question trailed away as she entered her small living

room and spied her sister's tense expression. Hailey perched on the edge of their dad's old recliner, her palms together and tucked between her knees. The chair was the only piece of furniture they'd kept after he died. That and the family's single photo album were all the Lansing girls had left of their dad.

Hailey's gaze darted Rachel's way as she paused just inside the room. Rachel's stomach gave a sickening wrench at the misery her sister couldn't hide. Only one person in the world produced the particular combination of alarm and disgust pinching Hailey's lips together.

Rachel turned her attention from her sister's stricken gaze to the tall man who dominated her couch. He'd grown fleshy in the four years since she'd last seen him, his boyish good looks warped by overindulgence and the belief that the world owed him something. He still dressed like the son of a wealthy and powerful business owner. Charcoal slacks, a white polo, blue sweater draped over his shoulders. He looked harmless until you got close enough to see the malicious glee in his eye.

"What are you doing here?"

He smiled without warmth. "Is that any way to greet the man you swore to honor and cherish until death you do part?" His gaze slid over her without appreciation. He ran an index finger across his left eyebrow. "You look good enough to eat."

Devour, more like. And not in a pleasant way. Brody Winslow enjoyed sucking people in with his smooth talk and clever charades, and using them up. Once upon a time, that had been her. She'd been taken in by the expensive car he drove and big house he lived in. Not until it was too late did she realize that some of the best liars came from money.

"What are you doing here?"

"I came to collect the money you owe me."

"You've been paid what I owe you this year. Nothing's due for another nine months."

"See, that's where we've got a little bit of a problem. I need the fifty grand now."

"Fifty…" She crossed her arms over her chest so he wouldn't notice the way her hands shook. "I can't pay you the full amount now."

He looked around her house. "Seems like you're doing pretty well."

"I bought the house through a special program that allowed me to put zero money down. I've barely got five percent equity and no bank is going to give me a second mortgage for that. You're just going to have to wait. I'll get the next installment to you in nine months."

"That's not working for me." He pushed himself off the couch and headed toward her.

She flinched as he brushed past her on his way to the window that overlooked her driveway.

"Nice car. It's got to be worth something."

"It's leased."

He shot her a look over his shoulder. "What about that business of yours?"

She bit her tongue rather than fire off a sharp retort. Making him mad wasn't going to get him out of her house or her life. The man was a bully, plain and simple. And he'd figured out where she lived and what she was doing for a living.

"The business is barely breaking even." A deliberate lie, but it wasn't as if her simple lifestyle betrayed the nest egg she'd been building. For so much of her adult life, she'd been on the edge of financial disaster. Having a bank balance of several thousand dollars gave her peace, and she'd fight hard not to give that up.

"I get it. Times are tough for you. But I need that money.

You're going to have to figure out how to get it for me or times are going to get even tougher for you and your pretty baby sister." He patted her cheek and she flinched a second time. "You hear what I'm saying?"

"I hear."

"And?"

"I'll get you what I can." As difficult as it would be to give up her financial cushion and postpone moving Lansing Employment Agency into a bigger, fancier office, she'd make the sacrifice if it meant keeping Brody out of her and Hailey's life. "Now, get out."

Brody laughed and headed for the front door.

Rachel followed him across the room and slid the deadbolt home before his tasseled loafers reached her front walk. She didn't realize how loud her heart thundered in her ears until Hailey spoke. She had trouble hearing her sister's apology.

"He must have followed me home from work," she said. "I'm so sorry."

"It's not your fault. We weren't going to hide from him forever."

"We've managed for four years."

"Only because he never came looking." Rachel sat down on the recliner's arm and hugged her sister. Hailey was shaking. Her confident, bright sister had been alone with Brody and afraid. "Why did you open the door to him?"

"He followed me into the house when I came home from work. I didn't realize he was there until he shoved me inside."

Rachel rested her cheek on her sister's head. "I'm sorry I didn't get home sooner."

Hailey shrugged her off. "Why do you owe him fifty thousand dollars?"

"I borrowed some money to start up the employment agency." It was a lie, but Rachel didn't want her sister to worry. The burden was hers and hers alone.

"Why would you do that?" Hailey demanded. "You know how he is."

Rachel shrugged. "No bank is going to lend a high school graduate with big ideas and a sketchy business plan the sort of money I needed. Besides, he owed me something for the five years I put up with him." She tried to reassure her sister with a smile, but Hailey had regained her spunk now that Brody was gone.

"Those years were worth a lot more than fifty thousand." Hailey levered herself out of the chair and whirled to confront Rachel. Her brows launched themselves at each other. "What are we going to do? How are we going to come up with the fifty grand?" Hailey's pitch rose as her anxiety escalated.

Rachel stood and took her sister's cold hands to rub warmth back into them. "There is no we, Hales. It was my decision to borrow the money and it's my debt to repay."

"But—"

"No." Rachel gave her head an emphatic shake and stood. She could out-stubborn her sister any day. "You are not going to worry about this."

"You never let me worry about anything," Hailey complained. "Not how we were going to get by after Aunt Jesse took off, not paying for college, not anything."

"I'm your big sister. It's my job to take care of you."

"I'm twenty-six years old," Hailey asserted, her tone aggrieved. "I don't need you to take care of me anymore. Why won't you let me help?"

"You already helped. You graduated from college with straight As and got a fabulous job at one of Houston's top CPA firms. You pay for half the groceries, do almost all the cooking and even your own laundry." Rachel grinned to hide the way her mind was already furiously working on a solution to the Brody problem. "I couldn't ask for more. Besides, once I pay Brody the money, he'll be out of our lives once and for all."

"But how are you going to come up with the money?"

"I'll try to get a bank loan. They might not have been willing to loan me money four years ago when I was starting up, but Lansing Employment Agency has a profitable track record now."

Perched on a guest chair in the loan officer's small cubicle, Rachel knew from the expression on the man's face what was coming.

"Economic times have hit us hard, Ms. Lansing." For the last four days she'd been listening to similar rhetoric, a broken record of no's. "Our small business lending is down to nothing. I wish I had better news for you."

"Thank you, anyway." She forced a smile and stood. A quick glance at her watch told her she'd run over her allotted hour lunch break.

This morning she'd wired her twenty-five thousand dollar nest egg to her lawyer with instructions to give the money to Brody. For the last five years, she'd been paying him ten thousand a year, double what she'd agreed to in their divorce settlement. Reimbursement for a debt she didn't owe. Punishment for divorcing him. No, Rachel amended, punishment for marrying him in the first place.

Returning to the Case Consolidated Holding offices, she slid into her desk and shoved her purse into a bottom drawer a second before Max's scowl peered at her from his office.

"You're late."

Rachel sighed. "Sorry. It won't happen again. Did you need something?"

"I need you to be at your desk for eight hours."

She tried again. "Something specific?"

"Get Chuck Weaver on the phone. Tell him I needed his numbers three hours ago."

"Right away."

As she was dialing, her cell started to ring. Since Chuck wasn't answering, she hung up without leaving a voice mail and answered her mobile phone.

Brody's voice rasped in her ear. "Did you get the money?"

"I wired twenty-five thousand to my lawyer this morning."

"I said fifty."

Demanding bastard. "It's all I could get." She kept her voice low to keep from being overheard. "You'll just have to be happy with that."

"Happy?" He chuckled, the sound low and forced. "You don't seem to get it. I need the whole fifty thousand now."

"I get it," she said. "You've been on a losing streak."

She hadn't known about his gambling until the second year of their marriage. A shouting match between him and his father clued her in to his destination when he vanished on the weekends. Frankly, she'd been disappointed. She'd thought he was having an affair. Had hoped he'd fallen in love with someone else and would ask for a divorce.

"That's none of your business."

"You need to get some help."

"You need to get me the rest of my money." He disconnected the call.

Rachel blew out a breath and pushed back from her desk. She had to clear her head. It wasn't until she stood up that she realized someone watched her. Max wore an inscrutable expression, but his shoulders bunched, tension riding him hard. He had the sexy overworked COO look going today. Coat off, shirt sleeves rolled up and baring muscled forearms. She stared at his gold watch to keep her gaze from wandering to his strong hands, and her mind from venturing into the memory of how gently he'd caressed her skin.

"Chuck Weaver wasn't in his office," she said, burying her shaking hands in her pockets. "I'm going to run to the ladies room. I'll have him paged when I get back."

Max shut off her torrent of words with a hard look. "Come into my office. We need to talk."

At his command, Rachel froze like an inexperienced driver facing her first spinout.

"Just give me a second," she protested, her eyes shifting away from him as if looking for an escape.

"Now." Max strode into his office and waited until she entered before he shut the door, blocking them from prying eyes. "Who was that on the phone?"

"No one."

"It sure sounds as if you owe no one a great deal of money." Her evasion irritated him.

He didn't want to care if she was in trouble, but couldn't ignore the alarm bells that sounded while he listened to her side of the phone call. With ruthless determination, he shoved worry aside and focused on his annoyance. The fact that she was in a bad spot wasn't his concern. Her ongoing distraction from her job was.

"You had no right to eavesdrop on my private conversation," she returned, belligerent where a moment earlier, she'd been desperate and scared.

He anchored one hand on the wood door to keep from launching across the room and shaking her until her teeth rattled. "You seem to forget whose name is on the door."

Her stubborn little chin rose, but she wouldn't make eye contact.

"It's none of your concern."

That was the wrong thing for her to say. "When they're calling here it becomes my concern."

Her defiance and his determination stood toe to toe, neither giving ground.

She broke first. Her gaze fell to his wingtips. "It won't happen again."

"Can you guarantee that?"

With her hands clenched to white-knuckle tightness at her side, she pressed her lips into a thin rosy line. Her nonanswer said more than words.

Frustration locked his vocal cords, making speech impossible. He sucked in a calming breath, keenly aware he was venturing into something that was none of his business. If he had an ounce of sense, he'd back off and let her deal with whatever mess she'd stepped in. Unfortunately for him, below his irritation buzzed a hornet of disquiet. He ducked the pesky emotion the way he'd dodge the stinging insect, but it darted around with relentless persistence.

"Do you need help?" He wrenched the offer free of his better judgment. The ramifications of involving himself in her troubles were bound to bite him in the…

"No." Her clipped response matched his offer in civility and warmth.

They glared at each other. Two mules with their heels dug in.

He should be glad she'd turned him down. Instead, her refusal made him all the more determined to interfere.

"Stop being so stubborn. Let me help you. How much do you owe?"

Her eyes never wavered from his, but she blinked twice in rapid succession. "I don't need your help."

"But I need things to run smoothly. I can't afford for you to be distracted by money problems. I assume that's what you've been dealing with on your extended lunch breaks."

"I've got everything under control."

"That's not the way it sounded just now." Max shoved

away from the door and stalked in her direction. He had no idea what he planned to do when he reached her. Something idiotic, no doubt, like take her in his arms and kiss her senseless.

The scent of her filled his nostrils. Some sort of nonfloral fragrance that made him think of clean sheets bleached by the sun. He was assailed by the image of her remaking the bed in their beach bungalow after their frantic lovemaking had ripped the sheets from the mattress.

His irritation faded. "You sounded upset."

Her eyes widened at whatever note of concern she heard in his voice. "I'm not going to let you help me."

Damned stubborn fool.

He caught her arm and pulled her across the gap between them. She came without resistance, her lips softening and parting as a rush of air escaped her. He wanted to sample those lips. Were they as pliant and intoxicating as ever?

"How are you going to stop me?" he demanded, cupping the back of her head to hold her still.

He dropped his head and claimed her mouth, swallowing her tart answer. He expected resistance. They'd been dancing around this moment for almost a week. The shoving match of his will against hers had inflamed his appetite for a similar battle between the sheets.

She moaned.

Her immediate surrender caught him off guard. It took him a second to change tactics, to stop taking and coax her instead to open to his questing kiss. She tasted like fruit punch, but went to his head like a Caribbean rum cocktail.

Long fingers darted into his hair. Her muscles softened. The flow of her lean lines against his frame was like waves on a beach, soothing, endlessly fascinating. With his eyes closed, the surf roaring in his ears, he remembered how it felt to hold her in his arms.

In a flash, all the memories of her that he'd locked away came back. Every instant of their time together played through his mind. His heart soared as he remembered not just the incredible sex, but the soul-baring connection they'd shared.

Then came her leaving. The ache that consumed him. His destructive anger.

Max broke off the kiss. Chest heaving, he surveyed the passion-dazed look in her azure eyes. Her high color. The flare of her nostrils as she scooped air into her lungs. He felt similarly depleted of oxygen. Surely that was the reason for his lightheadedness.

"That was a mistake," he said, unable to let her go.

Rachel took matters into her own hands. She shifted her spine straight and pushed on his chest. His fingers ached as she slipped free.

"That's supposed to be my line," she said, tugging her jacket back into order.

He inclined his head. "Be my guest."

Max retreated to the couch. Resettling his tie into a precise line down the front of his shirt, he laid his arm over the back of the couch and watched Rachel battle back from desire. She recovered faster than he'd hoped.

"That was a mistake." Crossing her arms over her chest, she leveled a narrow look his way. "One that won't be repeated."

"You misunderstand me," he said. "The mistake I referred to was letting the kiss happen here."

"What do you mean here? There's no place else it's going to happen."

He hit her with an are-you-kidding expression. "You're crazy if you think this thing between us is going to die out on its own."

"It will if you stop fanning the flames."

He had to fight from smiling at her exasperated tone. "Impossible. You set me on fire every time I get within twenty feet of you."

"I'm flattered."

Was she really? Her tight lips told a different story. "Don't be. I'm sure I get to you the same way." He plowed on, not giving her time to voice the protests bubbling in her eyes. "It's just a chemical reaction between us. Something ageless and undeniable. We can burn it out, but I don't see it just fizzling out."

"I really don't have the energy for this," she groused.

"Good. Stop fighting me and conserve your energy. I have a much better use for it."

Her arms fell to her sides. "Max, please be reasonable."

She'd stooped to pleading. He had her now.

"When have you ever known me to be reasonable?"

That wrung a grimace out of her. "Good point." She inhaled slow and deep; by the time the breath left her body, she'd changed tactics. "What'd you have in mind?" she questioned, retreating into humor. "A quickie in the copy room?" Pulling out her smart phone, she plied it like a true techno geek. "My schedule clears a bit at three. I can give you twenty minutes."

Max cursed. He should have anticipated she'd use humor to avoid a serious conversation. "I'll need more than twenty minutes for what I have in mind."

"You want more than twenty minutes," she corrected him, letting her thick southern accent slide all over the words. "You probably don't need more than…" She paused and peered at him from beneath her lashes. "Ten?"

Max rose from the couch and prowled her way. She turned her back as he stepped into her space. He loomed over her in order to peer at her phone's screen. So, she wanted to mess with him. Two could play at this game. A minute quiver betrayed her reaction to his proximity. Tension drained from his body. The chemistry between them was textbook and undeniable. His palms itched to measure her waist, reacquaint themselves with her breasts.

"I wasn't so much thinking of my needs as yours," he said, his voice low and intimate. "I know how much you like it when I take my time."

She sized him up with a sideways glance. "I thought this was the sort of thing you were trying to avoid doing with your assistant."

Max shook his head. "I was trying to avoid losing my freedom in one of your matchmaking schemes."

"You were trying to avoid marriage?" She slipped the phone back into its cradle at her waist. "Or falling in love?"

"Both."

"Because they don't always go hand in hand, you know."

"I'm all too familiar with that truth."

As she well knew. The four days they'd spent together hadn't been limited to learning about each other physically. Max had shared his soul, as well. Whether because they'd been two strangers sharing a moment with no thought of a future, or because being with her had thawed places long numb, he'd told her everything about his childhood and the problems with his family, delving into emotions he had no idea lurked beneath his skin.

She'd been a damn good listener. Made it easy to be vulnerable. He'd felt safe with her. And she'd left him. Gone back to her husband.

What an idiot he'd been.

"I'll go get Chuck Weaver on the phone," she said, retreating from his office.

It wasn't until he sat behind his desk and answered the call she put through that he realized she'd completely distracted him from getting answers about what sort of financial mess she was in.

Four

By six o'clock, the offices and cubicles around Rachel were dead quiet. Executing a slow head roll to loosen her shoulder muscles, she gusted out a sigh and saved the spreadsheet she'd been working on for the last couple of hours. Max had asked her to analyze the operations budget for one of the companies Case Consolidated Holdings owned in Pensacola, Florida. The company had been struggling with profitability for the last five years, and Max wanted her to figure out where they could trim expenses.

Whether Max knew it or not, she was the perfect person to figure out how to cut the fat. Ever since she'd lost her father and taken on the responsibility of her sixteen-year-old sister, money had been tight. She'd learned how not just to pinch a penny, but to turn it inside out and scrape every last bit of value out of the thing.

She cast a glance toward Max's office. Should she sneak out or say good-night? The kiss earlier had rattled her more than anything else she'd experienced in the last seven days and with Brody's unexpected reappearance and outrageous demand, it had been a doozy of a week.

As if summoned by her thoughts, Max appeared in the doorway.

"Leaving?" His low question boomed into the silence.

"It's six o'clock. We're the only ones here." She gulped as her words registered.

Pointing out to him that they were completely alone was probably not the brightest move after what happened between them today. The discovery that he intended to rekindle their affair made maintaining her cool a big challenge. If he'd decided this would be the perfect time to assault her willpower, it wouldn't be much of a skirmish.

That he still wanted her both worried and excited her. The heat between them remained as fierce as ever, and as much as he seemed to despise her for not being truthful five years ago, he was right when he said the passion between them hadn't been allowed to run its course back then.

Their four days together had been like an appetizer. One of those fancy ones that awakened the palate, but when you finish sampling, you're still hungry.

How long would the main course last?

A month?

Two?

Max leaned his shoulder against the door frame and regarded her through narrowed eyes. "I thought maybe we could have dinner and discuss your problem."

Translation, he wanted to probe her for more information about the phone call with Brody he'd eavesdropped on.

"You're the only problem I have," she muttered.

"I sincerely doubt that."

Rachel decided to let his remark pass unchallenged. "I can't have dinner with you. I have plans."

"A date?" His smooth tone gave away nothing, but his gaze gained an edge as he awaited her answer.

"Dinner with my sister." Why Rachel felt compelled to assure him she wasn't seeing anyone, she had no idea. Max wouldn't care if she was involved with someone. As long as she wasn't married, in his mind she was fair game. "She does all the cooking at home so I take her out once a week as a treat."

"I seem to recall she was in college when we first met. Did she graduate?"

"Right on schedule." Pride coated Rachel's voice. She might have done a lot of things wrong in her life, but somehow none of it had tainted Hailey. She'd turned out just fine. "She works for a CPA firm not far from here. Between work and her boyfriend, she's pretty busy, but we always make time one night a week."

An invitation to join them tickled the end of her tongue. Hailey would love to meet Max. Her sister fussed over Rachel's lack of a social life as if it was the worst thing in the world and would be giddy to know she'd spent four days in Gulf Shores, Alabama, having the most amazing sex of her life with a hottie like Max Case.

"I'll bet she's not as busy as you."

Was that a note of admiration in his voice? Rachel gripped her purse strap and fought the impulse to cross the five feet of space that separated them and smash her body against his. A throb of need pounded through her. Longing tightened her chest. Her breath grew shallow. If she met his gaze would she risk standing up Hailey for the first time ever?

His next words answered her question.

"Have a nice evening."

With her emotions a muddle of disappointment and relief, Rachel stood by her desk and watched him disappear into his office. Breathing became easier with him gone. Rachel muttered a curse.

She was way too infatuated with Max's tall, solid frame, smoky gray eyes and devilish smile for her own good. But as compelling as his sexy looks were, she could guard her heart against his outward charms. Her marriage to Brody had taught her that beauty was only skin deep.

A strong work ethic was another matter. His dedication to Case Consolidated Holdings touched a chord in her. A workaholic herself, she understood the need to put in long hours. It made her like him.

Which led her into dangerous waters.

This was bad. She'd been working for Max less than a week and almost every hour she caught herself featuring him in her daydreams. Pressure built beneath her skin every time they occupied the same space. How long could she hope to resist the hunger for his touch? Or should she?

That she'd asked the last question told Rachel it was only a matter of time before she wound up back in Max's bed.

She had to pass his open office door on her way to the lobby. Naturally she looked in as she went by. The image of him rubbing the back of his neck as exhaustion swept his features tugged at her, but she kept walking.

Nearing the elevator, she savagely shoved her thumb against the button with the down arrow. Damn him for getting under her skin. So what if he'd looked tired? So what if he'd been working late every night this week?

She cursed the urge to march back to his office and bully him into knocking off for the day even as she retraced her steps, poked her head into his office and asked, "Do you want to join us for dinner?"

Max looked up in surprise. For a split second, a smile tugged at his lips. "I don't want to intrude." But he was already getting to his feet.

"I'm sure Hailey won't mind." Her pulse accelerated as he advanced across the room. His gaze bored into her, and Rachel fought to subdue her body's reaction to the questions lurking in his gray eyes. "Aren't you going to grab your coat and briefcase?"

"I need to come back and finish up some things later."

A man after her own heart. "Okay."

With an entire elevator to themselves, he chose to set his back against the wall beside her. His shoulder grazed hers. The urge to lean against him swelled in her. How was it that four short days with him had left such an imprint on her body and soul? She knew without hesitation that they could tumble back into bed and pick up where they'd left off without a trace of awkwardness. The kiss this afternoon had proven that. He knew exactly how she liked to be touched. Remembered the precise spot on her back that made her knees turn to jelly.

"I've got a business trip to Pensacola scheduled Friday," he said, his brisk tone banishing her evocative musings. "I'd like you to come along."

Warning bells clanged. She cleared her throat. "Did Andrea accompany you on trips?"

"Rarely."

"Then you don't really need me, do you?" But she wanted to go. Wanted an excuse to spend more time alone with him. She knew the risks, but the thrill of being in his arms overrode prudence.

"On the contrary. You have a reputation for being able to read people. Isn't that how you make your perfect matches?"

Refusing to defend herself against his mockery, she watched the numbers light up above the door and wondered if she could get the elevator to descend faster by willpower alone.

"I could really use your opinion," he coaxed, altering his approach.

Rachel's defenses dropped at his softer tone. A quick check told her he was completely in earnest. Against her better judgment, she let herself feel flattered that he took what she did seriously. Very seriously, in fact.

"I'm really not sure I can be much help," she said as the elevator door opened.

"Let me be the judge of that."

Grimacing her acceptance, she stepped into the lobby. Max joined her after a slight hesitation. "We're walking?"

She pointed straight ahead. "The pub is a couple blocks that way. The fresh air will do you good."

"Fresh air?" he echoed doubtfully.

The hot July sun no longer baked the downtown Houston sidewalks, but heat continued to linger even in the shadows cast by the towering buildings. Rachel and Max strolled in silence toward their destination three blocks away—an Irish pub with great food and a relaxed atmosphere.

As they neared the pub, laughter and loud conversation reached them. Despite the day's humidity, the bar's outdoor seating was packed with business people enjoying happy hour after a long day. Max glanced at the windows, hung with neon signs advertising Guinness and Harp, and then the oval sign dangling over the front door.

"I've never been here before."

"Why am I not surprised?"

Max hit her with a hard look. "What's that supposed to mean?"

"It doesn't really seem like your kind of place. And why would you come all the way down here when you've got Frey's in the lobby of your building. That's more your style."

"And what do you think my style is?"

Snooty. Overpriced. Pretentious. "Sophisticated."

He actually laughed. A surprised chuckle that transformed his features into blinding handsomeness. White teeth flashed.

His gray eyes sparkled like sunshine on water. And his lips... those gorgeous lips relaxed into glorious, kissable curves.

Rachel almost groaned her appreciation.

"Did you forget the bar where we met? It was pretty low key." He got a faraway look as if his thoughts went backward to that moment five years earlier when they had locked gazes across a crowded bar.

Just like in the movies. Rachel remembered that first jolt of awareness from twenty feet away. Of course, it had been nothing compared to the sizzle when he'd come over and leaned close to tell her his name. Goose bumps broke out at the memory. Two hours later they'd been in his hotel room ripping each other's clothes off. She'd never experienced a moment that intense or right with anyone else.

"The food is great here," she said. "The pints are cold. What more do you need?"

Max opened the heavy wood door for Rachel. As she passed, he asked, "Does your sister know about us?"

Us?

Rachel's heart stopped at Max's use of the pronoun.

Inside the pub's front door was a small foyer that led to a second set of doors. The space kept the sultry outside from infiltrating the air-conditioned inside. Rachel paused between the doors and took advantage of the quiet to answer Max.

"Are you asking does she know that I had a four-day affair with you that ended badly and that you've bullied me into working as your assistant?"

"Yes."

"No."

"Hmmm." Max reached past her for the inside door handle. His body bumped against hers and started a waterfall of sparks running down her spine.

"What does that mean?" She stopped and half turned to confront him.

"It means you keep a lot of stuff to yourself."

She knew he referred to the fact that she hadn't mentioned her marital status to him five years ago. Despite knowing he had a right to be furious about that, his censure stung. "And what's wrong with that?"

"People get hurt."

People or him?

Don't be silly. They'd known each other four days. Not long enough to develop deep feelings. It had been abundant chemistry that had made those four days sizzle. Sure, there'd been some sort of connection above and beyond the physical, but no one fell in love in four days.

"If I don't share everything that's only because I'm doing what I think is best." And she'd kept some whoppers from Hailey. Stuff that if it came out, her sister would be upset. Rachel didn't like keeping Hailey in the dark. She did it to protect her.

"Best for whom?"

Before Rachel could answer, the door behind them opened and three guys in their mid-twenties appeared in the doorway, their good cheer shattering the tension in the small space and forcing Rachel and Max to move forward.

She stepped into the crowded bar, conscious of Max pressed against her back. Happy hour was in full swing. The sounds of merrymaking bounced off the pale brick walls and dark paneling. The space was illuminated by etched glass chandeliers and lighted beer signs. The bartender waved hello as Rachel made her way past the bar in search of her sister. Hailey worked in the building so she was always first to arrive and secure a table. Rachel found her staking out a booth in the back corner. The noise level improved back here. A dark beer sat on the table in front of her. She stared into it as if reading her future in the mahogany foam.

Rachel stopped beside the table. "Hi," she croaked. "I brought company."

Hailey looked up in surprise, her eyes widening as she noticed the tall figure looming behind Rachel.

"I'm Max." A hand reached past Rachel, aimed toward her sister. "You must be Hailey."

Max's solid torso pressed against Rachel's back. She hummed as delight poured through her veins like warm caramel. Only when she saw the hundred unspoken questions setting fire to her sister's keen blue eyes did she stuff a cork in her wanton emotions.

"Nice to meet you," Hailey murmured, unable to tear her gaze from Max. "Very nice."

Regretting her invitation, Rachel slid into Hailey's side of the booth and nudged her toward the wall, leaving the opposite seat open. This meant she would have the pleasure of staring at Max the whole meal, but wouldn't need to endure the tantalizing brush of his arm, shoulder or thigh against hers.

"Rachel has told me all about you," Max said, shooting a smug look her way.

"Is that so?" Hailey plunged an elbow into Rachel's side. "I'm afraid she hasn't mentioned you at all. How do you two know each other?"

"She's working as my executive assistant."

"Why is she doing that?" Hailey quizzed. "She's in the business of placing people, not taking jobs herself."

Rachel felt the heat of her sister's curiosity. Her cheeks warmed as she glared at Max. "It's just for a little while."

"Rachel knows how very particular I am and offered herself until my regular assistant gets off maternity leave."

His double entendre was a cheap shot to Rachel's midsection. Her stomach clenched. She had not offered herself to him in any way, shape or form. Not yet. She clenched her teeth to contain a hiss of exasperation.

"How are you doing that and running your company?"

"I'm managing."

"Is this why you haven't been home all week?"

"I've been home. It's just been late." Rachel lifted her shoulders in an offhanded shrug. "And I've been heading out early. It only seems as if I haven't been there."

"How long do you intend to keep this up?"

"As long as I have to."

Hailey ran out of questions about the same time as Jane, their usual waitress, set a glass in front of Rachel then smiled expectantly at Max.

"I'll have what she's having." He indicated Rachel's drink.

"A black and tan it is," Jane said.

Hailey pushed a menu at him. "I already know what I'm having."

While Max glanced at the menu, Rachel exchanged a nonverbal warning with Hailey, who merely grinned.

Decision made, Max closed the menu and leaned his forearms on the table. Hailey received the brunt of his attention as he said, "Your sister tells me you're a CPA."

"For almost three years now."

"Is that how long you've been in Houston?"

"We came here a year before that. From Biloxi." Hailey leaned back and framed her glass in a circle made by thumbs and forefingers. "How about you, are you from Houston?"

"Born and raised. Except for the years I spent away at school."

"And what business are you in?"

"My family owns Case Consolidated Holdings. My brothers and I run it."

"I'm familiar with the company." Hailey nodded in approval and nudged her knee against Rachel's. "And what do you do there?"

"I'm the chief operating officer."

"Are you two done giving each other the third degree?" Rachel interrupted.

"Not quite," Max said, his gaze never leaving Hailey. "Your sister has been agitated for the last couple days. Is she in some sort of trouble?"

"Max! That's none of your concern."

Hailey's gaze clung to Max as if he was a knight on a white horse come to save the day. Rachel clamped her fingers around her sister's arm to keep her from spilling about Brody and his demands for money.

"I think your sister wants to tell me what's going on."

"It's not a big deal. I've simply had to postpone moving my offices into a better location." She kept her voice and expression as bland as white rice.

"Why is that?"

"I had a little financial setback. Nothing disastrous. It's something that comes with being an entrepreneur. You should know that. Aren't you having a little difficulty of your own since Nathan showed up? I've been hearing stories of arguments that almost came to blows."

Max blew out a disparaging breath. "It sounds worse than it was."

"Who's Nathan?" Hailey asked.

"My half brother. He came to work for the company a year ago and he's been a pain in my ass ever since." Max sipped at his drink, appearing as if he'd said everything he intended to on the subject.

Hailey rested her elbows on the table and her chin on her clasped hands. "Why is that?"

While Max explained about an acquisition they'd decided not to make, Rachel watched him unnoticed. Max's animation and the multilayered nuances of his tone and facial expressions were vastly different from his older brother's stoicism. His passion had captivated her from the start, stirring her enthusiasm for whatever he was interested in. Like some smitten female, she could sit in silence and let him go on and on just to enjoy the way his eyes glowed with excitement and the way he punctuated his words with hand gestures.

"But enough about me," Max declared abruptly. "Let's talk about your sister. Is she dating anyone?"

Rachel came out of the clouds with a thump. "That's none of your concern."

Max's eyes swung in her direction. "It is my concern." His tone had gone deadly serious. "I'd like a clear field this time."

His intensity roused goose bumps on Rachel's arms. She sat on her hands to avoid rubbing the telltale reaction away and gritted her teeth against the shiver tickling her spine.

"What do you mean a clear field this time?" Hailey asked, leaning forward. "How long have you two known each other?"

"We met five years ago," Max admitted.

"In Biloxi?"

"Gulf Shores."

Rachel squirmed as Hailey went completely still. She should have told her sister something about meeting Max in Gulf Shores. At the time, she didn't want Hailey to know how miserable she'd been with Brody.

Her marriage had been anything but a love match. Brody had offered her security and a way to get her sister through college, not his undying devotion. In exchange, she'd agreed to work as his executive assistant and turn her paycheck over to him. Since he took care of her needs, she had little use for the money she earned working for him.

It wasn't until she signed her first tax return that she got a glimpse of how much money she was making working for Brody's family business. She was earning almost three times what an executive assistant should. Way more than he was paying out for Hailey's room and board. And when she asked him where the money was going, she discovered the sort of situation she'd gotten herself into.

She wasn't in a marriage. She was nothing more than a pawn in Brody's desperate attempt to keep his father from finding out how his gambling addiction had taken over his life. When Rachel found out the truth, she was told in no uncertain terms that she'd better keep her mouth shut or her happy little world would vanish. She and her sister would be back out on the street. Rachel knew that keeping her husband's secret was a small price to pay to keep Hailey in college.

But then, things started to get worse.

Brody grew more erratic. He would disappear for days at a time and when he was home, he seemed hunted. He missed family events and Rachel covered for him, but his parents were relentless in their questions. He came home from one weekend with bruises and admitted that he owed a lot of money to a casino. Money grew tight. They were behind on their mortgage. Her credit cards were declined.

The summer before Hailey's senior year, Rachel had enough. She took off, determined to divorce Brody and figure out another way to pay for Hailey's last year of college. Without cash or a plan, she wasn't likely to get very far. Heading to Gulf Shores had made sense. She'd grown up there. It was home. For two days, she'd hung out and contemplated what a mess she'd made of her life.

Then, she'd met Max. Those four days with him gave her a taste of how love was meant to be. Supportive, deeply connected, full of endless possibilities. She'd been a fool to marry Brody. She'd taken the easy way out of her problems and instead, made things worse.

Brody had tracked her down through a call to Hailey. His arrival had shattered the peace Rachel had found. She'd returned home with him because he'd threatened to tell Hailey about their marriage. Rachel couldn't let that happen.

Hailey would feel horrible if she thought Rachel had sacrificed her own happiness and peace of mind so that Hailey could go to a good college. Rachel was no more going to burden her sister with guilt than she would burden her with four years of college debt.

An awkward silence had settled over the table. Rachel could almost hear Hailey's thoughts as she sifted through the subtext of the conversation.

"I remember that trip," Hailey said. "It was the summer before my senior year. You were really different when you came back. Quiet. Except when you were trying too hard to be upbeat. You never mentioned you met someone."

With Max watching her, his expression a cement wall, Rachel swallowed a mouthful of her drink. "Max and I met at The Lucky Gull and hung out for a few days. It was…"

Rachel's eyes slid sideways toward her sister. She kept her face as expressionless as possible. She'd kept the truth about her troubled marriage from Hailey for the same reason she'd protected her sister before and after their father died. As the big sister, Rachel was responsible for Hailey's well-being.

"Casual," Max supplied, his voice as smooth as butter. "No big deal. We enjoyed each other's company for a short time and went our separate ways."

If he intended for this description of their affair to cause her damage then his aim was flawless.

"Casual," Rachel agreed, increasingly worried that her feelings for Max were anything but.

Five

While the sisters talked about plans for the upcoming weekend, Max tucked into a delicious dinner of shepherd's pie and pondered what the hell he hoped to accomplish by digging into Rachel's life. What was it about her that kept him from just leaving well enough alone? Because as soon as he got her away from her sister, he intended to get to the bottom of what was going on.

Was he looking for ammunition to use against her because five years after the fact he was still angry about being an unwitting accomplice in her infidelity? Sure, he had a hard time letting go of things that bothered him, but he'd only known her four short days. Not enough time for his emotions to get engaged. They'd had fun. Lots of great sex. The connection between them might have seemed real, but it had been a vacation fantasy.

As the debate raged inside him, Max grew less certain of his rationalization.

He'd come away from that long weekend in Alabama a changed man. Before he'd met Rachel he'd been an easygoing bachelor, happy to date a series of women with no distrust of love. After their time together, he closed himself off to emotions and made sure anyone he dated knew he wasn't interested in getting serious.

Until recently, he'd assumed his motivation for doing so was born out of being lied to by Rachel. In the last few days, he'd come to realize it stemmed from the fact that he'd experienced the four most amazing days with her and couldn't imagine feeling that way with anyone ever again.

A shriek went up across the table from him. Max's gaze shot to Rachel. The delight that glowed in her sapphire eyes and flushed her creamy skin rosy catapulted her from merely lovely to truly gorgeous. Happiness banished the shadows masking her eyes. The genuine love for her sister revealed her true heart. She was as beautiful on the inside as on the outside.

Her effect on him put his chest in turmoil. Heart and lungs competed for space in his ribcage. As he contemplated what a foolish move it had been to pull her back into his life, Rachel threw her arms around her sibling.

"Where's the ring?" Rachel demanded, snatching her sister's left hand and frowning at her bare fingers.

"Being sized." Hailey wore a concerned frown as she peered at her sister. "Are you sure you're okay with this?"

"Okay?" Rachel echoed, her pitch lower as excitement gave way to confusion. "I'm thrilled. Leo is a great guy. You two have been dating for two years. Why wouldn't I be okay?"

"Because we won't be living together anymore."

"And you're worried about me being on my own?" Rachel laughed. "Are you kidding? I can't wait to turn your bedroom into a home office."

Whether or not Hailey picked up on her sister's bravado, Max heard it loud and clear. Rachel was thrilled for her sister, but that didn't mean that she was ready for the major change in her life. It didn't take a genius to see that the sisters were tight, or that Rachel regarded her younger sibling as a child she was responsible for.

"Congratulations," Max interjected when the sisters paused for breath. "Have you set a date?"

Hailey answered after a quick glance at Rachel. "November fifteenth."

"So soon?" Rachel sagged in dismay. "There's so much to do before then."

"No, there's not. We're going to have a small wedding, just immediate family."

"But that's not your dream. And you've been saving for a huge blowout wedding since the day Leo asked you out."

Hailey held her sister's gaze, her expression determined. "Leo and I discussed it and we really don't want a huge wedding."

"But that's what you've been saving for. Your dream wedding."

"We want you to have the money."

A-ha!

Max's palm hit the table hard enough to cause plates and glasses to bounce, but the sisters were so focused on their battle of wills, neither turned his way. Confirmation that something was going on with Rachel's finances.

"You're being ridiculous," Rachel insisted, her tone scolding. "I'm not taking your money. You earned it. If you don't want a big wedding, use it as a down payment on your dream house."

"But what about—"

"It's okay," Rachel interrupted, gripping her sister's arm. She followed it up with an emphatic, "Really."

Max leaned forward with interest and pinned Hailey with his gaze. "Why would your sister need money?"

"Quit poking your nose into my business," Rachel said before Hailey could answer. "She has this silly idea that she should repay me for taking care of her all these years and paying for her college. It's ridiculous. I love her. That's why I did it. I wasn't expecting anything back."

There was more to it than that. Max could tell from Hailey's sudden silence and Rachel's fierce scowl.

"If you need money, I can help you out." He'd expected her definitive head shake. "Call it a personal loan. No strings attached."

He couldn't resist adding the latter. The way Rachel glared at him sent his libido into overdrive. He imagined her thinking of all the ways he'd use the loan to gain the upper hand in their arguments, as well as other areas. Her expression had never been more transparent. He studied her, his level gaze causing her color to rise. At last she locked eyes with him. The hard glint in their depths warned him to back off.

Sensing Rachel would continue to deny him answers until he got her alone, Max dropped the matter. Then, deaf to the protests of the two independent career women across from him, he settled the bill.

They exited the restaurant only to discover the day's heat had lingered into evening. Rachel's gaze followed her sister as Hailey headed off to where she'd parked her car. The shadows were back in her eyes.

"She's on top of the world," Max remarked, pacing beside Rachel as she retraced the path they'd taken an hour earlier.

"She's really happy."

Max cursed the strong desire to put his arms around Rachel and kiss her sadness away. "But you're not."

"Of course I am." She adjusted her purse strap. "I'm thrilled."

"For her, but not for yourself."

She wrapped silence around her like a muffler and shot him a look that would have taken down a lesser man.

"Not that I blame you for feeling sad," he persisted. "You've taken care of her all her life. It's got to be hard to let go."

"My feelings don't belong in the conversation."

Impatience rose in Max. Five years ago, he'd found her mysteriousness appealing. Until he'd discovered the reason behind it. How bad were the secrets she was hiding today?

"Why not? Surely it can't hurt to talk to me about what's bothering you."

"Nothing is bothering me."

In other words, she wanted him to back off. Too bad his disquiet over her financial troubles was a pest he couldn't ignore.

"That's not true. You've got financial problems."

She stopped at an intersection and faced him. "I'm going that way." Her finger pointed up a street perpendicular to the one they'd been walking along. "You need to go that way."

"I'm not going to let you walk alone to your car."

Despite the storm brewing in her blue eyes, she smiled. "I walk alone to my car every day. I don't need your manly presence at my side to keep me safe."

"Whatever."

He snagged her arm just above the elbow and stepped into the crosswalk. She resisted his manhandling for three strides before breaking free.

"I don't need you to walk me anywhere."

"Stop being so damned independent and let me help you."

She was breathing hard as they reached the sidewalk on the other side. Frustration poured off her in waves. She whirled to confront him. "I don't need your help."

"How about Hailey's help? Why does she really want to give you—?"

She stopped the rest of his question with an open-mouth kiss that left him reeling. Up on her toes, her fingers fisted in his hair, she plunged her tongue into his mouth in a determined bid to divert his line of questioning.

It worked.

Max gathered her slim form tight against his body. He slipped one hand between their bodies, her breast his goal, when a horn honked nearby, reminding him they were standing in the middle of a city street.

Panting, he raked his lips across her cheek. The heavy air had coated her skin with a fine sheen of perspiration. She tasted salty.

"Come back to my place."

"I can't." Her hands retreated from his back, sliding away from his body with haste. "I have a ton of work to catch up on at the agency."

"Take tomorrow morning off and do it then."

"You don't understand." Heaving a sigh, she shook her head and turned aside. "My boss is a complete tyrant."

Max caught her arm and tugged her back into his arms. "A bear, is he?"

She arched her eyebrows and peered up at him. "Always roaring and throwing his arms around in a threatening manner. It's awful."

"Maybe there's a reason why he's like that."

"Such as?"

"Sexual frustration?"

A golden chuckle rippled through her. "Not possible. You should see all the women he dates. There's a list of them on my computer. All their preferences. Their favorite restaurants. Favorite flowers. Favorite music. Even their preferred jewelers. I think he's getting plenty of action."

At her recitation, Max's grip loosened enough that she was able to free herself and put several feet between them. He hadn't considered that she'd have access to Andrea's files and information about his personal life. Sure, he knew a lot of women. Dated a lot of women.

"Did it ever occur to you that he dates all those women because he's searching for something missing in his life?"

"Ms. Right?" She shook her head, tugged her suit jacket straight and raised her chin. "I don't think that's what he's looking for. He's a confirmed bachelor. No woman stands a chance of capturing his heart." Rachel sent a breezy smile winging toward him and headed away. "See you tomorrow, boss."

Max stood where she'd left him, a sour feeling in his gut. At some point today he'd set his toes on the line he'd drawn five years ago in the sand of an Alabama beach. He'd sworn then that he'd never forgive Rachel for her lies. He hadn't understood the powerful connection between them or his vulnerability to it.

Today, in the face of his compelling need for her, Max felt anger and resentment losing their grip on him. How long before his heart was in danger? The smartest thing would be to cut her loose and stop playing this dangerous game. But his whole body ached at the thought of never again tasting her kisses or hearing the sounds of her pleasure as he drove into her.

Max pivoted and headed toward the Case Consolidated Holdings offices.

Who said he had to deny himself the opportunity to enjoy her body? Making love to her. Forgiving her. Falling for her, even. None of these things would result in the loss of his '71 Cuda.

He'd only lose his bet with Jason if he married her. And that was a trap he could avoid with ease.

* * *

At four in the afternoon, a Pensacola, Florida parking lot was the last place Rachel wanted to be. No breeze stirred the stifling air radiating from the sun-baked blacktop. The sky was a perfect blue, unspoiled by clouds. Rachel brushed sweat from her brow and half trotted to keep up with Max's long stride. The dense Florida humidity made her white blouse stick to her skin. Every inch of her felt uncomfortably damp. Only her mouth was dry. The parched sensation had begun the instant they'd emerged into the harsh afternoon sunlight, and Max had transformed from Case Consolidated Holdings' difficult chief of operations to the charming devil she'd toppled into bed with five years ago.

"That's got them running scared," he declared, even, white teeth flashing in a rakish grin. He stripped off his suit coat and flipped it over his shoulder. "When you pulled out your analysis of their numbers, Carlton got so red in the face, I thought he was going to pass out."

Eyes glued to the large brown hand tugging at the knot on his tie, Rachel told her hormones to settle down. Her chastising had no effect on her unruly body. "Are you really going to transfer operations to the Birmingham plant if they don't bring their costs down?"

Bright shards of silver danced in his gray eyes. "Of course not." With a very un-Max-like flourish, he held the rental car door open for her. This was the most relaxed she'd seen him. "They just need to realize that things can't continue the way they've been going." He leaned his forearms on the door and watched as she tossed her briefcase into the back. "It's hotter than hell out here," he remarked, his gaze sliding over her. "Aren't you going to ditch that jacket you're wearing?"

Not on her life. The last thing she wanted to do was relax around Max.

"No need," she replied, ignoring the way his knowing smile made her pulse jerk. "The car has air-conditioning."

"Suit yourself."

Rachel kept her head turned toward the passenger window as Max drove the car back to the airport, but her attention wasn't on the streets of Pensacola. She was running the last week through her mind.

Since the dinner with Hailey and the kiss afterward, the tenor of their working relationship had changed. Max had become less professional and more friendly. His hand had developed a distracting habit of brushing her arm, landing on her shoulder, or sliding into the small of her back at odd moments. Nothing as overt as her action the other night when she planted a big kiss on him, but the subtle touches made her acutely aware of how sensitive she'd become to his every slow breath, sidelong glance, and nuance of posture.

"Are you hungry?"

Max's question snapped her out of her daydream. A glance at the dashboard clock told her she'd been lost in thought for half an hour. "Where are we? I don't remember the trip from the airport taking so long this morning."

"I thought we'd take a little detour before heading back to Houston."

A detour? What was he up to? She recalled his last question. Did he want to prolong their time together by taking her to dinner?

"You don't need to feed me. I can make it back to Houston."

"About that."

She wasn't sure if it was his words or his tone that sent her uneasiness into overdrive. "About what?" Before long, the sign appeared for Highway 292 confirming her unspoken fear. "Where are we going?"

"The beach."

"Which beach?" she asked.

"Gulf Shores."

She'd known the answer before he spoke. Naturally, he'd pick the place where it all began. He wanted closure. What better way to get that than recreate the fantasy of those four days and let their romance run its course? And fantasy is exactly what it had been. She'd been running from reality. Being with Max then had been a frantic grab at the joy her life had been missing since she'd married Brody. She'd never been happier before or since.

Curses exploded in her mind like fireworks. This was going to end badly for her. Worse than the first time when she'd convinced herself the magic of those days had been all about the best sex of her life. Now, she knew better. Max was a complex man who both frustrated and fascinated her. What she felt for him went way beyond the purely physical. She felt a spiritual connection to him. And when that was ripped away, she would no longer be whole.

"I can't." She surveyed his profile and noted the steely set of his jaw. His lips might be relaxed into a half smile, but he was not in a cooperative frame of mind. "I've got things I need to do."

"What sort of things?" He raised dark eyebrows, daring her to lie.

"Things."

"I thought you said your schedule was clear this weekend."

"I never told you that."

"True. I must have overheard you talking to Hailey about how much you were looking forward to a weekend with nothing to do."

"You eavesdropped?"

"Eavesdropped is such a negative word."

"Listened in. Snooped. Spied. Take your pick." Her accusations bounced off him like bullets off Superman.

"It's not like you left me much choice. Perhaps if you were more willing to tell me what's going on in your life."

Rachel ignored his not-so-subtle dig. "I'm not going to sleep with you if that's what you think is going to happen this weekend." With a disgruntled huff, she folded her arms over her chest.

He took his eyes off the road long enough to show her he didn't believe that for one second. "Who are you trying to convince? Me or you?"

She ground her teeth together because she had no snappy comeback. Already her body was softening in anticipation of the feel of his lips against her skin, his hands finding where she burned for him.

"I suppose with all the dating you do, you're pretty confident when it comes to getting a woman into bed," she muttered, unable to leave well enough alone.

"I'm confident you'll wear yourself out resisting what your body wants." He reached across and took her hand in his, fingers sliding over hers with intoxicating results. He lifted her hand and lightly brushed to his lips across her knuckles.

She sighed at the gentle tug of his warm, moist mouth against her skin. She felt a damp heat between her thighs and resisted the urge to squirm on her seat as he ministered to the inside of her wrist, tongue flicking out to probe her staccato pulse.

"Pay attention to your driving." She used her free hand to pry herself out of his grasp. Much more of that delicious sucking and nibbling and she would put that hand of his where it would do her the most good. "I don't want to get into an accident."

With a low, sexy chuckle, he returned his full attention to the traffic around them.

Even with the air conditioner running at full blast, Rachel felt uncomfortably warm. Since willing her body to cool and settle wasn't working, she peeled off her jacket and released the top two buttons on her blouse. Raking her fingers through her hair, she disturbed the gel she'd used to restrict the waves into a sleek hairstyle. She rolled up her sleeves, took off her clunky jewelry, kicked off her shoes and shed her professional image.

"I suppose I'm falling right into your trap by saying I have nothing to wear but the clothes on my back."

"Normally, this would be where I'd tell you that I intend to keep you naked all weekend." Max glanced over at her, eyes burning with carnal promises. "But I had Hailey pack a bag for you. It's in the trunk."

Her own sister had betrayed her. Rachel's chest ached as she rested her elbow on the door and her head on her palm. "You thought of everything."

"I like to prepare for all contingencies."

Off to their left, sunlight sparkled on the Gulf of Mexico. A familiar sight from her childhood. Rachel flinched away from the sharp stab of nostalgia. Was it possible her father had been dead ten years? She missed him every time she sat in his scruffy old recliner or pan fried grouper the way he'd taught her.

They'd been a happy family—she, Hailey and their dad. Both Rachel and her father had worked hard to make sure Hailey never missed the mother that had run out shortly before Hailey turned two. Rachel remembered her as a sharp voice and little else. Her dad hadn't talked about her and there weren't any pictures of her in the house. The lack of a mother hadn't bothered Rachel until she turned thirteen and realized she didn't know much about becoming a woman. If she'd had a mother to advise her, would she have made so many stupid choices?

"Are you all right?" Max had caught her wiping away a tear.

"The sun's in my eyes." She lowered her visor and blinked

rapidly to clear moisture so she could see. "I wish I hadn't forgotten my sunglasses back in Houston."

Max whipped his off. "Take mine."

"You need them to drive."

"I'll be okay."

"Thanks." She slipped them on, appreciating the UV protection as well as the shield against Max's curiosity. "I'll buy a pair when we stop."

It was an hour's drive from Pensacola to Gulf Shores. Rachel recalled making the trip in reverse with her high school friends in those happy days before her father died. They'd head up to the "big city" to catch a movie or go shopping. There'd been a huge sense of freedom in getting in the car and going.

Her decision to take Hailey to live with Aunt Jesse in Biloxi after their dad died had robbed her sister of those sorts of fun times. If only she hadn't been so afraid to take on the responsibility of supporting her and her sister. At the time it seemed sensible to seek out the help of an adult. Of family. Too bad she didn't know what a loser their aunt was until it was too late.

Max's warm fingers stole over the fist balled on her thigh. "You know, it won't kill you to talk to me."

The soothing slide of his skin against hers caused her to release the breath she'd bottled up. She loved holding hands with him. They'd done a lot of that during those days at the beach. In fact, she doubted they'd gone more than five minutes at a time without touching. When they'd been out in public, most people had taken them as newlyweds, asking if they wanted their picture taken together.

To Rachel's surprise, Max had played along. Despite his claims that he never intended to marry, he'd sure enjoyed playing the part of smitten bridegroom.

What he never knew was that she'd asked one couple to

take their picture and email it to her. She'd stared at it every day until Brody found it on her computer and deleted it.

"I didn't tell you last time, but Hailey and I grew up around Gulf Shores. Dad was a deep-sea fishing guide. The best in the county."

He cocked his head. "How come I didn't know that?"

She shrugged. "You did most of the talking that weekend."

"I guess I did." His forehead creased. "That's not going to happen again."

"Are you sure?" she teased, forcing lightness she didn't feel into her tone. "You're kind of an egomaniac."

Rachel's doubts about spending this weekend with Max were coming to a boil once more. Last time, they'd been able to drop their guards and completely enjoy each other with no reservations or baggage between them. Intimacy had come easy because they'd been strangers.

Max's fingers tightened on hers. "Don't do that."

"What?" Her stomach crashed to her toes.

"Push me away with humor."

"Was I funny? You'd be the first person to say so." Rachel heard herself and ejected a sigh. "You're right. I'm sorry. I've never been good at playing with others." Amusement stirred at Max's impatient snort. "You know, now that I've gotten started, I don't think I can stop."

"I think you can," Max said, all serious. "Why don't you start by telling me why you and your sister left Gulf Shores?"

Max could try to dig up all the details about her past he wanted in an effort to rediscover the connection they'd briefly enjoyed five years ago, but he'd find out pretty quickly that the walls she'd spent the last ten years erecting wouldn't come down without a prolonged siege. And time was something they didn't have. A couple days, a couple weeks maybe, and he'd lose interest in her.

"Our dad died when I was eighteen and Hailey was sixteen. He was shot during a convenience-store robbery in Foley, Alabama. He had a girlfriend up there that he visited a couple times a month. They hadn't been dating long, but I had the feeling he really liked her."

"Had you met her?"

Rachel shook her head. "No, he didn't like bringing anyone around. He didn't want us to get attached to anyone in case things didn't work out." She watched beach houses slide past the window, barely recognizing the area with all the new construction that had taken place, but she knew they were getting close. "Our mom left when we were little. Dad didn't want to set us up to get hurt again."

"He sounds like a great father."

"The best." Remembering there had been tension between Max and his father, she didn't elaborate on all the wonderful things about her dad. "He put his life on hold to look after Hailey and me. I didn't realize how much until after he was dead and all his friends started telling stories of job offers he'd turned down because he wanted us to grow up in a community like Gulf Shores. There'd even been a woman he'd wanted to marry, but she had a big career somewhere up north and he wanted to keep us down here."

"Sometimes there are obstacles to a relationship that can't be overcome."

Like how she'd neglected to tell Max she was married? She probably should have ended things with him when she'd learned about his father's affair. After twenty years, Max couldn't let go of his resentment that his father had loved someone other than Max's mother. Even worse, Brandon Case had loved the child of that union as much as he'd loved his legitimate sons.

"And sometimes people are just plain stubborn. Hailey and I could have grown up anywhere and been just fine. I think Dad was afraid to trust anyone after the way my mom left us."

"Trust once broken is often impossible to heal."

And yet, here they were. Rachel let her head fall back against the headrest. This weekend was going to be a disaster. Why hadn't she pitched a fit until she convinced Max to take her home?

Because she wanted to be with him, no matter the cost to her heart and soul? She was a fool.

"You're right about that," she said. "Especially when people refuse to change." The sun dipped into the clouds looming on the horizon and Rachel pulled off the sunglasses. She handed them back to Max. "Looks like we might get some rain tonight."

"I checked the forecast for the weekend and it promised sunshine both days."

"Forecasts aren't always accurate."

"Let's just say, I'm feeling optimistic."

Was he, now. "Optimistic enough to only book one hotel room?"

Max answered her question with a blazing smile.

Six

Letting her stew about their destination amused Max for the next half hour. The silence gave him time to mull over what he'd learned about her. He'd known she'd taken care of Hailey and helped her by paying for college. It just never occurred to him how young she'd been when she'd taken on the responsibility of her sister.

As they entered the city limits of Gulf Shores, Rachel sat forward in her seat, her expression growing animated. Had she been back in the last five years? Many times he'd imagined her here. Pictured her long blond hair whipping around her face as she walked the beach or sat having breakfast at Jolene's Hideaway.

The car streaked past the beach cottages where they'd spent their four days together. Rachel's gaze snagged on the cluster of pale peach structures, her head turning as she kept her sights locked on them. Curiosity and confusion melded in the turbulent blue depths of her eyes as they came to rest on him.

"We're not staying there?"

"No."

"Then where?"

"You'll see."

They quickly left the main strip behind, hotels, restaurants and shops giving way to beach homes. Leggy structures built on pilings lined the road, their colors pale representations of the surrounding landscape.

"I thought you said we're staying in Gulf Shores," she persisted.

"We are."

"But the hotels are all back there." She gestured over her shoulder, indicating the town now a mile behind them.

"I own a house here." He didn't need to glimpse her expression to know he'd surprised her. Beside him, her body tensed. "I bought it four years ago."

A year after they'd met. It made sense to purchase property since he'd taken to visiting the town once a month. All in the hopes of finding her again. Proof positive that he was a fool. She'd been married. She'd returned to her husband. Yet he'd returned to the scene of the crime like some lovestruck idiot. Over and over.

When it occurred to him that he was behaving exactly like his father's mistress—a woman he despised for her weakness—that he was willing to take whatever scraps of Rachel's life he could because living without her made him miserable, he'd stopped coming to Gulf Shores for three months. But in the end, his longing for her had been too strong.

Naturally, all this was wrapped up in logic and justified by sound reasoning about rising property values and his need for a vacation home. But each time he returned to the beach house, he couldn't hide the truth from himself. He was here because he hoped Rachel would return to him.

"This is yours?" Rachel's question broke the quiet. She'd rolled down her window and a light breeze wafted in, bringing the rhythmic crash of surf and the scent of brine. "I don't get it. Your weekends are filled with racing. Why'd you buy a house out here? It's a lot of money for something you never use."

"I like the beach." More than ever now that she was here. "Let's go inside, I'll show you around."

Max had chosen the house for it's open floor plan and the location, but as Rachel exclaimed over the granite countertops and stainless appliances in the gourmet kitchen, he decided he might have had a woman in the back of his mind when he'd had the kitchen and bathrooms updated.

As they concluded the tour of the main part of the house and headed toward the bedrooms, Rachel tugged her overnight bag from his grasp and marched into the guest bedroom. He saw that she expected him to argue. Why bother when words would have little effect on her? She was afraid of what the chemistry between them would lead to. Oh, not the lovemaking. The hungry look in her eye told him that her desire for him matched his longing for her. But she was worried how their relationship would change after this weekend.

"I'm going to grab a shower," he told her. "See you in thirty."

When he returned to the small bedroom, he found Rachel in the midst of unpacking. She'd also showered and now wore a pale blue sundress that bared her slender arms and showed off her delicate collarbones. Her damp hair lay flat against her head, the bright gold darkened to bronze. Tiny silver butterflies swooped below her ears.

"Nice," he murmured, gaze snagged on the frothy scrap of red satin and black lace laid out beside her suitcase.

"That is not mine." She shook her head. "And I wouldn't have packed it for a weekend getaway with you."

"Why not?" He made no effort to resist a grin.

She rolled her eyes. "Because it wouldn't have lasted more than ten seconds, so what would be the point in putting it on?"

"Try it on and I'll demonstrate the point."

Max gathered her into his arms and dropped his lips onto hers. He'd meant it to be just a hot, quick kiss, a suggestion of what would come later, but she melted against him and he lingered. He tasted yearning and reluctance in her kisses. Both excited him. He couldn't wait for that moment when passion torched her hesitation and she let herself go.

Dropping his hands to her backside, he cupped his palms over her sweet curves and pulled her hard against the unruly tension in his groin. Her shiver told him she was on the verge of surrender. His stomach took that inopportune moment to growl.

A different sort of growl rumbled his throat as she laughed and flattened her hands against his chest to push him away.

"Sounds like the beast is hungry," she said.

Before she could move out of reach, he caught her hand and pressed it over the erection straining against his zipper. "The beast is starving."

For a series of heart-pounding seconds she cupped him, fingers trailing along his length, and Max found his knees starting to give way. But before he could swoop in for a deep, exploring kiss even hotter than the last one, she twisted free and fled out the door.

"Come on, Max," she called over her shoulder, cheeks flushed, her half smile taunting him. "You promised me dinner."

Ten minutes later, her eyes glowed as they drove into the parking lot of the restaurant she'd recommended. Reluctance, eagerness, anxiety and yearning passed across Rachel's features, and Max wondered what memories this place roused. He took her hand as they started up the steps to the enormous deck that wrapped around the outside of the waterfront restaurant. With spectacular views of the Gulf of Mexico, the deck was wide enough to accommodate two rows of tables set for four and a generous aisle between. Despite the heat, families and couples occupied every table.

Weathered wood boards squeaked beneath their weight as Max held the door open for her to enter the restaurant. Once inside, the cries of gulls and the soothing pulse of the gulf gave way to the chatter of the crowd occupying the tables in the enormous restaurant. Walls of windows on three sides provided stunning views of the beach and offered the opportunity to watch the day draw to a close in spectacular shades of orange and red.

Rachel approached the hostess stand and spoke to the woman who was directing her wait and bussing staff with crisp instructions. "Hi, Mary."

The woman looked around and her face lit up with astonishment. "Rachel Lansing. You darling girl. Come here and give me a hug."

At first Rachel looked overwhelmed by the warm welcome, but adapted with enthusiasm.

"Max. This is Mary. She owns the Pelican's Roost. I used to work here back in my high school days."

"She was one of our most popular girls."

"Yes," Max murmured. "I'm sure she was."

Mary lifted a disapproving eyebrow at his dry remark. "Not like that. She was a good waitress. Always smiling. Never got an order wrong and she could charm the crankiest customers. And we get a lot of those during season."

"I wasn't all that," Rachel demurred. "Dad taught me the value of hard work, that's all."

"Yes," Mary said with a sigh. "God rest his soul. So, where are you living these days? The last time you were here was five or six years ago, wasn't it? You were living in Biloxi, I think."

"I live in Houston now. I run my own business. Lansing Employment Agency."

"And is this handsome fellow your husband?"

Color brightened Rachel's cheeks as she shook her head. "He's a client, actually. We were in Pensacola on business."

To Max's bemusement, he resented being described as Rachel's client. But what did he expect, that she'd announce to the world that they were soon to be lovers? Or ex-lovers? Their relationship, past, present and future, was too complicated to be easily labeled.

"Do you want to sit inside or on the deck?" Mary gathered menus.

"Outside." Rachel grabbed Max's hand as the restaurant owner headed off and tugged to get him moving. "Is that okay with you?"

"Outside's fine."

He squeezed her hand and shook off his pensive mood. This weekend was supposed to be about two uncomplicated days of sex, conversation and laughter. No need to muck it up with a bunch of pesky emotions that would confuse things. Keep it light. Keep it casual.

"Everything looks good," he said, scanning the menu with only half his attention. The rest was caught, spellbound, by the whimsical curve of her lips as she set her arm on the railing and peered at the water. "What do you recommend?"

"I'm having the raw oysters, followed by the pan-fried grouper." She leaned forward and whispered, "Don't tell Mary, but it's not as good as my dad used to make." Then, she resumed speaking in her regular tone. "And for dessert, peach cobbler because nobody makes cobbler like the Pelican's Roost."

"Sounds good."

And it was. Thirty minutes later, Max set down his fork after cleaning up every last peach cobbler crumb and exhaled. "Everything was fantastic. Why didn't we come here five years ago?"

"We had a hard time getting dressed and going anywhere," she reminded him with a cagey grin.

That was true. They'd been insatiable. But looking back with a clearer head, he remembered it was Rachel who'd resisted his offers to investigate the local restaurants. The one time they had gone out for dinner, she'd directed him to a town fifteen miles farther along the coast. He realized now that she hadn't wanted to explain being with a man not her husband.

Then it struck him that this was how Nathan's mother must have felt. Always hidden away. Always coping with the fact that she was the dirty little secret in her lover's closet. Max had spent most of his teenage years hating his father's mistress, blaming her for the problems in his parents' marriage. With twenty years of resentment propping up his perception, he was dismayed to feel a twinge of sympathy for the woman.

As he drove back to his house, Rachel's nerves became more and more obvious. She half jumped out of her skin after he parked the car in the driveway and touched her arm.

"How about we take a walk on the beach?" he offered.

"But I thought…?" she began, obviously flabbergasted.

"That I was going to pounce on you the second we got back?" He wrapped his arm around her slim waist and pulled her snug against his side. He had no intention of telling her that his body was revved up to make love, but his emotions were playing sentimental tricks on him. "I thought you'd be more receptive after a sunset stroll."

"How thoughtful of you to consider my romantic needs." Beneath her dry tone he heard a throb of anxiety.

Max dropped a kiss on her head. "Just shut up and enjoy the moment."

Her chuckle vibrated against his ribs, easing the tension. They shed their shoes by the beachside stairs that led to his deck and stepped onto the warm sand. Fine white grains slipped between his toes as they strolled along the beach. The moon had risen early and shone as a narrow, white crescent against the deepening blue of the eastern sky. Max estimated it was somewhere close to low tide because they were able to walk on the hard, packed sand near the water's edge. The breeze was too light to push the waves onto the beach with any force.

"Thank you for bringing me here this weekend," Rachel said. "I didn't realize how much I missed the beach until now."

"Why'd you move away?"

She paused so long before answering, Max began wondering if she'd heard his question.

"After Dad died we went to live with his sister in Biloxi." She settled into her story like someone perched on the edge of a soft couch, too afraid to get comfortable. "Hailey wanted to stay and graduate with her friends, but I insisted we'd be better off if we were close to family."

"So, you don't have any family around here? What about your mother?"

"I barely remember her. She left when I was four and Hailey was two. Didn't have much use for us. At least that's what Daddy said." She slipped into a drawl that sounded very much like the local accent.

That's when he realized she'd stripped as much Alabama out of her accent as she could at some point since leaving here.

"And you never knew your grandparents?"

"I never knew anyone from Mom's side of the family. Sometimes it felt as if Hailey and I had been left on Daddy's doorstep."

"What about your other grandparents?"

"We met them a few times. They lived in Iowa and came down to visit from time to time until my grandmother got Alzheimer's and had to be put in a nursing home."

This was more of her background than she'd shared before. Five years ago, she'd sidestepped every question he'd directed at her. She'd been so accomplished at keeping the conversation focused on him that he hadn't been aware how little he knew about her until she was gone.

What had prompted her to open up to him now? Was she starting to trust him a little? Trust him enough to tell him about her problems?

They walked west in companionable silence, enjoying the play of rich oranges and purples across the sky. The clear night allowed the sun to glow red for a long time before it disappeared below the horizon. As daylight faded, they retraced their steps.

As peaceful as he felt with a soft, curvaceous Rachel relaxed against his side, the closer they got to his beach house, the more anticipation tightened his nerves into bowstrings. His earlier decision to take things slow now became the biggest mistake he'd made in months. Why had he taken Rachel first to dinner then on this long walk on the beach when they could have grabbed takeout and eaten dinner off each other's naked bodies?

Need tightened his gut as he watched Rachel dust sand off her feet on the deck. Patience snapping, he caught her hand and pulled her into the house.

"I can't wait another second to kiss you," he said, closing and locking the sliding glass door. Putting his arms around her, he tugged her hard against his body.

A breathy laugh escaped her. "Then I guess we'd better get started."

His lips captured hers in a fervent kiss that paid homage to her vulnerability while giving her a glimpse of how waiting had fueled his impatience. She met his demand with no sign of her earlier hesitation. Her arms came around his neck. He cupped her head and held her still for a deep, exploring kiss hotter than any they'd exchanged. She arched her back, pushing her lower half against his erection, letting him feel her urgency.

"Make love to me, Max." She tugged his shirt free of his pants and found his skin burning for her. "The romance has been nice, but I need you inside me."

In complete agreement, he drew her down the hall toward the master bedroom. Flinging aside the comforter, Max stripped off his shirt and kicked off his shoes. Despite the cool air blowing across his naked shoulders, he felt feverish. Kissing Rachel set him on fire. Making love to her threatened to reduce him to ash.

"Max."

He turned at the sound of his name and caught Rachel staring at him, her hand behind her, sliding down the sundress' zipper. The look in her eyes stopped his breath. The uncertainty lurking in their velvet blue depths was gone, replaced by confidence. She looked radiant in the rapidly fading evening light.

The smile she offered him was equal parts bold and encouraging. "Are you going to stand there and watch or help?"

She didn't need to ask twice. He brushed the straps off her shoulders and the dress fell to a pool at her feet. Clad in a lavender bra and matching panties, she stood still for his inspection, her chest heaving with each ragged breath.

"Beautiful." He played his fingertips along her collarbones

and then dragged reverent caresses along the bra straps to the edge of the bra. "Your skin is like silk."

She placed her palms on his abs and fanned the fire banked these five years. But he'd promised himself he'd take it slow. He wanted to learn every inch of her skin again.

Her fingers crept down his stomach, past his belly button to the low ride of his waistband. Beneath the buttons that held his jeans together his erection strained toward her questing touch. A groan erupted as she freed him. His hard length speared at her belly, searching for the soft, hot sheath that awaited him. Before he guessed her intentions, she grasped him in her hands.

Sensation exploded through him. A guttural moan tore from his throat as she closed her hand around him. The years fell away. There was no awkwardness in her caresses. She remembered exactly how he liked to be touched. Before her ministrations could cause a premature end to their fun, he swept her into his arms and deposited her on the bed.

"I get to play first," he told her, rolling her beneath him and pinning her hands above her head.

Her thighs parted as he inserted one leg between them. She bent her knee and rocked her hips, grinding her pelvis against him in a slow, sexy wiggle that short-circuited his willpower.

He captured her mouth with his again, his tongue easing past her full lips to sample the exotic pleasures that awaited him beyond. Frantic mewling noises erupted in her throat as she tugged to free her hands. He released her, having better uses for his fingers than holding her captive.

"Better," she murmured, hands riding his shoulders and back with provocative flair.

Taking his time, he drove her mad with feather-light kisses across her soft, fragrant skin. Inch by inch, he eased his way down her body, revisiting all her ticklish spots and the ones that made her gasp. Five years had gone by, but he knew her body as well as he knew his own. Maybe better.

His teeth latched on to the lace edge of her bra. Tugging at the material caused her to hiss impatiently through her teeth. He buried his smile between her breasts, trailing his tongue up one round curve just above the line of silk. He wrapped his fingers around her straps and eased them off her shoulders, but made no attempt to draw the material lower. Her breath came in erratic pants as he retraced his tongue's path, this time dipping below the fabric.

"You're being awfully darned slow about getting me naked," Rachel complained, arching her back to reach her bra catch.

It loosened, but kept her covered. She pushed hard on his shoulder, rolling him onto his back. He grabbed her hips and brought her with him. The bra fell, exposing her small, perfect breasts.

Max palmed them with a sigh of sheer joy. Her bra sailed somewhere off to his left as he began relearning the shape of her. Already her nipples had peaked into dark buds. Max half closed his eyes in satisfaction at the hitch in her breath as he fondled her.

Below where she sat, his erection prodded against her lavender panties, seeking entrance. She leaned forward and rocked her hips. His sensitive head slid against the silk of her underwear, so close to her heat he thought he might go mad with wanting.

She reached behind her and seized him. Max's mouth fell open in shock at the intense pleasure that washed over him. A groan ripped from his chest as her fingers played over the head of his erection. His focus narrowed to her hand and the acute agony denying himself the satisfaction his body craved.

He pulled her hands away and meshed her fingers with

his. He closed his eyes to block out her happy smile and the passion glowing in her half lidded gaze.

Not one of the women he'd been with since the day she'd left had brought him to the edge this fast. Control had never been a problem for him until Rachel had entered his life. Max sucked air into his lungs, struggling to clear the fog of passion before something happened they would both regret.

"Condom," he rasped out.

"Where?" She sounded as impatient as he felt.

"Front pocket."

She stabbed both hands into his pockets and plucked out a condom. "You came prepared," she said, dismounting.

The bed sagged to his left. Max shoved down his pants and opened his eyes in time to see a naked Rachel rip open the foil packet with her teeth and poise the condom over the tip of his erection. Clenching his teeth, Max let her finish the task without his help while his hands fisted into the bed sheets.

The time for subtlety and patience ended. With his heart thundering a frantic cadence, Max sat up, flipped Rachel onto her back and slid into her with one long thrust.

The perfection of Max buried deep inside her robbed Rachel of breath. Five years was a long time to go without being complete. And complete was how she felt in Max's arms. No other man reached past her defenses and captured her heart the way he did.

"You feel amazing," he said, voice husky and raw as if overused. The timbre rasped against her nerve endings with delightful results. "I'm sorry I didn't take it slower. I wanted to."

"You always wanted to delay the good stuff," she groused, but couldn't hide her smile.

He dropped a kiss on her mouth. "And you were always rushing me."

"Like this?" She placed her feet on the mattress and rocked her hips into his.

"Exactly like that."

But he began to move with her and the incredible slide of his thick length in and out of her body transported her beyond speech. She peaked fast, the climax shocking her with its intensity and duration.

"What the hell?" she muttered as his body continued to move against hers, stronger now. "Where did that come from?"

"Where they all come from."

He kissed her hard and long, the play of his tongue mimicking the movements of his lower body. To her intense disbelief, pleasure began to spiral upward again. Impossible. She was sated, exhausted by the intensity of her orgasm, yet another loomed on the horizon. Max slipped his hand between their bodies, finding the knot of sensitive nerves and plying it to great effect.

"Come for me again," he demanded. "Come hard. I want to hear it."

Faster and harder he thrust. Teeth bared, breath coming in heavy pants, he moaned her name, sounding as if it ripped from deep within his soul.

"Yes," she clutched his shoulders, driving her nails in as another orgasm rippled outward from her womb. "Yes, Max. Now."

And he came. She watched it unfold. Her inner muscles clenched in aftershocks as he bucked against her, wild and ferocious in his release. It thrilled her that she'd done this to him. For him.

He collapsed onto her with a gush of air and rolled them onto their sides. With Max still locked deep within her body, she bound his legs with her thigh, needing to keep them connected as long as possible.

"I'd forgotten how it was," he murmured, his palm damp against her sweat-soaked cheek.

She laughed then. It burst from her like the trill of a happy songbird. "So did I."

Time and self-preservation had dulled her memories of him. Of this. How else could she have gotten on with her life? And now that she'd tasted the amazing passion between them again, how was she supposed to walk away a second time?

When he pulled out of her arms and headed into the bathroom, she rolled onto her stomach and buried her face in the pillow. The sight of so much male perfection had aroused her all over again. She tingled with glee at the thought that he was hers, and hers alone, all weekend.

And after that?

The question clawed its way out of her subconscious and roosted in the front of her mind. Max was never going to marry. Even if his father's infidelity and mother's acceptance of it hadn't given him a sour view of the institution, there'd always been misgivings lingering in the back of his mind. Hesitations that had bloomed into full-blown skepticism after she'd made him an unwitting participant in betraying her marriage vows. Which meant, even if he changed his mind about marriage, he'd never change his mind about her.

Sunday morning, Max leaned his forearms on the balcony railing off the master bedroom and watched the rising sun shift the color of the sky from soft pinks and lavenders to a bright coral and gold. The wind had picked up overnight, and blew against his face, carrying the scent of brine to his nostrils. A jogger went by, nodding to a couple walking hand in hand as he passed. Farther east along the beach, a black lab chased a stick into the surf, bounding into the water with great enthusiasm.

Behind him, Rachel slept like someone who'd spent an exhaustive night making passionate love. He caught himself grinning. He'd worn her out. And she'd worn him out, but not enough to still the thoughts circling and bashing together in his head like bumper cars.

Last night, his mother had called. She was working on the seating arrangements for her thirty-fifth wedding anniversary party next weekend and wondered whether or not he was bringing a date. He should have told her he was flying solo; that had been his plan when he'd first learned his parents were renewing their vows and planning a big celebration.

His thoughts coasted to the naked woman slumbering in the room behind him.

If he asked Rachel to accompany him, the invitation would alter the texture of their relationship. No longer could he pretend that his interest was purely driven by sexual need. If he introduced her to his family, they'd be approaching something that resembled dating. Is that what he wanted?

Five years ago, before finding out she was married, he'd been ready to head down that road. Four short days with her had caused him to consider what his future would be like with her in it.

This weekend wasn't supposed to be about starting fresh. It was supposed to be about settling old business and Rachel seemed on board with that. Why alter course and sail into a storm when the skies before him were a calm blue?

He could tell himself that he was simply taking her for moral support. Both his brothers would be accompanied by their wives, and there was something about the way Sebastian and Nathan regarded him these days that felt a whole lot like pity. As if life was so much better for them. Both of their wives had them wrapped around their slender fingers. With children on the way, they were as trapped as two men could be. So why the hell did they seem so damned blissful?

Slender arms circled him from behind. Against his back, the soft press of Rachel's breasts, encased in thin silk, jump-started his body. Her hands played over his chest as her lips trailed over his shoulder. He closed his eyes, savoring the sweet seduction of her caresses until her teeth grazed the tender skin below his armpit and her fingers dove below the waistband of his pajama bottoms.

Lust surged, but instead of losing himself in sensual oblivion, he caught her wrists to stop the sexy exploration and trapped her hands in his. "Come with me to my parents' anniversary party next weekend."

"I don't think that's a good idea." Her body tensed as he dragged her around to face him. "You don't want your family getting to know me."

No, he didn't.

"My mother thinks I'm bringing a date." He drew a fingertip along her spine and felt her shiver.

She pushed against his chest. "I'm sure you can find someone to take in the next few days."

At her resistance, every bit of his ambivalence vanished. "I asked you."

Bending down, he hoisted her onto his shoulder and strode back toward the rumpled king-size bed, her fists hammering on his back all the while. He dumped her onto the mattress and slid his gaze from her ankles to her well-kissed mouth and stormy gaze. Gorgeous.

He set his knee on the mattress beside her right hip and pinned her in place with a stern look. "And we're not leaving this room until you agree."

Seven

Rachel hid a yawn behind her hand as Max turned the corner and arrived on her street. With her work schedule, she was accustomed to sleeping less than eight hours a night. But usually she lazed in bed on Sunday mornings and caught up on her rest. This Sunday morning she'd been in bed, but it hadn't exactly been lazy or restful.

As they neared her house, she automatically checked for Hailey's car in the driveway. She didn't really expect to see it there. Hailey had been spending more and more time with Leo. It wouldn't be long before they moved in together. Especially now that they were engaged.

Rachel sighed. She was going to miss having her sister around. The years Hailey spent at college were different. Then, Rachel had acted as parent. She'd shouldered financial responsibility for her sister's schooling, worried about how her studies were going, and planned for the future. Now, Hailey was a capable, accomplished woman in charge of her life. She'd taken charge of her dreams. Soon, she would be making plans with her husband. Rachel's role had been reduced to that of loving sister and nothing more.

It left her feeling a little lost.

Enter Max. Was she using him to fill a void? Being with him certainly filled a place inside her that had been empty for a long, long time.

He swung into her driveway and stopped behind her car. He stared through the windshield in silence for a long moment. "I don't want to drop you off and go home to an empty house."

Why did he always know exactly what to say to melt her insides?

"Inviting you in is not an option." She rushed a shaky hand through her tousled hair. "We'll just end up…" She flipped her hand in a circular motion. "You know."

He laughed. Her heart expanded at his relaxed expression and the silver shards that sparkled in his gray eyes. Max happy was like watching the most gorgeous sunrise ever. Just being in proximity to him in his current mood made her feel lighter than air.

"What if I promise to keep my hands off you?"

"You can stay for dinner," she said. "Although, it might have to be pizza because I don't know if we have any food in the house."

"Why don't you see what's there. We can always run to the store."

Rachel got out of the car, amused by the thought of Max in a grocery store. He had a housekeeper to shop, cook and clean for him. She had a hard time picturing him pushing a cart down the pasta aisle and deciding between linguini and bow ties.

"What's so funny?" he demanded, snaking his hand around her waist as they headed toward the side door that led into her kitchen. He crowded her on the steps, his solid muscles bumping her curves in tender affection.

Her body reacted accordingly, awakening to each cunning brush of hip and shoulder. "The thought of you shopping for groceries." She dug her keys out of her purse and slid her house key into the lock. It had been acting up lately so she needed to jiggle it a bit to get the tumbler to align properly.

Beside her, Max stiffened. "Someone slit your tires."

"What?"

Before she could turn around, he was off the steps and prowling around her car like a pride leader who'd had his territory invaded by a stray.

"All four of your tires are flat." His gaze shot to her. Worry pulled his mouth into a hard line. "You need to call the police."

"No." Her mind worked furiously. Brody had sounded more intense than usual during his last phone call, pushing her because the guy he owed money to wasn't satisfied by a partial payment. Did her slashed tires mean Brody's debt had become hers?

"What do you mean *no?*"

Seeing Max's surprise, she scrambled for an explanation. "I'm sure it's just neighborhood kids acting up. I'll call a tow truck and get new tires."

"This is serious vandalism," Max persisted. "You need to report it."

And explain her troubles in front of Max? Not likely. Besides, she didn't know for sure this had anything to do with Brody and his money problems. "It's not worth the hassle. The police won't be able to track down the culprits."

"You don't know that."

"It probably happened in the middle of the night when everyone was asleep so there won't be any witnesses. I'll have the tires replaced. It's no big deal."

Max set his hands on his hips. "Has this sort of thing happened in your neighborhood before?"

"Not to me," she hedged.

"Something's going on that you're not telling me. I don't like it."

"Nothing is going on. It's just some stupid vandalism." Her voice grew more strident as Max continued to press. Rachel gathered a long breath and aimed for calmer speech. "Let's go inside. I need to find someone who can fix the car or I won't make it to work on time tomorrow. And you know how difficult my boss is if I'm late." She tried for humor but it fell flat in the face of Max's scowl.

He took her by the elbow and walked her into the house. Once the door was shut and locked, he pulled out his cell phone and dialed a number. It turned out to be a friend that owned a repair shop. Rachel retreated to her bedroom while Max arranged to have her car picked up and the tires replaced.

Her heart pounded with vigorous force against her ribs as she dropped her overnight bag on the bed. A quick check told her Max was still on the phone. She shut the door and took her cell into the adjoining bathroom.

"Someone slashed my tires," she said when Brody answered.

"Yeah, well, I told you this guy plays rough."

"This is your problem, not mine. Did you tell him where I live?"

"It was that or he was going to beat me up."

Coward. She let her disgust come through in her tone as she said, "You're a bastard for making me a part of your problem. Did you explain to him that I don't have any more money to give you or him?"

"You could ask that rich boyfriend of yours," Brody responded, sounding so much like a whiney six-year-old that it was all Rachel could do to not hang up on him.

How had Brody found out about Max? And if her ex had told the goon about her, would Brody send him in Max's direction next? She had to stop that from happening.

"I already asked him," she lied. "He broke up with me over it, so there's no money coming from him."

"Ask again. Do whatever you have to do to convince him to give you the money."

"He won't speak to me and I'm done talking to you. If anything else happens, I'm going to the police."

"You're a bitch," Brody snarled, changing tactics. "He won't stop coming after you."

"You tell him he'd better." Or she'd what? Rachel's hands shook, making the phone bump against her ear. She couldn't believe this was her talking. But then, she'd never been this mad before, and with Max in the other room, she felt safe. "And if you don't," she continued, "he will be the least of your problems. I'll come after you myself."

Now, she did hang up. And her knees gave out. She sat on the toilet seat until her hands stopped shaking. Then, she returned to the kitchen where Max stood beside her small breakfast table, feet spread, arms crossed, a determined expression on his face.

She ignored his militant stance and peered into the refrigerator. Hailey had gone shopping at some point during the week. Rachel sighed in relief. She couldn't face going past her car's four flat tires right now.

She pulled out two plastic-wrapped packages and turned toward Max. "Steak or pork chops?" she asked with false brightness. Either could be grilled and served with red potatoes and a fresh salad.

"It doesn't matter. We're not staying here for dinner. Grab some clothes. You're coming home with me."

Dismay flooded her. She stuck the pork chops back in the refrigerator, hiding her expression from him. "Steak it is."

"Didn't you hear me?"

"I heard you, but I'm not going anywhere."

"You could be in danger."

"Because my tires were slit?" she scoffed, but very real panic fluttered in her gut.

"Because I don't think it was a random bit of vandalism."

"And why is that?"

"Who'd you go into the bathroom to call, Rachel? I heard you talking to someone when I came in to see if you were all right."

Of course he'd followed her into the bedroom. He was worried about her. Warmth pooled in Rachel's midsection. No one had worried about her since her father had died. It would be so easy to drop her guard and tell Max all her troubles. He would help her take care of Brody. And then he would walk away because when he found out she was keeping secrets from him about her ex-husband a second time, he would be angry with her all over again.

"I was talking to Hailey."

"And you had to go into the bathroom and shut the door to do that?" He scowled. "What sort of fool do you take me for?"

Rachel worried the inside of her lower lip. "I can't talk about this with you."

"Can't or won't?"

She couldn't face the cold fury in his eyes. Her heart worked hard in her chest as the silence stretched. "Both," she said at last, her voice catching on a jagged breath. "It's none of your concern."

His eyes narrowed. "I care about you. Why don't you think it's my concern?"

"Care?" Her heart swelled as hope poured into it. But what did Max's admission mean?

"You sound surprised."

"More confused. I don't know what you expect of me."

"I don't expect anything."

"But you do. You expect me to let you into my life."

"I want to help with whatever's going on."

"I don't need your help."

Frustration built inside him like a sneeze. She watched it pull his lips into a tight line and bunch his muscles. He frowned. He glared.

"You're getting it whether you like it or not. Pack."

This wasn't going well. "No."

"Rachel."

"Look, this thing between us. It's supposed to be about hot sex until the passion burns out. You didn't sign up for providing moral support and I didn't ask for a white knight to rescue me."

"That's what you think I'm doing?"

"Isn't it? After what happened between us five years ago, you admitted you don't trust me. Are you saying you've changed your mind?"

His stony stare gave away none of his thoughts. "The way you've been behaving tonight gives me no reason to."

She couldn't let him see how much his admission hurt. "Maybe we should return our relationship to that of boss and assistant without benefits."

"Is that what you want?" He asked the question in a deadly tone, soft and calm.

Rachel shivered. If she gave him a truthful answer, she'd open her heart up to be hurt. He'd know how much she cared for him, what having him in her life meant to her.

"It might be for the best." She turned back to the refrigerator, unsure her whopping big lie would stand up to his scrutiny.

Max came up behind her and held the door closed. "Might be?" His breath tickled her nape. The sensation raised the hairs along her arm. "Are you saying you don't care if I walk out the door and we never see each other again? Because that's what's going to happen. And if I go, don't bother showing up at work tomorrow. Consider your contract terminated."

"That's unfair."

"Maybe, but that's the way I roll."

"All because I won't let you take charge of my problems? That's ridiculous."

"No, what's ridiculous is that you won't let me help you."

She turned and put her back against the counter, feeling the bite of the Formica in the small of her back. "I don't let anyone help me."

"Not your employees?"

"I pay them to do a job."

"Hailey?"

Rachel shook her head. Crossing her arms gave her a little breathing room as his chest loomed closer. "I've taken care of her all my life."

"Who takes care of you?"

"I do." And she was damned proud of that fact.

His voice softened. "Everyone needs help from time to time."

"Not me."

"Why?"

"Because, every time I turn to someone for help they take advantage of me." She slid sideways away from him putting some distance between them.

"You think I'm going to take advantage of you?"

"Maybe." She didn't really. Of course, she hadn't thought

Aunt Jesse or Brody would leave her worse off financially than before she'd accepted their help, either.

"You can't be serious?"

Fool me once, shame on you. Fool me twice, shame on me. She'd be a complete idiot if she got fooled a third time.

"Given my financial situation, you probably think that it's far more likely that I'd take advantage of you than the other way around." She hardened her heart against the longing to fling herself into his arms and tell him everything. Once upon a time it had been so easy to trust. But she'd learned the hard way not everyone had her best interests at heart. "But I can't take that chance."

"You don't trust me?"

Instead of answering, she shrugged.

Max blew out his breath. "If anyone in this relationship deserves not to trust, it's me."

"I never asked you to trust me," she reminded him. "I'm sorry if I've upset you, but I need to do this myself." She tried a smile. "And what's wrong with that? You and I both know this thing between us is going to burn out eventually. It'll be easier to part ways if I don't owe you anything."

"I wouldn't expect you to owe me."

"I wouldn't feel comfortable taking help without being able to pay you back."

Max wasn't usually at a loss for words, but he seemed to be struggling with what to say to her now. Rachel imagined he was sorting through his conflicting impulses. Continue to push into her life and become the guy she could rely on, the one who would be there when things got difficult or uncomfortable. Or just enjoy the physical side of their relationship and be the guy that moved on before things got too complicated.

"Do you want me to find someone to come in for me starting tomorrow?"

The way his eyes widened, he hadn't expected her to be so matter-of-fact about ending things. He didn't know how much armor she'd wrapped around her heart or how many times she'd smiled in the face of heartbreak.

"No." He scrubbed at his unshaven cheek and studied her from beneath long, dark lashes. "Get in when you can. We're not done with this. Not by a long shot."

Rachel nodded, her throat too tight to speak as she watched him disappear out her door. For a long time her legs were too unsteady to move. By the time she walked to her large front window and sank to the floor, Max's car was long gone. She rested her chin on the sill and wished he could hear her silent plea for him to come back, take her in his arms and tell her everything was going to be okay.

A half an hour ticked by before she gave up hope. Max couldn't help her because she wouldn't let him. If she was miserable, she had only herself to blame.

Max drove out of Rachel's neighborhood, his gut on fire. He hadn't been this mad since Nathan decided to join the family business a year ago. But at least then, his anger made sense. His half brother had been pushing his way into a family where he didn't belong since their father brought him home twenty years ago.

Max had no real reason to be mad at Rachel. She didn't want his help. So what? She had an independent streak a mile long. He'd known that about her since they first met.

Did he really think she owed him an explanation about the things going on in her life? What were they to each other? Lovers. Casual ones at that. He'd told her they had no future. He'd given her a clear picture of his boundaries. Now he was upset because she didn't need him?

Max gunned the engine and pulled out into traffic.

This was for the best. It would be easier in the long run if they didn't draw out the goodbyes. A clean break. Just like last time.

Only here he was. In deeper than last time. On fire. Singed body and soul by emotions only she aroused. Around every corner, more secrets. More lies. And his need for her showed no sign of abating any time soon.

The next morning he arrived at the office tired and cranky. However, his surly mood brightened slightly at the sight of Rachel at her desk looking just as exhausted. She didn't greet him as he neared, but her tight expression told him she was acutely aware of his presence. To his dismay, he was relieved to see her. Happy, in fact. The sight of her shouldn't lift his spirits. He was still mad at her.

"I told you to take your time getting in this morning," he said, accepting the cup of coffee she held up to him.

"I know. And I appreciate it, but Hailey brought me in."

"Did you tell her what happened?"

Rachel shook her head. "She saw my car and she was no more happy about it than you were."

"Why am I not surprised?"

She appeared so miserable it took all his considerable willpower to keep from sweeping her into his arms and kissing away the worry lines between her brows. Instead, he jerked his head toward his office.

"Come in for a second."

She hesitated. "Is this about work? Because from here on out, that's all I want to talk to you about."

"Yes. It's about work. I have a difficult situation with an employee and I'd like your opinion on how to handle it."

Once he had her inside his office, he shut the door and gestured her into one of his guest chairs. Then he strode to the window and stood staring out over downtown Houston. Behind him, he heard her soft sighs and the creak of wood as she shifted in the chair, impatient for him to begin.

"Last night you said people had taken advantage of you. What happened?"

"You said you had a situation with an employee."

"You're an employee." Max turned and let his gaze catch on hers. "We have a situation."

"I'm a contractor working for you."

"Same difference."

"And nothing about this situation has to do with our professional relationship."

"It has everything to do with my ability to concentrate on work."

"I'll quit."

"It won't change my ability to get my job done. Five years ago, you walked out of my life and never looked back. That's not going to happen again."

"What are you saying?"

Yes, what was he saying? "That I want to see where this goes. And I want to start by learning about your past and your present. Maybe that way we can have a future."

"It will never work between us."

He snorted. Any other woman he'd ever dated would have been dancing for joy at what he'd just offered. He had to pick the one woman more skittish about commitment than he was. "What makes you so certain of that?"

"The biggest problem is you can't trust me."

"And you don't trust me," Max countered, still smarting from that revelation. "That puts us on the same page."

She crossed her arms over her chest. "We're not even in the same bookstore."

"Let's see if we can change that. Tell me who took advantage of you that makes you so skittish about accepting help."

She opened her mouth, but no words came out. A second later, she bit her bottom lip. Max waited while she grappled with what story to tell him and how much to tell. Letting her sort it out without prompting tested his patience, but he kept silent. At last, she seemed to come to some sort of decision. Her breath puffed out.

"Aunt Jesse." She closed her eyes. "My dad's sister."

"What happened?"

Instead of forcing intimacy by sitting in the chair next to her, Max gave her space by keeping his big executive desk between them.

"I was eighteen when my dad died and still in my senior year of high school. Hailey was two years younger. Since our mom left when we were both young, I'd always thought of Hailey as my responsibility. She was diagnosed with asthma when she turned six. The first time she collapsed and turned blue, I don't think I've ever been so scared in my whole life. After that, I watched her like a hawk, making sure she had her inhaler with her at all times. She was my baby sister. I couldn't lose her, too."

Too? Max wondered if she knew what she'd given away with that one word. Her mother had disappeared when she was four. Rachel had felt the loss no matter what she was willing to admit to herself. And then her father died. Max suspected protecting herself against loss had become second nature. Pity the man who tried to break down those walls.

"Who took you in after your dad died?"

Rachel stared at her hands. "No one. I dropped out of school and went to work full-time to make ends meet until we received the money from Dad's insurance policy. He took it out because you can be as careful as anything when you're out on the gulf, but accidents happen. No one expected he'd be shot during a convenience-store robbery twenty minutes from home."

"You never graduated?"

She shook her head. "I got my GED. I needed to take care of Hailey. Only it was a lot more expensive than I was expecting. And I was working all the time. By the time we got the insurance money, I was exhausted and worried about how I was going to handle everything. We had no medical insurance and Hailey's asthma had been flaring up a lot more since Dad died. The medication was expensive. That's when I called Aunt Jesse."

"Was she able to help?"

"She told us to come live with her in Biloxi. We'd have a place to stay while Hailey finished high school. I could work and maybe go to a community college. The rest of the money could go toward a real college for Hailey. She was always the smarter one."

"So, what happened?"

"For a while everything seemed okay. Then one day Aunt Jesse came home and asked if she could borrow Dad's life insurance money for a couple days."

"And you gave it to her."

"It was supposed to be a loan until she got paid at the end of the week. I probably should have said no, but she took us in when we needed help and she was family." Rachel's bitter smile said more than her expression. "She took the money and disappeared. We were stuck in Biloxi with no money, no friends and no family."

Her story would have wrung sympathy out of the most jaded heart.

"Did you call the cops?"

"And tell them what? That I'd lent money to our aunt and she'd disappeared?"

"Did you look for her?"

Rachel shook her head. "For all she was our closest living relative, we knew nothing about her life or her friends. Or, we didn't until people showed up looking for her. That's when we found out she was dealing drugs and had some rather scary acquaintances."

"Did any of them hurt you?"

"No. After the first guy came knocking, we didn't stick around."

"What happened?"

"I had a waitressing job. I picked up more hours. We found a small studio apartment in a relatively safe neighborhood and scraped by." Rachel downplayed what must have been a scary time for her with a single shoulder shrug and a self-deprecating smile.

Max's admiration for her went up several dozen notches. "I'm sorry you had such a tough time of it."

Rachel's eyes hardened into sapphire chips. "It was my fault we were in the mess."

"How do you figure that?"

"Hailey begged me to stay in Gulf Shores. She wanted to finish high school with her friends. But I was too scared about being solely responsible for her to listen. I wasn't ready to be an adult. Don't you get it? I screwed up. If we'd stayed put, Aunt Jesse wouldn't have stolen the insurance money. It would have been so much easier."

"You were eighteen. Cut yourself some slack."

"Life doesn't cut you slack," she said. "Life comes at you hard and fast and you either meet it head-on, duck, or get blindsided. I've promised myself not to get blindsided again."

Yet Max had the sense that something had blindsided her recently. Something that wasn't him. Something she wouldn't let him help her with.

"You said people *helped* you."

"What?"

"Last night. You said people. That's plural. Who else took advantage of you?"

She offered him a sad smile. "Sorry. I only reveal one major mistake from my past at a time. Tune in next week for the continuing saga of Rachel Lansing's journey into bad judgment."

"Don't shut me out. I want to know everything about you." Max hated the way she kept deflecting his questions. It created a chasm between them when all he wanted was to get close to her. "You know you can trust me."

"Of course I do. It's just that I get depressed when I think about all the mistakes I've made. Can't we talk about something else?"

As much as he wanted to push harder, he recognized the stubborn set of her mouth and knew they would only end up fighting if he bullied her for answers.

He tossed a file across the desk toward her. "Take a look at the Williamsburg numbers in their strat plan. They don't add up. I didn't have time to check it over this weekend and I'm supposed to be on a conference call with them at eleven."

Her relief at being back on professional footing was so palpable she might have stood up and given a double fist pump. Max watched her head out of his office, a slim silhouette in her long pencil skirt and fitted jacket. He wanted to take her in his arms and promise he wouldn't let her down the way others in her life had. But was that something she'd believe when he wasn't sure himself if it was something he could deliver?

Eight

Rachel sat down at her desk and opened the file she'd been working on before Max summoned her into his office. The numbers blurred on the page. She sat back and rubbed her eyes, then reached for her tall coffee with the three shots of espresso. Max was a bad influence on her in more ways than one.

What had possessed her to tell him about Aunt Jesse?

She owed him no explanations. The intimacy they'd developed was physical, not emotional. Yet, she couldn't deny that sharing the story had lifted a little weight off her shoulders. Not much, but enough to help her get through the day. To clear her mind for how she would handle things with Brody. She simply had to find the twenty-five thousand she still owed him.

You could borrow the money from Max. If you asked, he'd help.

And have to explain to him about Brody and why she'd

married him. As if his opinion of her wasn't bad enough already, Max could add opportunist and user to her list of flaws. Besides, she didn't want her ex-husband to come between them again. Although, at the rate she was screwing things up on her own, it wouldn't matter what she told Max. Given the way their conversation had gone last night, he was probably done with her right now.

Rachel made notes on the file Max had asked her to look at and checked in with Devon to see if anything had come up. He was proving to be a great manager despite his reservations about taking on the responsibility. Maybe this meant she could take a long weekend for herself after everything was over. Four days with nothing to do and no worries sounded like heaven.

But was it reality? Since coming to work for Max, she'd been drifting in a fantasy world. The time for daydreams was over.

Right at eleven, Max's conference call began with the general manager of their Williamsburg operations. While he was asking the questions she'd posed about their numbers, his second line lit up. Rachel answered the call. It was Andrea.

"How are things going?" Rachel winced in sympathy at the loud cries in the background.

"As well as can be expected with a baby who's up all hours of the night with colic."

"I hope things get better soon."

"Me, too."

"Max is on a conference call at the moment. Do you want me to have him call you?"

A long pause preceded Andrea's response. "No. I'll try him again later."

Rachel picked up on the other woman's change of tone. "Is something wrong?"

"Not wrong." But something was up. Rachel could hear it in Andrea's voice.

"Anything I can help you with?"

"Look, I don't exactly know how he persuaded you to fill in for me, but you should probably find someone to take over on a permanent basis."

"You're not coming back?"

"Ned and I discussed it on and off since the middle of my pregnancy. Max is great, but he works such long hours." Andrea tried for cheerful but her tone fell flat. "Now with Ben not sleeping, I'm even more exhausted than I was before he was born. We just think it would be better if I stayed home for his first year. Maybe longer if we decide to get pregnant again right away."

"That makes sense to me." Rachel's mind raced. She needed to call Devon right away about possible candidates for a permanent position. "You have to make your family your priority." If anyone understood that, she did.

Andrea's laugh released some of her tension. When she spoke next, she sounded less like she was carrying fifty pounds of salt on her shoulders. "Thanks, Rachel. I hope Max hasn't been too hard on you. I know what he's like when things don't go exactly to his plan."

"Well, don't worry about that anymore. You just concentrate on that baby of yours. He's the important one."

"Thanks."

Rachel ended the call and dialed Devon, giving him the heads-up that they were now dealing with a permanent placement.

"What are you up to now?" a deep voice demanded from behind her.

Rachel glanced over her shoulder and spied Max standing in his doorway. Her pulse jumped as it always did when he was around. He had an annoying habit of sneaking up on her.

"I've got to go," she said to Devon, and hung up. She glanced toward the phone and noticed his line was no longer lit up. "That was a short conference call."

"After I used your notes to point out to them where their numbers still weren't good enough, they decided to go back and reassess. We're scheduled to talk this afternoon. Who was that on the phone?"

"Devon. Andrea called a few minutes ago. She's not coming back. We've got three candidates for you to interview."

His gaze swept her features, settled on her mouth for a moment longer than the rest, then reconnected with her eyes. "How fast can you get them here for interviews?"

"It would go faster if I could work from my office. I need access to my files. My notes. Those are at my office."

"Then go."

And just like that it was over. His abrupt dismissal left her floundering in dumbfounded silence.

What was it about Max that turned her from a hardheaded business woman into a sentimental fool?

A lean, muscular body made to drive a woman mad in bed.

A personality that was one-third angry bear, one-third stubborn mule and one-third cuddly tiger.

But it was the way he looked at her as if she was the only woman he'd ever desired that turned her insides to mush. How could she help but fall under his spell?

It was a short three blocks back to the building that housed Lansing Employment Agency, and Rachel used the time to gather her scattered emotions into a nice neat ball. Sharp pains began in her stomach as she swallowed the desire to cry or shout out her unhappiness. Max was done with her. What had she expected? A tearful goodbye?

Devon was on the phone as she went past his office. Knowing he would be full of questions, she took a deep breath and tucked all emotion away.

"What are you doing here?" he asked from her doorway moments after she dropped into her executive chair. "Did you quit or did we get fired?"

"Neither." After playing assistant for Max these last four weeks, she'd forgotten how wonderful it felt to be the one in charge. "Max wants to interview potential candidates as soon as possible. It'll go faster if I'm here."

"You're on the verge of netting us another big commission and yet you don't look happy."

"Of course I'm happy."

But to her intense dismay, tears filled her eyes. Devon stared at her in stunned silence, before rushing in and kneeling beside her chair.

"What happened? Was it Max? Did he upset you? Do you need me to go kick his ass?"

The thought of five-foot, nine-inch Devon kicking anyone's ass, much less Max's, made her chuckle. Shaking her head, she straightened her shoulders and shook off her melancholy.

"No. Nothing like that. I did something really stupid."

"I don't believe that for a second. You're one of the most savvy businesswomen I've ever met."

"I slept with Max."

"Ah," Devon said cautiously.

"What do you mean, *ah?*"

"I'm not surprised, that's all. You said you'd known him before. So what happened?"

Telling Max about Aunt Jesse earlier today had caused a crack in her self-imposed isolation. She'd felt better, lighter, after sharing her struggles in the aftermath of her father's death. Drawing on Max's strength had helped make the memories less painful. No matter how much she isolated herself, she wasn't alone. Telling Devon about Max could provide the same sense of relief.

"He and I met five years ago in Alabama."

The whole story poured out of her. She explained about her affair with Max. She talked about her financial problems with Brody. She told Devon about keeping everything from Hailey and about her slashed tires. Max's offer of help and her subsequent refusal.

"I understand everything," Devon said. "Except the part where you won't tell Max about the trouble your ex-husband is causing."

Rachel dabbed at the tears that had overflowed onto her cheeks. "My being married to Brody is what caused Max to despise me the last time. I don't want him involved in case Brody sets the loan shark on him."

"So, all your problems stem from the fact that you're trying to keep your sister and Max from worrying about you and pushing them away in the process."

"That's not fair."

"But it's what you're doing."

"So, what am I supposed to do? Explain to Hailey that I stayed married to Brody even though he was stealing from me to pay his gambling debts? That I was then so desperate to get free that I let myself agree to a ridiculous divorce agreement that compelled me to pay back the hundred thousand dollars it cost for her college education? And that I'm being harassed by Brody and whatever goon he owes money to?"

"For starters."

"I can't. I've spent my entire life protecting her. Don't ask me to stop now."

Devon shook his head. "She was a kid back when all the bad stuff happened. She's an adult now. Tell her the truth and let her be someone you can lean on."

"She's getting married. She's starting a fresh new life." Rachel shook her head and dried her eyes. "I don't want her to have to worry about the past."

Devon blew out a breath. "I can see why Max got angry with you."

Despite his neutral, slightly sad tone, Rachel felt as if she'd been slapped. "He wanted nothing from our relationship except sex."

That was a cop-out. She didn't really believe that's all she and Max had. But it was more comfortable to cling to that notion than to open herself up to hope and end up getting hurt.

"He invited you to his parents' anniversary party."

Part of her longed to believe Devon's optimistic take on her and Max. Spending time with him made her happier than she'd ever been. But he'd insisted from the start that he wasn't with her for the long term. And his track record bore that out.

"He's between women at the moment."

Devon stared at her for a long time. "Or maybe he's found the one he wants."

"Or maybe," she countered stubbornly, "he hasn't. And he just likes to stick his nose in where it doesn't belong."

"You don't really believe that's all there is to it."

"I can't afford to believe anything different." Despair was close to swallowing her unsteady composure.

"So, you're going to push him away?"

Rachel picked up her pen and twirled it. "After what happened last night and today, I don't think I'm going to have to."

To her surprise and despite their rocky week, when Saturday night rolled around, Rachel found herself at Max's side as they ascended the steps of his parents' home in the western suburb of Houston, a gated community with wall-to-wall mansions. She had no clear idea how she had arrived at this moment. Sure, she'd given her grudging acceptance that morning in Gulf Shores so he'd stop torturing her body with seductive caresses that got her motor revved up, but took her nowhere.

But after their argument at her house and how disinterested he'd been about her leaving Case Consolidated Holdings…

She figured he was done with her.

Then late Wednesday night, he'd shown up at her office with the sea glass bracelet he'd bought her five years earlier. When she'd gone back to Mississippi, she'd left the bracelet behind because it was a talisman representing hope and joy. By returning to her marriage, she didn't believe she deserved such a keepsake.

She couldn't stop wondering why Max had kept the bracelet all these years. Did it mean he'd never stopped caring about her? What if it had no significance at all? Every question battered the armor surrounding her heart. Sleep came only after hours of tossing and turning. Her appetite had dropped off. She caught herself daydreaming at work while Devon worked harder than ever.

And Brody called her often to remind her how impatient he was.

Her life felt like it was spinning out of control and she wasn't sure how much longer she could hang on.

"Stop fidgeting," Max advised. He set his hand at the small of her back, his touch soothing. "You look fine."

Rather than let him see how ragged her emotions were, Rachel retreated into sarcasm. "Fine?" She glazed the word with contempt. "What makes you think any woman wants to be told she looks fine?"

To her intense annoyance, his lips twitched. His relaxed

mood made it hard to keep her glare in place. Why did the man have to make her so damned happy?

"You look gorgeous."

Her harrumph resulted in a full-blown grin.

"I really shouldn't be here," she said for about the hundredth time. "This isn't a business associate or a group of friends, this is your family."

He'd never given her a satisfying answer about his true motive for badgering her to accompany him. In the end, she'd let him convince her to attend the party, but dug in her heels when he insisted she also be there for the family-only renewal of vows that had taken place earlier that afternoon at the church where his parents had originally been married.

"You're here because I didn't want to go through this alone."

His explanation made perfect sense. She was a stand-in because he was between women. She knew better than to call them girlfriends. Max dated, but he didn't get involved. Casual affairs were more his style.

So, what were they doing?

Since Wednesday, she'd gone home with him after work and spent the night at his house. They watched TV. They made dinner. They made love. Playing house. Getting to know each other better with each hour that passed. The chemistry wasn't burning out the way he'd said it would. In fact, it was getting hotter by the day.

Nor was either of them trying to cool things off or slow things down.

Two months, she kept telling herself. That's how long his relationships usually lasted according to the notes in Andrea's computer. She wouldn't think any further into the future than that.

A maid opened the front door as they approached. The grand, two-story foyer Max nudged her into was half the size of her house. She gaped like a girl from a small beach town. Meeting wealthy executives at their offices didn't prepare her for the reality of what money could buy.

"Did you grow up here?" she asked, trying to imagine three energetic boys roughhousing around the expensive furniture and exquisite antiques.

"No. Mom and Dad downsized after they kicked the chicks out of the nest."

Her breath rushed out. "Downsized?"

"This house only has four bedrooms."

"Only." Apparently, her answers were limited to two syllables.

"Come on. Let's go congratulate the happy couple." The mischief vanished from his eyes as he steered her deeper into the house.

With Max's arm around her waist, Rachel floated through the large, perfectly decorated rooms in a haze of anxiety and awe. Her nervousness was tempered by a couple things. First, the beige silk cocktail dress she'd splurged on might have come off the rack of her favorite consignment store, but it was a designer original and she needed that boost of confidence as they passed by women wearing thousands of dollars worth of gowns and jewelry. Second, most of the furniture had been upholstered in tones of cream, beige and gold. That meant she could sit down and virtually disappear.

"There's Mom. Let me introduce you."

She hung back as Max leaned forward and kissed his mother on the cheek. Dressed in a beaded cream gown with diamonds at her ears, wrist and around her neck, Susan Case looked every inch a wealthy socialite, but the smile she beamed at her son looked warm and genuine enough to put Rachel at ease.

"Mom, this is Rachel Lansing. Rachel, my mother, Susan."

Rachel stretched her lips into a smile, hoping her nerves didn't show, and shook the soft hand Susan Case offered. "It's really nice to meet you," she said. "Max talks about you a lot."

"Have you two been dating long?"

"Oh, we're not dating," Rachel insisted in a rush. "I own an employment placement service. I'm helping him find an assistant to replace Andrea."

"I see." But it was obvious she didn't.

Rachel didn't miss the curious glance Susan sent winging toward her son. Beside her, Max radiated displeasure. Well, what did he expect? That she was going to explain the complicated arrangement between them when she wasn't exactly sure how to define it herself?

"How is the hunt for a new assistant going?"

"He's turning out to be a difficult man to please." She shot Max a warning look to shut down whatever protest he was about to make.

"Is he, now," Susan murmured wryly. "Well, I'm sure you'll figure out how to make him happy."

Rachel flushed at the subtext of Susan's remark and wished a sinkhole would develop beneath her feet. Before she mustered a response, a tall man with dove-gray eyes stepped into the trio's circle and wrapped a possessive arm around Susan.

"Good evening." Brandon Case extended his free hand to Rachel. "My son is lucky to have such a lovely companion this evening."

Rachel smiled at Brandon Case as she shook his hand, unable to stop herself from basking in the man's charm. At her side, Max stiffened slightly.

"Congratulations on your thirty-fifth anniversary," she said. Max's tension heightened her own anxiety and the next words that came out of her mouth, she wished back immediately. "What's your secret?"

Susan dipped her head in acknowledgement. "To a long marriage?" She gazed up at her husband. A gentle smile curved her lips. She was obviously very much in love with the man she'd married. "I think you need to be able to forgive each other and laugh together."

Such simplicity took Rachel's breath away. Was that really all there was to it? She thought about her own marriage. She and Brody had failed at both. She couldn't recall a single time when they'd laughed together. In the beginning, they'd gotten along, but it had never been joyful the way it was with Max.

A slight indent had developed between Max's brows at his mother's words. "And that's it? All the pain just magically melts away? Trust is restored with a chuckle?"

Rachel put her free hand on Max's arm and squeezed in sympathy. She'd been so busy thinking about herself this week, she hadn't considered how hard this renewal of vows and anniversary celebration would be on Max. He'd never gotten over his father's infidelity. And now she saw that he was also angry with his mother for staying with a man who'd betrayed her.

"Of course not," Brandon retorted, his gray eyes hard as they rested on his son. "What I did to your mother wasn't forgiven overnight. It took years before she began to trust me again. And now that she does, I would never do anything else to hurt her."

"Max, this is a party," his mother said, her voice showing no signs of stress. "My anniversary party. Please behave."

As the tableau played out before her, Rachel had a hard time swallowing past the lump in her throat. Seeing Max's expression darken and knowing why he was so upset made her realize she'd been a fool to wonder if the passion they shared might lead to something more.

If twenty years had passed without him forgiving his parents their shortcomings, she'd been a fool to hope he would ever forgive her.

Laughter and forgiveness.

His mother was kidding herself. For years she'd turned a blind eye to her husband's second life with the woman he couldn't bring himself to live without. She should have included sacrifice in the mix of ingredients that kept a marriage going. Because, in his opinion, if she hadn't sacrificed her pride, her self-confidence, and her peace of mind, she would have divorced Brandon a long time ago. Instead, her husband had violated her trust with his infidelity and yet she'd stayed.

She'd stayed because she loved him.

And she'd taught Max a valuable lesson about trust, marriage and love. He wouldn't make his mother's mistakes. He wouldn't trust. He wouldn't marry. He wouldn't love.

The first two he could control. It was the last that worried him.

Coming here tonight with Rachel brought home his own weakness. He'd grown preoccupied with a woman who behaved like his father, keeping secrets, sharing only the surface of her life, not the emotions that drove her actions. How could he trust her? What hidden bombs lurked beneath her composed exterior, waiting to detonate at the worst possible time?

A couple weeks ago he'd wagered an extremely valuable car that he wouldn't marry. Falling in love had been the furthest thing from his mind. But that's before Rachel had brought up all the unresolved issues between them. Telling himself that it was nothing more than passion that needed to run its course was a speech he was having a harder and harder time selling. What he felt for her ran deeper than desire. It had sunk its claws into his soul.

He couldn't control his fierce need for her. Just like his father couldn't control whatever had made him stay married to one woman and love another for more than twelve years. Max had become just like his father. He'd grown up despising Brandon because he'd let his emotional need for Nathan's mother damage his marriage, and in Max's eyes, destroyed his credibility and his character.

Her hand slipped into his to draw him along to the buffet. The simple contact tugged his pulse into a sprint.

Being with Rachel made a mockery of his principles. Yet the idea of walking away was sheer agony. He'd believed the only solution would be to purge his need for her. And the only way he knew to do that was to keep her in his bed until he grew tired of her.

Who was he kidding? He grew more attached to her every day.

On their way to the backyard where a dining tent had been set up to accommodate the guests, they were intercepted by a dateless Jason.

"I don't believe we've met." Max's best friend took Rachel's hand and bent forward to smile into her eyes. "I'm Jason Sterling, and you are way too gorgeous to waste your time on my friend here."

Max stiffened at his friend's flirtatious manner. They'd competed over women a time or two, but once either staked his claim, the other immediately backed off. A growl started building in Max's chest as Jason's gaze dropped from Rachel's face to scope out the rest of her.

"Rachel Lansing," she said. "I know your father. How are he and Claire doing?"

"They're doing great, thanks to you. My father's never been happier." Jason's keen eyes surveyed them. "Are you two dating?" A vile grin curved his lips as he looked to Max for confirmation.

"Something like that." Max stared down his friend, warning Jason to keep further comments to himself, and slid his hand into the small of Rachel's back.

Jason looked positively delighted. "How long has this been going on?"

"We're just old friends," Rachel said, offering her own version of their relationship.

"Are you, now?" Jason looked entirely too pleased with himself as he turned to Max. "I got an offer on my '69 Corvette yesterday. Looks like I should take it. I have a feeling there's a new car in my near future."

The taunt infuriated Max. "I've got room in my garage for the 'Vette. Maybe I'll take it off your hands."

Jason just laughed and turned his charm back on Rachel. "Will you sit next to me at dinner?"

"She's with me," Max growled.

"I thought you two were just old friends."

Max stepped between Rachel and Jason, bumping his best friend in the process. "You're supposed to bring a date to events like this, not poach someone else's." It wasn't until he'd settled Rachel at the table and taken his place beside her that his annoyance with Jason dulled to a nagging irritation.

Snarling like a guard dog was not the usual way he kept other men from sniffing around his dates. On the other hand, he wasn't sure he'd ever cared enough to warn anyone off before.

Rachel's hand settled on his thigh. His attention jerked in her direction.

Her eyes were soft with questions. "What was that about?"

"It was just Jason being Jason." For some reason he didn't want to explain about the bet.

"Why did you tell him we were just old friends?"

"I guess it's a little bit of a stretch." Her lips thinned as she pressed them together. "Why did you give him the impression we're dating?"

"Aren't we?"

"I don't think so." She settled her napkin on her lap. "The term seems too tame for what we're doing."

And wasn't she right about that. He remembered how she'd looked this morning in his robe, the dark blue terrycloth contrasting with her pale skin and matching the midnight blue of her eyes. With her hair soaked from her shower, she'd let him pull her close then shook herself like a dog after a swim. He'd retaliated by dumping her onto the mattress and making her all sweaty again. Then, he'd joined her for her second shower of the morning.

Desire seared him, hot and consuming. He laid his arm across the back of her chair and leaned close. When she glanced his way, he captured her gaze and gave her a glimpse of his hunger. To his intense satisfaction, her lips parted and her cheeks flushed.

With the amount of time they'd spent together in the last week, his body shouldn't be clamoring to ditch the party and take her home, but her touch set off a chain reaction inside him. Two things kept him in place. His mom would kill him if he left, and he was eager to take Rachel in his arms on the dance floor.

He covered her hand with his. Their fingers meshed. His emotions settled. The temperature of his desire dipped from raging boil to slow simmer.

On the opposite side of the table Jason watched him through narrowed eyes. Max knew what his friend was thinking, but he was dead wrong. As Sebastian stood to deliver the first toast, Max let his gaze roam around the tent. All the usual suspects had been invited. Immediate family, extended family and friends. About two hundred people in all. Including his illegitimate half brother, Nathan, who sat two tables over with his very pregnant wife, Emma.

For a moment, Max fought irritation. Nathan's presence shone a spotlight on Brandon's infidelity and made a mockery out of celebrating thirty-five years of marriage. Max had never understood how his mother had allowed her husband to bring Nathan into her home after his mother died. Sure, it was the decent thing to do and his mother was kind and generous, but it had to have killed her to explain to all her friends about the twelve-year-old boy with Brandon's gray eyes. Yet to the best of Max's recollection, he'd never heard a cross word between his parents on the subject. He'd never know if his mother had forgiven her husband, or if she'd just decided to bear the humiliation for the sake of her marriage.

He and Sebastian hadn't followed her example of tolerance toward Brandon and their half brother. Even now, twenty years later, Max couldn't come to peace with his father or Nathan. The anger and resentment bubbled far below the surface like a dormant volcano.

And caught up in all those negative emotions were his feelings for Rachel. He couldn't completely let go of the way she'd deceived him all those years ago. Nor could he turn a blind eye to the secrets he knew she kept from him now.

The secrets that were bound to tear them apart.

"What are you doing out here?"

Max looked up from the steering wheel of the '71 Cuda and spied Rachel standing in the doorway that led from the garage into his back hallway. They'd returned from the party fifteen minutes ago and while she'd disappeared into the bathroom to change clothes and brush her teeth, he'd retreated to the one place in the house that had the most soothing effect on him.

"I'm enjoying my latest purchase."

Rachel stepped into the garage, her three-inch heels giving her long legs a positively sinful appearance. She wore the red and black baby-doll nightie Hailey had packed for the trip to Gulf Shores. That weekend, his appetite hadn't afforded her the chance to wear it. He recalled her opinion about the futility of wearing the thing. That he would have it off her in ten seconds.

"Wouldn't you enjoy it more if you took it for a drive?" She stopped near the front of the car and bent down to slide her palms up the hood. The black lace edging her neckline gaped, baring her round breasts. Beneath his intent regard, her nipples puckered against the gown's thin fabric.

The combination of muscle car and half-dressed Rachel was irresistible. He was instantly hard.

"Feel like going for a ride?" He got out of the car and prowled toward her.

She plucked a condom from inside her bodice and held it up. "Maybe later."

He put his arms around her, hands riding the sexy curve of her butt to the nightgown's hem. "How about now?"

He loved the flow of the material over her warm curves and the contrast between the scratchy lace and her silky skin. But he adored the heat between her thighs even more. And the low moan of longing that rumbled through her as he dipped his fingers into the moisture awaiting him there.

She pressed hot kisses to his neck as her fingers dipped inside the elastic waistband of his underwear and slid them down his thighs. He kicked free of the material, groaning his appreciation as her hands rolled the condom on his hot shaft.

Her mouth was open and awaiting his kiss as he lifted her off her feet, savoring the damp slide of her hot, sweet center against his belly. Gently, he placed her on the car's hood, past caring what damage he might do to the very expensive collectible. He only gave himself a second to enjoy the sight of

Rachel splayed across the yellow hood, but the mental snapshot was unforgettable.

The elastic band kept the bodice snug against her chest and allowed the rest of the material to billow around the top of her thighs. However, the nightie was so short that when he'd set her on the car, the fabric rode up, exposing her concave belly and the thatch of dark blond curls at the juncture of her thighs. Nothing looked as gorgeous as she did at the moment.

He stepped between her legs and gathered her butt in his hands. Fastening his mouth on her, barely hearing her gasp past the roar in his ears, he feasted on her. She tasted incredible. Mewling sounds erupted from her parted lips as her fingers clutched his shoulders. He laved her with his tongue, penetrating deep while she writhed within his grasp. He drove her toward orgasm without mercy, ignoring her incomprehensible protests. Maybe later he would give her a turn at him. Right now, he wanted to put his mark on her body and soul.

When she was close to the edge, he slipped two fingers inside her and watched her explode. She screamed his name. Her nails bit into his shoulders as her back arched and her heels found purchase on the bumper. Shudder after shudder pummeled her body, wringing every single sensation possible out of her. Only when she went completely limp did he cease his erotic assault and kiss his way up her body.

Sliding his hands under the elastic beneath her breasts, he rode the material up over her head. She blinked and stared at him, dazzled.

"No fair," she complained. "I was going to do that for you."

"Later," he promised, riding the curve of her breast with his lips.

"It'll have to be much later," she agreed, sifting her fingers though his hair. "Because I can't move at the moment."

"That's okay. You just lie back and let me do all the work." He opened his mouth over her nipple, swirling his tongue around and flicking it over the sensitive tip. Her body jerked as he grazed his teeth against her flesh.

"Whatever you say." She closed her eyes. A half smile curved her lips. She looked the picture of utter contentment.

His heart turned over. It was happening to him all over again. He was falling beneath her spell. Her palms glided along his biceps as he nudged against her entrance. She was so slick, he almost drove straight in. But a week of intense lovemaking had taken the sharp edge off his driving need. He intended to savor every inch of their joining. To take his time enjoying the tight sheath that seemed made just for him.

And to watch her expression as he did so.

For it seemed the only time she truly dropped her guard and let him in was when he was buried inside her. That's when she couldn't fight what she needed or hide her thoughts.

He eased forward, delighting in the play of happy emotions across her features. When he was fully embedded, she surrendered a smile of sheer delight and opened her eyes. Plummeting into their blue depth, Max sank past her doubts and fears to her true heart. Jewel bright, her joy welcomed him. Pure and fierce it connected him to her.

"Again," she coaxed, cradling his face between her hands. "I love the feel of you sliding inside me."

He was happy to oblige her. She crooned her delight as he completed another long slow thrust. It was then that she wrapped her legs around his hips and began moving with him. He increased his rhythm. Pleasure built in slow waves as he took his time and gave her more of exactly what she liked.

And when he came, the pressure, swelling low in his back, exploded through him like a concussion bomb. The waves of pleasure caught Rachel and pulled her into bliss along with him. He lowered his head and touched his lips to hers, fusing their mouths together in a kiss of tender passion.

"Best ride of my life," he murmured against her neck as his heart labored and his lungs pumped.

Her nails grazed along his back to the base of his spine. "Better than racing around the track at a hundred twenty miles an hour?"

"Much, much better."

With his body mostly recovered, he gathered her in his arms and carried her back to bed. Once there, she snuggled at his side, her head on his shoulder, hand on his chest. Peace swept over him. He liked falling asleep next to this woman. Sleepovers were something he usually frowned on. They suggested a level of intimacy he avoided with all the women he dated.

Rachel was different. She knew they had no future. Only the present. They weren't dating. They were lovers. Lovers without expectations. She understood and accepted the limits of their relationship.

Because after much soul-searching tonight, he'd decided it was all he could offer her.

Nine

Max finished interviewing the last of the candidates Rachel had sent him. His respect for her ability to match employer to employee had increased over the last two days. She'd even scheduled the four women in order of their compatibility for both him and the type of work he would have them do, starting with the most likely candidate first and finishing with the woman he liked least.

They were all beautiful. Single. Intelligent. A month ago, fantasizing about any one of them could have occupied him for hours.

Today, his thoughts centered around one woman. Rachel. With her wise and witty opinions of the four candidates melding with his impression of them, he couldn't help but appreciate their similar thought patterns. Already he missed her sitting outside his door. He hadn't realized how often he'd walked past her desk so that he could deliver a remark guaranteed to make her grin or frown at him.

"Thank you for coming by on such short notice," he told the last candidate as he handed her off to his temporary assistant. A capable woman in her fifties, she'd been sent by Rachel to fill in for a few days. "Cordelia, can you show her out?" To his chagrin, he'd already forgotten the candidate's name.

"Of course." Cordelia stood. "And there's a young woman waiting for you in the lobby. Hailey Lansing."

Curious why Rachel's sister would have come to see him, Max headed for the lobby.

"Hailey?" He approached her with a smile. "To what do I owe the honor of your visit?"

Rachel's sister rose to her feet and took the hand he extended. Her brows darted together. "Thanks for seeing me like this. I probably should have called."

Something about Hailey's grave expression and obvious agitation put Max's instincts on red alert. Here was his chance to find out what was really going on with Rachel. She might never forgive him for going behind her back, but if he had to lose her, at least he could say that he'd done everything he could to straighten out whatever had gone wrong in her life.

"Let's get out of here." He gestured toward the elevator. Whatever Hailey had to say involved her sister and he thought it might go down easier with a single-malt scotch.

As the elevator door closed on them, Hailey twisted her engagement ring around and around on her finger and shot him an uncomfortable half smile. "You're probably wondering why I came to see you."

"You could say that."

Given Rachel's proclivity for keeping her problems hidden from everyone in her life, he was dying to know what had brought Hailey to his doorstep. And why she was wringing her purse strap like a dishcloth.

He escorted her across the lobby to the restaurant that occupied a large chunk of the first floor. Known for its fabulous cuisine and rich ambiance, it was a favorite place for those in the surrounding buildings to bring clients. It was also packed for happy hour, but at three in the afternoon, it was early enough that Max was able to find them a table in a quiet corner of the bar.

The waiter brought his usual and Hailey surprised him by ordering a martini.

At his expression, she offered him a weak smile. "It's been a long week."

Even though it was only Wednesday, Max agreed. "What can I help you with?"

"My sister."

Of course. "I thought that might be why you came by." He let an ironic smile kick up one side of his lips. "She's no longer working for me directly."

"I know."

"Then, I'm not sure what I can help you with."

The waiter placed their drinks before them. Hailey took a long sip of her martini before answering. "I found out from our neighbor last night that someone slashed Rachel's car tires."

Max stared into the amber depths of his drink. "Yes, I know. It happened sometime between Friday night when I picked her up and Sunday evening when I dropped her off."

"I knew it." Hailey flashed her straight, white teeth in a triumphant grin.

"Knew what?"

"That you two were involved. The sexual tension between you that night at dinner was hot."

Max leaned back and redirected the conversation where he wanted it. "Rachel said the neighborhood kids slashed her tires."

"That's what she told me, too, but I know better." Hailey's hunched shoulders suggested she was worried.

Alarm sizzled along his nerve endings. "Then who do you think is responsible?"

"Her stupid ex."

"I didn't realize he lived in Houston." Why hadn't Rachel told him? Why did he even bother asking? She held secrets tighter than a cold-war spy.

"As far as I know, Brody still lives in Biloxi. And my sister doesn't like admitting past mistakes. Brody was a big one."

"Why is that?"

"Because he was a complete jerk. You'd never know it to look at him. He dresses like he's harmless and he can turn that boyish charm of his on and off like a faucet, but beneath the surface, he's creepy."

Something beyond sisterly loyalty tightened Hailey's expression into a stiff mask. Seemed she had a few secrets of her own. But it was the fear that Max glimpsed in her eyes that pumped him full of adrenaline.

"You're not as good at hiding things as your sister. Tell me why he was a complete jerk."

"I didn't spend much time around him, just my last year of high school. And even then, I was cheerleading and on the yearbook staff so I wasn't home much." She took a deep breath and continued. "I didn't like the way he treated Rachel when I wasn't around."

"How did you know how he treated her if you weren't there?"

"Sometimes they didn't know I was home. I spent a lot of time in my room with the door closed. Brody was always on her about putting me first. He said that he was her husband and she should make his needs her priority. I'm ashamed to admit that I was really glad to head off to college. And once I was gone, I stayed away as much as I could, taking summer courses and working." Her chin sank toward her chest. "Part of me hated to leave Rachel alone in that house, but I knew if I showed her I could take care of myself, she could concentrate on her marriage."

"So, he was abusive."

"Not physically. He was too much of a coward to go after her. But I heard them fighting a couple times." Hailey's expression hardened. "Nothing Rachel couldn't handle. My sister's tough. But that's no way to live."

Max acknowledged that with a weary exhalation. "I agree." He didn't like the picture developing in his head. And it made him rethink how angry he'd been with her all those years ago for going back to her ex-husband.

"I guess it's wrong of me to say bad things about him when he paid for my education and everything. That's why I've been paying him back a little every year. I don't want to feel indebted to him at all."

"How much have you paid him?"

"Not much. About twenty thousand."

Max whistled. "That's a pretty big chunk for someone just out of school."

"I still owe him almost eighty." Hailey drew circles around the rim of her martini glass with her finger. "I wish I had it so I could be done with the guy."

"Why did you agree to pay him anything?"

"When Rachel asked him for a divorce he made it pretty clear that he wasn't going to let her go." Hailey winced. "He agreed to let her have a divorce if I paid him back the money he'd shelled out for college."

"That's blackmail."

"It was the only way he'd let her go without a major battle."

Max was liking Rachel's ex-husband less and less with each bombshell Hailey dropped. How had Rachel fallen for a guy like that? Granted, she'd been young, and probably a bit desperate, but had she mistaken gratitude for love? Or was he only hoping that her feelings for such worthless scum hadn't run deep?

"Let me lend you the money to pay off Rachel's ex-husband."

Hailey looked appalled. "That's not why I wanted to talk to you. What you must think of me."

She looked ready to walk out on him. Max put a hand on her arm to calm her. The sisters were very much alike. He hoped her fiancé had a clue what he was getting into. "I think you're charming. And crazy to repay someone like your ex-brother-in-law."

Her features settled into a mutinous expression she'd learned from her sister. "I pay my debts."

"Of course you do," he soothed. "And that's why I offered you the loan. Rachel's ex sounds unstable. I would just feel better if he was out of both of your lives for good."

Hailey shook her head. "Forget about me. It's not me he's harassing. Would you be willing to help Rachel in the same way?"

"Of course." He was insulted she even needed to ask. "But she won't tell me what's wrong much less accept my help. In fact, we had a big fight about it."

"But enough to break up over?"

"No." But it was why he feared their relationship might be over. Pain stabbed his chest. "Why do you ask?"

"Because she's been moping around lately like you two were done." The look she leveled at him was fierce and concerned. "I hope you mean to stick around. The last time you walked away she was different."

"I didn't walk away. She did. She got in a car with her ex-husband. She left me." Was he going to let her walk away from him again? The decision to fight for her had been gaining momentum in his subconscious. He might have noticed sooner if he'd stopped behaving like a pigheaded idiot. "Why did you assume I left her?"

"When we met, I recognized you from a picture she kept on her computer of the two of you. She hadn't looked that happy since before Dad died. I couldn't imagine her giving that up." Hailey's voice trailed away. She looked rattled.

As rattled as Max felt. Those days with Rachel had been the best moments of his life. But Rachel had gone back to her husband. And now he was back in her life again.

Max couldn't lose her this time. "How can I help?"

"She borrowed money from Brody to start the business. He showed up a couple weeks ago to collect the full amount. She paid him, but I don't think she had enough to pay him all of it."

"Is that why he's harassing her? How much is left to pay?"

"I think around twenty-five thousand."

Peanuts. Such a small amount shouldn't cause this much drama.

"Are you sure Brody's hanging around because of the money she owes him?"

"Why else?"

"Maybe he wants her back. You said he was possessive and gave her a hard time about the divorce. So much that you two left town to escape him. If he tracked her down after five years only to call for the money she owes him, why hasn't he come after you, too?"

Hailey's eyes widened. "Do you think he might come after me?"

He hadn't meant to upset her further. "Not if he hasn't already. No. I think this is personal." And if it was, Max was going to make sure Brody stayed out of Rachel's life for good. "Do you have a phone number for this guy?"

"I took it off Rachel's cell."

"Give it to me. I'll take care of him."

Ten

Rachel's office phone rang and her stomach dropped. Ten days had gone by since she'd gone with Max to his parents' anniversary party. Two days ago Max had hired his new assistant. She hadn't heard from him once since. Had her contact with him started and ended with his employment needs? If so, what had the amazing sex on Saturday night been about? Good-bye?

Hearing the phone ring had become torture. Any call could be Max. How should she act with him? Professional? Friendly? What should she say? Were they moving to a different level?

But he never called and she wasn't sure where they stood.

Nevertheless, every time she picked up the phone, her heart lurched as if it was trying to escape her chest.

"Rachel Lansing."

"Well, if it isn't my beautiful girl."

Rachel shuddered. Brody had always called her that and

never meant it. She'd never been his idea of beautiful. Just his idea of someone he could manipulate.

"What do you want, Brody?"

"I want you to meet me."

She rolled the phone cord around her finger. "Why? I already told you I can't pay you anything. There's no need for us to meet."

"The guy I owe money to isn't going to give up unless you tell him that."

"Why do I need to tell him anything? And what makes you think he's going to believe me any more than he believed you?"

"He just wants to meet you."

Rachel didn't like this one bit. "It has to be somewhere public." With lots of security guards within earshot.

"How about that place in the lobby where your boyfriend works? We could have drinks. Catch up."

"He's not my boyfriend." The restaurant in the lobby of Max's building? "Not there. Choose some other place."

"Can't. I already told the guy we'd meet in the bar. Be there at three."

He hung up. Rachel stared at the phone in her hand, consumed by the urge to slam it repeatedly on the edge of her desk. Acid burned her stomach. What was going on? Had Brody told the guys about her connection to Max? Would they follow him to his car one night and slash more than his tires?

Rachel wanted to scream in frustration. She couldn't let anything happen to Max. If that meant meeting Brody and the thug he owed money to, so be it.

Exactly at three, she pushed through the lobby doors and headed toward her rendezvous with Brody and his loan shark. For about the hundredth time she wondered what the hell she was doing. These were dangerous men. But it was a public place. And if it got her off the hook then it would be worth her trouble.

She spotted Brody before she reached the restaurant. He was deep in conversation with another man who faced away from her. She'd recognize those broad shoulders and the arrogant stance anywhere. Max. Her heart hit her toes as the worst of her imagined scenarios began to play out.

Max handed Brody a thick envelope and slid a folded piece of paper into an inner pocket of his suit coat before heading toward the elevator without ever noticing her standing in stunned immobility in the middle of the enormous lobby.

Brody spotted her as soon as Max headed for the elevator. A broad smirk transformed his boyish good looks into engaging handsomeness. The effect was lost on Rachel. She stalked over to him.

"What were you doing with Max?" She pitched her voice low, conscious that Max stood twenty feet away waiting for the elevator.

Brody waggled the envelope. "Collecting the money you owe me."

"Give me that." She made a swipe at the envelope, but Brody lifted it out of her reach.

"I don't think so."

"That money doesn't belong to you."

"The hell it doesn't." Brody's smug smile made her grind her teeth.

"Where's the guy who's been threatening me?"

Brody laughed. "You're such a sap. There never was anyone. I knew you needed motivating so I made him up."

"No guy?" She shook her head, confused. "But you owe someone the money?"

"Nope. I needed the fifty grand to buy into this poker game a buddy of mine is running. I knew you wouldn't give me the money unless you thought I needed help. I remember how scared you were when I owed money to Chuckie back when we were married."

"Poker?" Was she that much of a sucker? Shame overrode her other emotions for a moment. Then she grasped what Brody had done. "You terrorized me and my sister over a stupid poker game?"

Rachel saw red. She raised her fists, ready to beat him silly, but spotted Max returning across the lobby toward them. Her hands fell to her sides, the fight draining out of her.

Max stepped between her and Brody. "Get out of here," He addressed the command to her ex. "And don't let me catch you anywhere near Rachel or her sister ever again."

He might be a bully with her, but Max's threat made him pale. However, when Max made no further move against him, Brody sneered at Rachel and departed across the lobby toward the street.

Frustration surged as Rachel watched her ex-husband getting away. "Damn it, Max." She turned the full brunt of her irritation on him. "What the hell did you do?"

"I paid your debt with your ex. You don't have to worry about the guy ever showing up again."

Dismay consumed her. "You paid my debt? I didn't ask you to do that." Now she was in his debt. Someplace she'd sworn never to be.

"Yours and Hailey's. He's out of both of your lives forever."

Rachel stared at him, some of her anger draining away. "Hailey didn't owe him any money."

Max nodded. "She did. She was paying him back for her schooling."

"What?" Rachel struggled to breathe as the weight of these new revelations crushed her.

"It was the only way she could get him to leave you alone. He agreed to stay out of your life if she reimbursed him the hundred thousand for her college education." Max frowned down at her. "Only you had to go and borrow money to start your agency and bring him back in."

She ripped her wrist from his grasp. "I didn't borrow money from him," she snarled. "I told Hailey that so she wouldn't know what was really going on." Bitter laughter tore from her throat. "What a bunch of idiots we all are. I was already paying Brody back for her schooling. It was part of our divorce decree. He played all of us. You. Me. Hailey." She set her back against a nearby pillar as strength left her limbs. "How much did you give him?"

Max didn't look the least bit worried about what she'd just told him. "A hundred and five thousand dollars."

Rachel gaped at him. "What? Why so much?"

"The twenty-five you owed him plus the eighty Hailey still owed."

"How much had she paid him already?" She shut her eyes, fought tears, and awaited the answer.

"Twenty."

Helpless fury welled up inside her, but she didn't have the energy to vent it. Hailey had been paying Brody behind Rachel's back? That hurt.

"Rachel?" Concern tempered Max's tone. "What the hell is going on?"

She looked up at him. His brows had come together in a concerned frown that made her stomach turn cartwheels. From deep inside her mind, Devon's words surfaced.

Or maybe he's found the one he wants.

Her heart ached for it to be true, but Rachel shied away from the foolish hope.

"I need to get out of here," she said. "I need to find Brody and get that money back."

Max caught her arm. "I don't want you anywhere near him."

"I can't owe you."

"You don't."

"I do. You paid my debt."

"To get him out of your life, forever. If you hadn't shown up today you'd never have known about our deal." Max's steel gray eyes sliced at her. "Isn't that the way you work? Keeping everyone in your life in the dark about what's going on with you."

"That's not fair. I was only trying to protect Hailey."

"Fair? Do you think it was fair of you to keep the truth from your sister? She was paying your ex-husband a hundred thousand dollars to protect you."

Rachel gasped. "She didn't need to do that. I had everything all worked out."

"Only she didn't know that, did she? You were too busy keeping her wrapped in cotton to realize that by isolating her, you made her vulnerable."

"I was trying to keep her safe."

"And she was trying to help you. But you couldn't let her. You can't accept help from anyone."

Max's accusations lashed at her. Unable to deny that they made sense, she retreated into her convictions. What he said rang true, but it was only half the story.

"For good reason."

"Care to share?"

She recoiled. Telling Max about the mistakes she'd made with Brody would substantiate every negative thought he'd ever had about her. Rachel wasn't convinced she was strong enough to watch his concern die, but what choice did she have?

"So you agreed to pay him for Hailey's education."

"I didn't borrow money from Brody to start up the business. I was paying him so he would agree to a divorce."

"How much?"

"A hundred thousand dollars."

"Why so much?"

"That's how much it cost to put Hailey through college." All at once, the secrets she'd lived with for years could no longer be contained. "Brody used me to keep his gambling a secret from his father. While I was married to him, he put me on the payroll for more than what I should have been earning. I was supposed to use the money for Hailey's school, but most of the time, there wasn't enough because he was losing the money playing poker. To get what I needed, I waitressed on the weekends he was gone."

"He was stealing money from the company."

"I guess."

"How much of Hailey's education did you pay for by waitressing?"

"By the end, I was paying for all of it." She circled her hand in a vague gesture. "That's when I wanted out. But Brody hired the best divorce attorney in Biloxi and contested everything. I was desperate enough to agree to anything to get away from him."

"I don't understand why you let him do that to you."

"Because I was young and scared. When I met Brody, I'd been taking care of Hailey by myself for a year and slipping a little further behind every month. Our apartment was a dump. We clipped coupons and barely scraped by. Most days I didn't see how I was going to make it to the next paycheck. Then Brody swept into my life. He seemed like a dream come true. Wealthy, handsome, charming, and he saw me as the perfect patsy. Stupid and gullible." Rachel turned away from Max, unable to face her failure reflected in his eyes. "I guess some things haven't changed. I came here today because he said that I needed to meet with the guy who slashed my tires and convince him that I wasn't going to be able to come up with any more money. Only there wasn't any guy threatening Brody."

"He lured you here to see me giving him the money. He wanted to hurt you."

He wanted to humiliate her. To demonstrate he'd always be smarter than her. "How did you know about him? About the money I owe him?"

"Hailey. She was worried about you and came to me for help. Did you know she was paying your ex for her tuition?"

"What?" This was a complete disaster. Now she had to have a long, painful talk with her sister. "Why would she do that?"

"Brody convinced her the only way he would give you a divorce is if she paid him back for tuition."

"She did it because we were worried about you. Why can't you just say thank you for the help?"

Failure buzzed around her head like a swarm of black flies. She'd screwed up again. Self-loathing flared, setting fire to her irritation.

"I didn't ask for her help or yours."

"Maybe everything would have turned out better if you had." Max's gaze warned her to stay silent as she opened her mouth to disagree. "You brought this whole mess on yourself and on us because you had to do it all yourself. You couldn't reach out for help. You couldn't accept assistance when it was offered. Instead, you alienated Hailey and me and made it so your ex-husband could cheat both of us."

"You'll get every penny back," she retorted, her face hot while the rest of her body shivered with chill. "If it takes me until the day I die, I'll pay you back every cent."

"I don't care about the money. I only care about you." He reached for her, but Rachel flinched back. It was instinctive reaction to Max's earlier scolding, but his gray eyes became like a wintry sky, dense and ominous. "Only you won't let me do that."

And to Rachel's profound dismay, he turned on his heel and walked away from her. She wrapped one arm around her waist and ground the knuckles of her other hand against her lips to keep from calling him back. The set of his shoulders told her he was completely done with her.

As he should be.

He was right. This was all her fault. She'd made nothing but one mistake after another since the day her father died. She'd trusted the wrong people. She'd allowed fear to make her weak. And when she learned to be strong, she swung so far in the other direction that she'd put up walls that kept out even the people she loved.

She didn't blame Max for walking away. In fact, she was a little surprised he hadn't run as far and fast as he could to get away from her. She owed him more than she could repay. Not just the money he'd given Brody, but for stepping in on her behalf as well as on Hailey's.

What a fool she was to have shut him out. She was an even bigger fool to let fear of rejection stand in the way of her chasing after him now.

Max went straight to the parking garage. His footfalls ricocheted around the concrete structure, mimicking the echo in his empty chest. He'd called his new assistant and warned her he'd be gone the rest of the day. Taking off in the middle of the afternoon wasn't like him, but what was the point in trying to work when there was no way he could concentrate?

He eased his car up the exit ramp and rolled down the window to activate the garage's electronic gate. Heavy, humid air, stinking of exhaust, washed over him as his tires reached the street. He longed for the clean scent of the beach. But even that wouldn't soothe him for long. The fragrance would forever remind him of Rachel and their time together.

How could two people be so right for each other and so wrong at the same time?

The question made him think of his parents' past troubles, and before he knew his intention, the car was heading to the suburbs. He called ahead to make sure someone was home and his mother met him at the door.

"Your father is golfing," she said, drawing him through the house with her arm linked through his. "He appreciates playing so much more now that he's back to work part-time. I've never seen him so relaxed. He'll be back in an hour or so if you can wait around that long."

"I didn't come about business. I need to talk to you."

"Really?" Her surprise faded to concern as she scanned his face. "Is it something serious? You're not ill, are you? You look awfully pale. Are you sleeping?"

"Nothing like that." Max patted her hand to reassure her. "It's about Dad's affair." Max felt his mother's whole body stiffen. He kicked himself for being so blunt. "If it's too hard for you to talk about, I'll understand."

"No." The word swept out of her on a gust of air. "It's okay. I should be able to talk about it after twenty years, right?"

"It's okay if you can't."

She didn't speak until they'd entered the kitchen and she'd pushed him onto a stool at the breakfast bar. In his childhood home, the kitchen had been separate from the rest of the house, a place where the housekeeper prepared meals and he and Sebastian snuck snacks. In this house, the kitchen opened onto a large great room with overstuffed couches and an enormous flat-screen television. A sunroom had been transformed into a semiformal dining area for eight and a breakfast nook held a table that seated four.

Although the house possessed a formal dining room designed to entertain on a grand scale, the room was used infrequently. For holidays, birthdays and spontaneous dinners, the family gathered in this casual space.

From the refrigerator, his mother brought out white cheddar cheese, pâté, and olives. From the pantry, two types of crackers. By the time she handed Max a glass of crisp chardonnay, an empty plate and a napkin, he was grinning.

"What's so funny?" she demanded, handing him a cracker spread with pâté.

"I didn't realize it was happy hour."

"It's five o'clock somewhere." She waved her hand at him and sipped her own wine. "I tried a new recipe for the pâté. I'd like your opinion, but only if you rave about my wonderful cooking. Now, what did you want to know about your father's relationship with Marissa?"

Nathan's mother's name slipped off her tongue with ease as if she'd spoken it a thousand times.

"It really isn't the affair I'm interested in. I wanted to know why you forgave Dad after what he'd done to you." Max popped the cracker into his mouth and chewed. "Or maybe I should ask how you forgave him."

"I loved him."

"That's all there was to it?" Max couldn't shake his disappointment. He wanted a concrete, step-by-step plan that he could apply to his own difficulties with Rachel. "You didn't weigh your options then decide do it to keep the family together or because he promised never to do anything like that again?"

His mother shook her head. "No. I forgave your father for purely selfish reasons. I didn't want to live without him."

"Even knowing he hadn't been honest with you?" The question struck at the heart of what he couldn't grasp. "What assurance did you have that he wouldn't lie again?"

"None." His mother cocked her head. "I went on faith."

"That's it?" Damn it. The answer to such a complex problem couldn't be that simple. "After everything that happened you didn't want a guarantee?"

"What assurance do you have that someone will love you forever or that they ever intended to keep vows they made? 'Til death do us part. How many people believe in that anymore? The vows should say, ''til we're no longer willing to work on our marriage.'"

His mother's pragmatism left Max momentarily speechless.

"But you and Dad just renewed your vows. Why did you do that if you didn't believe in them?"

"Did I say I didn't believe in them? I took my vows to your father very seriously." She handed him a slice of cheese. "And just so you know, it was his idea to renew our vows. It's taken us a lot of work to get to where we are today. But I can say with confidence that your father and I are more in love and more committed to each other than we were the day we got married."

Max chewed on the cracker and pondered his mother's words.

He loved Rachel. There was no sense in denying it any longer. Her stubborn need to reject all outside help had given him the excuse he needed to hide from the truth in his heart. No matter how many secrets she kept from him, she wasn't deceitful because she was a bad person. She merely struggled to trust anyone. And after what she'd been through, could he blame her? He had his own issues with trust.

"Is this about that woman you brought to the party?" his mother asked, stepping into the silence. "I liked her very much." Her lips curved in a wry grin. "I got the distinct impression you did, as well. You two left here early enough."

Max felt a little like a teenager caught in the backseat of

the car with a half-naked girl. "We've been seeing each other for a few weeks."

"And she's important to you."

"Yes."

"But there's a problem of trust between you?"

"We met five years ago. She was married at the time, although I didn't find that out until after we..." He paused, groping for a delicate way to put it.

His mother played with her diamond tennis bracelet. "Spent some time together naked?" While he regarded her in dismay, she chuckled. "Oh, I wish you could see the look on your face right now."

Max dove back into the story. "I was so angry when I found out. With everything that happened with Dad you know I wouldn't have gotten involved with her if I'd known." Or would he? The chemistry between them had been hot and all consuming. Would he have walked away if she'd told him up front that she was in an unhappy marriage?

"She's divorced now, I take it."

"For four years. When we met, she didn't tell me she was married. I found out when her husband showed up to bring her home."

"And you overreacted because you've always taken issue with your father for cheating on me. If you love her, you can't continue to punish her for mistakes she made."

"I don't want to punish her." But wasn't his inability to trust her just as detrimental to their relationship?

"If you can't forgive her, you might have to give up and let her go."

But his mother hadn't given up and Max needed to know why. "Why didn't you leave?"

"Some things are worth fighting for. Your father was one of them."

"Even after he'd lied to you and had an affair?"

"Not just an affair," she told him, her voice and eyes steady. "He loved Marissa. I don't know why he never left me for her."

Max's temper simmered at the old hurts. "You didn't ask?"

"It was enough that he stayed."

He remembered those days. His mother had been depressed and on the verge of tears much of the time. Max hadn't understood what was happening between his parents until Nathan appeared, but he'd been mad as hell at his dad for upsetting his mom.

Max still didn't understand his mother's ability to forgive his father. Sure, she loved him and wanted to keep her family together, but she wasn't bitter or angry about the past. It was as if she understood she needed to let it go in order to be happy in the future.

"And he promised it would never happen again," his mother continued.

"You believed him?"

"Yes." She lifted her hand and showed off the five carat diamond ring Brandon had bought to renew their vows. "And we're still married because I did."

"I'm not sure I have it in me to forgive Dad."

"I wish you would. Hanging on to the past isn't healthy. You've let what happened between your father and me keep you from falling in love and getting married. Rachel seemed like a lovely woman. I can't imagine that you would care for her if she wasn't wonderful. Forgive them both. I think you'll find doing so will set you free."

"I'll think about it," Max muttered, but even as he said the words, he felt himself resist.

Rachel hadn't wanted to interrupt Hailey at work, but she desperately needed to talk to her sister. She called Hailey and invited her to dinner. Then, she went to the grocery store and bought what she needed to make their father's famous pan-fried grouper.

The domestic routine soothed her. She'd been rushing around so much these last few weeks, between her business and Max's office, fitting in a couple hours to cook and eat a meal hadn't been a priority.

It was time she slowed down.

By six o'clock when Hailey arrived, Rachel had made a mess of the kitchen but had fun doing it.

"Whoa. What's with this? You're cooking?" Hailey dropped her purse on the small breakfast table and surveyed the mess Rachel had made. She wrinkled her nose at the spilled flour, puddles of buttermilk and the array of spices and bowls that occupied every square inch of countertop. "Now I remember why I took over cooking. You are a disaster in the neatness department."

"Don't I always clean up when I'm done? Get changed and come open a bottle of wine."

"I'll be right back."

Only a twinge of guilt pinched Rachel as she directed her sister to the bottle in the refrigerator.

Hailey pulled it out and peered at the label. "Champagne? What are we celebrating?"

"I had some good news today."

"A new client?" Hailey worked off the foil and pried at the cork.

"Better." Rachel waited until her sister was fully engaged in wiggling the cork free before she unloaded her bombshell. "Max paid off Brody."

The bottle jerked. The cork shot out with a loud pop and dented the ceiling. Hailey stared at Rachel with her mouth open as foam flowed down the side of the bottle onto the floor.

"He did?"

"Any idea how Max found out that Brody was hassling me about money?"

"I told him." Hailey looked one part anxious and one part resolute. "Are you mad?"

Damn right she was mad. But confronting Hailey about seeking Max's help wasn't satisfying. Tension flowed out of her, leaving behind nothing. Not even regret.

"No. I'm angry with myself. I should have told you the truth instead of trying to protect you." Rachel's eyes burned as she reached into the cupboard and brought out two water glasses. The only pair of champagne glasses she'd ever owned had been bought for her wedding toast. She'd smashed them not long after her first anniversary.

Hailey poured the champagne. "I wish you had. It would have made things a lot easier for both of us."

"Here's to honesty between sisters from here on out." Rachel clinked her glass against Hailey's.

"I'll drink to that," Hailey said. "Tell me what happened today."

"Why don't you start by telling me what possessed you to go to Max."

Hailey shot her an accusing look over the rim of her glass. "You are mad."

"I'm not," she started, but her sister's impatient huff reminded her of their toast. "Okay, I'm not exactly mad at you. I get why you did it. I just wish you hadn't."

"I had to. Someone slashed your tires. That scared me."

Rachel flinched. "I had it under control."

"No, you didn't." Hailey's voice was hot as she countered Rachel's claim. "Just like you didn't have it under control after Dad died and Aunt Jesse took off on us. I know I wasn't out of high school, but you should have let me help."

"I was trying to protect you."

Hailey shook her head. "You always treated me like I was

made of glass. Just once I wanted you to lean on me, but you never did."

"I didn't realize it was that important to you," Rachel said, holding up her hands to fend off her sister's verbal battery. She'd always been proud of her sister, but never more than now. "Thank you for going to Max."

Hailey's temper evaporated. Her lips formed a half grin. "Wow, how'd that taste?"

"Bitter." Rachel finished the rest of her champagne in one swallow and held her glass out for a refill. "If you hadn't gone to him, Brody would have continued to pester us. He'd have taken more of your money. And I would forever be hopeful that Max might someday forgive me for not telling him I was married five years ago. I don't need to worry on any of those accounts any more."

"You and Max will make it work. That man has it bad for you."

"You didn't see him today. He never wants to see me again. Thanks to me he paid a hundred and five thousand dollars to a lowdown stinking liar."

"Why so much? You only owed him twenty-five."

"But you told Max that you'd promised to pay Brody for your college education."

Hailey gasped. "He wasn't supposed to do that."

"Now do you understand why I kept this from Max?" She slid the cooked fish onto two plates and dished out the broccoli she'd steamed. "He's not the sort of man to stand on the sidelines when he could save the day." Another reason why she loved him. Rachel blew out a breath. "He settled both our debts. I told him I'd pay him back the money. The problem is, you and I were both paying Brody off for your schooling. He was double dipping."

"I thought you were paying him back for a loan to start your business."

"No. Brody was cheating us. We paid him for your schooling twice."

"Twice?" Hailey looked horrified.

"I was paying him as part of our divorce decree. Now paying back Max will make it three times."

"That's insane. You're not going to do that. I'm not going to let you."

Rachel shoved a plate into her sister's hands. "Yes, I am."

"No, you're not. It was my mistake. I'm going to pay Max back."

"It was my fault for not telling you about my arrangement with Brody from the beginning. I'll pay Max back. You're getting ready to start your life with Leo. You don't want this sort of debt hanging over your head."

"And you've got a business to run. You shouldn't have to shoulder it, either."

Rachel had never seen her sister look so fierce or so determined. New respect bloomed. While she'd struggled with her business and finances, Hailey had become a strong, independent-minded young woman. Rachel was ashamed she hadn't noticed sooner.

"Okay."

Hailey's eyebrows shot up. "What do you mean, okay?"

"You're absolutely right that I don't want to be the one to pay Max back."

"You're going to let me do it?" Hailey nodded in satisfaction.

"Nope. I have a different idea altogether." Rachel rubbed her hands together and sent an evil grin winging toward her sister.

Hailey cracked a smile. "Anything you'd care to share?"

"Grab some silverware. We'll talk while we eat."

Eleven

Rachel stood on Max's front porch, her finger hovering over the doorbell. Her enthusiasm for the plan she talked over with Hailey had faded as she'd driven the twenty minutes to his house. What was she doing here? Max wouldn't want to help her after what had happened earlier today. Even if he answered the door, he'd probably slam it in her face as soon as he spotted her standing here.

Maybe he wasn't home. It was a Thursday night. Didn't he get together with his friends and go clubbing on Thursdays? She should have called. But what if he refused to answer?

She should have waited until Monday and caught him at his office. Of course, he might refuse to see her there, as well.

The door opened while lose-lose scenarios played through her mind like an action movie.

"Are you planning on standing out here all night?" Max asked. He blocked the doorway with his arm and nothing about his hard expression or his tense body language gave her hope. But suddenly Rachel's spirits rose.

"I guess I'll have to if you don't let me in."

His eyebrows rose. "What's the password?"

"You were right."

"That's three words."

She dug deeper. "I'm sorry."

"That's two words." A twitch at the corner of his mouth told her she was getting close.

"Help."

He reached out and dragged her inside. "That's it."

Lowering his head, he captured her mouth in a hard, unyielding kiss that melted away her worries. She wrapped her arms around his neck and kissed him back, giving full rein to her angst and fear of losing him.

He stripped off her shirt and dove his fingers beneath the elastic waistband of her skirt, pushing it down her hips until she stood before him in bra, panties and sneakers. Then, he scooped her into his arms and carried her down the hall to his bedroom.

The long walk gave her time to summon explanations or apologies, but Max's grim expression tied her tongue into knots. Make love to him now. Fight with him later. At least they would make another incredible memory for her to relive after they parted ways for good.

When he set her on her feet beside the bed, she grabbed the hem of his T-shirt and raised it past his flat stomach and powerful chest. He helped her by tearing it over his head. A purr-like sound vibrated her throat as she set her palms against his chest and backed him toward the bed.

Her fingers worked at the button and zipper of his jeans. She needed to taste him. The urgency made her clumsy and she let him rid himself of the rest of his clothes. Once he was naked, she dropped to her knees in front of him and sucked him into her mouth without finesse or preliminaries. He released a hoarse groan as her tongue circled him, discovering his texture and the best way to give him pleasure.

Before she brought him all the way to release, he stopped her and pulled her back to her feet. Placing a hot, sizzling kiss on her lips, he lifted her and deposited her on her back in the middle of the mattress. She kicked off her shoes. He followed her down and as his weight pressed her into the mattress, she ran the sole of her foot along his calf.

His fingers hooked around her underwear, stripping it down her legs. While he cast it aside, she took off her bra. The contact between her sensitized nipples and his hard chest set off a chain reaction of desire.

She lifted her hips toward the hand that teased between her legs, urging him to touch her with wild gyrations and garbled pleas. A half sigh, half moan broke from her as he slid his finger into her wetness and penetrated deep. She shuddered as he began to stroke her, each movement of his hand driving her further toward fulfillment. But that's not the way she wanted to go. Her nails bit into his wrist.

"Not like this," she gasped as his teeth grazed her throat. "Make love to me."

"If you insist."

He moved between her thighs, impaling her with one swift thrust. Hard and thick, he filled her over and over, the friction driving her crazy with wanting. Together they climbed. Higher and faster than ever before. When she came, the sensation rolled over her, wave after wave of intense pleasure. She floated back to earth in slow motion, the thundering of her heart keeping time with Max's thrusts as he surged toward his own climax.

Fascinated, she watched him come. His facial muscles locked in concentration. His eyes, half-closed, snagged with hers. He set his mouth against hers and plunged his tongue deep in a sexy kiss that stole her breath. Then his body drove into hers one last time and spasmed in release.

With her arms wrapped around his shoulders, Rachel held on to him and absorbed his aftershocks. Loving Max like this was easy. They knew exactly how to communicate in bed. She'd lost hope at being able to do so anywhere else.

All too soon, Max pushed away and dropped onto his back beside her. He lay with his forearm across his eyes, his chest rising and falling as his body recovered. Unsure if he would welcome her touch now that their frantic coupling was through, Rachel rolled onto her side and tucked her arm beneath her head.

Five minutes passed before he spoke.

"I'm glad you stopped by." Voice neutral. Expression hidden behind his arm. His mood an enigma.

"Me, too."

As much as she longed to cuddle up beside him and feel the reassuring weight of his arm settle around her, she'd made too many mistakes to hope that he felt tender or affectionate toward her.

"I was hard on you earlier," he continued. "I'm intolerant when I don't agree with someone. It's a bad habit of mine." He shifted his arm off his face and set it above his head. His gaze locked on the ceiling. "Or so my mother tells me."

"You were right to be angry. I screwed up. I should have been more up front with Hailey and with you. If I had, none of this would have happened." She paused. "It's my fault that Hailey gave Brody twenty thousand dollars. It's my fault that you gave him a hundred and five thousand. It's not right that he cheated you and I intend to get that money back."

At last, Max looked at her. The iron in his gray eyes made her wish he hadn't.

"How do you intend to go about that?" he demanded, his hard tone warning her he'd better like her answer.

She drew her knees up and bumped his thigh with them. The grazing contact eased the tension between them. "I'm going Biloxi to ask for it back."

"He went to a great deal of trouble to get the money in the first place," Max said, rolling onto his side so that they faced each other. "Have you considered what you'll do if he won't just give it back?"

She offered him a wan smile. "I was hoping you'd come along. I need your help." She held her breath and waited for some sign that he wasn't going to kick her and her crazy idea to the curb. "Please."

"You're asking me to help you?"

"Yes. I need you. I can't do this alone."

Max's arms snaked around her body, pulling her flush against him. With her thigh trapped between his and her head settled on his shoulder, his lips glanced off her forehead. "I'm glad you finally realized that."

The closer they got to Biloxi, the quieter Rachel became. And it wasn't just that she stopped talking. Her entire body stilled as if by remaining frozen, she could become invisible. Max kept glancing her way as they picked up a rental car at the airport and drove through the city.

He longed to reach out and offer her comfort, but she'd locked herself away and drawn the shutters. His fingers beat a tattoo on the steering wheel. The previous evening's connection had faded with the advent of dawn. She'd stood at the foot of his bed and worried the inside of her lip while he made arrangements for their flight to Biloxi.

"Say the word and we'll get right back on the plane and go home to Houston," Max offered.

In the seat beside him, Rachel started as if he'd jumped out and yelled "boo." Beneath his scrutiny she struggled a long moment before mastering the trace of panic in her dark blue eyes. Seeing her vulnerable for even that short second disturbed Max. She was awash in anxiety and trying like crazy to hide it. He was used to her strength and determination. Is this why she was so scared to ask for help?

"We've come all this way," she said. "We're not going back without that money."

Max nodded. He liked the way she said *we,* including him as part of her team, and appreciated what it had taken her to let him in.

"It's going to be okay. I won't let him hurt you ever again."

"I'm counting on that."

To Max's surprise, she reached out and grabbed his hand.

"Is that why you brought me along?" he teased. "Muscle?"

She stroked up his biceps, wrapping long fingers around his upper arm. "Well, you certainly have enough of them to qualify for that. But that's not why you're here."

"Then why?"

"Because I knew you'd want to come." She glanced his way and encountered his frown. Her elaborate sigh filled the car. "Fine. Because I wanted you to come. You make me feel safe in ways that no one ever has before." She pulled a face. "Happy now?"

"Deliriously."

Rachel's directions brought them into a commercial section of Biloxi. Max parked the car in a visitor's spot in front of Winslow Enterprises. As they entered the front door, he watched her gather courage. By the time they'd arrived at the front desk, her spine was straight and her eyes glinted with determination.

"Hello," he said to the receptionist. "I have an eleven o'clock meeting with Carson Winslow."

Rachel jerked in surprise. He could feel her gaze upon him.

"And your name?"

"Max Case."

While the receptionist spoke into the phone, Rachel grabbed on to Max's arm and drew him toward a seating area. "Why are we meeting with Brody's father?"

"I called him with a business proposition."

"Why?"

"You didn't seriously think Brody was going to just return the money because we asked him to, did you?"

From the expression on her face, she hadn't planned beyond demanding the money back.

Max shook his head. "You told me he's been gambling for years. He used you and the huge salary he paid you to hide his problem from his father. Why do you think he was so reluctant to give you a divorce?"

"Because any financial problems we had he could blame on me." Rachel blinked in dazed disbelief like a prisoner coming out of a dark cell. "What has he been doing since then?"

"I don't imagine he's quit gambling."

"Obviously not if he came to me for the cash he needed to get into a high-stakes poker game."

"Mr. Winslow said he'd be right up," the receptionist said with a polite smile before returning to stuffing envelopes.

"So, what's your plan? You're not going to ask Carson for the money, are you? Brody works hard to keep his father completely in the dark."

"And that will work to our advantage."

She frowned at his cryptic reply, but had no chance to ask for clarification because a thin, gray-haired man in his mid-sixties appeared in the doorway that led to the rest of the building.

"Follow my lead," Max murmured as he stepped forward with his hand extended. "Max Case. Thank you for taking a meeting with me on such short notice."

"Not at all. I was intrigued by your call."

"This is my associate." Max stepped to one side so Rachel came into view.

"Rachel?" Carson's smile faltered. "How are you?"

"I'm wonderful. And you?"

While pleasantries were exchanged between Rachel and her former father-in-law, Max observed the interplay with interest. There was no obvious animosity between the pair. Did that mean Carson had no idea what had transpired in his son's marriage?

"Let's head back to my office," Carson said.

Once inside the spacious corner office, Max wasted no time in getting to the point. "You've probably figured out by now that Rachel was the one who pointed me in the direction of Winslow Enterprises."

"I'll admit it clears up how we came to your attention."

Max smiled. "After doing some research on your company, I was able to determine that it's positioned to break out, but you lack the capital and the skilled management to take you to the next level."

Frustration and resignation tightened Carson's mouth into a grim line. Beside him, Rachel had gone so still, Max wondered if she was holding her breath. He matched her immobility, letting his words penetrate Carson's defenses. From what Max had gathered from his sources in Biloxi, ever since Carson had handed the business operations over to his son, the company was floundering.

Carson was at a crossroads. He needed to decide if he was going to let his son take over and risk the company's future, or sell the business and enjoy his retirement.

"What's going on in here?" an unfriendly voice demanded from the doorway.

Rachel shifted in her seat to confront her ex-husband. Her knees bumped Max's thigh. A tremor passed through her, heightening his determination to give her closure with her ex. By the time Max finished with Brody, the guy wouldn't dare bother Rachel or her sister again.

Carson hit his son with a meaningful look. "Max has come to us with a proposition."

"Is that so." Brody's lip curled. "And what is she doing here?"

Rachel inclined her head, all nervousness mastered. With a half smile, she said, "If it wasn't for me, Max would never have become interested in Winslow Enterprises."

The return of Rachel's confidence eased Max's tension.

"Of course, my brothers are not convinced that your company is large enough for us to pursue. But after we get a look at your books, I'm sure they will be persuaded."

Brody's gaze bounced between his father and Max. Anger melted into uncertainty. "Well, it's not for sale."

"You don't get to make that decision," Carson reminded him, his voice tight with reproof.

"Why not? You've put me in charge, haven't you?" Brody seemed to have forgotten that this family squabble was in front of witnesses.

His father's gaze flicked in Max's direction. "We'll discuss this later. Right now I'm going to take Max on a tour of the facility."

"Let me do it," Brody said.

The tension between father and son tainted the air like exhaust as Brody led the way out of the office. But instead of taking Max and Rachel on the tour his father had suggested, Brody steered them into a conference room and shut the door.

"You've got a lot of nerve showing up here," he snarled.

"*We've* got a lot of nerve?" Rachel began, her fingers curled into claws as if she'd like to rip her ex-husband's eyes out. "You bastard. I want the money you stole from Hailey."

"I don't know what you're talking about."

"She's been paying you for her college."

"So?"

"We agreed as part of our divorce settlement that I would pay you for her education. You had no right to go behind my back and demand money from her, as well."

Brody laughed. "Too bad."

"I want every penny back that she gave you."

"Not going to happen."

"You haven't had time to lose all of it."

"I haven't lost any of it."

"Good. Then you can return the hundred thousand you stole from my sister."

"I didn't steal anything from Hailey or you. She agreed to pay me."

"Because she didn't know I was already paying you."

"And whose fault is that? You were always so determined to keep her in the dark about everything. Our marriage. Her education. You made it so easy for me to tell her anything I wanted and have her believe it."

Max decided it was time to step in. "Return the money."

Brody heard the threat loud and clear. "Or what?"

"Or I'm going to make your father an offer on his business he can't refuse and a team of accountants will show up to do due diligence and your father will learn just how much money you've embezzled from this company over the years."

"I don't know what you're talking about." But Brody's bluff fell flat.

Max snorted in disgust. "I can see why you lose at poker as often as you do," he said. "What do you think is going to happen when your father realizes that you haven't kicked your little problem the way you claim you have?"

"You've been stealing from the company?" Rachel looked almost sorry for her ex-husband.

"More so after you two divorced," Max interjected.

"Have you lost your mind?" Rachel questioned. "After he paid off your gambling debt with the Menks brothers, he swore if you gambled again he would sell the company and cut you off without a cent."

Max chipped in. "Imagine how unhappy he would be to hear that you never had any intention of quitting."

"You have no idea what you're talking about."

"Don't I?" Max couldn't believe the guy thought anyone would believe the words coming out of his mouth. "My brother used to be a professional gambler. When he reached out to his contacts they put him in touch with a number of people you've borrowed money from. Your associates were happy to shed light on your past dealings with them." Max shouldn't have enjoyed twisting the knife as much as he was, but this guy had mistreated Rachel and deserved everything he was getting. "And they've agreed to have a chat with your father if I ask them to."

"You're bluffing." Brody's eyes were blind with panic.

"I don't gamble," Max told him. "That means I never bluff. Every negotiation I go into, I'm holding a royal flush. I never lose."

"Everyone loses sometimes."

"The only one who loses today is you. Get the money."

"I don't have it with me." Brody's tone was close to a whine. Despite the air-conditioned comfort of the room, a bead of sweat trickled down his temple.

"Pity." Max set his hand on the small of Rachel's back and turned her toward the conference-room door.

"Wait."

Max turned the knob and opened the door to reveal Carson Winslow. The older man was frowning.

"I thought Brody was going to take you on a tour."

"He's been telling us how much the company means to

him," Max said. "I didn't realize he was so passionate about the business."

From the way Carson regarded his son, the current owner of Winslow Enterprises hadn't, either. "Well, that's good to know."

"Thank you for your time."

Carson shook his head in confusion. "You're leaving? But we never discussed the reason for your visit."

"I had hoped for a more amiable meeting." Max shook hands with the elder Winslow. "However, Brody made his position clear. He's not interested in doing business with me. I'm sure in time he'll regret making such a rash decision." He hit Rachel's ex with a hard stare.

It took a couple seconds for Brody to understand that Max intended to carry out his threat of informing Carson of his son's gambling. Brody glared at Max.

Seeing the unfriendly exchange, Carson turned on his son. "That wasn't your decision to make."

"Take it easy, Dad." Brody put up his hands. "Max just misunderstood my reservations. If I can have a couple minutes with him in private, I'll explain myself better."

While Rachel and Carson headed for the reception area, Max followed Brody down the hall and into his office, wondering what sort of scheme Rachel's ex would come up with now to save his hide.

To Max's surprise, Brody opened his briefcase and took out an envelope.

He tossed it at Max. "Here it is. A hundred grand. Count it if you want."

Max did. "Looks like it's all here."

"This means we're done. You'll leave me alone?"

"As long as you leave Rachel and Hailey alone, you'll never hear from me again."

"Good."

As he neared the lobby, Max caught Rachel's eye and gave her a tiny nod. Her eyes brightened with unshed tears. His heart turned over in his chest. He wanted nothing more than to wrap her in his arms and hug her hurt away. But with Carson looking on, Max limited himself to a brief smile.

"Did you get Hailey's money back?" she quizzed the instant they emerged into the hot Mississippi afternoon.

He handed her the envelope. "A hundred thousand. Just what you asked for."

She pulled out twenty thousand and gave him back the balance.

"I don't think Brody wants to risk his comfortable little world collapsing around him," he said, watching her face as she held her sister's money.

"I probably could have gotten back all the money you paid him."

Rachel shook her head. "I couldn't spend the rest of my life looking over my shoulder, waiting for him to reappear because he thinks he was cheated out of what's rightfully his." She gave him a sad smile. "You won't be around to protect me forever."

They started their relationship again with the understanding that it was temporary, but it stung hearing her talk about a future without him in it.

"If he's so bad, why did you go back to him after we met?"

"I went back to him because he said he'd tell Hailey why I really married him. I didn't want her to be ashamed of me."

"Sweetheart, she loves you, and she's proud of you. Nothing you did could change that."

"But I couldn't take care of her. She was my responsibility and I was failing."

"You were barely able to take care of yourself." Max wrapped his arm around her shoulders and hugged her. "Cut yourself some slack. You did the best you could. No one could fault you for that."

They hadn't gone more than a mile before Max glanced over and saw Rachel's cheeks were wet with tears. He pulled into the first parking lot he came to and parked the car. The instant he shut off the ignition, she leaned against his shoulder. Max twisted in his seat and drew her into his arms.

"It's going to be okay now," he said. "He'll never bother you again."

Cupping her head, he nuzzled her cheek and absorbed her shudders against his chest. He soothed her with long caresses up and down her back until her breath settled into a steady rhythm.

"I can't believe it's really over." She rested her head on his shoulder for a minute longer, before pushing away and wiping her cheeks. "Take me home."

While Max drove back to the airport, Rachel got on her cell phone and gave Hailey a blow-by-blow of the confrontation with Carson and Brody. He only half listened to her voice. The other half of his attention chewed on his reaction to Rachel asking him to take her home.

He knew she meant home to Houston and her house. But he couldn't shake the bone-deep longing to take her back to a home that they'd make together. What was he thinking? Living together? Marriage? Was he ready to take that step? And with Rachel?

His mind cleared.

Of course with Rachel. He'd loved her since the moment they'd met. He'd been thinking of a future with her. No wonder he'd been so crushed to discover she was already married. That she loved someone else.

And now?

Was he ready to let go of past mistakes and start anew? He was. But first he had to settle a little unfinished business with his father. Max knew he'd never be able to move into the future with the old resentment chained to his ankles like a concrete block. He owed Rachel a fresh start.

As the plane lifted off the ground and low clouds obscured her view of Biloxi, Rachel let her head fall back against the seat. She could have been one of those clouds, as light as she felt at the moment. Today, a chapter of her life had ended. A door closed between past and present. She never had to return to Biloxi or think about Brody ever again.

She glanced at the man beside her. Seeing him in action earlier had made her glad he was on her side. He'd been decisive and intimidating. She'd enjoyed watching him outclass her ex-husband. For the first time in ten years she felt completely free.

"You're smiling," Max said, taking her hand and grazing his lips across her knuckle.

"Savoring the victory."

"I had no idea your divorce had been that contentious."

"My entire marriage was that way. When Brody was losing, he was miserable and made everyone around him the same way."

"No wonder you got out."

"I didn't love him."

Max nodded. "After all you'd been through, I understand why you wouldn't."

"Not in the end." The need to unburden herself was probably going to backfire, but he had seen part of the truth. He might as well know it all. "From the start." She plunged on, needing Max to understand what she'd gone through. "I know it was wrong, but you have to understand how it was. I was afraid. I didn't know how much longer I was going to be able to keep feeding us, much less send Hailey to college. When Brody came along, he seemed nice and wanted to help. I told myself I was in love with him when he proposed, but I think I was so relieved at the idea of having a real home again, I lied to myself and to him. I used him."

"People get married for all sorts of reasons. Not all of them are right." Max's eyes were clear and free of reproach.

"You don't hate me?" Rachel couldn't believe she'd been wrong all along. "I married a man I didn't love because I was scared and wanted financial security. Don't you think that makes me a terrible person?"

"No." Max frowned. "Is that what you've been worried about all this time? That if I knew you'd made a mistake at twenty that it would somehow diminish you in my eyes?"

"You already hated me for not telling you I was married five years ago."

"Hated." He echoed the word and rubbed his eyes. "I never hated you. I said some harsh things when I found out because I was angry. But I never hated you."

"Not even a little?"

When he didn't answer right away, Rachel waited, her breath lodged in her chest. He had something on his mind, an emotion that he needed to distill into words.

"You know my father cheated on my mother."

"Yes."

"It nearly destroyed our family. Mom went through a really tough time when Sebastian and I were kids. I had a hard time watching her be unhappy and not being able to do anything about it. I swore I would never involve myself in any sort of extramarital affair. It's one of the reasons I don't want to marry. I can never cheat on my wife if I don't have one."

Rachel stared at their linked fingers. "I never should have started anything with you."

"Don't say that. This isn't your problem, it's mine. And I'm not sure if I'd known from the start that you were married if I would have been able to walk away."

"Of course you could have. You just said that having an affair was something you swore never to do."

"That's what eats at me. When tested, my convictions failed."

"But they didn't. You didn't know I was married until the end."

"And when I did know, that didn't stop me from wanting you." Max's bitter half smile tore at Rachel's heart.

"So, what are you saying? That if I'd stayed, we could have had a future together." She couldn't help the doubt that crept into her tone. "That's a nice happy ending, Max, but you and I both know that it never would have happened. You would have forever resented me for luring you into something that deep down you didn't want."

"You don't know that."

"I saw your face at your parents' anniversary party. You haven't forgiven your father for what he did to your mother twenty years ago. Those same resentments would have colored our relationship. Every time you look at me you see my infidelity. Just like you see your father's."

She saw the truth in his eyes. It sliced deep into her heart. To conceal the wound, she leaned forward and kissed his cheek.

"I don't want that between us," he said.

"Neither do I." Her throat tightened. "It just is."

Twelve

The conversation on the plane ride home ate at Max long after he dropped Rachel at her house. The lingering kiss she'd given him had tasted like goodbye. Her sad smile, a sign marking a dead end.

Being told that he was an unforgiving bastard had never bothered him before. Only Rachel could make him question what good he was doing himself or anyone else by holding twenty-year-old mistakes against his father.

Restless and unable to face his empty house, he called his dad and found him at the golf course once again. However, when Max arrived, Brandon had just finished the round and was having a drink at the clubhouse before returning home.

"Max," Brandon said, getting up to shake his son's hand. "What brings you here?"

"I wondered if we could talk privately."

"Sure." Brandon excused himself from his friends and led the way to the bar. An Astros game filled the television screen behind the bartender. As soon as Max had ordered a whiskey, Brandon asked, "What's wrong? Problems with your brothers again?"

"Nothing like that."

Despite the fact that Max had recently decided a cease fire in the office was more conducive to productivity, his resentment toward the relationship between Nathan and their father persisted. Brandon had always favored Nathan. And why not? He'd been born to the woman Brandon adored. Unlike his first two sons.

Max wondered if that's what had bothered him all these years. His father had never seemed present when Max and Sebastian were kids. And then Nathan came along and suddenly there were family dinners and vacations. Brandon was around more because he preferred Nathan to his older sons and wanted to spend time with him. At least that's what Max's young mind had decided. He saw now that jealousy had buried that idea in his subconscious and tainted his relationship with his father.

"Your mom told me you came by and asked about my affair with Marissa."

Max and his father had always been blunt with each other. Mostly because Max lacked Sebastian's diplomatic skills or Nathan's charm.

"Your affair hurt her."

"I know." Brandon stared into Max's eyes without flinching. "It's something I'll never be able to make up for, even if I spend the rest of my life trying."

"But she forgave you."

"She's a saint. That's one of the reasons why I love her." Brandon's gaze turned to flint. "And don't for a second think I don't. I was wrong to promise her my fidelity and break that trust, but I loved her when we married and I've loved her every day since. Some days better than others."

For the first time ever, Max saw his father's remorse and the conflict that must have raged in him all those years. He hadn't had a string of affairs. He'd loved two women. One he'd married. The other he'd been unable to give up despite knowing his affair hurt both the women in his life.

"Why is this coming up now?" Brandon asked.

Because he'd hung on to his anger at his father and let the woman he loved walk away. He thought about what his mother had said about him overreacting to Rachel being married. If he'd gone after Rachel and found out the sort of bad situation she was in, he might have convinced her to return with him to Houston. If he'd supported her instead of turning his back in anger, she could have started fresh with him. How much pain could have been avoided if he hadn't been so quick to judge her?

"I'm sorry," he told his father. "I should have followed Mom's example and let go of my anger years ago."

For a long moment, Brandon looked too stunned for speech. "You shouldn't apologize," he said at last, his deep voice scored with regret. "I'm sorry I put you, your brother and my wife through hell." Brandon looked older than he had in the year since his surgery. "I've been waiting a long time for you to stop hating me."

"It took falling in love with a very stubborn woman to make me understand that my anger hasn't done me any good."

"Rachel." Brandon's head bobbed in approval. "I was glad to see you two together at our anniversary party. She brought Missy and Sebastian together, you know. If she hadn't found Missy to be his assistant, I don't know what would have happened to your brother. He's happier than I've ever seen him. We have Rachel to thank for helping make that happen."

And that was it in a nutshell, Max realized. Rachel had helped Sebastian. She'd found him the perfect assistant. The perfect mate. Helping was what she did best. Behind the scenes, often at great personal sacrifice.

His heart expanded as an idea took hold.

It was past time someone did something for her in return.

A new client, Devon had said. He'd sent a text to her phone with an address and suite number, but no contact name. She'd called him back, but he hadn't picked up at work and wasn't answering his cell phone. Not surprising. It was past five o'clock on a Friday night. He had a social life. As did Hailey and pretty much everyone else on the planet.

Everyone except her.

In the two weeks since returning from Biloxi, she'd thrown herself into work. Exhaustion helped her sleep, but nothing prevented the dreams where she chased Max through a maze of long, dark hallways, following the sound of his voice, but never able to catch up to him.

She didn't need a professional to analyze her dreams. As much as she longed to be with him, Max was out of reach.

Stepping out of the humid Houston afternoon into the cool comfort of the building's enormous lobby, Rachel felt the first tingle of excitement in weeks. Landing a client in this building would mean big commissions. This was prime downtown real estate, the sort of place she'd hoped to lease for Lansing Employment Agency.

In fact, six months ago, she'd looked here, but the available space, perfect for her needs, had been snapped up the day after she'd toured. With a gym and a whole host of retail and service providers on the first floor, it was a huge step up from the older building near the edge of downtown that she was in now. Rachel let a wistful sigh escape as she rode the elevator to the eighth floor.

The suite had no identifying name on the outside. Not surprising. She'd passed quite a few unmarked offices on the way. Pushing through the door, she hesitated just inside.

No one occupied the reception desk. The space beyond had an empty feel to it. Granted, it was after the normal workday on a Friday, but she'd expected some sign of life.

"Hello?" She felt uncomfortable searching out her contact in the empty office. "It's Rachel Lansing, I believe we had an appointment."

"Surprise!" Out of two offices burst Hailey and Devon. They threw their arms around each other's shoulders and laughed, enjoying her shock.

"What are you doing here?" she demanded, confusion making her cross.

"I work here," Devon explained. "Come see my new office."

"You quit?" Tears popped into her eyes. She couldn't lose Hailey, Max and Devon in the space of a month.

"No." Devon shook his head, his smile bigger than ever.

Rachel took a deep breath, her hurt easing toward confusion. "I don't understand."

"These are our new offices."

She must have misheard him. "Our new what?"

"Offices," Hailey chimed in, rushing forward to enfold Rachel in an enthusiastic hug. "What do you think?"

"That I've died and heaven is an office suite in the best building in downtown Houston."

A pop came from behind Devon, the distinct sound of a cork leaving a champagne bottle.

"Come see your office," Hailey said.

Rachel resisted her sister's tugging. "This is a great idea," she said. "But I've crunched the numbers a hundred different ways and I can't afford to move in here."

"You can," a deep, masculine voice assured her. Max came

down the hall, carrying four flutes of champagne. "Thanks to your sister."

Seeing him wrenched her heart in six different ways. The days of no communication had been excruciating. She had reached for the phone a hundred times and dialed his number at least a dozen. Loving him and knowing that he could never forgive her was agony.

She turned away from his handsome face and stared at her sister. "Hailey, what does he mean?"

"He means that I took the money I got back from Brody and put it toward your offices."

Rachel's spirits plummeted. "Hailey, no. You shouldn't have done that."

"Don't even go there. You put me through school. You suffered with Brody for five years. Let me do something for you."

"But you're getting married. You should use the money for your wedding or a house."

"I'm marrying a man who understands how amazing my sister is and supports my desire to help her with something she's been working toward for four years."

"In other words," Devon piped up. "Say thank you, Rachel."

"Thank you," Rachel echoed, with the slightest touch of irony. Tears burned her eyes. Emotion tightened her throat. She wrapped her arms around Hailey and hugged her hard. "Thank you," she repeated, unable to speak above a whisper.

"Here," Max handed her a glass of champagne, his eyes glinting with satisfaction. Devon handed Hailey a glass. "To Lansing Employment Agency. May it continue matching executives with assistants for many years to come."

They clinked glasses. Rachel sipped her champagne, and then watched the bubbles to avoid staring at Max. Two weeks and two feet separated them. She felt as giddy as a teenager, and just as awkward.

"I have you to thank for this, as well, don't I?" she asked him.

"I might have made a few inquiries."

She suspected he'd done more than that. She wouldn't be surprised if he'd vouched for her, as well. What prompted him to help her? Heaven knew she'd been nothing but a thorn in his side since reappearing in his life. He'd been eager enough to drop her off after their trip to Biloxi. She'd put every scrap of love she felt for him into that kiss and he'd walked away without a backward glance.

"Thanks." She put her hand on his arm. Lightning shot from her fingertips to her toes, awakening every nerve it passed. "You have no idea what this means to me."

"I think I do."

The room fell away as she got lost in the possibilities swimming in his eyes. He took a half step closer, filling her nostrils with his crisp masculine scent, swamping her with the heat from his body and the pull of his charisma.

"Max, I'm sorry about everything."

He plucked her glass from her numb fingers and set it on the receptionist desk. "You have nothing to be sorry for."

"Brody. The money."

"Gone and returned." His hands slid around her waist, drawing her against him. "I'm the one who's sorry."

"For what?"

"For making you the scapegoat for my problems with my father." He drew his thumb against her cheek. "Being with you, I felt things that made me question what I believed was right. For years I'd been angry with my father for cheating, and with his mistress for refusing to give him up. I resented my mother because she clung to love when self-preservation should have told her to walk away. Wanting you demonstrated that I was no better than them. I was ready to sacrifice my principles to have you in my life."

"But you were so angry when you found out I was married."

"I was angry because you went back to your husband."

"I didn't think I had a choice." And now she understood what a mistake she'd made.

"You put Hailey's needs above your own. How can I be angry about that?"

Rachel snuggled against his chest, hiding her tears from him. For the first time in forever, her life was perfect. She wanted to savor the moment. All too soon, Max pushed her to arm's length. She dabbed at the corners of her eyes with the back of her hand and sniffled.

Glancing around, she realized the offices were empty. "What happened to Hailey and Devon?"

"I think they had someplace else to be."

"Is this really all mine?" She still couldn't believe what Hailey and Max had done for her.

"All yours."

"When I didn't hear from you after getting back from Biloxi, I thought we were done."

"I needed a little time to settle my past where it belonged."

"And now?"

"Put to rest."

As nice as all this sounded, she wasn't sure what happened next. "I'm glad." She pushed aside her doubts about the future and concentrated on enjoying her present. "Can I buy you dinner to celebrate?"

"I have an errand to run, but after that, I'm free."

"How long will it take? Shall I meet you somewhere?"

"Not long. I could use your help, if you don't mind."

"Sure."

They exited the suite, Rachel taking care to lock the door

behind her. The hand Max placed against the small of her back spread warmth throughout her entire body. Contentment radiated to every nook and cranny, bringing light to the darkest recesses of her soul.

He gave her an address and directions before they parted on the downtown street. Still floating in her happy bubble, she scarcely noticed the rush-hour traffic as she crept toward the suburbs. By the time she parked in front of an elegant colonial in one of Houston's older, affluent neighborhoods, she'd decided whatever form Max wanted their relationship to take, she'd enjoy being with him as long as he wanted her around.

While she wondered who lived in the house, Max drove up past her in a familiar yellow convertible and parked in the driveway. Her cheeks heated as she recalled what had happened on the hood of that car. Mystified by the reason he was driving one of his rare cars, she crossed the lawn toward him.

He'd discarded his suit coat and tie and rolled up his sleeves. She took the hand he held out to her and let him lead her toward the front door.

"What are we doing here?" she asked as they waited for the owner to answer their knock.

"You'll see."

His mischievous grin told her he wasn't giving anything away. A second later, she was distracted by the blond man who opened the door. Jason Sterling, Max's best friend. His gaze bounced from Max to her to the car in the driveway.

He paled beneath his tan.

"Oh, man, I never thought I'd see the day." Jason stepped back to let them enter the house. "Are you sure you want to do this?"

"Never more sure of anything in the world." He tossed his keys to Jason and wrapped his arm around Rachel's waist, guiding her into the foyer.

She gazed up at him, deciding she'd never seen him so relaxed. "Why did you give Jason your car keys?"

"Not just the keys," Jason said.

"The car."

"But you love that car," she exclaimed. "Why would you sell it?"

Max raised his eyebrows. "I didn't sell it."

"I won it."

Rachel regarded the two men for a long moment, watching the silent interaction between them. "Won it how?"

Before Max could answer, Jason waggled his head in dismay. "I thought you loved that car."

"I love this woman more."

Rachel's breath stopped. Without his arm propelling her forward, her feet would have stopped as well. Instead, she kept going, stumbling over the transition from hardwood floor to area rug. Max's strong arm supported her. His steady calm soothed her flustered emotions.

She regained her balance, physically and spiritually, and stared up at him in awe. "You do?"

"Of course he does," Jason grumbled. "He's giving up the find of a lifetime because of you."

Max shot his best friend a sour look. Jason retaliated with a disgruntled glare of his own. The undercurrents in the room darted around her like agitated birds. Rachel wasn't sure what was going on, but she sensed she was at the heart of it.

"You don't have to give up your car for me."

Max took her hands in his and deposited kisses in both palms. "I'm not giving it up for you. I'm giving it up because I lost a bet."

"What sort of bet?"

"I bet him he'd marry whoever your agency placed as his assistant," Jason explained.

The absurdity of it made her laugh. "You were serious

about all that?" she asked him. "I thought for sure you'd made it all up as payback for what I did to you five years ago."

"No," Jason said. "We were completely serious. Do you have any idea how many men have married the assistants you've placed with them?"

"You're both insane."

"Nine." Jason crossed to a table with three crystal decanters and poured himself a shot out of one. When he gestured toward them with the bottle, both she and Max shook their heads. "Nine perfectly happy bachelors have fallen in love. Including my father. His brother. And now my best friend. All because of you."

"I wasn't perfectly happy," Max insisted.

Rachel turned on Jason. "You're behind his idiotic idea that I run a matchmaking service? You can't seriously think I have anything to do with those couples falling in love."

Jason scowled at her. "You match executives and assistants. A lot of them get married."

His claim was so preposterous she didn't know how to refute it. "That's crazy."

"Is it?" Jason gestured behind her.

Rachel turned. To her astonishment, Max dropped to one knee and produced a ring from his pocket. "Rachel Lansing. Will you marry me?"

Rachel covered her gasp with both hands as she stared from the man she adored to the ring he held out to her. The large diamond sparkled, hypnotizing her. Her thoughts began to circle. Max wanted to marry her. He loved her. They would live together in his big house and have lots of babies. At least she hoped they would. She had no idea of his views on children. Or any of a hundred things that couples heading toward marriage talked about.

"Answer him," Jason bellowed, his impatience spilling over.

"Yes."

Grinning, Max slid the ring on her finger. He got to his feet and cupped her face, drinking from her lips, long and deep.

By the time they came up for air, Jason had collapsed onto the couch and was staring at the empty glass in his hand.

"What's wrong with him?" Rachel whispered, nudging her head toward Jason. "He looks like he's lost his best friend."

Max's grin was pure mischief. "He's sad because he's a miserable, lonely bachelor."

"Does he need an executive assistant?"

Jason came off the couch with a roar. "Don't you dare."

Laughing, Max and Rachel retreated from the house. As Max drove her car back to his place, Rachel leaned her head against the seat rest and admired the ring on her hand. "Do you think there's anything to Jason's claim of matchmaking?"

"No." His scoffing tone was at odds with his uncertain frown. "But maybe in the future all the assistants you place at Case Consolidated Holdings should be old and married."

Rachel laughed. "I think that can be arranged."

* * * * *

HIS TEMPORARY MISTRESS

CATHY WILLIAMS

To my three daughters, Charlotte, Olivia and Emma and their continuing support in all my endeavors...

CHAPTER ONE

So it was bad news. The worst possible. Damien swivelled his leather chair so that it was facing the magnificent floor-to-ceiling panes of glass that afforded his office suite such spectacular views of London's skyline.

The truism that money couldn't buy everything had come home to roost. His mother had been given the swift and unforgiving diagnosis of cancer and there was nothing a single penny of his bottomless billions could do to alter that bald fact.

He wasn't a man who ever dealt in *if onlys*. Regret was a wasted emotion. It solved nothing and his motto had always been that for every problem there was a solution. Upwards and onwards was what got a person through life.

However, now, a series of *what ifs* slammed into him with the deadly precision of a heat-guided missile. His mother's health had not been good for over a year and he had taken her word for it when she had vaguely told him that yes, she had been to see her GP, that there was nothing to worry about…that engines in old cars tended to be a little unreliable.

What if, instead of skimming the surface of those assurances, he had chosen to probe deeper? To insist on bringing her to London, where she could have had the best possible medical advice, instead of relying on the uncharted territory of the doctors in deepest Devon?

Would the cancer now attacking her have been halted in its tracks? Would he not have just got off the phone to the consultant having been told that the prognosis was hazy? That they would have to go in to see how far it had spread?

Yes, she was in London now, after complicated arrangements and a great deal of anxiety, but what if she had come to London sooner?

He stood up and paced restlessly through his office, barely glancing at the magnificent piece of art on the wall, which had cost a small fortune. For once in his life, guilt, which had been nibbling at the edges of his conscience for some time, blossomed into a full-scale attack. He strode through to his secretary, told her to hold all his calls and allowed himself the rare and unwelcome inconvenience of giving in to a bout of savage and frustrating introspection.

The only thing his mother had ever wanted for him had been marriage, stability, a good woman.

Yes, she had tolerated the women she had met over the years, on those occasions when she had come up to London to see him, and he had opted to ignore her growing disappointment with the lifestyle he had chosen for himself. His father had died eight years previously, leaving behind a company that had been teetering precariously on the brink of collapse.

Damien had been one hundred per cent committed to running the business he had inherited. Breaking it up, putting it back together in more creative ways. He had integrated his own vastly successful computer firm with his father's outdated transport company and the marriage had been an outstanding success but it had required considerable skill. When had he had the time to be concerned over lifestyle choices? At the age of twenty-three, a thousand years ago or so it seemed, he had attempted to make one serious lifestyle choice with a woman and that had spectacularly crashed and burned. What was the problem if, from then onwards, his choices had not been to his mother's liking? Wasn't time on his side when it came to dealing with that situation?

Now, faced with the possibility that his mother might not have long to live, he was forced to concede that the single-minded ambition and ferocious drive that had taken him to the top, that had safeguarded the essential financial cushion his mother deserved and required, had also placed him in the unpalatable situation of having disappointed her.

And what could he do about it? Nothing.

Damien looked up as his secretary poked her head around the door. With anyone else, he wouldn't have had to voice his displeasure at being interrupted, not when he had specifically issued orders that he was not to be disturbed. With Martha Hall, the usual ground rules didn't work. He had inherited her from his father and, at the age of sixty-odd, she was as good as a family member.

'I realise you told me not to bother you, son...'

Damien stifled a groan. He had long ago given up on telling her that the term of affection was inappropriate. In addition to working for his father, she had spent many a night babysitting him.

'But you promised that you'd let me know what that consultant chap said about your mother...' Her face was creased with concern. She radiated anxiety from every pore of her tall, angular body.

'Not good.' He tried to soften the tone of his voice but found that he couldn't. He raked restless fingers through his dark hair and paused to stand in front of her. She would have easily been five ten, but he towered over her, six foot four of pure muscular strength. The fine fabric of his hand-tailored charcoal trousers and the pristine white of his shirt lovingly sheathed the lean, powerful lines of a man who could turn heads from streets away.

'The cancer might be more widespread than they originally feared. She's going to have a battery of tests and then surgery to consolidate their findings. After that, they'll discuss the appropriate treatment.'

Martha whipped out a handkerchief which she had stored in the sleeve of her blouse and dabbed her eyes. 'Poor Eleanor. She must be scared stiff.'

'She's coping.'

'And what about Dominic?'

The name hung in the air between them, an accusatory reminder of why his mother was so frantic with worry, so upset that she was ill and he, Damien, was still free, single and unattached, still playing the field with a series of beautiful but spectacularly unsuitable airheads, still, in her eyes, ill equipped to handle the responsibility that would one day be his.

'I shall go down and see him.'

Most people would have taken the hint at the abrupt tone of his voice. Most people would have backed away from pursuing a conversation he patently did not want to pursue. Most people were not Martha Hall.

'So have you considered what will happen to him should your mother's condition be worse than expected? I can see from your face that you don't want to talk about this, honey, but you can't hide from it either.'

'I'm not hiding from anything,' Damien enunciated with great forbearance.

'Well, I'll leave you to ponder that, shall I? I'll pop in and see your mother when I leave work.'

Damien attempted a smile.

'Oh, and there's something else.'

'I can't think what,' Damien muttered under his breath as he inclined his head to one side and prayed that there wouldn't be a further attack on his already overwrought conscience.

'There's a Miss Drew downstairs insisting on seeing you. Would you like me to show her up?'

Damien stilled. The little matter of Phillipa Drew was just something else on his plate, but at least this was something he would be able to sort out. Had it not been for the emergency with his mother, it would have been sorted out by now, but...

'Show her up.'

Martha knew nothing of Phillipa Drew. Why would she? Phillipa Drew worked in the bowels of IT, the place where creativity was at its height and the skills of his highly talented programmers were tested to the limit. As a lowly secretary to the head of the department, *he* had not been aware of her existence until, a week previously, a series of company infringements had come to light and the trails had all led back to her.

The department head had had the sternest possible warning, meetings had been called, everyone had had to stand up and be counted. Sensitive material could not be stolen, forwarded to competitors... The process of questioning had been rigorous and, eventually, Damien had concluded that the woman had acted without assistance from any other member of staff.

But he hadn't followed up on the case. The patent on the software had limited the damage but punishment would have to be duly meted out. He had had a preliminary interview with the woman but it had been rushed, just long enough for her to be escorted out of the building with a price on her head. He had more time now.

After a stressful ten days, culminating in the phone

call with his mother's consultant, Damien could think of a no more satisfying way of venting than by doling out just deserts to someone who had stolen from his company and could have cost millions in lost profits.

He returned to his chair and gave his mind over completely to the matter in hand.

Jail, of course. An example would have to be set.

He thought back to his brief interview with the woman, the way she had sobbed, begged and then, when neither appeared to have been working, offered herself to him as a last resort.

His mouth curled in distaste at the recollection. She might have been a five foot ten blonde but he had found the cheap, ugly working of the situation repulsive.

He was in the perfect mood to inform her, in a leisurely and thorough fashion, that the rigours of the British justice system would be waiting for her. He was in the perfect mood to unleash the full force of his frustration and stress on the truly deserving head of a petty criminal who had had the temerity to think that she could steal from him.

He pulled up all the evidence of her ill-conceived attempts at company fraud on his computer and then relaxed back in his chair to wait for her.

Downstairs, in the posh lobby of the most scarily impressive building she had ever entered, Violet waited for Damien Carver's secretary to come and fetch her. She was a little surprised that getting in to see the man in the hallowed halls of his own office had been so easy. For a few misguided seconds she nurtured the improbable fantasy that perhaps Damien Carver wasn't quite the monster Phillipa had made him out to be.

The fantasy didn't last long. No one ever got to the

stratospheric heights of success that this man obviously had by being kind, forgiving and compassionate.

What was she doing here? What was she hoping to achieve? Her sister had stolen information, had been well and truly suckered by a man who had used her to access files he wanted, had been caught and would have to face the long arm of the law.

Violet wasn't entirely sure what exactly the long arm of the law in this instance would be. She was an art teacher. Espionage, theft and nicking information couldn't have been further removed from her world. Surely her sister couldn't have been right when she had wailed that there was the threat of prison?

Violet didn't know what she would do if her sister wasn't around. There were just the two of them. At twenty-six, she was four years older than her sister and, whilst she would have been the first to admit that Phillipa hadn't always been an easy ride, ever since their parents had died in a car crash seven years previously, she loved her to bits and would do anything for her.

She looked around her and tried to stem the mounting tide of panic she felt at all the acres of marble and chrome surrounding her. She felt it was unfair that a simple glass building could fail to announce such terrifyingly opulent surroundings. Why hadn't Phillipa mentioned a word of this when she had first joined the company ten months ago? She pushed aside the insidious temptation to wish herself back at the tiny house she had eventually bought for them to share with the proceeds left to them after their parents' death. She valiantly fought a gut-wrenching instinct to run away and bury herself in all the school preparations she had to do before the new term began.

What on earth was she going to say to Mr Carver?

Could she offer to pay back whatever had been stolen? To make some kind of financial restitution?

Absorbed in scenarios which ranged from awkward to downright terrifying, she was startled when a tall grey-haired woman announced that she had come to usher her to Damien Carver's office.

Violet clutched her bag in front of her like a talisman and dutifully followed.

Everywhere she turned, she was glaringly reminded that this was no ordinary building, despite what it had cruelly promised from the outside.

The paintings on the walls were dramatic abstract splashes that looked mega-expensive…the plants dotting the foyer were all bigger and more lush than normal, as though they had been routinely fed on growth hormones…the frowning, determined people scurrying from lift to door and door to lift were younger and more snappily dressed than they had a right to be…and even the lift, as she stepped into it, was abnormally large. She dodged the repeated reflection of her nervous face and tried to concentrate on the polite conversation being made.

If this was his personal secretary, then it was clear that she had no idea of Phillipa's misdeeds. On the bright side, at least her sister's face hadn't been reprinted on posters for target practice.

She only surfaced when they were standing in front of an imposing oak door, alongside which two vertical sheets of smoked glass protected Damien Carver from the casual stares of anyone who might be waiting in his secretary's outside office.

Idly tabulating the string of idiotic mistakes Phillipa Drew had made in her half-baked attempt to defraud his company, Damien didn't bother to look up when his door was pushed open and Martha announced his unexpected visitor.

'Sit!' He kept his eyes glued to his computer screen. Every detail of his body language suggested the contempt of a man whose mind had already been made up.

With her nerves unravelling at a pace, Violet slunk into the leather chair directly in front of him. She wished she could direct her eyes to some other, less forbidding part of the gigantic room, but she was driven to stare at the man in front of her.

'He's a pig,' Phillipa had said, when Violet had offhandedly asked her what Damien Carver was like. Violet had immediately pictured someone short, fat, aggressive and unpleasant. Someone, literally, porcine in appearance.

Nothing had prepared her for the sight of one of the most beautiful men she had ever seen in her life.

Raven-black hair was swept away from a face, the lines and contours of which were finely chiselled. His unsmiling mouth filled her with cold fear but, in a strangely detached way, she was more than aware of its sensual curve. She couldn't see the details of his physique, but she saw enough to realise that he was muscular and lean. He must have some foreign blood in him, she thought, because his skin was burnished gold. He made her mouth go dry and she attempted to gather her scattered wits before he raised his eyes to look at her.

When he finally *did* turn his attention to her, she was pinned to the chair by navy-blue eyes that could have frozen water.

Damien looked at her for a long time in perfect silence before saying, in a voice that matched his glacial eyes, 'And who the hell are you?'

Certainly not the woman he had been expecting. Phillipa Drew was tall, slim, blonde and wore the air of some of the women he had dated in the past—an expression of smug awareness that she had been gifted with an abundance of pulling power.

This woman, in her unflattering thick black coat and her sensible flat black shoes, was the very antithesis of a fashion icon. Who knew what body was lurking beneath the shapeless attire? Her clothes were stridently background, as was her posture. Frankly, she looked as though she would have given a million dollars to have been anywhere but sitting in his office in front of him.

'I'm Miss Drew... I thought you knew...' Violet stammered, cringing back because, without even having to lean closer, she was still overwhelmed by the force of his personality. She was sitting ramrod-erect and still clutching her handbag to her chest.

'I'm in no mood for games. Believe me, I've had one hell of a fortnight and the last thing I could do with is someone finding their way into my office under false pretences.'

'I'm not here under false pretences, Mr Carver. I'm Violet Drew, Phillipa's sister.' She did her best to inject some natural authority into her voice. She was a teacher. She was accustomed to telling ten- and eleven-year-olds what to do. She could shout *Sit!* as good as the next person. But, for some reason, probably because she was on uncertain ground, all sense of authority appeared to have abandoned her.

'Now why am I finding that hard to believe?' Damien vaulted upright and Violet was treated to the full impact of his tall, athletic body, carelessly graceful as he walked around her in ever diminishing circles. Very much like a predator surveying a curiosity that had landed in his range of vision. He withdrew to perch on the edge of his desk, obliging her to look up at him from a disadvantageous sitting position.

'We don't look much alike,' Violet admitted truthfully. 'I've grown up with people saying the same thing. She inherited the height, the figure and the looks. From my mother's side of the family. I'm much more like my dad was.' The rambling apology was well rehearsed and spoken on autopilot; God knew she had trotted it out often enough, but her mind was almost entirely occupied with the man in front of her.

On closer examination, Damien could see the similarities between them. He guessed that their shade of hair colour would have been the same but for the fact that Phillipa had obviously dyed hers a brighter, whiter blonde and they both had the same bright blue eyes fringed with unusually dark, thick eyelashes.

'So you've come here because...?'

Violet took a deep breath. She had worked out in her head what she intended to say. She hadn't banked on finding herself utterly distracted by someone so sinfully good-looking and the upshot was that her thoughts were all over the place.

'I suppose she sent you on a begging mission on her behalf, did she?' Damien interjected into the lengthening silence. His lip curled. 'Having discovered that her sobbing and pleading and wringing of hands didn't cut it, and having tried and failed to seduce me into leniency, she thought she'd get you to do her dirty work for her...'

Violet's eyes widened with shock. 'She tried *to seduce you*?'

'A short-sighted move on her part.' Damien swung round so that he was back in front of his computer. 'She must have mistaken me for the sort of first-class idiot who could be swayed by a pretty face.'

'I don't believe it...' And yet, didn't she? Phillipa had always had a tendency to use her looks to get her own way. She had always found it easy to manipulate people into doing what she wanted by allowing them into the charmed space around her. Boys had always been putty in her hands, coming and going in a relentless stream, picked up and discarded without a great deal of thought for their feelings. Except, with Craig Edwards, the shoe had been on the other foot and life had ill prepared her to deal with the reversal. Violet was horribly embarrassed on her sister's behalf.

'Believe it.'

'I don't know if she told you, but she was used by a guy she had been dating. He wanted to get access to whatever files he thought you had on...well, I'm not too sure of the technical details...'

'I'll help you out there, shall I?' Damien listed the range of information that had fortunately never found its way into the wrong hands. He sat back, folded his hands behind his head and looked at her coldly. 'Shall I give you a rough idea of how much money my company stood to lose had your sister's theft proved successful?'

'But it *didn't*. Doesn't that count for *something*?'

'What argument are you intending to use to try and save your sister?' Damien drawled without an ounce of compassion. 'The *got-sadly-caught-up-with-the-wrong-guy* one or the *but-it-didn't-work* one? Because I can tell you now that I'm not buying either. She told me all about the smooth-talking banker with an eye to the main chance and a plan to take a shortcut to a career in computer software by nicking my ideas, except your sister, from the brief acquaintance I had with her, didn't exactly strike me as one of life's passive victims. Frankly, I put her down as a co-conspirator who just didn't have the brains to pull it off.'

Violet looked at him with loathing. Underneath the head-turning good looks, he was as cold as a block of ice.

'Phillipa didn't ask me to come,' she persisted. 'I came because I could see how devastated she was, how much she regretted what she had done...'

'Tough. From where I'm sitting, it's all about crime and punishment.'

Violet paled. 'She's being punished already, Mr Carver. Can't you see that? She's been sacked from the first real job she's ever held down...'

'She's twenty-two years old. I know because I've memorised her personnel file. So if this is the first real job she's ever held down, then do you care to tell me what she's been doing for the past...let's see...*six years*...? Ever since she left school at sixteen? If I'm not mistaken, she led my people to believe that a vigorous training course in computers was followed by exemplary service at an IT company in Leeds... A glowing written and verbal reference was provided by one *Mr Phillips*...'

Violet swallowed painfully as a veritable expanse of quicksand opened up at her feet. What could she say to that? Lie? She refused to. She looked at the hatefully confident expression on his face, the look of someone who had neatly led the enemy into a carefully contrived trap. Phillipa had said nothing to her about how she had managed to secure such a highly paid job at a top-rated company. She knew how now. Andrew Phillips had been her sister's boyfriend. She had strung him along with promises of love and marriage as he had taken up his position at an IT company in Leeds. He hadn't been out of the door for two seconds before she had turned her attention briefly to Greg Lambert and then, fatally, to Craig Edwards.

'Well?' Damien prompted. 'I'm all ears.' A part of him was all too aware that he was being a little unfair. So this girl, clearly lacking in guile, clearly well intentioned, had plucked up the courage to approach him on her sister's behalf. Not only was he in the process of shooting her down in flames, but he was also spearheading the arrow with poison for added measure.

The past few weeks of stress, uncertainty and unwelcome self-doubt were seeking a target for their expression and he had conveniently found one.

'Look—' he sighed impatiently and leaned forward '—it's laudable of you to come here and ten out of ten for trying, but you clearly need to wake up to your sister's true worth. She's a con artist.'

'I know Phillipa can be manipulative, Mr Carver, but she's all I have and I can't let her be written off because she's made a mistake.' Tears were gathering at the back of her eyes and thickening her voice.

'My guess is that your sister's made a number of mistakes in her life. She's just always been able to talk her way out of them by flashing a smile and baring her breasts...'

'That's a horrible thing to say.'

Damien gave an elegant little shrug of his shoulders and continued to look at her in a way that made her whole body feel as though it was burning up. 'I find that the truth is something best faced squarely.' Except, he privately conceded, that was something of a half truth. He had nonchalantly refused to face the truth about his mother's concerns over his lifestyle, preferring to stick it all on the back burner and turn a blind eye.

'So what happens now?' Violet slumped, defeated, in the chair. It had been a vain hope that she could appeal to his better nature.

'I'll take advice from my lawyers but this is a serious charge and, as such, has to be dealt with decisively.'

'When you say *decisively*...' She was mesmerised by

the icy, unforgiving lines of his face. It was like staring at someone from another planet. Her friends were all laid-back and easy-going. They cared about humanitarian issues. They joined protest marches and could argue for hours over the state of the world. The majority of them did charity work. She, herself, visited an old people's home once a week where she taught basic art. She had only ever mixed with people who thought like her. Damien Carver not only didn't think like her, she could tell that he was vaguely contemptuous of what she stood for. Those merciless eyes held no sympathy for anything she was saying. She could have been having a conversation with a block of marble.

'Jail.' Why beat about the bush? 'A learning curve for your sister and an example just in case anyone else thinks they can get away with trying to rip me off.'

'Phillipa wouldn't last a day in a prison cell...'

'Something she should have considered before she decided to try and hack into my computers to get hold of sensitive information,' Damien responded drily.

'It's her first offence, Mr Carver... She's not a criminal... I understand that you won't be giving her any references...'

Damien burst out laughing. Was this woman for real? 'Not *giving her references*? Have you heard a single word I've just said to you? Your sister will be put into the hands of the law and she will go to prison. I'm sure it won't be a hardcore unit with serial killers and rapists but that's not my problem. You can go visit her every week and she can productively use the time to reflect on the wisdom of a few personality changes. When she's released in due course back into the big, wide world, she can find herself a menial job somewhere. I'm sure the process of rehabilitation will be an invaluable experience for her. Of course, she'll have a criminal record, but, like I said, what else could she have expected?' He reached into one of the drawers in his massive desk, fetched out a box of tissues and pushed it across to her.

Violet shuffled out of her chair and snatched the box from his desk. Her eyes were beginning to leak. What else was there to say?

'Don't you have *any* sense of compassion?' she whispered in a hoarse undertone. 'I promise I'll make sure that Phillipa doesn't put a foot astray *ever again*...'

'She won't be able to when she's behind bars. But, just out of curiosity, how would you manage to accomplish that feat anyway? Install CCTV cameras in her house? Or flat? Or wherever it is she lives? As long-term solutions go, not a practical one.'

'We share a house,' Violet said dully. She dabbed her eyes. Breaking down was not the way to deal with a man like this. She knew that. Men like him, *people* like him, only understood a language that was similar to the one they used, the harsh and ugly language of cold, merciless cruelty. He wouldn't appreciate a sobbing female and he just wouldn't get the concept of loyalty that had driven her to confront him face to face in his own office.

Unfortunately, being tough and aggressive did not come naturally to Violet. She might have possessed a strength of character her sister lacked, but she had never had the talent Phillipa had for confrontation. 'And I would never dream of spying on anyone. I would keep an eye on her...make sure she toed the line...' Easier said than done. If Phillipa decided to try and defraud another company, then how on earth would she, Violet, ever be able to prevent her? 'I've been doing that ever since our parents died years ago...'

'How old are you?' The connections in his brain were beginning to transmit different messages now. He stared at her carefully. Her eyes were pink and her full mouth was still threatening to wobble. She was the picture perfect portrait of a despairing woman.

'Twenty-six.'

'So you're a scant four years older than your sister and I guess you were forced to grow up quickly if you were left in the role of caretaker... I'm thinking she must have been a handful...' For the first time in weeks, that feeling of being oddly at sea, at the whim of tides and currents over which he had no control, was beginning to evaporate.

Wrong-footed by the sudden change of tempo in the conversation, Violet met those fabulous navy eyes with a puzzled expression. She wondered whether this was a prelude to another rousing sermon on the salutary lessons to be learnt from incarceration. Maybe he was about to come out with another revelation, maybe he was going to inform her in that cold voice of his that Phillipa had done more than just make a pass at him. She was already cringing in mortification at what was to come.

'She went off the rails a bit.' Violet rushed into speech because, as long as she was talking, he wasn't saying stuff she didn't want to hear. 'It was understandable. We were a close family and she was at an impressionable age...'

'And you weren't?'

'I've always been stronger than Phillipa.' He was still staring at her with that speculative, unreadable expression that made her feel horribly uneasy. 'Phillipa was the spoiled one. I got that. She was a beautiful baby and she grew into a beautiful child and then a really stunning teenager. I was sensible and hard working and practical...'

'You must be hot in your coat. Why don't you remove it?'

'I beg your pardon?'

'The central heating here is in perfect working condition. You must be sweltering.'

'Why would I take my coat off, Mr Carver? When I'm going to be leaving in a short while? I mean, I've said everything there is to say and I've tried to appeal to your better nature, but you haven't got a better nature. So there's no point in my being here, is there? It doesn't really matter what I say, you're just going to tell me that Phillipa needs to be punished, that she's going to go to prison and that she'll come out a reformed person.'

'Maybe there's another discussion to be had on the subject…'

Violet hardly dared get her hopes up. She looked at him in disbelief. 'What other discussion, Mr Carver? You've just spent the past forty-five minutes telling me that she's to be held up as an example to your other employees and punished accordingly…'

'Take the coat off.'

Violet hesitated. Eventually she stood up, awkwardly aware of his eyes on her. She harked back to what he had said about her sister trying to seduce him. She had heard the contempt in his voice when he had said that. She wondered what his thoughts would be when he saw *her* without the protective covering of her capacious coat, and then she sternly reminded herself that what she looked like was irrelevant. She had come to plead her sister's case and she would take whatever sliver of compassion he might find in his heart to distribute.

Damien watched the unflattering coat reveal a baggy long-sleeved dress that was equally unflattering. Over it was a loose-fitting cardigan that reached down to below her waist.

'So the question is this…with your sister facing a prison sentence, what would you be prepared to do for her?'

He let that question hang in the air between them. Her eyes, he absently thought as she stared at him in bewilderment, weren't quite the same shade of blue as her sister's. They were more of a violet hue, which seemed appropriate given her name.

'I would do anything,' Violet told him simply. 'Phillipa may have her faults but she's learnt from this. Not just in the matter of trying to do something she shouldn't, but she's had her eyes opened about the sort of men she can trust and the ones she can't. In fact, I've never seen her so devastated. She's practically locked herself away...'

Damien thought that a few days of self-imposed seclusion before rejoining the party scene was a laughable price to pay for a criminal offence. If that was Violet Drew's definition of her sister's *devastation* then her powers of judgement were certainly open to debate.

'So you would do anything...' he drawled, standing to move to the window, briefly looking out at the miserable grey, muted colours of a winter still reluctant to release its grip. He turned around, strolled to his desk where he once again perched on the side. 'That's good to hear because, if that's really the case, then I would say that there's definitely room to negotiate...'

CHAPTER TWO

'NEGOTIATE? HOW?' VIOLET was at a loss. Would he ask her for some sort of financial compensation for the time his people had spent tracking Phillipa down? If no money had actually been lost, then she could hardly be held accountable for any debt incurred and, even if money had actually been lost, then there was no way that she could ever begin to repay it. Just thinking of all the money his company nearly did lose was enough to make her feel giddy.

This was not a situation that Damien liked. As solutions went, it left a lot to be desired, but where were his choices? He needed to prove to his mother that she could have faith in him, that he could be relied upon, whatever the circumstances. He needed to reassure her. If his mother wasn't stressing, then the chances of her responding well to treatment would be much greater. Who didn't know that stress could prove the tipping point between recovery and collapse in a case such as this? Eleanor Carver wanted him settled or she would fret over the consequences and that was a worst case scenario waiting to happen. He loved his mother and, after years of ships-in-the-night relationships, it was imperative that he now stepped up to the plate and presented her with a picture of stability.

The grim reality, however, was that he had no female friends. The women in his life were the women he dated and the women he dated were unsuitable for the task at hand.

'My mother has recently been diagnosed with cancer...'

'I'm so sorry to hear that...'

'Stomach cancer. She's in London at the moment for tests. As you may know, with cancer, its outcome can never be predicted.'

'No. But...may I ask what that has to do with me?'

'I have a proposal for you. One that may be beneficial to both of us.'

'A proposal? What kind of proposal?'

Damien looked steadily at the woman in front of him. On almost every level, he knew this was, at best, questionable. On the other hand, looking at the bigger picture, didn't the value of the ends more than make up for the means? Sometimes you had to travel down an unexpected road to get to the desired destination.

And now a virtual stranger, a woman he would not have looked at twice under normal circumstances, was about to be ushered into his rarefied world to do him a favour and he was well aware that she would be unable to refuse because her own protective instincts for her sister had penned her into a place in which she was helpless.

'For some time, my mother has had certain...misgivings about my lifestyle...' He realised that he had never actually verbalised any of this to anyone before. He wasn't into the touchy-feely business of sharing confidences. It was reassuring to know that Violet Drew didn't actually count as someone with whom the sharing of confidences was of any significance. He wasn't involved with her. It wasn't as though she would attach herself to anything he said and use it as a way of insinuating herself into a relationship. And yet...he still had to fight a certain hesitancy.

He impatiently swept aside his natural instinct for complete privacy. Hell, it wasn't as though he was in a confessional about to admit to an unforgivable mortal sin!

'Has she?'

'If you're wondering where this is going, then you'll have to hear me out. One thing I'm going to say, though, is that nothing I tell you leaves this room. Got it?'

'What are you going to say?'

'My mother is old-fashioned...traditional. I'm thirty-two years old and, as far as she is concerned, should be in a committed, serious relationship. With a...ah...let's just say a certain type of woman. Frankly, the sort of woman I wouldn't normally look at twice.'

'What sort of women do you look at?' Violet asked, because his remark seemed to beg further elaboration. Looking at him, the answer was self-explanatory.

'Let's just say that I tend to spend my time in the company of beautiful women. They're not the sort of women my mother has ever found suitable.'

'I still don't know what this has to do with me, Mr Carver.'

'Then I'll spell it out. My mother might not have long to live. She wants to see me with someone she thinks is the right sort of woman. Currently, I know no one who fits the bill...'

Enlightenment came in a blinding rush. 'And you think that *I* might be suitable for the role?' Violet shook her head disbelievingly. How on earth would anyone ever buy that she and this man were in any way involved? Romantically? He was aggressively, sinfully beautiful while she...

But of course, she thought, that was the point, wasn't it? Whilst his type would be models with legs up to their armpits and big, long hair, his mother obviously had a different sort of girl in mind for him. Someone more normal. Probably not even someone like *her* but maybe he figured that he didn't have time on his side to hunt down someone more suited to play the part and so he had settled for her. Because he could.

Damien calmly watched as she absorbed what he was saying. 'You're nothing like anyone I've ever dated in my life before, ergo you'll do.'

'I'm sorry, Mr Carver.' Violet wondered how such physical beauty could conceal such cold detachment. She looked at him and couldn't tear her eyes away and yet he chilled her to the bone. 'For starters, I would never lie to anyone. And secondly, if your mother knows you at all, then she'll see right through any charade you have in mind to…to…pull the wool over her eyes.'

'Here's the thing, though, Miss Drew…your sister is facing a prison sentence. Is that what you really want? Do you honestly want to condemn her to the full horrors of a stint courtesy of Her Majesty?'

'That's awful! You can't *blackmail* me…'

'Whoever said anything about blackmail? I'm giving you an option and it's an extremely generous one. In return for a few days of minor inconvenience, you have my word that I'll call the dogs off. Your sister will be able to have her learning curve without having to suffer the full force of the law, which you and I both know is what she richly deserves.' He stood up and strolled towards the impressive window, looking out for a few seconds before returning to face her. 'I wouldn't want you to think for a minute that I won't do my utmost to make sure your sister is punished should you decide to play the moral card. I will.'

'This is crazy,' Violet whispered. But she had a mental snapshot of beautiful Phillipa behind bars. She didn't possess the inner strength to ever survive something like that. She was a woman who was reliant on her beauty to get through life and that had left her vulnerable. Maybe she did indeed need to have a forceful learning curve, but prison? Not only would it destroy her, but if she ever found out that she, Violet, had rejected an opportunity to save her, then would their relationship survive? There was no large extended family on whom to rely, no one to whom either of them could turn for advice. A few second and third cousins up north…and then just old friends of their parents, most of whom they no longer saw.

'No one does stuff like this.' She made a final plea. 'Surely your mother would rather you go out with the sort of women you like rather than pretend to be with someone you don't.'

'It's not quite as simple as that.' Damien raked his fingers through his hair, suddenly restless as the need for yet more confidences was reluctantly dragged from him. 'Of course, if it were a simple case of my mother not approving of my choice of woman, then it would be regrettable, but something we could both live with.'

'But…?'

'But I have a brother. Dominic is six years older than me and he lives at home with my mother in Devon.' Damien hesitated. Nine years ago, before time and experience had done its work, he had been stupid enough to fall for a woman—so stupid that he had proposed to her. It had been an eight-week whirlwind romance that had largely taken place in bed. But she had been intelligent, a career woman, someone with whom he could envisage himself enjoying intellectual conversations. And then she had met Dominic and he had known within seconds that he had made a fatal error of judgement. Annalise had tried to cover her discomfort, and he had briefly and optimistically given her the benefit of the doubt until she had haltingly told him that she wasn't sure that she was ready to commit. He had got the message loud and clear. She could commit to him, but she would not commit to him if he came with the baggage of a disabled sibling, someone he would have to look after when his mother was no longer around. Since then, he had made sure that he kept his relationships with women short and sweet. He had never taken any of them to Devon and only a few had ever met his mother, mostly when he had had no choice.

He had to fight back his natural instinct to keep this slice of his life extremely private. It was a place to which no one was invited. However, these were circumstances he could never have foreseen and, like it or not, he would have to give the woman in front of him some background detail. It wasn't a great position in which to find himself. He restively began to prowl the room while Violet distractedly watched him. There were so many things to process that her brain seemed to have temporarily shut down and, instead, her senses were making up for the shortcoming, had heightened so that she was uncomfortably and keenly aware of the flex of every muscle in his body as he moved with economic grace around her, forcing her to twist in the chair to keep her eyes on him.

'My brother was born with brain damage,' he told her bluntly. 'He's not completely helpless, but he's certainly incapable of leading a normal life in the outside world. He is wheelchair-bound and, whilst he has flashes of true brilliance, he is mentally damaged. My mother says that he was briefly starved of oxygen when he was born. The bottom line is that he is dependent on my mother, despite the fact that he has all the carers money can buy. She believes that he needs the familiarity of a strong family link.'

'I understand. If you're not settled or at least involved with someone your mother approves of…she feels that you won't be able to handle your brother if something happens to her…'

'In a nutshell.'

Looking at him, Violet had no idea how he felt about his brother. Certainly he cared enough to subject himself to a role play he would not enjoy. It pointed to a complexity that was not betrayed by anything on his face, which remained cool, hard, considering.

'It's never right to lie to people,' Violet said and the forbidding lines of his face relaxed into a cynical smile.

'You don't really expect me to believe you, do you? When you spring from the same gene pool as your sister?'

'There must be some other way I can…make amends for what Phillipa's done…'

'We both know that you're going to cave in to what I want because you have no choice. Ironically, your position is very much like my own. We're both going to engage in a pretence neither of us wants for the sake of other people.'

'But when your mother discovers the truth…'

'I will explain to her that we didn't work out. It happens. Before then, however, she will have ample opportunity to reassure herself that I am more than capable of taking on the responsibilities that lie with me.'

Violet's head was swimming. She shakily got to her feet, but then sank back down into the chair. He was right, wasn't he. She *was* going to cave in because she had no choice. They both knew it and she hated the way he had deprived her of at least having the opportunity to come to terms with it for herself.

'But it would never work,' she protested. 'We don't even like each other…'

'Liking me isn't part of the arrangement.' Damien circled her then leant forward to rest both hands on either side of the chair and Violet squirmed back, suffocating in a wave of intense physical awareness of him. Everything about him was so overpowering. There was just *so much* of him. She found it impossible to relax. It was as if she had been plugged into an electrical socket and her normally placid temperament had been galvanised into a state of unbearable, strangulating tension.

'But your mother will see that straight away...she'll *know* that this is just a farce...'

'She'll see what she wants to see because people always do.' He needed her to. He knew he had not been a perfect son. His mother had never complained about the amount of time he spent away. She had always been fully understanding about the way work consumed his life, leaving very little room for much else, certainly very little room for cultivating any relationship of any substance, not that he had ever been inclined to have one. Her unprotesting acceptance had made him lazy. He could see that now but then hindsight was a wonderful thing.

He pushed himself away and glanced at his watch. 'I intend to visit my mother later this evening.' This time when he looked at Violet, it was assessingly. 'I'm taking it that you will agree to what I've suggested...'

'Do I have a choice?' she said bitterly.

'We all have choices. In this instance, neither of us are perhaps making the ones we would want to, but...' he gave an eloquent shrug '...life doesn't always play out the way we'd like it to.'

'Why don't you just hire an actress to play the part?' Violet glared resentfully at him from under her lashes.

'No time. Furthermore, hiring someone would open me up to the complication of them thinking that there might be more on offer than a simple business proposition. They might be tempted to linger after their job's been done. With you, the boundaries are crystal-clear. I'm saving your sister's skin and you owe me. The fact that you don't like me is an added bonus. At least it ensures that you won't become a nuisance.'

'A *nuisance*, Mr Carver?'

'Damien. However gullible my mother might be, calling me *Mr Carver* would give the game away.'

'How can you be so...so...cold-hearted?'

Damien flushed darkly. As far as he was concerned, he was dealing with a situation as efficiently as he could. Drain it of all emotion and nothing was clouded, there were no blurry lines or grey areas. His mother was ill... she was anxious about him...desperate for him to produce someone by his side whom she could see as an anchor... His task was to come up with a way of putting her mind at rest. It was the way he tackled all problems that presented themselves to him. Calmly, coolly and decisively. It was an approach that had always served him well and he wasn't going to change now.

He pushed the ugly tangle of confusion and vulnerability away. He had always felt that he was the one on whom his mother and Dominic needed to rely. After his father's death, he had risen to the challenge of responsibilities far beyond any a boy in his twenties might have faced. He had jettisoned all plans to take a little time out and had instead sacrificed the dream of kicking back so that he could immerse himself in taking over the reins of his father's company. His only mistake had been to fall for a woman who hadn't been able to cope with the complete picture and, in the aftermath, he had wasted time and energy in the fruitless pastime of self-recrimination and self-doubt. He had moved on from that place a long time ago but negative feelings had never again been allowed to cloud his thinking. Indecision was not something that was ever given space and it wasn't about to get any now.

'How I choose to deal with this situation is my concern

and my concern only. Your role isn't to offer your opinion; it's to be by my side in two days' time when I go and visit my mother. And you asked me what I meant by *a nuisance*...' There was no chance that she would become a liability. They were two people who could not have been on more opposing ends of the scale. If she hadn't told him that she didn't like him, then he would have surmised that for himself. It was there in the simmering resentment lurking behind her purple-blue eyes and in her body language as she huddled in the chair in front of him as if one false move might propel her further into his radius. Of course it didn't help that she considered herself there under duress, but even when she had first walked into his office she had failed to demonstrate any of those little signals that heralded interest. No coy looks...no encouraging half smiles...no fluttering eyelashes...

He wasn't accustomed to a reaction like this from a woman and, in any other situation, he might have been amused, but not now. Too much was at stake. So, whatever he thought, he would make his position doubly clear.

'A nuisance would be you imagining that the charade was real...getting ideas...'

Violet's mouth fell open and she went bright red. Not only had he blackmailed her into doing something she knew was wrong, but he was actually suggesting, in that *smug, arrogant* way, that she might start...*what, exactly*...? Thinking that he was seriously interested in her? Or imagining that she was interested in *him*?

He really was, a little voice whispered in her head, quite beautiful but she would never be interested in a man like him. Everything about him, aside from those staggering good looks, repelled her. Her soft mouth tightened and she looked back at him with an equal measure of coolness.

'That wouldn't happen in a million years,' she told him.

'The only reason I'm even consenting to this is because I don't have a choice, whatever you say. And how do I know that you'll keep your side of the deal? How do I know that you won't take proceedings against my sister after I've done what you want…?'

Damien leaned forward. Every line of his body threatened her. 'How do I know that you won't turn around and tell my mother what's actually going on? How do I know that you'll deliver what I need you to? I guess you could say that we're going to be harnessed to one another for a short while and we're just going to have to trust that neither of us decides to try and break free of the constraints… Now, we need to discuss the details…' He strode towards his jacket, which had been tossed over the back of the leather sofa against the wall. 'It's lunchtime. We're going to go and grab something and start filling in the blanks.'

He expected her to follow. Was he like that with *all* women? Why on earth did they put up with it? She had to half run to keep up with him, past the grey-haired secretary who looked at them both with keen interest as she was ordered to cancel all his afternoon appointments, and then back down to the foyer where, it now seemed like a million years ago, she had sat in a state of nervous panic waiting to be shown to his office.

She couldn't fail to notice the way everyone acknowledged his presence as he strode ahead of her. Conversations halted, backs were straightened, small groups dispersed. There was absolutely no doubt that he ran the show and she wondered how her sister could ever have thought that she could get away with trying to steal information from him. Perhaps she had never personally met him, but surely Phillipa would have realised, even if only through hearsay, that the man was one hundred per cent hard line? But then Phillipa had been busy losing her head to a guy who had spotted a way in to making a quick buck via a back door. Her sister, for once, had found herself being the victim of manipulation. Chances were she hadn't been thinking at all.

Her coat was back on because she had expected them to be walking to wherever he was taking her for lunch, but in fact they headed down to a lift that carried them straight to an enormous basement car park and she followed him to a gleaming black Aston Martin which he beeped open with his key.

'Tell me the sort of food you like to eat,' he said without looking at her.

'Is that the first step to pretending we know one another?'

'You're going to have to change your attitude.' Damien was entirely focused on the traffic as he emerged from the underground car park into the busy street outside. 'Two people in a relationship try to avoid sniping and sarcasm. What sort of restaurants do you go to?'

He slid his eyes across to her and Violet felt a quiver of something sharp and unidentifiable, something that slithered through her like quicksilver, making her skin burn and prickling it with a strange sensation of *awareness*.

This was a business deal. They were sitting here in this flash car, awkwardly joined together in a scheme in which neither wanted to participate but both were forced to, and she could do without her nervous system going into semi-permanent free fall.

She needed to hang on to her composure, however much she disliked the man and however much she scorned his ethics.

'I don't,' she told him evenly. 'At least not often. Sometimes after work on a Friday night. I'm an art teacher. I haven't got enough money to eat out in fancy restaurants.'

She wanted to burst out laughing because not only did they dislike each other, but they were from opposite sides of the spectrum. He was rich and powerful, she was… almost constantly counting her pennies or else saving and the only power she had was over her kids.

Damien didn't say anything. He had never gone out with a teacher. He leaned towards models, who moaned about not being paid enough…but usually it meant for the purchase of top end sports cars or cottages in the Cotswolds rather than fancy meals out. Most of them wouldn't have been caught dead in cheap clothes or cheap restaurants. They earned big bucks for strutting their stuff on catwalks. In their heads, there was always a photographer lurking round the corner so getting snapped looking anything but gorgeous and being anywhere but cool was unacceptable.

'When you say *fancy*…' he encouraged.

'What do *you* call fancy?' she asked him, because why should she be the one under the spotlight all the time?

He named a handful of Michelin-starred restaurants which she had heard of and she laughed with genuine amusement. 'I've read about those places. I don't think I'd make it to any of them, even for a special occasion.'

'Really,' Damien murmured. He altered the direction of his car.

'Really. Your mother will be very curious to discover what we see in one another. How would we have met in the first place?' For a few seconds she forgot how much she disliked him and focused on the incongruity of the two of them ever hitting it off. 'I mean, did you just see me emerging from the school where I work and decide that you wanted to come over for a chat?'

'Stranger things have been known to happen.'

But not much, Violet thought. 'Where are we going, anyway?'

'Heard of Le Gavroche?'

'We can't!'

'Why not? You said you've never eaten out at a fancy restaurant. Now's your big opportunity.'

'I'm not dressed for somewhere like that!'

'Too late.' He made a quick phone call and an attendant emerged from the restaurant to take the keys to his car. 'I eat here a lot,' Damien explained in an undertone. 'I have an arrangement that someone parks my car and brings it back for me if I come without my driver. You can't wear the coat for the duration of the meal. I'm sure what you're wearing is perfectly adequate.'

'No, it's not!' Violet was appalled. The surroundings weren't intimidating. Indeed, there was a charm and old-fashioned elegance about the place that was comforting. Damien was greeted like an old friend. No one stared at her. And yet Violet couldn't help but feel that she was out of her depth, that she just didn't look the part. She had dressed for what she had thought was going to be a difficult interview. The clothes she wore to work were casual, cheap and comfortable. She wasn't used to what she was now wearing—a stiff dress that had been chosen specifically because it was the comforting background colour of dark grey and because it was shapeless and therefore concealed what she fancied was a body that was plump and unfashionable.

'Are you always so self-conscious about your appearance?' was the first thing he asked as soon as they were seated at one of the tables in a quiet corner. He eyed her critically. He had never seen such an unflattering dress in his life. 'In addition to allowing your sister to walk free, you'll be pleased to hear that you'll benefit from our deal as well. I'm going to open an account for you at Harrods. I have someone there who deals with me. I'll give you her name, tell her to expect you. Choose whatever clothes you want. I would say a selection of outfits appropriate for visiting my mother while she's in hospital.' He looked at her horrified, outraged expression and raised his eyebrows. 'I'm being realistic,' he said. 'I may be able to pull off the *opposites attract* explanation for our relationship, but there's no way I can pull off a sudden attraction for someone who is completely disinterested in fashion.'

'How *dare* you? How *dare* you be so rude?'

'We haven't got time to beat around the bush, Violet. My mother won't care what you wear but she *will* smell a rat if I show up with someone who doesn't seem to care about her appearance.'

'I do care about my appearance!' Violet was calm by nature but she could feel herself on the verge of snapping.

'You have a sister who's spent her life turning heads and you've reacted by blending into the background. I don't have to have a degree in psychology to work that one out, but you're going to have to step into the limelight for a little while and you'll need the right wardrobe to pull it off.'

'I don't need this!'

'Are you going to leave?'

Violet hesitated.

'Thought not. So relax.' He pushed the menu towards her. 'You teach art at a school…where?' He sat back, inclined his head to one side and listened while she told him about her job. He was taking everything in. Every small detail. The more she talked, the more she relaxed. He listened to her anecdotes about some of her pupils. He made encouraging noises when she described her colleagues. She seemed to do a great deal of work for precious little financial reward. The picture painted was of a hard-working, diligent girl who had put the time and effort in while her pretty, flighty sister had taken the shortcuts.

Violet realised that she had been talking for what seemed like hours when their starters were placed in front of them. Having anticipated a meal comprised of pregnant pauses, hostile undertones and simmering, thinly veiled accusations and counter accusations, she could only think that he must be a very good listener. She had forgotten his offensive observation that she didn't take care of herself, that she had no sense of style, that she needed a new wardrobe to meet his requirements. She wanted to defensively point out that wearing designer clothes was no compensation for having personality. She was tempted to pour scorn on women who defined themselves according to what they wore or what jewellery they possessed. It took a lot of effort to rein back the impulses and tell herself that none of that mattered because none of this was real. They weren't embarking on a process of discovery about each other. They were skimming the surface, gleaning a few facts, just enough to pull off a charade for the sake of his mother. That being the case, she didn't need to defend herself to him, nor should she take offence at anything he said. His request that she buy herself a new wardrobe was no different from being told, on applying for a job working for an airline, that there would be a uniform involved.

'What sort of clothes would your mother expect me to show up in?' Once more in charge of her wits, Violet paid some attention to the food that had been placed in front of her. Ornate, as beautifully arranged as a piece of artwork, and yet mouth-wateringly delicious. 'I don't own many dresses. I have lots of jeans and jumpers and trousers.'

'Simple but classy might be good...'

'And how long would I be obliged to play this part?'

Damien pushed aside his plate to lean forward and look at her thoughtfully. Down to business. Although he had to admit that hearing about her school days had been entertaining. It made a change to sit in a restaurant with a woman who wasn't interested in playing footsie with him under the table or casting lingering looks designed to indicate what game would be played when the footsie was over. He wondered whether she had ever played footsie with a man, which made him speculate on what body was hidden under her charmless dress. It was impossible to tell.

'There will be a series of tests spanning a week. Maybe a bit longer until treatment can be transferred to Devon.'

'I expect your mother will be anxious to get back to her home... Can I ask who is looking after your brother at the moment?'

'We have a team of carers in place. But that's not your concern. You will be around while she is in London. As soon as she leaves for Devon, your part will be done. I will return with her and, during that time, I will eventually break the news that we are no longer a going concern. At that point, I intend to demonstrate that she has nothing to be worried about...' He looked at her flushed heart-shaped face and his eyes involuntarily wandered down to the swell of full breasts straining against the unforgiving lines of the severe dress she had chosen to wear.

Violet sensed the shift of his attention from his unemotional checklist of facts to her body. She didn't know how she was aware of that because his face was so unreadable, the depth of his deep blue eyes revealing nothing at all, and yet she just *knew* and she was appalled when her body reacted with a surge of intense excitement that shocked and bewildered her.

Unlike her sister, Violet's history with men could have been condensed to fit on the back of a postage stamp. One fairly serious relationship three years previously, which had ended amicably after a year and a half. They had started as friends and no one could accuse them of not having tried to take it a step further, but, despite the fact that, on paper at least, it made sense, it had fizzled out. Back into the friendship from whence it had sprung. They kept in touch and since then he had married and was living the fairy tale in Yorkshire. Violet was happy for him. She harboured the dream that she too would discover her fairy tale life with someone. She was certain that she would know that special someone the second he stepped into her life. In the meantime she kept her head down, went out with her friends and enjoyed the company of the guys she met in a group. She didn't expect to be thrown unwillingly into the company of a man of whom she didn't approve and feel anything for him bar dislike. Certainly not the dark, forbidden excitement that suddenly coursed through her body. It was a reaction she angrily rejected.

'You will agree that you'll be profiting immensely from your side of this deal...' More food was brought for them although his eyes never left her face. She had amazing skin. Clear and satiny-smooth and bare of make-up, aside from some remnants of lipgloss which he suspected she had applied in a hurry.

'You still haven't told me where we're supposed to have met.' Violet looked down and focused on yet more artfully arranged food on her plate, although her normally robust appetite appeared to have deserted her. She was too conscious of his eyes on her. Having given house room to the unwelcome realisation that there was something exciting about being in his presence, that that excitement swirled inside her with a dark persuasive force that she didn't want, not at all, she now found that she had to claw her way back to the level of composure she needed and wanted.

'At your school. It seems the least convoluted of solutions.'

'Why would you be in a school in Earl's Court, Mr Carver? Sorry, *Damien*…'

'I know a lot of people, Violet. Including a certain celebrity chef who is currently working on a programme of food in schools. Since I've set up a small unit to oversee the opening of three restaurants, all of which will be staffed by school leavers who have studied Home Economics or whatever it happens to be called these days, then it makes perfect sense that I might be in your building.'

'You haven't really, have you?' Violet was unwillingly impressed that he might be more than an electronics guru. 'I mean become involved in a set-up like that…'

'Why do you find that so hard to believe?' He shrugged. Did he want to tell her how satisfying he found this slice of semi charity work? Because certainly he didn't expect to see much by way of profit from the exercise. Did he want to explain that he knew what it felt like to have someone close who would never hold down a job? He was almost tempted to tell her about his long-reaching plan to source IT projects within his company for a department that would be fitted out to accommodate the disabled because he knew from experience how many of them were capable and enthusiastic but betrayed by bodies that refused to cooperate.

'Don't bother to answer that—' he brushed aside any inclination to deviate from the point '—this isn't a soul-searching exercise. Nor do we have the time to get into too much background detail. Like I said. You smile and leave the rest to me. Before you know it, you'll be on your merry way and everyone will be happy.'

CHAPTER THREE

'But *how*? *How* did you manage to do it? I know I keep going on about it, but it's just so...incredible!'

Phillipa was sitting across the kitchen table from Violet. In front of her inroads had already been made into a bottle of white wine. She had greeted the news of Damien Carver's unexpected leniency yesterday with stunned disbelief, incredulity, anger that Violet might be stringing her along and, finally, she had taken it on board, although Violet could tell that her vague explanations hadn't quite passed muster.

'I begged and pleaded,' Violet said for the umpteenth time. 'When did you start drinking? It's only five-thirty!'

'*You'd* be drinking too if you were in my position,' Phillipa said sulkily, unwinding her long legs, which had been tucked under her, and standing up to stretch in a lazy, languorous movement like a cat. Stress had not affected Phillipa the way it would other people. She still managed to look amazing. Although it wasn't hot inside the house because the thermostat was rigidly controlled to save money, she was wearing a thin silky vest and a matching pair of silky culottes. Violet assumed that they had been one of the many presents she had received from Craig as he had manoeuvred to get her on board with his plan.

From what Violet had gathered, he had disassociated

himself from Phillipa and denied all knowledge of what she had done. Nevertheless, he was, she had been told only an hour before by her clearly gleeful sister, who had recovered well from her devastation, out of a job and planning on leaving the country. He hadn't deleted her fast enough from his Facebook account to prevent her from maliciously charting his progress but he had as soon as she had posted a message informing the world that he was a crook and a bastard and that if anyone bought that phoney crap about better opportunities abroad then they were idiots.

'I don't suppose you managed to persuade him to let them give me a reference, did you?' Phillipa asked hopefully and Violet stifled a groan of pure despair. 'Okay, okay, okay. I get the picture. But...thanks, sis...'

'You don't have to keep thanking me every two seconds.'

'I know I can be a nightmare.' She hesitated, thought about pouring herself another glass of wine and instead reached for a bottle of water from the case on the ground next to her. 'But I've really had time to think about... everything...and I've been in touch with Andy... So I may have used him just a teeny bit in getting me that job, but he's a good guy...'

A good guy who hadn't been thinking with the right part of his body when he fudged you a dodgy reference, Violet thought.

'And he's been given the sack,' Phillipa continued glumly.

'Was he very angry with you?' She shook her head, reluctantly amused at the half smile tugging the corners of her sister's mouth.

'He adores me.'

'Even after the whole Craig Edwards fiasco?'

'I explained that I just hadn't been thinking straight at

the time... Well, we all make mistakes, don't we? Anyway, seeing that we're both out of a job...we've decided to pool our resources...'

'And do what, Pip?'

'Don't be cross, but he has a good friend out in Ibiza and we're going to take our chances there. Bar work. Some DJing...loads of opportunities... I hocked all that stuff that creep gave me; well, why should I return any of it? When he nearly got me behind bars?'

Violet sat down heavily and looked at her sister. Like a married couple, they had been hitched together for better or for worse ever since their parents had died. She was twenty-six years old and had never known what it might be like to live on her own, without having to accommodate anyone else, without having to compromise, without having to tailor her needs around her sister's. Phillipa had always done her thing and Violet had picked up whatever pieces had needed picking up. She had been the shoulder to cry on, the stern voice of discipline, the nagging quasi parent, the worried other half.

'When would you go?'

'I'm heading up to Leeds in the morning and then we'll take it from there. Andy's got to sort out the lease on his flat...get his act together... You don't mind, do you?'

'I think it's a brilliant idea.' Already her mind was leaping ahead to the following afternoon, when she would be meeting Damien's mother in hospital for the first time. She realised that she had been holding a deep breath, worrying about the possibility of Phillipa asking questions, demanding to know where she was going... Stuck at home, still smarting from losing her job under ignominious circumstances, Phillipa was bored and restless...a lethal combination given the fact that she, Violet, would be trying hard to keep a secret. If Violet was clued up to her sister's foibles, then her sister was no less talented at spotting hers, and an inability to keep a secret was high on the list of her weaknesses. Now, at least, there would be one less thing to stress about.

And perhaps this was a rut... Wasn't there always a point in time when apron strings needed to be cut?

She thought of Damien's casually dismissive remarks about her relationship with her sister and gritted her teeth to block out the mental images of him that seemed to proliferate at speed and without warning. She couldn't think of anyone else, ever, who had managed to infiltrate her head the way he had. From the minute they had parted company, half her waking time had been occupied with thoughts of him and it infuriated her that not all of them were as virulently negative as she would have liked. She harked back to the cold, arrogant words leaving his mouth and then she recalled what a sexy mouth it was...she thought of that hard slashing gesture he had made with his hand when he had condemned Phillipa to jail and then, in a heartbeat, she couldn't help but recall what strong forearms he had and how the dark hair had curled around the dull silver matt of his watch...

Enthused by a positive response, Phillipa was off. Ibiza would be great! She was sick of the English weather anyway! The club scene was brilliant! She'd always wanted to work in one! Or in a bar! Or anywhere, it would seem, where computers were not much in evidence.

She left early the following morning, with promises that she would be in touch and saying she would have to return anyway to pack some things, although she could just always buy out there because they wouldn't need much more than some T-shirts and shorts and bikinis...

Deprived of her sister's ceaseless chatter, which had veered from the high of realising that she wasn't going to be prosecuted to the bitterness of acknowledging that she'd been thoroughly used by someone she had thought to be really interested in her, Violet was reduced to worrying about her forthcoming meeting with Damien.

He had informed her, via text, that he would meet her in the hospital foyer.

'Visiting hours start at five,' he had texted. *'Meet me at ten to and don't be a second late.'*

If the brevity of the text was designed to remind her of her indebtedness to him and to escalate the level of her already shredded nerves, then it worked. By the time she was ready to leave for the hospital, she was a wreck. She had spent far too long choosing what to wear. Damien's offer of a complete new wardrobe from Harrods to replace the one he obviously thought was dull, boring and inadequate, had been rejected out of hand and she was left with only casual clothes, one of her three dresses having already been used up on her interview with him. Having sneakily checked him out on the Internet, she had had a chance to see first-hand the sort of women he went for. Tall, leggy beauties. The captions informed her that they were all models. She actually recognised a couple of them from magazines. Was it any real surprise that he had suggested funding a new wardrobe for her? His mother would have to seriously be into the concept of opposites attracting if there was any chance that they would be able to pull off the charade he had signed her up for. She was short, with anything but a stick-like figure, long, unruly hair that resisted all attempts to be tamed and, as she had quickly discovered after five seconds in his presence, was never destined to be the sort of subservient yes girl he favoured.

She wore jeans. Jeans, a cream jumper and her furry boots, which were comfortable.

He was waiting for her in the designated place at the

hospital. Violet spotted him immediately. He had his back to her and was perusing the limited supply of magazines in the small gift shop near the entrance.

For a few seconds, she had the oddest sensation of paralysis. She could barely take a step forward. Her heart began to beat faster and harder, her mouth went dry and she could feel the prickly tingle of perspiration break out over her body. She wondered how she could have forgotten just how tall he was, just how broad his shoulders were. He had removed his trench coat and held it hooked by a finger over one shoulder. His other hand was in his trouser pocket. Even in the environment of a hospital, where people were too ensconced in their own private worlds of anxiety and worry to notice anything or anyone around them, he was still managing to garner interested stares.

He turned around and Violet was pinned to the spot as he narrowed his eyes on her hovering figure. She was still wearing the shapeless, voluminous coat she had worn when she had come to the office to see him on her begging mission, but now her fair hair was loose and it spilled over her shoulders in waves of gold and vanilla. Against the black coat, it was a dramatic contrast. He doubted she ever went to the hairdresser for anything more than a basic cut, and yet he knew that there were women who would have given an arm and a leg to achieve the vibrant, casually tousled effect she effortlessly had.

'You're on time,' he said, striding towards her, and Violet instinctively fell back. 'My mother is looking forward to meeting you. I see you didn't take advantage of the offer of a shopping spree.'

'I think that either someone will like me or not like me, but hopefully it won't be because of what I happen to be wearing.' She fell into step beside him. Although she tried her best to maintain a healthy distance, there was a magnetism about him that seemed to want to draw her closer, a powerful pull on her senses that defied reason. She had to resist the strangest urge to look across at him and to just keep looking.

He was explaining that his mother had wanted to find out everything about her, that he had been sketchy on detail but had fabricated nothing at all. She had been intrigued to find out that he was dating a teacher, he said.

'And did we meet in the canteen at school?' Violet asked politely as she walked briskly to keep up with him.

'I thought I'd leave it to you to come good with the romantic touches,' Damien told her drily.

'Doesn't it upset you at all that you're lying to your own mother?'

'It would upset me more to think that her health might be compromised because she was worried about my stability.' He glanced down at her fair head. She barely reached his shoulder. He could feel her reluctance pouring through every fibre of her being and he marvelled that she could be so morally outraged at a simple deception that was being done in the best possible faith and yet forgiving of her sister, who had committed a far greater fraud. He wondered whether that was the outcome of family dynamics. Just as quickly as his curiosity reared its head, he dismissed it. He wasn't in the habit of delving too deeply into female motivations. He enjoyed women and was happy to move on before simple enjoyment could become too fraught with complications. And yet this wasn't just another female to be enjoyed, was she? In fact, enjoyment didn't actually feature on his list when it came to Violet Drew.

They had taken the lift up to the floor on which Eleanor Carver had a private room. It was a large teaching hospital with a confusing number of lifts, all of which seemed to have different, exclusive destinations to specialised departments.

'I don't know anything about *you*,' Violet said in a sudden rush of panic. She tugged him to a stop before they could enter the room where his mother was awaiting her arrival. 'I mean, I know about your brother…but where did you grow up? Where did you go to school? What are your friends like? Do you even *have* any friends?'

She had pulled him to the side, where they were huddled by the wall as the business of the hospital rushed around them.

'Now that's just the sort of thing that's guaranteed to make my mother suspicious,' Damien murmured, looking down at her into those remarkable violet eyes. 'A girlfriend who thinks that her guy is such a loser that he can't possibly have any friends. You're supposed to be crazy about me…' He reached out and trailed his finger along her cheek and for a few heart-stopping seconds Violet froze. She literally found that she couldn't breathe. The noise and clatter around her faded into a dull background blur. She was held captive by deep blue eyes that bored into her and set up a series of involuntary reactions that terrified and thrilled her at the same time. She could still feel the blazing path his finger had forged against her skin and belatedly she pulled away and glared at him.

'What are you doing?'

'I know. Crazy, isn't it? Actually touching the woman who is supposed to be head over heels in love with me. You didn't think the charade would just involve you sitting across the bed from me and making small talk for half an hour, did you?'

'I… I…'

'The occasional gesture of affection might be necessary. It'll certainly make up for the fact that we're practically strangers.' Damien pushed himself away from the wall against which he had been indolently leaning. He thought of Annalise, the wife who never was. He had fully deluded himself into thinking that he had known her. In fact, it turned out that he hadn't known her at all. He had seen the perfect picture which had been presented to him and he had taken it at face value. He had committed himself to the highly intelligent, beautiful career woman and had failed to probe deeper to the shallow upwardly mobile social climber. So the fact that he and his so-called girlfriend were strangers hardly made the union less believable as far as he was concerned.

Violet hadn't banked on gestures of affection. In fact, she had naively assumed that she *would* just be sitting across a hospital bed from him and making small talk with his mother.

'There's no need to look so uncomfortable,' he drawled lazily.

'I'm not uncomfortable,' Violet hurriedly asserted. 'I just hadn't thought about that side of things.'

'There *is* no that side of things. There's the pretence of affection.'

'Oh yes. I forgot. You only like women who are decked out in designer gear and have the bodies of giraffes!'

Damien threw back his head and laughed and a few heads turned to stare for a couple of seconds. 'Are you offended because you're not my type?' He thought of Phillipa. How on earth could two sisters be so completely different? One brash and narcissistic, the other hesitant and self-conscious? Yet, curiously, so much more genuine? Intriguing.

Violet blushed furiously. 'I think we've already established that *you're* not *my* type either!' she bristled. 'And shall we just go in now?'

'Is your moment of panic over?'

'I really dislike you, do you know that?'

'You bristle like a furious little bull terrier...'

'Thank you very much for that!'

'And entering the room with that angry expression isn't going to work...'

Violet's mouth was parted as she prepared to respond appropriately to that smug little smile on his face. His mouth covered hers with an erotic gentleness that took her breath away. He delicately prised a way past her startled speechlessness and his tongue against hers was an invasion that slammed into her with the force of a hurricane. It was the most sensational kiss she had ever experienced and all she wanted to do was pull him closer so that she could continue it. Her skin burned and she felt a pool of honeyed dampness spread between her legs. She wanted the ground to open up and swallow her treacherous body whole as he gently eased himself away to push open the door to his mother's room.

He was smiling broadly as he entered and she could not have looked more like a woman in love. He had kissed her at the right time and the right place and her flushed cheeks and uneven breathing and dilated pupils were telling a story that had no foundation in fact.

He wanted his mother to believe that they were all loved up and Violet smarted from the realisation that one clever kiss had done the job. Eleanor Carver was smiling at them both, her arms outstretched in a warm gesture of welcome.

She was smaller than Violet had imagined. Whilst her son was well over six feet tall, Eleanor Carver was diminutive in stature. She looked impossibly frail against the bed sheets but her eyes were razor sharp as she rushed into inquisitive chatter.

'Don't excite yourself, Mother. You know what the consultant said.'

'He didn't say anything about not exciting myself! Besides, how can I fail to be excited when you've brought me this delightful girl of yours to meet?'

Violet stood back and watched as Damien fussed around his mother. He was so big and so powerful and yet there was a gentleness about him as he bent down to kiss her on the cheek and make sure that she was propped up just right against the pillows. It was as though he had slowed his pace to accommodate her and it brought an unwelcome lump to Violet's throat.

'He's like a mother hen now that I'm cooped up here.' Eleanor smiled and patted him on the hand.

Violet smiled back and thought that he was more fox in the coop than innocent hen and, as if he could read her mind, Damien grinned at her with raised eyebrows.

'Violet would be the first to agree that I'm the soul of sensitivity...' He moved so that he was standing next to her and she tried not to stiffen in alarm as he slipped his arm around her.

'I'm not *entirely* sure that's the description that springs to mind...' Violet unbuttoned her coat and slipped it off. In the process, she managed to edge skilfully past him to the chair next to the bed.

Still grinning as he imagined some of the descriptions she might have had in mind for him, he wasn't prepared for the hourglass figure that took his breath away for a few shocking seconds. This was not what he had expected. He had expected frumpy, slightly overweight...someone who could perhaps do with shedding a few pounds. Was it because his expectations had been so wildly at variance with the voluptuous curves on offer now that he felt the sudden thrust of painful response? Or had his diet of thin, leggy models left him vulnerable to the sort of curvy, full-breasted figure that had once haunted his testosterone-fuelled teenage dreams?

Out of the corner of his eye, he caught his mother watching him and he stopped staring to move and stand behind Violet so that he could rest both his hands on her shoulders.

From this position, he felt no guilt in appreciating the bounty of her generous breasts. She was small in stature and a positive innocent compared to the hardened, worldly, sophisticated women he dated. She didn't have a clue how to play the games that eventually led to the bedroom. He thought that if she *did* know them, then she would refuse to play them. So the lush sexiness of her body was all the more of a turn-on. Standing behind her, he could barely drag his eyes away from her gorgeous figure.

It wasn't going to do. This wasn't about attraction or sex. This was an arrangement and he didn't need it to be complicated because his testosterone levels had decided to act up.

He pulled over the other spare chair and sat next to her because staring down at her was proving to be too much of an unwelcome distraction.

His mother had launched into fond reminiscing about his childhood. Halting her in mid-stream would have been as impossible as trying to climb Everest in flip flops, so he allowed her to chatter away for as long as she wanted. He hadn't seen her so animated since she had been diagnosed and, besides, as long as she was chatting, she wasn't asking too many detailed questions. Eventually he looked at his watch and gave a little cough to indicate departure time. He would have to admit that Violet had done well. She had certainly shown keen interest in every anecdote his mother had told and had been suitably encouraging in her remarks, whilst managing to keep them brief. Watching her out of the corner of his eye, he could appreciate what he had failed to previously when he had been too busy putting his plan into action and laying down the rules and boundary lines. She was a naturally warm, empathetic person. It was what had driven her to come and see him in defence of her sister when she must have been scared witless. It was what made her smile with genuine warmth at his mother as she triumphantly reached the punchline of her story involving him, two friends and a bag of frogs.

'We really should be going, Mother. You mustn't over tire yourself.'

'Life will be very limited for me if I can't get excited and I can't get too tired, darling. Besides, there are so many questions I want to ask you both…'

Violet sneaked a surreptitious glance at Damien's hard, chiselled profile and the memory of that kiss snaked through her, bringing vibrant colour to her cheeks. Of course he hadn't been *turned on*. As he had made abundantly clear on more than one occasion, he dated supermodels. She had been chosen to play a part because she was at his mercy and because she *wasn't* a supermodel. He had kissed her like that in order to achieve something and it had worked.

It filled her with shame that *she* had been turned on. She cringed in horror at the realisation that she had wanted the kiss to go on…and on…and on… She wondered where her pride had gone when she could be held to ransom by a man she loathed to do something of which she heartily disapproved and yet, with a single touch, find her willpower reduced to rubble.

'Damien's barely told me anything about how you two met… He said that it was a couple of months ago…but that he didn't want to say anything for fear of jeopardising the relationship...'

'Did he?' Violet glanced across, eyebrows raised. 'I didn't realise that you felt so...vulnerable...' Her voice was sugary-sweet.

Damien rested his hand over hers and idly stroked her thumb, which sent her pulses racing all over again, but, with his mother's eyes on them, what could she do but to carry on smiling?

'It's a lovable trait, isn't it? Darling?' he murmured, looking her straight in the eyes and reaching to cup the nape of her neck with his hand, where he proceeded to sift his fingers through her hair.

'So how did you meet?' Eleanor asked with avid curiosity.

'Darling—' Damien continued to caress her until every part of her body was tingling in hateful response '—why don't you tell my mother all about our...romantic first meeting...?'

'It really wasn't that romantic.' Violet tried to shift away from the attentions of his hand, which was something of a mistake as he promptly decided to switch focus from her hair to her thigh. 'Actually, when I first met your son, I thought he was rude, arrogant and overbearing...'

Damien responded by squeezing her thigh gently with his big hand in subtle warning.

'He...er...came to the school for a...er...meeting with our head of Home Economics...' The pressure on her thigh was ever more insistent but, instead of turning her off, it was having the opposite effect. How on earth could her body be so wilful? When had that ever happened? She felt faint with a dark, forbidden excitement that went against every grain of common sense and reason. She wanted to squeeze her thighs tightly shut to stifle her liquid response but was scared that if she did he would duly take note and know exactly what was going on with her rebellious body. He was, after all, nothing like the guys she knew. He was a man of the world and, even on short acquaintance, she suspected that he was as knowledgeable and intimate with the workings of the female mind as it was possible for any man to be. The thought of him second-guessing that she found him sexually attractive was mortifying.

'Do you remember how bossy you were with poor Miss Taylor?' she asked, scoring points wherever she could find them and trying hard to ignore what his hand was doing to her. Out of sight of his mother's eyes because of the positioning of the chairs, his roaming hand came to rest on her thigh just below the apex where her legs met. When she thought of how that hand would feel just there, were it against bare skin, were he able to brush the downy hair with his fingers, her brain went into instant meltdown.

'We all got the impression that you were terribly important—too important to be time wasting at a school because the CEO couldn't make it... I'll admit, Mrs Carver, that my first impressions of your son were that he was a tad on the arrogant, conceited, bossy side...thoroughly unbearable, if you want the truth...'

'And yet you couldn't tear your eyes away from me,' Damien murmured in quick retaliation. He smiled and leaned across to feather a kiss on the corner of her mouth, making sure to keep his hand just where it was. 'Don't think I didn't notice when you thought I wasn't looking...'

'Ditto,' Violet muttered in feeble response because what else could she do, short of launching into a scathing attack on everything she had decided was awful about him?

'So true.' Damien allowed himself the luxury of looking at her with lazy, speculative eyes. 'And how could I ever have guessed that underneath your shapeless clothes was the figure of a sex goddess...?'

Violet went bright red. Was he joking? Continuing with their subtle duel of words which carried an undertone that his mother would not have clocked? Was he *laughing at her*? What else? she wondered, hot and flustered under the scrutiny of his deep blue eyes. She kept her gaze pointedly averted, looking at his mother with a smile that was beginning to make her jaws ache, but every inch of her was tuned in to Damien's attention, which was focused all on her. One hundred per cent of it. She could feel it as powerfully as if a branding iron had been held to her bare skin.

'Hardly a sex goddess... There's no need to tell lies...' she mumbled with an embarrassed laugh, while trying to play half of the loving couple by awkwardly leaning towards him and at the same time taking the opportunity to snap her legs firmly shut on a hand that was getting a little too inquisitive for her liking.

'You're just what my son needs, Violet,' Eleanor confided with satisfaction. 'All those girls he's spent years going out with... I expect you have a potted history of Damien's past...?'

'Mother, please. There's no need to go down that road. Violet is very much in the loop when it comes to knowing exactly the sort of women I've dated in the past...aren't you, darling...?'

'And I find it as strange as you do, Mrs Carver, that someone as intelligent as your son could have been attracted to girls with nothing between their ears. Because that's what you've said, haven't you, dearest? I'm sure they were very pretty but I've never understood how you could ever have found it a challenge to go out with a mannequin...?'

Damien smiled slowly and appreciatively at her. Touché,

he thought. She had been gauche and awkward when she had come to him with her begging bowl on her desperate mission to save her sister's skin but he was realising that this was not the woman she was at all. Warm and empathetic, yes—that much was evident from the way she interacted with his mother. She had also been prepared for him to walk all over her if she thought it would help her sister's cause. However, freed from the constraints of having to yield to him in the presence of his mother, her true colours were emerging. She was quick-tongued, intelligent and not above taking pot shots at him under cover of a smiling façade and the occasional glance that tried to pass itself off as loving.

He found that he liked that. It made a change from vacuous supermodels. Certainly, a charade he had been quietly dreading now at least offered the prospect of not being as bad as he had originally imagined and, ever creative when it came to dealing with the unexpected, he had no misgivings about making the most of a bad deal. So she thought that she'd get a little of her own back by having fun with double entendres and thinly cloaked pointed remarks? Well, two could play at that game and it would certainly add a little spice to the proceedings.

'You're so right, my dear...' Eleanor's shrewd eyes swung between the pair of them. Their body language... their interaction...her son was set in his ways...so where did Violet Drew fit in...? How had the inveterate womaniser become domesticated by the delightful schoolteacher who seemed willing to trade punches...? And where were the airheads who simpered around him and clung like leeches? Sudden changes in appetite were always a cause for concern, as her consultant had unhelpfully pointed out. So what was behind her son's sudden change in appetite? For the first time Eleanor Carver was distracted from her anxiety about her cancer. She enjoyed crosswords and sudoku. She would certainly enjoy unravelling this little enigma.

'Of course…' she glanced down at the wedding ring she still wore on her finger and thoughtfully twisted it '…there *was* Annalise…but I expect you know all about her…?' She yawned delicately and offered them an apologetic exhausted smile. 'Perhaps you could come back tomorrow? My dear…it's been such a pleasure meeting you.' She warmly patted Violet's outstretched hand. 'I very much look forward to getting to know you much, much better… I want to find out every little thing about the wonderful girl my son has fallen in love with.'

CHAPTER FOUR

So who was Annalise?

Violet was pleased that she had not been tempted to ask the second they had left his mother's room. She didn't know, didn't care and was only going to be in his company for a short while longer in any case.

Infuriatingly, however, the name bounced around in her head over the next week and a half, as their visits to the hospital settled into a routine. They met at a predetermined time in the same place, exchanged a few meaningless pleasantries on the way up in the lift and then played a game for the next hour and a half. It was a game she found a lot less strenuous than she had feared. Eleanor Carver made conversation very easy. Little by little, Violet pieced together the life of a girl who had grown up in Devon, daughter of minor aristocratic parents. Childhood had been horses and acres of land as a back garden. There had been no boarding school as her parents had doted on their only child and refused to send her away and so she had remained in Devon until, at the age of seventeen and on the threshold of university, she had met, fallen head over heels in love with and married Damien's father, an impossibly dashing half Italian immigrant who had wandered down from London with very little to offer except ambition, excitement and love. Eleanor had decided in seconds that all three were a better bet than a degree in History. She had battled through her parents' alarm, refused to cave in and moved out of the family mansion to set up house in a little cottage not a million miles away. In due course, her parents had come round. Rodrigo Carver might not have been their first choice but he had quickly grown on them. He offered business advice on the family estate when fortunes started turning sour and his advice had come good. He had a street smart head for investment and passed on tips to Matthew Carrington that saw profits swell. In return, Matthew Carrington took a punt on his rough-diamond son-in-law and loaned him a sum of money to start up a haulage business. From that point, there had been no turning back and the half Italian immigrant had eventually become as close to his parents-in-law as their own daughter.

Violet thought that Eleanor Carver probably believed in fairy tale endings because of her own personal experience. Whirlwind romance with someone from a different place and a different background...a battle against the odds... Was that why she had accepted her son's sudden love affair with a woman who could have been from a different planet?

She had posed that question to Damien only the day before and he had shrugged and said that he had never considered it but it made sense; then he had swiftly punctured that brief bubble of unexpected pleasure by adding that it was probably mingled with intense relief that she had been introduced to a woman who wouldn't run screaming in horror at the thought of wellies, mud and the great outdoors.

For once, Violet arrived at the hospital shop ahead of schedule and was glancing through the rack of magazines when she heard him say behind her shoulder, 'I didn't get the impression that you were all that interested in the lifestyles of the rich and famous...'

She spun round, heart beating fast, and in that split second, realised that the hostility and resentment she had had for him had turned into something else somewhere along the line. She wasn't sure what, but the sudden flare of excitement brought a tinge of high colour to her cheeks. When had she started *looking forward* to these hospital visits? What had been the thin dividing line between not caring what she wore because why did it matter anyway, and taking time out to choose something with him in mind? She had always felt the sparrow next to her sister's radiant plumage. She couldn't compete and so she had never tried. She had chosen baggy over tight and buttoned up over revealing because to be caught up in trying to dress to impress was superficial and counter-productive. So when had that changed?

Everything they said in that room and every fleeting show of affection was purely engineered for the sake of his mother and yet she found that she could recall each time he had touched her. She no longer started when his hand slid to the back of her neck. A couple of days ago he had casually tucked some of her hair behind her ear and she had caught herself staring at him, mouth half open, transfixed by a rush of violent confusing awareness, as if they had suddenly been locked inside a bubble while the rest of the world faded away. His mother had snapped her out of the momentary spell but it was dawning on her that lines were being crossed. She just didn't know what to do about it. She would have to find out just how long the charade was destined to continue. Yes, she had made a deal but that didn't mean that she could be kept in ignorance of when the deal would come to an end. Her life was on hold while she pretended to be his girlfriend. She needed to find out when she would be able to step back to reality.

'Aren't we all?' she snapped, taking a step back and bumping into someone behind her. Flustered, she muttered apologies and then looked straight into Damien's amused blue eyes. Usually he came straight to the hospital from work. Today was an exception. He wasn't in his suit but in a pair of black jeans and a thick cream jumper. She couldn't peel her eyes away from him.

'My apologies. Shall I buy the magazine for you?'

Violet discovered that she was still clutching the magazine and she wondered why because she had had no intention of getting it. 'Thank you, but there's no need. I was just about to buy it myself.'

'Please. Allow me.' He made an elaborate show of studying the cover of the magazine. 'I dated her,' he mused, but his interest stopped short of flicking through the magazine to look further.

If that passing remark was intended to bring her back down to earth, it certainly succeeded and Violet was infuriated with herself for the time she had taken choosing which pair of jeans to wear and which jumper. Ever since he had made that revealing remark about her body, and even if it had been meant for the benefit of his mother, she had chosen her snuggest jumpers to wear, the ones that did the most for a figure like hers. Now she was reminded of just the sort of body he looked at and it wasn't one like hers.

'What's her name?' Violet wondered if it was the mysterious Annalise his mother had dropped into the conversation on that first evening.

'Jessica. At the time, she was on the brink of making it to the catwalk. Seems she got there.' He paid for the magazine and handed it over to her.

'I'm not surprised. She's very beautiful.'

And once upon a time, Damien thought, she would have encompassed pretty much everything he sought in a woman. Compliant, ornamental and inevitably disposable.

He looked down at the argumentative blonde staring up at him with flushed cheeks and a defiantly cool expression and felt that familiar kick in his loins. The complication which he had been determined to sideline was proving difficult to master. He wondered whether it was because denial was not something he had ever had the need to practice when it came to the opposite sex. When he had concocted this plan, he had had no idea that he might find himself at the mercy of a wayward libido. He had looked at the earnest, pleading woman slumped despairingly in the chair in his office and had seen her as a possible solution to the problem that had been nagging away at him. Nothing about her could possibly have been construed as challenging. There had not been a single iota of doubt in his mind that she might prove to be less amenable than her exterior had suggested.

While it was hardly his fault that his initial judgement had a few holes, he still knew that the boundaries to what they were doing had to be kept in place, although it was proving more challenging than expected. Every time he touched her, with one of those passing gestures designed to mimic love and affection, he could feel a sizzle race up his arm like an electric current. Those brief lapses of self-control were unsettling. Now, as they began moving out of the hospital shop, he stopped her before they could head for the lift.

'We need to have a chat before we go up.'

'Okay.' This would be an update on how long their little game would continue. Perhaps he had had word back from the consultant on the line of treatment they intended to pursue. When she thought of this routine coming to an end, her mind went blank and she had to remind herself that it couldn't stop soon enough.

'We could go the cafeteria but I suggest somewhere away from the hospital compound. Walking distance. There's a café on the next street. I've told my mother that we might be a bit later than usual today.'

'There haven't been any setbacks, have there?' Violet asked worriedly, falling into step beside him. 'A couple of days ago your mother said that they were all pleased with how things were coming along, that it seems as though the cancer was caught in time, despite concerns that she might have left it too late...'

'No setbacks, although my mother would be thrilled if she knew that you were concerned...are you really? Because there's just the two of us here. No need for you to say anything you don't want to. No false impressions to make.'

'Of course I'm concerned!' She stopped him in his tracks with a hand on his arm. 'I may have agreed to go through this charade because my sister's future was at stake, but your mother's a wonderful woman and of course I would never fake concern!'

Damien recognised the shine of one hundred per cent pure sincerity in her eyes. For a second, something very much like guilt flared through him. He had ripped her out of her comfort zone and compelled her to do something that went against the very fabric of her moral values because it had suited him. He had thrown back the curtain and revealed a world where people used other people to get what they wanted. It wasn't a world she inhabited. He knew that because she had told him all about her friends in and out of school. Listening to her had been like lifting a chapter from an Enid Blyton book, one where good mates sat around drinking cheap boxed wine and discussing nothing more innocuous than the fate of the world and how best it could be changed.

Still, everything in life was a learning curve and being introduced to an alternate view would stand her in good stead.

'How is your sister faring in Ibiza?' he asked, an opportune reminder of why they were both here.

Violet smiled. 'Good,' she confided. 'Remember I told you about that job she wanted? The one at the tapas restaurant on the beach?' Despite the artificiality of their situation, she had found herself chatting to Damien a lot more than she had thought she might. Taking the lift down after visiting his mother, wandering out of the hospital together, he in search of a black cab, she in the direction of the underground...conversation was always so much less awkward than silence. And he was a good listener. He never interrupted and, when he did, his remarks were always intelligent and informative. He had listened to her ramble on about her colleagues at work without sneering at them or the lives they led. He had come up with some really useful advice about one of them who was having difficulties with a disorderly class. And he had cautioned her about worrying too much about Phillipa, had told her that she needed to break out of the rut she had spent years constructing and the only way to do that would be to walk away from over-involvement in what her sister was getting up to. If Phillipa felt she had no cushion on which to fall back, then she would quickly learn how to remain upright.

Had she mentioned Phillipa and the job at the bar? Damien thought. Yes. Yes, she had. Well, they saw each other every day. The periods of time spent in each other's company might have been concentrated, but they conversed. It would have been impossible to maintain steady silence when they happened to be on their own. Admittedly, she did most of the conversing. He now knew more about the day-to-day details of her life than he had ever expected to know.

'I remember.' No references needed for a bar job. Good choice.

'Well, she got it. She's only been there two days but she says the tips are amazing.'

'Let's hope she's not tempted to put her hand in the till,' Damien remarked drily but there was no rancour in his eyes as they met hers for a couple of seconds longer than strictly necessary.

'I've already given her a lecture about that,' Violet said huffily.

'And what about the partner in crime?'

'He wasn't a *partner in crime*.'

'Aside from the forging of references technicality.'

'He's working on restoring a boat with his friend.'

'He knows much about boat restoration?'

'Er...'

'Say no more, Violet. They're obviously a match made in Heaven.'

'You're so cynical!'

'Not according to my mother. She complimented me on my terrific taste in women and waxed lyrical about the joys of knowing that I'm no longer dating women with IQs smaller than their waist measurements.'

They had reached the café and he pushed open the door and stood aside as she walked past him. The brush of his body against hers made her skin burn. So his mother was pleased with her as a so-called girlfriend. She thought back to the eye-catching brunette on the magazine cover. He must find it trying to have pulled the short straw for this little arrangement. He could have been walking into a café, or into an expensive restaurant because hadn't he already told her that the women he dated wouldn't have been caught dead anywhere where they couldn't be admired, with a leggy brunette dangling on his arm. Instead of her.

He ordered them both coffee and then sat back in his chair to idly run his finger along the handle of the cup.

'Well?' Violet prompted, suddenly uncomfortable with the silence. 'I don't suppose we're here because you wanted to pass the time of day with me. It's been nearly two weeks. The new term is due to start in another ten days. Your mother seems to be doing really well. Have you brought me here to tell me that this arrangement is over?' She felt a hollow spasm in the pit of her stomach at the prospect of never seeing him again and then marvelled at how fast a habit, even a bad one, could be turned into something that left a gaping hole when there was the prospect of it being removed.

'When I told you that our little deal would be over and done with in a matter of days, I hadn't foreseen certain eventualities.'

'What eventualities?'

'The consultants agree that treatment can be continued in Devon.'

'And that's good, isn't it? I know your mother is very anxious about Dominic. She speaks to him every day on the telephone and has plenty of contact with his carers, but he's not accustomed to having her away for such a long period of time.'

'When did she tell you this?'

'She's phoned me at home a couple of times.'

'You never mentioned that to me.'

'I didn't realise that I was supposed to report back to you on a daily basis...'

'You're *supposed* to understand the limitations of what we have here. You're *supposed* to recognise that there are boundaries. Encouraging my mother to telephone you is stepping outside them.'

'I didn't *encourage* your mother to call me!'

'You gave her your mobile number.'

'She asked for it. What was I supposed to do? Refuse to give it to her?'

'My mother plans on returning to Devon tomorrow. She'll be able to attend the local hospital and I will personally make sure that she has the best in house medical team to hand that money can buy.

'That's good.' She would miss Eleanor Carver. She would miss the company of someone who was kind and witty and the first and only parent substitute she had known since her own mother had died. There had been no breathtaking revelations to the older woman or dark, secret confessions, but it had been an unexpected luxury to feel as though no one expected her to answer questions or be in charge. 'I guess you'll be going with her.'

'I will.'

'How is that going to work out for you and your work? I know you said that it's easy to work out of the office but is that really how it's going to be in practice?'

'It'll work.' He paused and looked at her carefully. 'The best laid plans, however...'

'I hate to sound pushy but would you be willing to sign something so that I know you won't go back on what you promised?'

'Don't you trust me?' he asked, amused.

'Well, you *did* put me in this position through some pretty underhand tactics...'

'Remind me how much your sister is enjoying life in sunny Ibiza...' Damien waved aside that pointed reminder of his generosity. 'Naturally, I will be more than happy to sign a piece of paper confirming that your sister won't be seeing the inside of a prison once our deal is over.'

'But I thought it was...' Violet looked at him in confusion.

'There's been an unfortunate extension.' He delivered that in the tone of voice which promised that, whatever he had to say, there would be no room for rebuttal. 'It seems that your avid attention and cosy chats with my mother on the phone have encouraged her to think that you should accompany me down to Devon.'

'What?' Violet stammered.

'I could repeat it if you like, but I can see from the expression on your face that you've heard me loud and clear. Believe me, it's not something I want either but, given the circumstances, there's very little room for manoeuvre.' Could he be treated to anyone looking more appalled than she currently was?

'Of course there's room for manoeuvre!' Violet protested shakily.

'Shall I tell her that the prospect of going to Devon horrifies you?'

'You know that's not the sort of thing I'm talking about. I...I...have loads to do before school starts...classes to prepare for...'

Damien waited patiently as she expounded on the million and one things that apparently required her urgent attention in London before raising his hand to stop her in mid-flow.

'My mother seems to think that having you around for a few days while her treatment commences would give her strength. She's aware that you start back at school in a week and a half.' She had no choice but to do exactly what he said; Damien knew that. When it came to this arrangement, she didn't have a vote. Still, he would have liked to have her on board without her kicking and screaming every inch of the way. And really, was it so horrific a prospect? Where his mother lived was beautiful. 'She's not asking you to ditch your job and sit by her bedside indefinitely.'

'I know that!'

'If I can manage my workload out of the office, then I fail to see why you can't do the same.'

'It just feels like this is…getting out of control…'

'Not following you.'

'You know what I mean, Damien,' Violet snapped irritably. 'I thought when I accepted this…this…*assignment*… that it was only going to be for a few days and it's already been almost two weeks…'

'This situation isn't open to discussion,' Damien said in a hard voice. 'You traded your freedom for your sister's. It's as simple as that.'

'And what about when I leave Devon? When do I get my freedom back?' Violet hated the way she sounded. As though she couldn't care less about his mother or her recovery. As though the last thing in the world she wanted was to help her in a time of need. And yet this wasn't what she had signed up for and the prospect of getting in ever deeper with Damien and his family felt horribly dangerous. How could she explain that? 'I'm sorry, but I have to know when I can expect my life to return to normal.'

'Your life will return to normal—' he leaned forward, his expression grim and as cold as the sea in winter '—just about the same time as mine does. I did not envisage this happening but it's happened and here's how we're going to deal with it. You're going to put in an appearance in Devon. You're going to enjoy long country walks and you're going to keep my mother's spirit fighting fit and upbeat as you chat to her about plants and flowers and all things horticultural. At the end of the week, you're going to return to London and, at that point, your presence will no longer be required. Until such time as I inform you that your participation is redundant, you remain on call.'

Violet blanched. What leg did she have to stand on? He was right. She had effectively traded her freedom for Phillipa's. While her sister was living a carefree existence in Ibiza, she was sinking ever deeper into a morass that felt like treacle around her. She couldn't move and all decision-making had been taken out of her hands.

'The more involved I get, the harder it's going to be to tell your mother...that...'

'Leave that to me.' Damien continued to look at her steadily. 'There's another reason she wants you there in Devon,' he said heavily. 'And, believe me, I'm not with her on this. But she wants you to meet my brother.' His mother had never known the reasons for his break-up with Annalise, nor had she ever remarked on the fact that, after Annalise, he had never again brought another woman down to the country estate in Devon. The very last thing he wanted was a break in this tradition, least of all when it involved a woman who was destined to disappear within days.

'That's very sweet of her, Damien, but I don't want to get any more involved with your family than I already am.'

'And do you think that *I* do?' he countered harshly. 'We both have lives waiting out there for us.' The fact that control over the situation had somehow been taken out of his hands lent an edge to his anger. When his mother had suggested bringing Violet to Devon, he had told her, gently but firmly, that that would be impossible. He cited work considerations, made a big deal of explaining how long it took to prepare for a new term—something of which he knew absolutely nothing but about which he had been more than happy to expound at length. He had been confident that no such thing would happen. His fake girlfriend would not be setting one foot beyond the hospital room.

His mother had never been known to enter into an argument with him or to advance contrary opinions when she knew how he felt about something. He had been woefully unprepared for her to dig her heels in and make a stance, ending her diatribe, which had taken him completely by surprise by asking tartly, 'Why don't you want her to come to Devon, Damien? Is there something going on that I should know about?'

Deprived of any answering argument, he had recovered quickly and warmly assured his mother that there was nothing Violet would love more than to see the estate and get to know Dominic.

'You will need a more extensive wardrobe than the one you have,' he informed her because, as far as he was concerned, there was nothing further to be said on the matter. 'You need wellies. Fleeces. Some sort of waterproof coat. I'm taking it that you don't have any of those? Thought not. In that case, you're going to go to Harrods and use the account I've already talked to you about.'

'Do you know something? I can't wait for all of this to be over! I can't wait for when I no longer have to listen to you bossing me about and reminding me that I'm in no position to argue!' Over the past few days she had been lulled into a false sense of security, of thinking that he wasn't quite as bad as she had originally thought. She had watched him interacting with his mother, had listened as he had soothed the same concerns on a daily basis without ever showing a hint of impatience. She had foolishly started feeling a weird connection with him.

'Is that how you treat everyone?' she blurted, angry with herself for harbouring idiotic illusions. 'Is that how you've treated all the women you've been out with? Is that how you treated Annalise?' It was out before she had a chance to rein it in and his eyes narrowed into chips of glacial ice.

'Was that another topic under discussion with my mother?'

'No, of course not! And it's none of my business. I just feel...frustrated that my whole world has been turned upside down...'

'Excuse me if I don't feel unduly sympathetic to your cause,' Damien inserted flatly. 'We both know what was at stake here. As for Annalise, that's a subject best left unexplored.' Without taking his eyes from her face, he signalled for the bill.

'You can't expect me to spend a week in your mother's company and not have an inkling of anything to do with your past.' She inhaled deeply and ploughed on. 'What do you expect me to say when she talks about you? It's going to be different in Devon. We'll have a great deal more time together. Your mother's already mentioned her once. She's sure to mention her again. What am I supposed to say? That we don't discuss personal details like that? What sort of relationship are we supposed to have if we never talk about anything personal?'

She stared at him with mounting frustration and the longer the silence stretched, the angrier she became. He might be the puppet-master but there were limits as to how tightly he could jerk the strings! She foresaw long, cosy conversations with his mother when her only response to any questions asked, aside from the most basic, would be a rictus smile while she frantically tried to think of a way out. She would be condemned to yet more lying just because he was too arrogant to throw her a few titbits about his past.

'I don't *care* what happened between the two of you. I just want to be able to look as though I know what your mother's on about if she brings the name up in conversation. Why are you so…so…*secretive*?'

Damien was outraged that she had the nerve to launch an attack on him. Naturally there was a part of him that fully understood the logic of what she was saying. Undiluted time spent with his mother in front of an open fire in the snug would be quite different from more or less supervised snatches of time spent next to a hospital bed during permitted visiting hours. Women talked and it was unlikely that he could be a stifling physical presence every waking minute of the day. That said, the implicit criticism ringing in her voice touched a nerve.

Bill paid, he stood up and waited until she had scrambled to her feet.

'Are you going to say anything?' She reached out and stayed him with her hand. 'Okay, so you've had loads of girlfriends. That's fine.'

'I was going to marry her,' Damien gritted.

Violet's hand dropped and she looked at him in stupefied silence. She couldn't imagine him ever getting close enough to any woman to ask for her hand in marriage. He just seemed too much of a loner. No…it was more than that. There was something watchful and remote about him that didn't sit with the notion of him being in love. And yet he had been. In love. Violet didn't know why she was so shocked and yet she was.

'What happened?' They were outside now, heading back towards the hospital. Her concerns about going to Devon had been temporarily displaced by Damien's startling revelation.

'What happened,' he drawled, stopping to look down at her, 'was that it didn't work out. I didn't share the details with my mother. I don't intend to share them with you. Any other vital pieces of information you feel you need to equip yourself with before you're thrown headlong into my mother's company?'

'What was she like?' Violet couldn't resist asking. In her head, she imagined yet another supermodel, although it was unlikely that she could be as stunning as the one on the cover of the magazine.

'A brilliant lawyer who has since become a circuit judge.'

Well, that said it all, Violet thought. It also explained a whole host of things. Such as why a highly intelligent male should choose to go out with women who weren't intellectually challenging. Why his interest in the opposite sex began and ended in bed. Why he had never allowed himself to have a committed relationship again. He had been dumped and he still carried the scars. She felt a twinge of envy for the woman who had had such power over him. Was he still in touch with her? *Did he still love her?*

'And do you bump into her? London's small.'

'Question time over, Violet. You now have enough information on the subject to run with it.' Damien's lips thinned as he thought of Annalise. Still hovering in the wings, still imagining that she was the love of his life. Did he care? Hardly. Did he bump into her? Over the years, with tedious and suspicious regularity. There she would be, at some social function for the great and the good, always making sure to seek him out so that she could check out his latest date and update him on her career. He never avoided her because it paid to be reminded of his mistake. She was a learning curve that would never be forgotten.

Violet saw the grim set of his features and drew her own, inevitable conclusions. He had been in love with a highly intelligent woman, someone well matched for him, and his marriage proposal had been rejected. For someone like Damien, it would be a rejection never forgotten. He had found his perfect woman and, when that hadn't worked out, he had stopped trying to find another.

What they had might be a business arrangement, but everything he had ever had with every woman after Annalise had been *an arrangement*. Arrangements were all he could do.

'I'll get some appropriate clothes,' Violet conceded. 'And you can text me with the travel info. But, at the end of the week, it's over for me. I can't keep deceiving your mother.'

'By the end of the week, I think you will have played your part and I will officially guarantee that your sister is off the hook.'

'I can't wait,' Violet breathed with heartfelt sincerity.

CHAPTER FIVE

THE HOUSE THAT greeted Violet the following evening was very much like something out of a fairy tale. Arrangements for Eleanor's transfer had been made at speed. Her circumstances were special, as she was the principal carer for Dominic, and Damien, with his vast financial resources, had made sure that once the decision to transfer was made, it all happened smoothly and efficiently.

In the car, Violet had alternated between bursts of conversation about nothing in particular to break the silence and long periods of sober reflection that the task she had undertaken seemed to be spinning out of control.

She was travelling with a stranger to an unknown destination, removed from everything she knew and was familiar with, and would have to spend the next few days pretending to be someone she wasn't. If she had known what this so-called arrangement would have entailed, would she have embarked on it in the first place? Regrettably, yes, but knowing that didn't stop her feeling like a sacrificial lamb as the powerful car roared down the motorway, eating up the miles and removing her further and further from her comfort zone.

While Phillipa was taking time out in Ibiza, doing very little in a tapas restaurant and no doubt enjoying the attention of all the locals as she wafted around in sarongs and summer dresses, here she was, sinking deeper and deeper into a situation that felt like quicksand, all so that her sister could carry on enjoying life without having to pay for the mistakes she had made.

'Maybe she *should* have had her stint in prison,' Violet said, apropos of nothing, and Damien shot her a sideways glance.

Locked in to doing exactly what he required of her, he could sense the strain in the rigid tension of her body. She would rather be anywhere else on earth than sitting here in this car with him. Naturally, he could understand that. More or less. After all, who wanted to be held hostage to a situation they hadn't courted, paying for a crime they hadn't committed? Yet was his company so loathsome that she literally found it impossible to make the best of a bad job? She was pressed so tightly against the passenger door that he feared she might fall out were it not for the fact that the doors were locked and she was wearing a seat belt.

There had been times over the past week and a half when some of her resentment had fallen away and she had chatted normally to him. There had also been times when, in the presence of his mother, he had touched her and his keenly attuned antenna had picked up *something*—something as fleeting as a shadow and yet as substantial as jolt of electricity. Something that had communicated itself to him, travelling down unseen pathways, announcing a response in her that she might not even have been aware of.

'You don't mean that,' he said calmly.

'Don't tell me what I mean! If it weren't for Phillipa I wouldn't be here now.'

'But you are and there's no point dwelling on what ifs. And stop acting as though you're being escorted to a torture chamber. You're not. You'll find my mother's estate a very relaxing place to spend a few days.'

'It's hardly going to be a *relaxing situation*, is it? I don't feel *relaxed* when I'm around you.' When she thought about seeing him for hours on end, having meals in his company, being submerged in his presence without any respite except when she went to bed, she got a panicky, fluttery feeling in the depths of her stomach.

Without warning, Damien swerved his powerful car off the small road. They were only a matter of half an hour away from the house and the roads had become more deserted the closer they had approached the estate.

'What are you doing?' Violet asked warily as he killed the engine and proceeded to lean back at an angle so that he was looking directly at her. In the semi-darkness of the car, with night rapidly settling in around them, she felt the breath catch painfully in her throat. Apprehension jostled with something else—something dark and scary, the same dark, scary thing that had been nibbling away at the edges of her self-control ever since he had told her about Devon.

'So you don't feel relaxed around me. Tell me why. Get it off your chest before we reach the house. Okay, you're not here of your own free will, but there's no point lamenting that and covering old ground. It is as it is. Have you never been in a position where you had to grit your teeth and get through it?'

'Of course I have!'

'Then tell me what the difference is between then and now.'

'You're scary, Damien. You're not like other people. You don't *feel*. You're so...so...*cold*...'

'Funny. Cold is not a word that any woman has ever used to describe me...'

Violet felt her heart begin to race and her mouth went dry. 'I'm not talking about...what you're like in bed with women...'

'Would you like to?'

'No!'

'Then how would you like me to try and relax you?'

Violet couldn't detect anything in his voice and yet those words, innocuous as they were, sent a shiver of awareness rippling up and down her spine. She had a vivid, graphic image of him relaxing her, touching her, making her whole body melt until she was nothing more than a rag doll. Was this the real reason why she was so apprehensive? Terrified even? At the back of her mind, was she more scared of just being alone with him than she was of playing a game and acting out a part in a place with which she was unfamiliar? Did her own responses to him, which she constantly tried to squash, frighten her more than *he* did?

It didn't seem to matter than he was cold, distant, emotionally absent. On some level, a part of her responded to him in ways that were shocking and unfamiliar.

She could feel the lazy perusal of his eyes on her and she wished she hadn't embarked on a conversation which now seemed to be unravelling.

'I'm just nervous,' she muttered in a valiant struggle to regain her self-composure. 'I'll be fine once we get there. I guess.'

'Try a little harder and you might start to convince me. You get along well with my mother. Is it Dominic?' The question had to be asked. He hadn't been in this position for a very long time. He had brought no one to Devon. He had vowed to never again put himself in the position of ever having to witness a negative reaction to his brother. However, this was an unavoidable circumstance and he felt the protective machinery of his defences seal around him like a wall of iron.

'What are you talking about?' Violet was genuinely puzzled.

'Some people feel uncomfortable around the disabled. Is that why you're so strung out?' It had taken Annalise to wake him up to that fact, to the truth that there were people who shied away from what they didn't know or understand, who felt that the disabled were to be laughed at or rigorously avoided. The ripple effect of those reactions were not contained, they always spread outwards to the people who cared. It was good to bring this up now.

'No!'

'Sure about that, Violet? Because you know me, you know my mother...the only unknown quantity in the equation is Dominic...'

'I'm *looking forward* to meeting your brother, Damien. The only person who makes me feel uncomfortable is *you*!' This was the first time she had come near to openly admitting the effect he had on her. She glared at him defensively, feeling at once angry and vulnerable at the admission and collided with eyes that were dark and impenetrable and sent her frayed pulses into overdrive.

All at once and on some deep, unspoken level, Damien could feel the sudden sexual tension in the air. Her words might say one thing but her breathlessness, the way her eyes were huge and fixed on him, the clenching and unclenching of her small fists...a different story.

He smiled, a slow, curving, triumphant smile. Whilst he had privately acknowledged the unexpected appeal she had for him, whilst he had been honest about the charge he got from a woman who was so different in every possible way to the type of women he had become used to, he had pretty much decided that a Hands Off stance was necessary in her case.

But they were going to be together in Devon and, like an expert predator, he could smell the aroma of her unwelcome but decidedly strong sexual attraction towards him. She was as skittish as a kitten and it wasn't because she was nervous about spending a week in the company of his mother. Nor was she hesitant about his brother. He had detected the sincerity in her voice when he had suggested that she might be.

He took his time looking at her before turning away with a casual shrug and turning the key in the ignition. Her presence next to him for the remainder of the very short drive felt like an aphrodisiac. Potent, heady and very much not in the plan.

The drive up to the grand house was tree-lined, through wrought-iron gates which he could never remember being closed. Having not been to the estate for longer than he liked to think, Damien was struck by the sharp pull of familiarity and by the hazy feelings he always associated with his home life—the sense of responsibility which was always there like a background refrain. Having a disabled brother had meant that any freedom had always been on lease. He had always known that, sooner or later, he would one day have to take up the mantle left behind by his parents. Had he resented that? He certainly didn't think so, although he *did* admit to a certain regret that he had failed to extend any input for so long.

Was it any wonder that his mother had been so distraught when she had been diagnosed, that she might leave behind her a family unit that was broken at the seams? He had a lot of ground to cover if he were to convince her otherwise.

'What an amazing place,' Violet murmured as the true extent of the sprawling mansion, gloriously lit against the darkness, revealed itself. 'What was it like growing up here?'

'My parents only moved in when my grandfather died, and I was a teenager. Before that, we lived in the original cottage my parents first bought together when they were married...'

'It must have seemed enormous after a cottage...'

'When you live in a house this size you get used to the space very quickly.' And he had. He had lost himself in it. He had been able to escape. He wondered whether he had been so successful at escaping that a part of him had never returned. And had his mother indulged that need for escape? Until now? When escape was no longer a luxury to be enjoyed?

Not given to introspection, Damien frowned as he pulled up in the large circular courtyard. The house was lit up like a Christmas tree in the gathering darkness and they had hardly emerged from the car with their cases when the front door was flung open and Anne, the housekeeper who had been with the family since time immemorial, was standing there, waving them inside.

Violet wondered what her role here was to be. Exactly. Sitting by a hospital bed, she had known what to do and the impersonal surroundings had relieved her of the necessity of trying to act the star-struck lover. A few passing touches, delivered by Damien rather than her—more would have seemed inappropriate in a hospital room, where they were subject to unexpected appearances from hospital staff.

But here she was floundering in a place without guidelines as they were ushered into the grandest hall she had ever seen.

The vaulted ceiling seemed as high and as impressive as the ceiling of a cathedral. The fine silk Persian rug in the hall bore the rich sheen of its age. The staircase leading up before splitting in opposite directions was dark and highly polished. It was a country house on a grand scale.

The housekeeper was chatting animatedly as they were

led from the hall through a perplexing series of rooms and corridors.

'Your mother is resting. She'll be down with Dominic for dinner. Served at seven promptly, with drinks before in the Long Room. You've been put in the Blue Room, Mr Damien. George will bring the bags up.'

Looking sideways, Violet was fascinated at Damien's indifference to his surroundings. He barely looked around him. How on earth could he have said that a person could become accustomed to a house of this size? She had initially been introduced to Anne as his girlfriend and now, as though suddenly remembering that she was trotting along obediently next to him, he slung one arm over her shoulder as the housekeeper headed away from them through one of the multitude of doors, before disappearing into some other part of the vast family mansion.

'An old retainer,' he said, dropping his arm and moving towards a side staircase that Violet had failed to notice.

'It's a beautiful house.'

'It's far too big for just my mother and Dominic, especially considering that the land is no longer farmed.' He was striding ahead of her, his mind still uncomfortably dwelling on the unexpected train of thought that had assailed him in the car, the unpleasant notion that the grand house through which he was now confidently leading the way had been his excuse to pull away from his brother. He had never given a great deal of thought to his relationship with Dominic. Was he now on some kind of weird guilt trip because of the circumstances? Had he shielded himself from the pain Annalise had inflicted on him when she had rejected his brother by pulling ever further away from Dominic? He should have been far more of a presence here on the estate, especially with his mother getting older.

'It would be a shame to sell it. I bet it's been in your

family for generations…' She was barely aware of the bedroom until the door was thrown open and the first thing that accosted her was the sight of a massive four-poster bed on which their suitcases had been neatly placed. While he strode in with assurance, moving to stand and look distractedly through the windows, she hovered uncertainly in the background.

'Well?' Damien harnessed his wandering mind and focused narrowly on her.

'Why are both our suitcases in this room?' Violet asked bluntly. She already knew the answer to that one, yet she shied away from facing it. She hadn't given much thought to the details of their stay. In a vague, generalised way, she had imagined awkward one-to-one conversations with Damien and embarrassing economising of the truth with his mother, along with stilted meals where she would be under scrutiny, forced to gaily smile her way through gritted teeth. She hadn't gone any further when it came to scenarios. She hadn't given any thought to the possibility that the loving couple might be put in the same bedroom. She had blithely assumed that such an eventuality would not occur because surely Eleanor belonged to that generation which abhorred the thought of cohabitation under their roof. Eleanor was a traditionalist, a widow who still proudly wore her wedding ring and tut tutted about the youth of today.

'Because this is where we'll be sleeping,' Damien replied with equal bluntness. His unaccountably introspective and dark frame of mind had not put him in the best of moods. Having questioned his devotion as a son and on-hand supportive presence as a brother, the last thing he needed was to witness his so-called girlfriend's evident horror at being trapped in the same bedroom as him.

'I can't sleep in the same room as you! I didn't think that this would be the format.'

'Tough. You haven't got a choice.' He began unbuttoning his shirt, a prelude to having a shower, and Violet's eyes were drawn to the sliver of brown chest being exposed inch by relentless inch. She hurriedly looked away but, even though she was staring fixedly at his face, she could still see the gradual unbuttoning of his shirt until it was completely open, at which point she cleared her throat and gazed at the door behind him.

'There must be another room I can stay in. This place is enormous.'

'Oh, there are hundreds of other rooms,' Damien asserted nonchalantly. 'However, you won't be in any of them. It's a few days and my mother has put us together. Somehow I don't think she's going to buy the line that we're keeping ourselves virtuous for the big day.' He pulled off his shirt and headed towards his case on the bed, flipping it open without looking at her. 'We have roughly an hour before we need to be downstairs for drinks. My mother enjoys the formal approach when it comes to dining. It's one of her idiosyncrasies. So do you want to have the bathroom first or shall I?'

Violet hated his tone of voice. It was one which implied that he couldn't even be bothered to take her concerns into account. He was accustomed to sharing beds with women, she thought with a burst of impotent anger. In his adult life, he had probably slept with a woman next to him a lot more often than he had slept alone. It wasn't the same for her. Did he imagine that she would be able to lie next to him and pretend that she was on her own? The bed was king-sized but the thought of moving in the night and accidentally colliding with his sleeping form was enough to make her feel like fainting.

'I hate this,' she whispered, filled with self-pity that the last vestige of her dignity was being stripped away from her. 'You'll have to sleep on the sofa.'

Damien glanced at the chaise longue by the window and wondered whether she was being serious. 'I'm six foot four. What would you suggest I do with my feet?' He raised his eyebrows and watched as she struggled in silence to come up with a suitable response. 'I've spent hours driving. I'm going to have a shower. Don't even think of trawling the house for another bedroom.'

With that, he vanished into the adjoining bathroom, leaving Violet to fight off the waves of panic as she stared at her lonesome suitcase on the bed. Everything about the bedroom seemed designed to encourage a fainting fit, from the grandeur of a bed that would have been better suited to the lovers they most certainly were not, to the thick, heavy curtains which she imagined would cut out all daylight so that the intimacy of the surroundings became palpable.

Wrapped up in a series of images, she almost forgot that he was in the shower until she heard the sound of water being switched off, at which point she raced to her suitcase, extracted an armful of clothes and then stood to attention by the window, with her back pointedly turned to the bathroom door.

She heard the click of the door opening and then she froze as his voice whispered into her ear, 'You can look. I'm decently covered. Anyone would think that you were sweet sixteen and never been kissed.'

He was laughing as she unglued her eyes from his bare feet and allowed them to travel upwards to where he was decently covered in no more than a pair of boxer shorts and his shirt, which he was taking his own sweet time to button up.

If he called that *decently covered* then she wanted to

ask him what she might expect of him when the lights were switched off.

'I'll meet you downstairs,' she said coolly, at which he laughed a bit more.

'You wouldn't have a clue where to go,' Damien pointed out. Her face was flushed. Her hair, which had started the journey in a sensible coil at the nape of her neck, was unravelling. He could feel his mood beginning to lift, which was a good thing because he was ill equipped for negative thoughts. 'You'd need a map to find your way round this house. At least until you've become used to it. Most of the rooms aren't used but good luck locating the ones that are.' He reached into the cupboard where a supply of clothes, freshly laundered, were hanging, awaiting his arrival.

Once again, Violet primly averted her eyes as he slipped a pair of trousers from a hanger. She backed towards the door but he wasn't looking at her.

Good heavens! She would have to get her act together if she was going to survive her short stay here. She couldn't succumb to panic attacks every time they were alone together! She would need immediate counselling for post-traumatic stress disorder as soon as she returned to London if she did! He wasn't even glancing in her direction. If he could be unaffected by her presence, then she would follow his lead and everything would be smooth sailing. Two adults sharing a room wasn't exactly a world-changing event, she told herself once she was in the bathroom, having checked the door three times to make sure that it was locked.

She took a long time. She had bought a couple of dresses so that she didn't have to spend the entire stay in jeans and sweaters. This dress, a navy-blue stretchy wool one with sleeves to her elbows, was fitted, although she couldn't quite see how fitted because there was no long mirror in the bathroom. Nor could she do much with her make-up because the ornate mirror over the double sink was cloudy with condensation. Her hair, she knew, was fit for nothing except leaving loose. Her curls were out of control, a tangle of falling tendrils which she impatiently swept back from her face before taking a deep breath and opening the bathroom door.

He was sprawled on the bed, the picture of the Lord of the Manor waiting for his woman to emerge. His trousers were on, although, her inquisitive eyes made out, zipped but with the button undone. His long-sleeved jumper was dark grey and slim-fitting, so there was no escaping the lean, hard lines of his body.

One arm behind his head, Damien watched her with brooding eyes. It was the first time he had ever seen her in a dress that actually fitted. More than that, it clung. To curves that did all the right things in all the right places and lovingly outlined the sort of breasts that mightn't work on a catwalk but sure as hell worked everywhere else. He forgot about any tension that might lie ahead. He forgot those vague, never disclosed concerns that he had turned a blind eye to his brother for too long. Hell, he forgot pretty much everything as his eyes raked over her body and he felt the pain of an erection leaping to attention. Which made him hurriedly sit up.

She was running her fingers through her hair and wincing as she tried to gently unravel some of the knots. Then, without saying a word, she flounced over to her case and excavated a pair of high-heeled shoes which she self-consciously slipped on with her back to him.

'I'm ready.' She smoothed nervous hands along the dress. This wasn't the sort of thing she ever wore. She had always favoured baggy. She wondered whether her stupid brain had actually paid attention to that passing compliment he had given her about her figure and then decided that if it had, she was pathetic. But she still felt a thrill of excitement as he lazily scrutinised her before shifting off the bed, taking his time and moving at an even more leisurely pace to retrieve his watch from the dressing table.

'I hope I look okay...' Violet was mortified to hear herself say and she was even more mortified when, with deliberate slowness, he eyed her up and down and then up and down again for good measure.

'You'll do. New dress?'

'You can have it back when this stint is over.'

'What would I do with it?'

'I just wouldn't want you to think that I wanted anything from you but my sister's freedom.'

'I've always found martyrdom an annoying trait.'

Violet seethed on the way down, through another wilderness of rooms. En route, he gave her a potted history of the house and the land around it. She thawed. She was reluctantly charmed at the thought of an unknown half Italian coming to live there and passing on the mansion to his children, wrenching it away from the exclusive grasp of the landed gentry.

By the time they were finally at the sitting room where drinks were being served, she was more relaxed, and then she fully relaxed as Eleanor was helped down to make her entry, accompanied by Dominic and a young girl who tactfully left, having settled Eleanor in the chair by the fire.

She forgot about Damien. She knew that she should be making conspicuous efforts to play the adoring girlfriend but she became wrapped up in Eleanor and Dominic. She had been warned about Dominic's disability. She hadn't been told that although he was in a wheelchair, although his speech was often difficult to understand and although his movements were not perfectly controlled, he was smart and he was funny and shy. She sat very close to him, sipping her wine and leaning in so that she could pick up everything he said while Damien and his mother conducted a conversation, the wisps of which came floating her way. The need to think about selling the house...the difficulties of managing the various floors even if she made a full recovery...the value of having somewhere closer to civilisation where doctors and the hospital were not an unsafe car drive away if the weather was inclement.

He was the background voice of reason, the head of the family making sensible decisions, although, sliding her eyes across to him, she was aware of the frustration etched on his features at his mother's vague, non-committal replies to his persuasive urgings.

Every family had its stories to tell and she wondered if this was his. If he was so embedded in his role as protector that he failed to recognise any form of mutiny in the ranks. He obviously didn't think that his brother should have any input because the conversation was dropped the minute they were at the dinner table.

A carer helped Dominic with his food while Eleanor fussed and explained to her that that was normally her job.

'I'm a pain in the ass,' Dominic stammered.

Violet laughed and looked across to Damien, who was seated opposite her. 'You have that in common with your brother,' she said tartly and then flushed when he looked back at her with a slow, appreciative smile. Her heartbeat quickened. His glance lingered just that bit too long and she returned it with just a little too much dragging intensity.

After that, she was conscious of every little movement he made and tuned in to every word he said, even when her attention appeared to be elsewhere. She was aware of the quality of the food and the fact that she was being treated like a valued guest because, despite what Damien had said, Eleanor had long dispensed with formalities when it was just herself and Dominic and the wonderful girl who helped with him. Then they ate in the kitchen with dishes served by the housekeeper straight from Aga to plate.

'My son would know that if he visited with a bit more regularity,' Eleanor said with asperity. 'Perhaps you could see that as your mission—to get him away from London and his never ending workload...'

Watching her, Damien was impressed at how well she fielded the awkward remark, which implied a future that wasn't on the cards. He took in the way she communicated with Dominic. With ease, not patronising, without a hint of indulgence or condescension. Nor did she look to anyone to rescue her from what she might have felt was an uncomfortable situation.

Sipping the espresso that had been brought in for him, he mentally began to compare her natural responses to those of Annalise but it was an exercise he killed before it could take root. Such comparisons, he knew, were entirely inappropriate. That said, he murmured softly as they walked back up the stairs, Dominic and his mother having retired for the night, 'Very good...'

'Sorry?' Violet wished she could have stretched the evening out for longer—for as long as she could, like a piece of elastic with no breaking point—because now she faced the prospect of the shared bedroom. He certainly wasn't going to sleep on the chaise longue. *She* could try to, but chaises longues had not been designed for deep REM slumber. She might embarrass herself by falling off. Worse, she might *hurt* herself by falling off.

'Your performance tonight. Very good.'

'I wasn't performing.' They were now at the bedroom door and she stood back as he pushed it open and waited for her to precede him. 'You know I like your mother and your brother's amazing.' He was pulling off the luxurious, ornate spread that had been thrown over the bed, dumping it in a heap in the corner of the room. Violet's hands itched to fold it neatly, a legacy of having an untidy sister behind whom she had long become accustomed to tidying up.

He was beginning to unbutton his shirt, eyes still firmly focused on her, pinning her into a state of near paralysis.

Why couldn't he have found somewhere else to sleep? Or found *her* somewhere else to sleep? Surely, in a mansion the size of a hotel, they could have had separate sleeping quarters without the whole world detecting it? Why was she being placed in this position? It felt as though every sacrifice was being made by *her* and she was the one who directly benefited from none of it.

Anger at her helplessness to alter the situation made her eyes sting. She clung to the anger like a drowning person clinging to a lifebelt.

'I can see why your mother was so worried about Dominic when she was diagnosed,' Violet imparted recklessly and she immediately regretted the outburst when he stilled.

'Come again?'

'Nothing,' Violet mumbled.

'Really?' He was strolling towards her, lean, dark and menacing, and Violet stood her ground, stubbornly defensive. 'If you have something to say, why don't you come right out and say it? Only start something, Violet, if you intend to see it through to the end.'

'Well, you don't seem to really communicate with him. You leave it all to your mother. I heard you talking about selling the house with her and yet you didn't say anything to Dominic about it, even though he would be affected as well...'

Damien stared at her with cold fury. Had he just heard

correctly? Was she actually *criticising* his behaviour? Coming hard on the heels of his own unexpected guilt trip, he could feel rage coursing through his veins like a poison. Was she deliberately needling him?

'I don't seem to communicate with him...' was all that managed to emerge from his incredulous lips.

'You talk around him and above him and when you *do* talk directly to him, you don't really seem to expect an answer, even though you look as if you do.'

'I can't believe I'm hearing this.'

'No one ever tells you like it is, Damien.'

'And you mistakenly think that you're in a position to do so?' He watched as she lowered her eyes, although her soft lips were still pinched in a stubborn line. 'This may come as a cruel shock, but you're over-stepping your brief...'

When had he stopped listening to what his brother had to say? Was it when they moved to the estate? When acres of space removed the need for physical proximity? And then later, in London...with trips back to the estate infrequent obligations...his mother usually amenable to taking a bit of time out in London, travelling without Dominic... had distance crept through the cracks until he had simply forgotten how to communicate? Or, worse, had he selfishly been protecting himself by unconsciously withdrawing? You couldn't feel pain at other people's thoughtless reactions if you just never put yourself in that position in the first place, could you?

'I know I am!' Violet flung at him defiantly. 'But you can't expect me to come here and have no opinions at all on the people I meet! And besides, what do I have to lose by telling you the truth? Once I leave here, I'll never see you again! And maybe it's time someone *did* speak their mind to you!' She had courted an argument. It seemed safer to get into that bed with her back angrily turned away from him. But the shutter that fell over his eyes sent a jolt of unhappiness through her. She fought it off because why did it matter what he thought of her in the long run?

'I think I'll go downstairs and catch up on work.' Damien turned away from her, walked towards his laptop, which he had left on the chest of drawers, and Violet was unaccountably tempted to rush into a frantic apology for having crossed the line.

'Don't,' he threw over his shoulder with biting sarcasm, 'wait up.'

CHAPTER SIX

WHEN DAMIEN HAD considered the challenge of setting his mother's fears to rest and allaying her worry that he would not be able to cope with Dominic in her absence, he had envisaged a fairly straightforward solution.

He would take time off work to come to Devon. He would dispatch Violet after her week and, henceforth, he would assume the mantle of responsible son and dependable brother. How hard could it possibly be? He might have been a little lax in his duties over the years, but that was not for lack of devotion to his family. His work, every minute of it, was testimony to his dedication. They wanted for nothing. His brother had the very best carers money could buy. His mother enjoyed help on every front, from garden to house. She fancied roses? He had ensured that a special section of the extensive cultivated land was requisitioned for a rose garden fit to be photographed in a magazine. When she had been complaining of exhaustion only months previously, before the reason behind that exhaustion became known, he had personally seen to it that one of the finest chefs in the area was commissioned to cook exquisite meals and deliver them promptly so that she could be spared the effort of doing so herself. On the rare occasions when she ventured up to London, theatre tickets had been obtained, opera seats reserved, tables at the best restaurants booked.

Unfortunately, his clear cut route now to a successful outcome was proving elusive.

He adjusted his tie, raked his fingers through his hair and then hesitated. He knew that Violet was more than happy to meet him in the sitting room. After five days, she knew that house better than he did. How had that transpired? Because she was involving herself with his family. She and his mother appeared to have become best buddies. From his makeshift office in the downstairs library, he had a clear view of the back garden and had spotted them out there in the cold, slowly strolling and chatting. About what? He had casually asked her a couple of days ago and she had shrugged and delivered a non-answer. Was he going to push it? No. Ever since she had decided that it was her right to speak her mind, she had defied all attempts to smooth the strained atmosphere between them. In company, she was compliant and smiling. The second they were alone together, he was treated to the cold shoulder despite the fact that he had magnanimously chosen to overlook her outrageous, uninvited criticism of him.

He pulled the chair over to the window and sat down. At six-thirty in the evening, the room was infused with the ambers and golds of what had been a particularly fine and sunny day. In an hour, they would be leaving for a local restaurant. This had not been of his choosing. He would have been more than happy to have had a meal in, relaxed for ten minutes and then retired to catch up on his emails. But his mother had suggested it, to take her mind off the treatment which was due to commence at the weekend.

Or maybe, he mused darkly, Violet had suggested it... who was to say? His mind idly wandered over the events of the past few days. The clever way she had bonded with

Dominic, involving him in the art preparation she was doing for her class, letting him guide her through some computer stuff for a website she wanted to set up to display the work of her more talented pupils. His mother had taken him to one side and confided that she had never seen Dominic so relaxed with anyone.

'You know how wary he is of people he doesn't know...' she had murmured.

He didn't, in actual fact. Which had only served as a reminder of what Violet had said about his communication skills.

He scowled and then looked up as the door to the adjoining bathroom slowly opened.

Immersed in her thoughts, with a towel wound turban style around her newly washed hair and another towel wrapped round her body, barely skimming her breasts and thighs, Violet was not expecting him. In fact, she didn't register him at all sitting on the chair in the far corner of the room.

She was thinking about the past few days. Having a view on Damien and his relationship with his family seemed to have been the catalyst for the one thing she had been determined to avoid, namely involvement. She had told him what she thought about his relationship with his brother and, in so doing, she had unlocked a door and stepped inside the room. She hadn't wanted to have opinions. She had simply wanted to do her time and then disappear back to her life. Instead, she was becoming attached and she had no idea where that was going to lead. Damien was barely on speaking terms with her. They communicated in front of an audience but once the audience was no longer around, the act was dropped and he disappeared into that office of his, only emerging long after she was fast asleep.

The bed which she had looked at with horror, which had thrown her into a state of panic because she had had visions of rolling over and bumping into him, had turned out to be as safe as a chastity belt. She was not aware of him entering the room at night because she was fast asleep and she was not aware of him leaving it in the morning because she was still sleeping.

She pulled the towel off her head and shook her hair, then she walked towards the bedroom door and locked it because you could never be too sure. Damien would already be downstairs. He would be making an effort.

Just like that, her mind leapt past her own nagging worries and zeroed in on Damien. She no longer fought the way he infiltrated her head. One small passing thought and suddenly the floodgates would be opened and she would lose herself in images of him. It was almost as if the connections to her brain were determined to disobey the orders given and merrily abandon themselves to reformatting her thoughts so that he played the starring role.

Without even looking in his direction, she was still keenly aware of everything he did and everything he said. There was no need to look at him because in her mind's eye she could picture the way he looked, his expressions, the way he had of tilting his head to one side so that you had the illusion that whatever you were saying was vitally important.

He had stopped trying to corner his mother into making a decision about the house and whether it should be sold.

He had begun asking her about small things, like books she might have read and committees she belonged to in the village.

His conversation with Dominic was no longer a few words, some polite murmurings, a hearty pat on the shoulder and then attention focused somewhere else. Over dinner the evening before, she had heard him telling his brother about one of his deals which had run into unexpected problems with the locals because a vital factory had been denied planning permission, and the trouble they had taken to accommodate their concern.

Violet would rather not have noticed any of these details. She would rather he remained the one-dimensional baddy who barely had two words to say to her the second they were alone. She didn't want to leave this house only to find herself wondering how the rest of their lives all turned out. She wanted to be able to put them all out of her mind and yet, the more absorbed she became in their dramas, the more difficult she knew that was going to be.

Still frowning, she dropped the towel to the floor and stepped towards the wardrobe. Her hair felt damp against her back and she lifted the heavy mass with one hand and, at that very moment, she saw him.

For a few seconds Violet thought her eyes might be playing tricks on her. She froze, her arm still raised holding her hair away from her body. Her brain refused to accommodate the realisation that he wasn't safely downstairs but was, in fact, watching her as she stood in front of him, completely and utterly naked. When it did, she gave a squeak of absolute horror and reached for the discarded towel, which she wrapped tightly around her body. She was shaking like a leaf.

'What are you doing here?' She backed towards the bathroom door but, before she could make it to the relative safety of the bathroom, he was standing in front of her, barring her path.

For the first time in his life, Damien was lost for words. What was he doing there? Did it make any difference that it was his bedroom?

The thirty-second glimpse of her body had sent his libido into orbit. He was in physical pain and he fought to bring his senses back down to Planet Earth. The fluffy white towel was back in place, secured very firmly by tightly clenched fists, but in his mind's eye he was still seeing the voluptuous curves of her body. He had caught himself idly wondering what she looked like under the dresses and the jeans and the jumpers. Whenever he had entered the bedroom to find her asleep, the covers had been pulled tightly up to her neck as though, even in slumber, she was determined to make sure that she kept him out. The first time he had seen her in jeans, his imagination had been up and running and her deliberate attempts to keep him at arm's length had only served to increase its pace.

But nothing had prepared him for the mind-blowing sexiness of her curves. Her breasts, unrestrained by a bra, were far more than a generous handful. Her nipples were big pink discs that pouted provocatively and her stomach was flat as it planed downwards to the thatch of dark blonde hair between her thighs. All thoughts of self-denial were shattered in an instant. Every ounce of common sense that warned him against getting involved with a woman whose departure date from his life was any minute now, vanished like a puff of smoke.

'You have to go,' Violet said shakily. 'I want to get dressed.' She just couldn't look him in the face. Her body was burning at the thought of his eyes on it. Even with the towel secured around her, she still felt as though her nudity was on parade.

'I wanted to talk to you.'

'We can talk...later...your mother and Dominic...'

'Will be fine if they have to wait for us for a few minutes.'

He stood in front of her, as implacable as a solid wall of granite. Having made a concerted effort in the past few days to try and give her body as little option as humanly possible to feel any of that unnerving, unwelcome sexual awareness that seemed to ambush her at every turn, she was horribly aware of her racing pulses and the liquid heat pooling inside her. The silence stretched and stretched. She desperately wanted to get dressed and yet shied away from drawing attention to her nakedness under the towel.

'I need to get dressed,' she finally breathed and Damien stood aside.

Now that he had dropped all pretence of keeping life simple by not yielding to an attraction that seemed to have a will of its own, he could feel the stirrings of a dark, pervasive excitement coursing through him. Anticipation was a powerful aphrodisiac.

'Of course,' he murmured, stepping back further. 'We can talk later.' And they would.

Violet only realised that she had been holding her breath when she sagged against the closed bathroom door. Her breathing was thick and uneven. After days of standoff, she had felt those lazy eyes on her naked body and nearly collapsed. What did he want to talk to her about? She had heard the slam of the bedroom door, but she gave it a little while before poking her head out and establishing that the bedroom was empty.

She wanted to put that recollection of him sitting in that chair, looking at her as she blithely discarded the towel, to the back of her mind. Actually, she wanted to eradicate it completely, but it kept recurring as she got dressed and met the assembled party in the Long Room.

What had he thought of her? Had the reality of a body that wasn't stick-thin repulsed him? She had returned to her uniform of baggy clothes, a shapeless dress over which she had thrown a thick cardigan. The thought of drawing any more attention to herself made her feel sick. At least there would be more than just the four of them for the meal out. Eleanor had invited some of her friends. Damien's attention would be blessedly diluted. But, even amidst the upbeat conversation and the laughter, she was keenly aware of his eyes sliding over to her every so often. The conversation finally turned to Eleanor's treatment, which was due to start the following day.

'No one can tell me exactly how I'll be affected,' she confessed to one of her friends who had undergone a similar situation and was full of upbeat advice. 'Apparently, everyone reacts differently...but it'll be wonderful knowing that I'll have Dominic and Damien by my side...' She looked steadily at Damien. 'You *will* be staying on for a short while, won't you, darling?'

Damien smiled and gave an elegant, rueful and playfully resigned shrug. 'My office is up and running. It'll make a nice change looking through the window and not being treated to a splendid London view of office blocks...'

He did it so well, Violet thought, returning to her food. He was charm personified. Everyone was chuckling. There was general laughter when he launched into a wry anecdote about some of the urban myths surrounding a couple of the office blocks in the square mile.

When the laughter had died down, Eleanor turned to Violet. 'You must hate me for keeping Damien all the way down here in this part of the world...' she murmured.

Violet flushed. She hated those instances when she had felt horribly as though she was doing more than just play acting for a good reason, when she felt corralled into a corner from which she had no choice but to baldly lie.

'Oh, I shall be busy...you know...the new term starts soon and it's always hectic...' she offered vaguely.

'But you *will* come down on the weekends, won't you, my dear? You've been such a source of strength...'

'Well…sure, although…er…Damien mentioned something about having office stuff to do in London…in the coming weekends…'

'Did I?' Damien looked at her with a perplexed expression. 'I've been known to go to the office occasionally on a weekend, but…' he raised both hands in a gesture of amused surrender while keeping his eyes firmly pinned to Violet's flushed face '…even a diehard workaholic like myself knows when to draw the line…so I'll be down here unless something exceptional happens in London that requires my presence…'

'So that means that you'll be with us this weekend, my dear?' Eleanor was looking keenly at Violet's flushed face. 'I shall probably need some help around the house and it's so much nicer having someone around who knows us all rather than getting staff in. I do know you'll be busy at school…so please say if you'd rather not come…perfectly understandable…'

Violet felt the weight of expectation from everyone around the table and she sneaked a pleading glance at Damien, who returned her stare with an infuriatingly bland expression. 'I…' she stammered. 'I'm sure I should be able to…get away for the weekend…given the circumstances…' She smiled weakly. Even to her own ears, it was hardly the sound of excited enthusiasm but Eleanor was smiling broadly and reached over to pat her on her hand.

'Perfect! I shall probably be in a horizontal position most of the time but it should give you and Damien a really terrific opportunity to explore the village and the surroundings. I mean, you've hardly been out on your own since you got here and I may be an old lady but I'm not so old that I can't remember what it's like to be a couple of love birds…!'

Everyone laughed. Dominic said something salacious. Violet cringed.

She barely registered the remainder of the evening. She drank slightly more than was usual for her. By the time they eventually made it back to the house, it was after ten-thirty and her few glasses of wine had gone to her head.

'You need water,' Damien said, leading her towards the kitchen once Eleanor and Dominic had disappeared. 'And paracetamol...you drank too much.'

'Don't you dare lecture me on how much I drank, Damien!' She yanked her arm free of his supportive hand, stumbled, straightened and stopped to glare at him. 'How *could* you?'

Damien wondered whether she was aware that she was slurring her words. Ever so slightly. She had also, somewhere along the line, hurriedly done up her cardigan but misaligned the buttons and her hair was all over the place as she had insisted on opening her car window for a spot of fresh air.

'You're going to have to sit down if you're going to accuse me of something.' He led her towards a kitchen chair, sat her down and fetched her a glass of water and some tablets. 'Now...' he positioned his chair squarely to face her and leaned forward, resting his forearms on his thighs and staring at her with earnest concentration '...you were about to start an argument...'

Violet was mesmerised by his eyes. He hadn't shaved for the day and there was a dark shadow that promised stubble in the morning. She wanted to reach out and touch it. The temptation was so strong that she had to sit on her hand to suppress it.

'So tell me what I'm guilty of,' Damien prompted, 'but only when you've finished looking at me. I wouldn't want to rush that...'

Violet reddened and immediately looked away. 'So now I'm going to be coming here at the weekend,' she said in a rush. The feel of his eyes on her and the faint woody smell of his aftershave were doing disastrous things to her equilibrium, cutting a swathe straight through the cool detachment she had managed to maintain over the course of the past few days. After his reciprocal coldness, this sudden attention was as dramatic on her nerves as an open flame next to dry tinder.

'I do recall you agreeing to something of the sort.' Damien was enjoying her attention. Enjoying the way her eyes skittered away from his face but then were compulsively drawn back to stare at him. He realised how much he had disliked her coolness towards him. They might have found themselves sharing the same space for very dubious reasons, but proximity and their need to pretend had invested a certain edge to what they had. A little wine had now made her lower her defences and he liked that. A lot. He leaned a little closer, as though he didn't want to miss a single word of what she was saying.

'Are you telling me that you didn't mean it?' he asked in a vaguely startled voice, as though this angle had only now popped into his head. 'Perhaps I misconstrued the relationship you have with my mother. You two seemed to be getting along like a house on fire...'

'That doesn't have anything...to do with...anything...' Violet said incoherently. 'I *like* your mother very much. *That's* why I...why it's such *a mistake*...'

'Honestly not following you at all...'

'I was only supposed to be here until the end of the week...'

'You were. And you're free to go once your week here is over.' He sat back, angling his body to one side so that he could extend his legs. He linked his hands behind his head.

'You have a life happening back in London. Of course, I know that I could keep you hanging on, doing what I ask of you, because you would do pretty much anything to save your sister's skin, but...' He stood up and walked, loose-limbed, to fetch himself a bottle of water, which he drank in one go while he continued to stare at her.

'But?' Violet was still having trouble peeling her eyes away from him.

'But that could prove a never-ending situation. So once we're back in London, feel free to jump ship. I'll sign a guarantee that your sister won't be prosecuted. She will be free as a bird to roam the Spanish coastline doing whatever takes her fancy. And you can return to your life.'

'And what would you tell your mother?' Faced with the prospect of returning to her life, Violet was now assailed by a host of treacherous misgivings that this much-prized life, the one she had insisted was there, waiting to be lived, was not quite the glittering treasure she had fondly described. She didn't quite get it, but there had been a strange excitement to being in Damien's company. When she was around him, even when, as had been the case over the past few days, she was keeping her distance, she was still always so *aware* of him. It was as if her waking moments had been injected with some sort of life-enhancing serum.

'That's not your problem. You can leave that one to me.'

'I'd quite like to know,' Violet persisted. She should be grabbing at this lifeline. She knew that. 'I'm really fond of your mother, Damien. I wouldn't want to think...I wouldn't want her to...'

'Be unduly hurt? Become stressed out? Think badly of you? All of the above? Funny, but I wasn't getting the impression that you were overly bothered. After all, five seconds ago you were accusing me of deliberately blindsiding you by not announcing on the spot that you wouldn't be back here for weekends...'

'I thought you would *want* to start bracing your mother for...you know...the inevitable...'

'The day before she begins what could be gruelling treatment?'

'Well...'

'Dominic has become attached to you.'

'Yes...' Just something else to think about, just another link in the chain she would have to melt down when she walked away from his family.

'When my mother begins her treatment she'll probably be too weak to help with my brother...'

'He doesn't need *help* as such. I mean, he has his carers for the physical stuff...'

'But has always relied on my mother for everything else. If she's in bed, she won't be able to provide all of that.'

'Which could be where *you* step in,' Violet urged him.

Damien flushed darkly. This conversation wasn't meant to be about *him*. Her bright eyes were positively glowing with sincerity.

'I can't be on call twenty-four seven. I still have a business to run, even if it's from a distance.'

'You wouldn't have to *be on call* twenty-four seven. Dominic's perfectly happy doing his own thing. He's really got into that website I asked him to try and design... Besides, I've noticed...'

'What? What have you noticed?'

'You didn't like it the last time I spoke my mind.'

'Maybe I've realised that it's about time I stop trying to think of your mind as anything but a runaway train,' Damien mused under his breath.

'I don't think that's very fair.' All signs of tipsiness had evaporated. She felt as sober as a judge. Her hands were clammy as she rested them on her knees to strain forward.

'You speak your mind. Maybe I find that a refreshing change. So don't spoil the habit of a lifetime now by going coy on me.'

'Okay. Well, I've noticed that you're making a bigger effort with Dominic. I mean, when we got here, you were hardly on speaking terms with him.'

Considering he had asked her to speak her mind, Damien made a concerted effort to control his reaction to that observation. 'Go on,' he muttered tightly, through gritted teeth.

'You never really directly *talked* to him. You talked *at* him, then you turned your attention to someone else or something else. And yet,' she mused thoughtfully, 'your mother says you two used to be so close when you were growing up...'

So *that* was what they talked about, Damien thought tensely. They discussed *him*. He angrily swept aside the sudden undercurrent of guilt that had been his unwelcome companion over the past few days and rose to his feet.

'It's late. We should be heading up,' he said smoothly.

'*We*? Aren't you going to work?'

'I'll see you up to the bedroom first. My mother would be horrified if you missed your footing on the stairs because you had a little too much to drink and I wasn't there to do the gentlemanly thing and catch you as you fell...'

'You're annoyed with me because of what I've said...'

'You're entitled to have your opinions.'

'I never wanted to.' She rose a little clumsily to her feet and turned in the direction of the kitchen door.

'Never wanted to what...?'

His breath fanned her cheek as he leaned down to hear what she was saying.

'Have opinions. I never wanted to have opinions about you.' She felt giddy and breathless as he shadowed her out of the kitchen and into the series of corridors and halls that eventually led to the staircase up to the wing of the house in which they had been placed.

'I'm finding that so hard to believe, Violet,' he murmured in a voice that warmed every part of her. 'You *always* have opinions. When you first walked into my office, I took you for someone who had scrambled all her courage together to confront me but who, under normal circumstances, wouldn't have said boo to a goose. My mistake.'

Violet eyed the landing ahead of her. Bedroom to the right. She thought she had recovered from that momentary tipsiness induced by a little too much wine with dinner but now she felt dizzy and flustered and wondered if she had overestimated her sobriety after all.

She glanced down and her eyes flitted over his lean brown hand on the banister just behind her.

Her heart was beating wildly as they made it to the bedroom door.

'All teachers have opinions,' she managed in a strangled voice. She took a step back as he reached around her to push open the bedroom door.

'There's a difference between having opinions and being opinionated. You're opinionated.' His arm brushed her and, all at once, he felt himself harden at the passing contact. That forbidden excitement coursed through him, reminding him of what she had looked like standing in front of him, naked and unaware. He hadn't had a woman for over three months. His last relationship, short-lived though it had been, had crumbled under the combined weight of his unreliability and her need to find out where they were heading. Not even her stupendous good looks, her unwavering availability whatever the time of day or night, or the very inventive sex, could provide sufficient glue to keep them going for a little longer.

He firmly closed the door behind him and switched on a side light so that the bedroom was suddenly infused in a mellow, romantic glow.

'You're going downstairs to work now, aren't you?' Violet asked nervously and he gave her a rueful smile.

'I'm trying to kick back a little...I think it would reassure my mother that I'm capable of involving myself in family life and leaving the emails alone now and again... You do approve, don't you?'

Violet found herself in the unenviable position of having to agree with him, especially when she had stuck her head above the parapet to voice her positive opinions on just that point.

'So...if you'll excuse me, I'll go have a shower...' He began unbuttoning his shirt and was amused when she primly diverted her eyes. This was the very situation most women would have loved. Up close and personal with him in a bedroom. He caught the distinctly erotic aroma of inexperience and her shyness was doing amazing things for his already rampant libido.

He made sure not to lock the door but he took his time, washing his hair and emerging twenty minutes later to find her with all her accoutrements in her hands.

'Sure you don't need a suitcase to carry all that stuff through?' he enquired and Violet blushed.

'I wouldn't want to disturb you when I come out. Just in case you're sleeping.'

'Very thoughtful.'

Violet backed away, eyes pinned to his face, anywhere but his muscled body, which was completely naked but for the tiny towel he had slung around his waist and which was dipping down in a very precarious fashion.

Did he sleep in pyjamas? How would she know when he had spent the past few nights retiring to bed at after one in the morning and getting up before six to start his day? She certainly hadn't seen any lying about and she found that her mind was entirely focused on that one small technicality as she lingered in the bathroom for as long as she possibly could.

And for a while after she emerged into a pitch-black room, she actually breathed a sigh of relief that he was asleep. He was nothing more than a dark shadow on the bed. On the very *big* bed.

Barely daring to breathe, she slipped under the duvet and turned on her side away from him with movements that were exaggeratedly slow. *Just in case.*

'You never actually told me whether you'd decided to come next weekend or not. Our conversation must have become waylaid...'

Violet gave a squeak of horror that he was not only awake but, from the sound of his voice, bright-eyed and bushy-tailed. She heard him adjust his position on the bed and when he next spoke she knew that he was now facing her.

'I think we lost track of the point when you decided to congratulate me on my sterling efforts with my brother...' He reached out to place a cool hand on her shoulder and Violet's blood pressure soared into the stratosphere. 'I hate talking to someone's back.'

Violet froze. She felt trapped between a rock and a hard place. She was in this bed with this man and she either turned round to face him, thereby instantly diminishing the generous proportions of the bed, or else she remained as she was, with her back to him like a petrified object, desperately hoping that hand would go away and not do something more exploratory to urge her over onto her other side. She reluctantly shifted her position and was screamingly aware of the rustle of the duvet and the soft deflation of the pillow as her body shifted.

Her eyes had adjusted to the darkness in the bedroom and her mouth went dry when she realised that he was bare-chested. Propping himself up on one elbow, the duvet was down to his waist, allowing her an eyeful of his perfectly muscled, sinewy chest with its flat brown nipples and just the right amount of dark hair to make her breath catch painfully in her throat.

'That's better,' Damien said with satisfaction. 'Now I can actually see your face. So what's your decision to be?'

'Can't we discuss this in the morning?'

'I'm a great believer in not putting off for tomorrow what can be done today and that includes decisions.'

'I suppose it wouldn't hurt to come down next weekend,' Violet mumbled. Underneath the prim fleecy pyjamas, she could feel the heavy weight of her unconstrained breasts, which in turn made her remember that very moment when she had realised he had been watching her as she had emerged completely naked from the bathroom. Those twin attacks on her crumbling composure sent a wave of heat licking through her.

'My mother and Dominic will both be pleased.' Damien's voice was low and unbearably sexy. 'As,' he continued, 'will I...'

'You will? You don't mean that. You've barely spoken to me all week.'

'I might say the same for you. But we're talking now...'

'Yes...'

'Feels good, doesn't it?'

Violet could hear the rapid rush of her own breathing. His low, husky words were a backdrop to something else. She felt it with an instinct she wasn't even aware she possessed. He wasn't touching her but it felt as though he might be and, although she knew that he couldn't read her expression any more accurately than she could read his in the darkness, there was still a crackle of high voltage electricity between them that made the hairs on the back of her neck stand on end.

Was he going to make a move on her? Surely not! And yet…now was the time to briskly bring the conversation to an end by turning away. Sleep might be difficult to court with him lying right there next to her on the bed, but he would get the message that she had nothing more to say to him when she coldly turned away. And if she couldn't see him, then this weirdly unsettling *awareness* that was making her pulses race would be extinguished at source. He would probably be gone, as usual, before she woke up in the morning and they would be back to keeping a healthy distance from each other, only breaking it in front of his family.

Violet knew exactly what she should do and how she should react and instead, to her horror, she found herself reaching out to touch that hard, broad chest. Just one touch. Where on earth had that dangerous thought come from? How had it managed to slip through all the walls and barriers of common sense and self-protection she was frantically erecting?

And where had that soft gasping sound come from as her fingers rested briefly on his chest?

Damien felt a kick of supreme satisfaction. Never had a woman's touch felt so good. It was hesitant, timid, a barely-there sort of touch, and it ignited his blood, which was burning hot in his veins as he pulled her towards him…

CHAPTER SEVEN

His lips met hers and Violet was lost. While a part of her knew that this shouldn't be happening, the rest of her clung to him with shameful abandon. She couldn't get enough of touching him. She wanted to explore every inch of his body and then begin all over again. The urge was nothing like anything she had felt before in her life. For her, love-making always seemed a calm, pleasant business, but then her one and only lover had started life as a friend. Damien was certainly no friend and this was not calm. She feverishly traced the muscled contours of his shoulders and she could feel him smiling against her mouth.

She ran her foot along his calf and shivered as her knee came into contact with the rigidity of his erection. When he flipped her onto him, she arched and threw her head back as he undid the buttons of her top, to reveal breasts that dangled tantalisingly by his mouth. She straightened to fling the constricting fleece off her.

She looked down at him, breathing hard, her hair tumbling past her shoulders. His skin was golden-brown, a natural bronze that contrasted dramatically against her own paleness. She reached out and flattened the palm of her hand against him and felt the ripple of muscle under her fingers.

He pulled her into him and half groaned as her breasts

squashed against his chest. This time, his kiss was long, lingering and never-ending. It was a kiss that was designed to get lost in. It was a kiss that allowed no room for thought.

The warm fleece of her pyjama bottoms felt itchy and uncomfortable. Her underwear was damp with spreading moisture. She parted her legs and, through the fleece, she felt the hard jut of his erection.

'We shouldn't,' she moaned, instantly negating that passing thought by moving sinuously against him.

'Why? We both want it…'

'Because you want something doesn't mean that you should just go right ahead and have it…'

'Are you telling me that you want to stop?' She could no more do that than he could. Damien was aware of this with every fibre of his being. He pulled her back down against him, stifling any protest she might have come up with, and Violet ran her fingers through his hair. She loved the feel of its silky thickness. Touching him like this…it felt decadent, taboo, weirdly wicked. Even though she was supposed to be his girlfriend…

She felt like a Victorian maiden on the verge of swooning when he eased her up and hooked his fingers into the waistband of the pyjamas. Her breasts were tempting and luscious, but first…

He tugged the bottoms and watched with satisfaction as she quickly slipped them off. When she reached to do the same with her panties, he stayed her hand. He could see the dampness darkening the crotch as she straddled him and he placed his palm against the spot and moved it until he could feel the wetness seeping through to his hand.

'Enjoying yourself?' Anticipation was running through his veins. Making his blood boil. He intended to take things slowly, but it was hard. All he could think of was her settling on him, feeling her softness sheathing him and her tightness as she moved on him. 'Touch me.'

Violet quivered. The underwear had to come off. She was going crazy. She swung her legs over the side of the bed and kicked it free, then turned back to see him watching her with a little smile as he touched himself. He was huge. A massive rock-hard rod of steel nestled in whorls of dark hair. She was mesmerised by the sight of his hand lightly circling himself, moving lazily, biding his time until she could pleasure him.

'I'd rather *you* were doing this...'

Violet made her way over to him so that she was within touching distance...within licking distance...

Damien groaned and flung his head back, eyes closed, enjoying her tongue and mouth on him. He curled his hands into her hair, cupping her head. He had to steel himself against a powerful urge to let go, to release himself. He was in the process of physically losing control and he almost failed to recognise that fact because it was not something with which he was familiar. For him, making love had always been a finely tuned art form, where mutual pleasure rose along a predictable, albeit pleasurable, incline.

With a shudder, he reluctantly pulled her away from him and took a few seconds to gather himself.

Violet experienced a heady feeling of power. That this beautiful, desirable alpha male had to steady himself because of her...

She revelled in the unusual situation of really and truly, for the first time in her life, letting herself go. She felt as though she had had years of always having to be the one in control. Even in her one and only relationship, she had remained that person—the person who always thought before acting, the person who was always responsible. In giving Phillipa permission to be exactly the person she wanted to be, Violet, without knowing it, had tailored her own responses, had become the one who held back because *someone* had to, in the absence of parents.

Now...

She licked his rigid shaft once again and felt the roughness of veins against her tongue, a contrast to the silky smoothness at the top.

She had a moment's hesitation as her ever present common sense cranked into gear.

What was going on here? So yes, he was an intensely attractive man. It was perfectly understandable that she might be attracted to him. Attraction and lust had nothing to do with love and affection. She knew that now. But why on earth did *he* find *her* attractive? He was a man used to supermodels. She had seen pictures of them and, on his own admission, his first impressions of her had hardly been positive. So was he here now because a certain amount of boredom had met a similar amount of curiosity and the two, in this strangely charged situation, had combined to produce desire? Had the charade of playing their respective parts spilled over into reality?

For whatever reason, this man wanted her and for even more nebulous reasons, and against her better judgement, she wanted him. She knew what she should do. But suddenly she thought of her sister, flitting around in Ibiza, doing exactly what she wanted to do while she, Violet, remained behind to pick up the pieces. She thought of herself, always travelling in the slow lane, always taking care, while the fast-paced rush of the unexpected and the novel flew past her, leaving her in its wake.

Why, she wondered with a spurt of rebellion, shouldn't *she* jump on the roller coaster for once in her life? Why should she hold back at this eleventh hour? Would it be fair to herself? It certainly wouldn't be fair to *him*.

So what they had wouldn't last but what did she stand to lose? Damien meant nothing to her emotionally. He turned her on but she would always be able to walk away from lust because, sooner or later, her common sense would once again kick in, telling her that it was time to move on. When that time came, she would get back out there and jump back into the dating game, find herself a nice guy. She would never look back and have regrets that she had had her one window to be reckless and she had chosen to primly shut it and walk away.

She raised her head to meet his eyes and read the naked desire there.

'You're fabulous,' he said roughly, and Violet smiled and blushed because she couldn't think of a time when anyone had called her that.

'You're just saying that...'

'Don't tell me you haven't driven your fair share of men crazy before...' He raised himself, pulled her towards him and kissed her with driving urgency, stifling any confirmation. He didn't want to think of her with any other man. It was an unsettling and momentary pull of possessiveness that was completely alien to him.

His mouth never left hers as he found one breast and massaged its plumpness, finding the erect peak of her nipple to tease it until she was squirming.

In shocking detail, his voice rough and uneven, he told her exactly what he wanted to do with her, where he wanted to touch her, what he wanted her to feel.

Violet's skin burned hotly with the thrill of what he was saying. True, her experience when it came to the opposite sex was limited to one guy, but even so nothing could quite have prepared her for this sensory overload. His husky sex talk was doing all sorts of things in her mind while his hand, which had moved from her breast to caress the fluffy downy hair between her legs, was having a similar effect on her body.

She writhed and moaned softly, lowering herself to rake her teeth along his shoulder. He flipped her over so that he was now on top of her and she watched the progress of his dark head as he trailed a blazing path with his mouth along her shoulders to clamp on her nipple. Her nails dug into his shoulder blades then moved to tangle into his hair so that she could urge his mouth harder on her sensitised nipple.

He told her to tell him what she liked. Violet blushed furiously and thought that that was something she would never be able to do in a million years.

'So...' Damien was inordinately thrilled at her shyness. On so many levels he had been spot on when he had told her that she made a refreshing change. He had raised himself up now, his powerful body over hers, his hardness pressed against her, which made her desperate to open her legs and guide him inside. He laughed when she tried and told her that he was having none of that. Yet.

'You don't talk during sex...' He slipped two fingers inside her, felt her wetness and began teasing her, rubbing the throbbing little bud of her clitoris until she was gasping, only to move his attention elsewhere so that she didn't peak.

'Damien...'

'How do you expect me to know what turns you on if you don't tell me...?'

'You *know* what turns me on... You're...you're...'

'Doing it right now?'

'Please...'

'I like it that you're begging me...do you enjoy it when *I* talk...?' He whispered a few more things in her ear and Violet groaned. 'Well...?' His exploring fingers drove deeper inside her and she tightened her legs.

'Yes,' Violet whispered, then she shot him a devilish smile, 'although right now...there's other stuff I'd like you to do...'

'Tell me...'

'I...I can't...' She felt as green as a virgin.

'Of course you can,' Damien coaxed. It was taking a massive amount of willpower to maintain this leisurely pace. Her body pressed against his was beyond a turn-on and the slippery wetness between her legs was something he could barely think about because, if he did, he knew that he would lose control.

'I like it when you...suck my nipples...they're very sensitive...' Violet could feel her skin burning as though she was on fire. She felt forward and wanton and thoroughly debauched and she wondered how it was that she had never, ever been tempted to let go like this before. For a second she panicked at the notion that a man with whom she had nothing in common had been the one to rouse her to these heights.

'Your wish is my command...and I have other things in store for you...'

Violet decided not to think. She immersed herself in sensation after sensation as he suckled on her nipples, his tongue darting and rubbing and licking and then she gasped, shocked, as his wandering mouth travelled southwards. When she stammered that she had never...he couldn't possibly mean to...he laughed, deep-throated and amused, and proceeded to precisely what she had never...

His head between her legs made her want to cry out loud. Of their own volition, they parted to accommodate his ministrations and he was very thorough. He teased her with his tongue until she knew that she couldn't stand it any longer, then he angled his big body so that she could pleasure him just as he was pleasuring her.

Her legs were spread wide as he continued to feast on her. His tongue probed every bit of her and she did likewise to him, taking his bigness into her mouth, tasting it in every way possible. Only when she knew that they were both about to tip over the edge did he raise himself up, pulling apart only to ask her if she was protected. He was breathing heavily.

Why on earth would she be? Violet wanted to ask. But she knew that, for Damien, his relationships would always have been with women who travelled prepared. She was certain that had they fallen into bed in his house or flat or apartment, or wherever it was he lived, there would be ample supplies of condoms in a bedside cabinet. She shook her head. She searched his face for signs of impatience and frustration but there were none. Instead, he rubbed himself against her and murmured that full intercourse would have to wait.

'There are other ways to keep busy...'

Violet was lost for words at his generosity. She wasn't completely naive. She knew that a lot of men would have been angry, enraged even, to have had their pleasure curtailed, even if it wasn't the woman's fault. A lot of men were selfish. Contrary to first impressions, Damien clearly was not one of those men.

Something shifted inside her but it was something she didn't stop to analyse. Just at that moment, her brain wasn't up to doing anything analytical. Not when he was touching her once again, burying his head between her thighs, relentlessly teasing her throbbing clitoris with his tongue.

Their bodies seemed to fuse into one and when, finally, she climaxed, thrusting up against his greedy mouth, she felt utterly spent. She blindly reached for him, felt his hardness and curved her languorous body so that her mouth met it, so that she could take him to the same heights to which he had taken her.

Their bodies were slick with perspiration and the room filled with the miasma of sex. He tugged her off him before he came and she felt his ejection on her face and body. It mirrored her own wetness that glistened on his face. When they kissed as he returned to Planet Earth, it was the most sensuous thing she had ever done. She felt giddy from such complete loss of her self-control.

'I think tomorrow we might pay a visit to the chemist...' Damien was on top of the world. What was it about this woman? They hadn't even indulged in full intercourse and why kid himself, no amount of inventive touching could compare to the unique sensation of penetration. Yet he was infused with a feeling of absolute well-being. On a high. He wanted to start all over again, touching, tracing her body with his hands, tasting...

He pulled her against him and relished the softness of her full breasts squashed against his chest.

'I don't know how this happened...'

'Are you saying you wish it hadn't?'

'No,' Violet admitted truthfully, 'but I'm not the kind of girl who falls into bed with men...'

'Not even with the boyfriend you happen to be deeply in love with?'

It took a couple of seconds for it to register that he was teasing her. 'Ha, ha, very funny...' she said weakly. *But what happens next?* she wanted to ask. Except the question seemed strangely inappropriate.

'This complicates things...' she said instead.

It was precisely why he had made such a big effort not to go there. Even when he had acknowledged that he was attracted to her, even though he was a man who had never missed a step between attraction and possession, it was precisely why Damien had stepped back. Because he had acknowledged that to sleep with her would be to complicate an already complicated situation.

Now, with her sexy, luscious body pressed against his, there was no room in his head for thoughts of complications.

'That's one way of looking at it. On the other hand, you could say that it makes the situation much more interesting.'

'I'm not an interesting person.'

'Leave the character assessment to me...' He smoothed his hand over her thigh, slipped it underneath, sandwiching it between her legs, his own personal hand warmer.

Violet knew exactly what sort of character assessment he was talking about. It had nothing to do with her personality.

'So we're here...and we're sleeping together. You might say it adds a great deal more veracity to the situation. No need to pretend...'

Except, Violet thought, they were *still* pretending. Pretending an emotional connection that was absent, even though there was now a physical one.

'You're still frowning.'

'I can't help it.'

'Live for the present.'

'I've never been good at doing that. When our parents died, I was left in charge of Phillipa and the last thing I could afford to do was live for the present.'

'I get that,' Damien murmured. He wasn't one for soul-searching conversations but he was feeling incredibly relaxed. 'With a sister like her, you had to carry worries about the future for both of you.' He gently parted her legs and slipped his finger along the crease that protected her femininity like the petals of a flower.

'I can't...talk when you're doing that...'

'Fine by me. Touching and talking don't go hand in hand. At least...not unless the talking's dirty...which I've discovered turns you on...'

'But we have to talk...'

'Wouldn't you rather...'

'Damien!' She could feel her body tensing and building up to a climax. His caressing hand was doing all sorts of things to her and yet there was stuff that needed to be said.

'I know. Irresistible, isn't it? And you can feel how much it's turning me on as well...'

Violet wondered how it would be were they to make love fully, properly... Her imagination soared as the rubbing movements against the pulsating bud of her clitoris got faster and faster and when she came it was an explosion that left her drained.

She curled against him. 'What happens now...?' She hadn't wanted to pose the question but it was one that needed to be asked.

Damien stilled. Questions of that nature always left him cold. However, in a strange way, this was a far more straightforward situation. 'You come up next weekend. As agreed. But I won't be working till one in the morning and leaving the bedroom by six. It has to be said that the prospect of sojourns in the countryside has taken on a distinctly upbeat tempo.'

'But I'm not your real girlfriend...'

'Where are you going with this?'

'Do we communicate during the week?' She worried her lower lip as she tried to get her head round a relationship that wasn't a relationship. 'Or do we just become involved when we're here? I mean,' she added, just in case he got it into his head she would spend Monday to Friday pining for his company and putting her life on hold, 'what if I meet someone...? I have quite a busy social life. Teachers like going out after school. Most of us feel we need a drink after a day in the company of high energy kids.'

'Meet someone?' He shifted so that he could look down at her.

'I've been thinking about getting back into the dating scene. For some reason, it's always been difficult with Phillipa around. I guess she just took up so much of my energy. I spent so much time worrying about what she was getting up to and listening to her personal sagas that there never seemed to be much time left over for myself. With Phillipa in Ibiza now...'

Damien's brain had come to a screeching halt at the words *getting back into the dating scene*. They had just made love! He was outraged. How could she even be contemplating the prospect of some other guy when she was lying next to him, her body still hot and flushed after her climax that he had given her?

'Sorry, but that's not going to happen.' He flung himself back and stared up at the ceiling with its ornate mouldings which he could hardly make out in the darkness. He felt her shift next to him so that she, likewise, was staring up at the ceiling.

'I'm not following you...'

'Explain to me how, on the one hand, you say that you don't climb into bed with random men whilst on the other telling me that you want to start going to nightclubs and sleeping with whoever takes your fancy at the time...'

'That's not at all what I said!'

'No? It sounded very much like that to me. And I am very much offended that you would even think of raising a subject of this nature after we've spent the past hour and a half making love. In fact, you shouldn't even be *thinking* about other men. Right now, *I* should be the only man on your mind.'

'The game's changed,' Violet said calmly on a deep breath, 'and now there are different rules.'

'Enlighten me.'

'Why do you have to be so arrogant?'

'It's one of the more endearing aspects of my personality. You were going to tell me about these new rules.'

'I... For some weird reason I find I'm attracted to you.' She took a deep breath. 'You've told me that I should live in the present and I guess this is my one-off opportunity to do that. I never expected it to happen, but there you go.'

'So...other guys...out of the question. Nightclubs and sex after two drinks...likewise out of the question.'

'In which case, the same rules apply to you.'

Damien rolled to his side and looked at her. In accordance with a serious conversation, she had tucked the duvet right up to her neck.

'Gladly.' He pulled the duvet down, exposing her breasts and he gently nuzzled a rosy tip until it stiffened against his tongue. 'Gladly?' Violet tugged him up so that he was looking at her, although her body was aching for him to carry on doing what it had been doing so well.

'I'm a one woman kind of man...'

Violet wondered whether that was because he happened to be temporarily stuck far away from the action but then she conceded that, however arrogant and infuriating he could be, his ground rules would be fair.

'And besides...' he nibbled her lower lip, tugging it gently between his teeth '...this works...'

'You said you first thought that getting involved like this...'

'Falling into bed together and making love until we're too exhausted to move…'

'…would complicate things.' Violet didn't know what she wanted him to say. She had knowingly thrown caution to the winds and yet she still felt confused. She had never felt so physically satisfied—*never ever*—and yet the road ahead still seemed opaque and clouded with uncertainty. He might not want to put a label to what they now had, but effectively they were an item. For real. And yet why didn't it feel that way? And did she really expect him to set those niggling anxieties to rest?

'I wasn't thinking out of the box. I've found that women seem to associate fun in bed with meeting the parents and eventually shopping for a wedding ring. You…' seemingly of its own volition, his hand caressed her breast; he couldn't get enough of her '…fall into a different category. You know how the ground lies. I'm not looking for any kind of commitment. Been there, done that, won't be revisiting that particular holiday hotspot in the foreseeable future. But what's going on right now…mind-blowing…and I'm not one to throw around superlatives lightly…' He shot her a smouldering smile that made her toes curl. 'I won't be casting my net anywhere else and, if it makes you happy, you can communicate with me all you want to during the week. In fact, you'll need to be updated on my mother's progress. I'm sure she'll also get in touch. It would be abnormal for you to be ignorant of how she is doing. So I'm guessing all your questions have been sorted…'

They were having fun. Plus it was convenient. But he was trusting her not to get emotionally wrapped up. When he said that they would communicate during the week, she knew that their conversations would be about Eleanor, that there would be a specific reason for them to happen in the first place. They wouldn't be passing the time chatting about nothing much in particular. Violet decided that she was fine with that. She had never been the sort of person who kept the various sections of her life neatly boxed away and separated. This was how it was done. Of course, it would take a little getting used to but she would do it because, like it or not, she was greedy for the physical exhilaration he had introduced into her life, which, on that level, now seemed bland and nondescript in comparison.

She parted her legs and felt his hardness rub against her. No penetration but the sensation produced was still powerful and she moved in time to increase the pressure.

'And when things fizzle out between us...' she volunteered breathlessly.

'It's called the natural course of events.'

She could hardly imagine him being so deeply in love with a woman that he would want to take it to the very limit, that he would propose marriage. She couldn't get her head around the notion of him offering commitment rather than talking about the natural course of events. For a man as intensely proud and intensely passionate, she could understand how he could have been permanently damaged by the most significant relationship in his life going belly up. Eleanor had never broached the subject of Annalise again and neither had she. Damien's past was none of her business. This was the here and now. Everything he said made sense. This was her one opportunity to ditch her comfort zone and there was no point having a mental debate on the pros and cons of the clauses attached.

'We'll go our separate ways but as long as we're lovers you'll find, my darling, that I am exceedingly generous...'

'Your money doesn't mean anything to me.' She tried not to feel hurt at the implication that she could be shoved into the predictable mould of one of his women, eager to take whatever gifts were on offer. 'That's not why...I don't care if you own the Bank of England. I don't want anything from you.'

Damien thought that whilst she might say that now, her tune would change the second he presented her with her very first diamond-encrusted bracelet or top-of-the-range sports car.

'Frankly, my mother would expect it.'

'She already knows that I'm not the materialistic kind.'

'More confidences exchanged during one of your cosy tête-à-têtes?' But he liked her protestations of wholesomeness. What guy in his position wouldn't? Even if, sooner or later, the moral high ground took a bit of a beating? Greed and avarice were frequent visitors to his life. It was nice not to have them knocking on the door just yet.

'We don't *just* talk about you!'

'I'm hurt. I thought I was never far from your thoughts...' He moved fractionally against her and she squirmed and her eyes fluttered. To stop herself from losing control altogether once again, she reached down and firmly held him in her hand. The steel thickness of his girth made her shudder with wicked pleasure.

'You're not *in* my thoughts,' Violet denied vigorously. Having someone in your thoughts implied a *connection*. Even jokingly, she didn't want to go there, didn't want to let him think that he might be anything more to her than she was to him. 'You crop up in conversation with your mother because you're the person we have in common and, under normal circumstances, a girlfriend would be really happy to hear her stories about the guy in her life from his mother. It's natural that your mother would want to talk about you. Now, though, we talk about other things. Art, the garden, life in a small community, the treatment and what it might involve...and I don't just have conversations with your mother. I talk a lot to Dominic as well. He has a lot to say. You just have to be patient. He gets frustrated because he can't communicate as fluently as he'd like, but he's smart.'

Damien gently removed her hand from him. Reluctantly. Of course, warning bells shouldn't be ringing. They were, after all, singing from the same song sheet but still…just in case…

'Don't get too wrapped up, Violet.'

'What do you mean?'

'I mean…we might become more involved with one another than either of us anticipated or probably even wanted, and your role might have been extended beyond what I envisaged, but don't start nurturing ideas of permanence.'

'I wouldn't do that!' She pulled away from him. 'And you don't have to warn me! You've already made the parameters of what we have perfectly clear. I understand, Damien. It suits me! I'm not an idiot.'

'But you're forming links with my family,' Damien said drily.

'I'm *having conversations*!' But she could detect the coolness in his voice. This wasn't a gentle caution. This was a warning shot across the bows, a blunt reminder that she was not to go beyond the Keep Out signs he had erected around himself. If she did, and the message was clear though unspoken, she would be ditched. He would enjoy her but that was as far as things would go. In short, *don't start getting any ideas…*

'I'm a big girl. I know how to take care of myself. And because the women you've dated in the past might have wanted more from you than you were prepared to give, that's not the case with me. I've always been careful. I'm just having a go at what it feels like not to be careful for once in my life. And do you always have a list prepared of dos and don'ts when you start a…something? With a woman? Or is this specially for me because I happen to have met your family?'

Violet knew that she shouldn't be pursuing this. This wasn't part of her decision to *be daring for once in her life*.

'I'm always upfront when it comes to women. I let them know that I'm not in it for the long-term.'

'Because you've been hurt once doesn't mean that you have to spend the rest of your life keeping your distance.'

'Come again?' Damien said coldly.

'I'm sorry. I shouldn't have said that.' But had he laid down loads of rules and regulations for Annalise? No. She wasn't in the same category—of course she wasn't—but neither did she need to be subjected to a hundred and one boundary lines because he thought she was too gullible or too stupid to know how the land lay.

'Let's move on from this conversation, Violet. My past is not fertile ground for discussion.' And he was willing to let it go. His magnanimity surprised him because he categorically did not invite anyone's opinions on certain aspects of his life. Naturally, he didn't want to engineer an argument. He hadn't enjoyed the past few days of awkwardness. And also, for once, he was thinking with that part of his body which he always had under control. Never had elemental desire been so important a factor in his response.

'As I said, I understand the parameters and it suits me.'

'You're using me, in other words.' His voice was light and amused.

'No more than you're using me.'

Not quite the response he had expected. He gave a low laugh. Fair's fair, he thought. Wasn't it? He'd never had any woman admit to using him before. So what if the feeling didn't sit *quite right*? He wanted her. She wanted him. Trim away the excess and that was all that mattered.

CHAPTER EIGHT

DAMIAN REACHED INTO his jacket pocket and flipped open the lid of the black and gold box which had been nestling there for the past three hours.

A necklace with a teardrop pendant, a blood-red ruby, surrounded by tiny diamonds. He had chosen it himself. Well, why not? Suitable recompense for the past three and a half months, during which Violet had proved herself a superb and satisfying lover. He always gave gifts to his lovers. She might have thwarted every attempt he had made thus far on that front, rebutting his offers of a car, *because who needed to become snarled up in traffic, not to mention contributing to global warming whilst having to pay the Congestion Charge the second you needed it for anything really useful?* an expensive weekend in Vienna now that his mother seemed to be responding so well to her treatment programme, *can't, too much work, sorry,* some really expensive kitchen equipment because he had seen what she had, *no, thanks, a girl becomes accustomed to working with old, familiar pots and pans and ovens and fridges and microwaves...*

But this necklace was a fait accompli. She would have no choice but to accept it.

He snapped shut the lid of the box and returned it to

his jacket pocket before sliding out of his car and heading up to her house.

He had grown accustomed to the confined space in which she lived. Literally two-up, two-down. Phillipa was still doing whatever she was doing in Ibiza. He couldn't imagine the claustrophobia of actually having to share the place with another adult human being. Personally, it would have driven him mad. He was used to the vast open-plan space of his five-bedroom house in Chelsea. When he had moved there years ago, he had hired a top architect who had re-configured the layout of the house so that the rooms, all painted stone and adorned with a mixture of established art and newer investment worthy pieces, flowed into one another.

Violet's house was more in the nature of a honeycomb. Two weeks previously, he had offered to have the whole thing gutted and redone more along his tastes, but predictably she had looked at him as though he had taken leave of his senses and laughed. Alternatively, he had said, they could just spend more time at his place. He was now splitting his time between London and the West Country. Why not make love in luxury? But she had told him, in the sort of semi-apologetic voice that managed to impart no hint of remorse, that she didn't like his house. Something about it being sterile and clinical. He had refrained from telling her that she was the first woman to have ever responded to opulence with a negative reaction.

He pressed the doorbell and instantly lost his train of thought at the sound of her approaching footsteps.

From inside the house, Violet felt that familiar shiver of tingling, excited anticipation. After the first month, and once he had ascertained that Eleanor was responding well, Damien had split his time. He always made sure to spend weekends in the country and often Mondays as well, but he was now in London a great deal more and Violet liked that. On all levels, what she was doing was bad for her. She knew that. She didn't understand where this driving, urgent chemistry between them had sprung from and even less did she understand how it was capable of existing in a vacuum the way it did, but she was powerless to fight it. Having always equated sex with love, she had fast learned how easy it was for everything you took for granted to be turned inside out and upside down.

She had also fast learned how easy it was to lose track of the rules of the game you had signed up to.

When had she started living her week in anticipation of seeing him? Just when had she sacrificed all her principles, all her expectations of what a relationship should deliver on the high altar of lust and passion and sex?

She had told herself that she was throwing caution to the winds. That most of her adult years had been spent being responsible and diligent and careful so why on earth shouldn't she take a little time out and experience something else, something that wasn't all wrapped up with *doing the right thing*? She had practically decided that she *owed* herself that. That she was a grown woman who was more than capable of handling a sexual relationship with a man to whom she was inexplicably but powerfully attracted.

So how was it that it was now so difficult to maintain the mask of not caring one jot if he never discussed anything beyond tomorrow? If he assumed that whatever they had would fizzle out at some point? More and more she found herself thinking about Annalise, the wife that should have been but never was. He never mentioned her name. That in itself was telling because three weeks ago, on one of their rare excursions out for a meal at a swanky restaurant in Belgravia, he had bumped into a woman and had afterwards told her that he had dated her for a few months. The woman had been a flame-haired six-foot beauty, as slender as a reed and draped over a man much shorter and older. Afterwards, Damien had laughed and informed her that the man in question was a Russian billionaire, married but with his wife safely tucked away in the bowels of St Petersburg somewhere.

'Don't you feel a twinge of jealousy that he's dating a woman you used to go out with?' Violet had asked, because how could any man not? When the woman in question looked as though she had stepped straight off the front cover of a high-end fashion magazine? Damien had laughed. Why on earth would he be jealous? Women came and went. Good luck to the guy, although he had enough money to keep the lady in question amused and interested.

'Was she too expensive for you?' Violet had asked, which he had found even more amusing.

'No one's too expensive for me. I dumped her because she wanted more than money could buy.'

Violet had thought that that had said it all. The woman in question had wanted a ring on her finger. Damien, on the other hand, had wanted casual. Which was what he wanted with her and the only woman to whom those rules had never applied was the one woman who had broken his heart.

And yet, knowing all that, she could still feel herself sliding further and further away from logic, common sense and self-control. Forewarned wasn't forearmed.

She pulled open the door and her heart gave that weird skippy feeling, as though she were in a lift that had suddenly dropped a hundred floors at maximum speed.

It was Thursday and he had come straight from work, although his tie was missing and his jacket was slung over his shoulder.

'Damien...'

'Missed me?' Deep blue, hooded eyes swept over her with masculine appreciation. No bra. Ages ago, he had told her that it was an entirely unnecessary item of clothing for a woman whose breasts were as perfect as hers. At least indoors. When *he* was the male caller in question...

He had been leaning indolently against the doorframe. Now he pushed himself off and entered the tiny hallway, his eyes glued to her the whole time.

His smile was slow and lazy. With an easy movement, he tossed his jacket aside, where it landed neatly on the banister, then he wrapped his arms around her, drew her to him so that he could try and extinguish some of the yearning that had been building inside him from the very second he had set foot in his car. Her mouth parted readily and he grunted with pleasure as his tongue found hers, clashing in a hungry need for more.

Violet braced her hands against his chest and stayed him for a few seconds. 'You know I hate it when the first thing you do the very second you walk through the front door is...is...'

'Kiss you senseless...?' Damien raked his fingers through his hair. Frankly, he wasn't too fond of that particular trait himself. He didn't like what it said about his self-control when he was around her, but he chose to keep that to himself. 'Is that why the last time I came, we didn't even manage to make it up the stairs?' he said instead. 'In fact, if I recall...your jumper was off on stair two, I had your nipple in my mouth by stair four and by stair eight, roughly halfway up, I was exploring other parts of your extremely responsive body...'

Violet blushed. As always, it was one thing saying something and another actually putting it into practice.

Right now, although he had done as asked and had

drawn back from her, the one thing she wanted to do was pull him right back towards her so that they could carry on where they had left off.

It was only a very small consolation that these little shows of strength helped her to maintain the façade of being as casual about what they had as he was. She knew that she had to cling to them for dear life.

'I'm going to cook us something special.' She led the way to the kitchen and retrieved a cold bottle of beer from the fridge, which he took, tilting his head back to drink a couple of long mouthfuls.

'Why?'

Violet contained a little spurt of irritation. Shows of domesticity were never appreciated. He had never said so but, tellingly, his chef would often prepare food, which he would bring with him, stuff that tasted delicious and required an oven, a microwave and plates, or else takeaways were ordered when they had been physically sated. The ritual of eating was usually just an interruption, she sometimes felt, to the main event.

'I'm trying it out as a meal for my class to learn,' she lied and he shrugged and swallowed a couple more mouthfuls of beer before retreating to the kitchen table, where he sprawled on one chair, pulling another closer and using it as a footrest.

Violet bustled. Now that they weren't tripping over themselves, tearing each other's clothes off in a frantic race to make love, she wished that they were. Her body tingled at the knowledge that he was looking at her. She loved it when his eyes got dark and slumberous and full of intent.

'Tell me how your mother's doing,' she said, to clear her head from the wanton desire to fling herself at him and forget about the meal she had planned.

She listened as he told her about recent trips into the

village, her upbeat mood, which so contrasted with her despair when she had initially told him about the situation, recovery that was exceeding the doctor's expectations...

Violet half listened. Her mind was drifting in and out of the uncomfortable questions she had recently started asking herself. Occasionally she said something and hoped for the best. She was a million miles away when she jumped as Damien padded up towards her and whispered into her ear, 'Must be a complicated recipe, Violet. You've been staring into space for the past five minutes.'

Violet snapped back to the present and turned to him with a little frown. 'I've got stuff on my mind.'

'Anything I'd like to hear about?'

She hesitated, torn between not wanting to rock the boat and needing to say what she was thinking.

'No. Just to do with school.' She cravenly shied away from doing what she knew would ruin the evening.

'What can I do to take your mind off it...?' Just like that, Damien felt his tension evaporate. He thought he might have been imagining the thickness of the atmosphere, her unusual silence. He turned her back to the chopping board, where she had been mixing a satay sauce, and wrapped his arms around her from behind. 'Looks good. What is it?' He slipped one big hand underneath her loose top and did what he had been wanting to the moment he had set foot through the front door. He caressed one full breast, settling on a nipple, which he rubbed gently but insistently with the pad of his thumb. With his other hand, he dipped a finger into the sauce, licked some off and offered the rest to her. Violet's mouth circled round his finger and she shivered at the deliberate eroticism in the gesture.

She moved across to the kitchen sink, carrying some dishes with her, and he released her, but only briefly, before resuming his position standing right behind her.

Outside, with the days getting longer, darkness was only now beginning to set in. Her view was spectacularly unexciting. The back of the house overlooked the wall of another house; the outside space comprised of a pocket-sized back garden just big enough for Phillipa to lie down in summer and spend the day tanning without having to dismantle the washing line.

Their bodies, merging together, were reflected hazily back to them in the windows overlooking the garden and their eyes tangled in the reflection as he slowly pushed up her jumper until she could see both their bodies and the pale nudity of her breasts. She gasped and fell back slightly against him as he began massaging them, rhythmic, firm movements that pushed them up, making her large nipples bulge and distend.

'Damien…no…someone might see us…' Although that wasn't really a possibility. The one thing about the house and its location was that it was surprisingly private, given the fact that it was in London, where privacy was a rarity. The small back garden was fully enclosed with a fence and a fortuitous tree in the back garden of the neighbour opposite ensured limited view.

Damien continued rubbing her breasts, filling his hands with the heavy weight of them, bouncing them slightly, as though evaluating their worth.

'Get naked for me,' he murmured, nipping her neck and then trailing hot kisses along it.

'Get…what…?'

'Don't pretend you didn't hear. Get naked for me. Take your clothes off. Scratch that. Maybe I'll let you get away with just wearing an apron…'

'I'm not dressing up for your enjoyment!' But already the thought of his dark, intense eyes following her naked body as she moved around the kitchen was making her feel hot and bothered.

'I'm not asking you to dress up. I'm asking you to dress down...' He shifted her jumper up, over her breasts, and Violet responded by spinning round to face him, her bare breasts pushing against the hard wall of his chest.

She began unbuttoning his shirt. From a position of relative inexperience only months ago, she had grown in confidence. He might not have had it at his disposal to offer anything most women would have expected of a proper relationship, but he certainly had it within him to turn her into a woman who was no longer tentative when it came to responding in ways that would pleasure her.

She shoved her hands under his shirt and felt the abrasive rub of his chest, not smooth and androgynous, but aggressively masculine with its dark hair. Slowly, she pushed the shirt off his broad shoulders, running her hands expertly along the contours of his muscles until the shirt had joined her jumper on the kitchen floor.

He propped himself against the counter, caging her in, and took his time kissing her until her whole body was burning up and she could feel the damp heat pooling between her legs.

'Those jogging bottoms do nothing at all for your superb figure... They should be banned from your wardrobe...' He slipped his fingers underneath the stretchy waistband and tugged them down, allowing her to wriggle out of them, keeping his arms on either side of her so that her movements were restricted. When he looked down, he could see her generous breasts shifting as she moved, soft and succulent. Unable to resist, he captured one and lifted it until her nipple was pouting directly at him. Reluctantly he decided that a full-on assault would have to wait. He wanted to take his time. She had been in his head for days; frankly, from the last time he had seen her, which had been the previous week, and he wasn't going to rush things. He had spent hours fantasising about the next time they met and he intended to see at least some of those fantasies translated into sexy reality.

'Same goes for the underwear...'

'But it's beautiful lacy underwear...' Violet protested with mock hurt. 'Brand new! And very expensive...not the sort of underwear a hard-working teacher can afford too much of...'

'I'll buy you the store. Then you can save your hard-earned salary for other things...'

Violet traced the outline of his flat brown nipples, moistened her fingers with her tongue, traced them again, and relished the way he flexed in immediate, gratifying response.

'I like the underwear,' Damien asserted huskily as he looked down at the lacy lavender piece of nothing. 'I just don't like it on you at this particular moment in time...' He pointedly tugged the lace, then, without giving her time to protest, knelt in front of her.

Looking down with a little gasp, Violet saw the dark bowed head of a supplicant. Even if he was very far from being one. It was an incredible turn-on.

He gently urged her thighs slightly apart and then peeled the underwear back, revealing the lushness of her hair.

With a shudder, she braced herself against the counter, head flung back, knowing that if she wasn't careful she would come in seconds. As his tongue slipped into the groove of her wetly receptive sex, she could hear the faint slick sounds as he licked and explored, with his finger still holding the underwear to one side.

She clenched her fists and gritted her teeth in a mammoth effort not to come against his questing mouth.

She reached down to tug his hair and, on cue, he straightened. Her hands scrabbled helplessly at his trousers and he gave a deep throaty laugh and began to unzip them.

'We haven't made it to the food,' he murmured.

'But at least we're not on the staircase...' As if that said anything, as if it implied any more restraint. It didn't. She was as desperate for him now as she always was when he came through her door.

'No. The kitchen. Lots of scope for being inventive... although would you rather we ate the food than tried playing with it...?' Damien laughed at her shocked expression. She had only had one other lover. He had managed to get that out of her ages ago and, from the sounds of it, that one lover had hardly been sizzling in the bedroom stakes. Every time they made love, he felt as though he was coming to her as her first and the feeling that generated was beyond satisfaction. 'Okay,' he drawled, 'maybe next time. I could teach you some very inventive things that can be done with champagne and cherries...'

He removed his trousers and underwear in one smooth movement. The kitchen was warm and fragrant with the food that had already started cooking. Outside, night had finally drawn in. With the lights off, they were just two shadows touching, feeling and responding to one another.

He breathed in her uniquely feminine scent, something to do with a light floral perfume she wore. It wouldn't have suited everyone but it damn well suited her. Even when they were apart, he could recall the smell and it always managed to get him aroused. How was that possible? He half closed his eyes and was relieved that she couldn't witness that momentary lapse of self-control.

For a few seconds a streak of anger flared inside him. A confused, chaotic anger that resented the peculiar hold he sometimes thought she had over him. He lifted her, taking her by surprise, and sat her on the counter, shoving aside the remnants of food and cutlery still to be cleared.

'What are you doing?' Violet's voice was breathless as her rear made contact with the cool surface of the kitchen counter.

'I'm taking you.'

'But...'

He didn't say anything, instead holding her with one hand while he bent to retrieve the wallet from his trousers, home of at least one extremely useful condom if memory served him right. He was hard and erect, throbbing with an urgent need to sink into her body and feel it wrap itself around him like a glove.

Her hands were on his shoulders and her short pearly nails were digging into his flesh. Leaning back, her breasts were thrust out, nipples standing to attention. He paused briefly to take one into his mouth, sucking hard on it until she was whimpering and crying out and could no longer keep still. His leisurely lovemaking plan had taken a nosedive. Pushing open her legs and angling her just right so that she was ready to receive him, he entered her.

Pleasure exploded in her like a thunderbolt. She could feel every magnificent inch of him as he moved inside her, strong, forceful and with deepening intensity.

This was almost rough and yet it felt so good. She heard herself crying out and the sound seemed to be coming from someone else.

'Talk to me!' he demanded, curling his long fingers into her hair, tugging her into looking at him. Which she did, through half closed eyes because she was pretty much beyond focusing on anything but what he was doing to her.

'Damien!' He talked dirty to her but it was something she had not done in return. Some lingering element of prudishness always seemed to stand in the way.

'Tell me how you're feeling with me inside you!' He emphasised the order with a powerful thrust that made her slide a little way back on the counter.

Violet shivered with heady abandon. She clutched him and told him exactly what he was demanding to know. How it felt to have him in her, filling her up, taking away her ability to think. Her breasts ached for him. She wanted his mouth on them. She just couldn't get enough of him...

To her own ears, every word she uttered seemed to plunge her deeper and deeper into a vulnerable place. Would he pick that up? Was that finely tuned instinct of his sharp enough to pick up what wasn't being said behind the graphic descriptions? That she literally couldn't get enough of him, and not just on the physical, carnal plane, addictive though that was? That, for her, want was very much interlinked with need, which was dangerously close to...

Violet clamped shut her mouth, allowed herself to be carried away to oblivion. She cried out mindlessly as wave upon wave of glorious, unstoppable sensation ripped through her perspiring body, and he echoed her.

When he withdrew from her, turning to deposit the used condom in the bin, she scrambled off the counter and, for a few seconds, barely remembered the train of thought that had been running through her head just before she had climaxed.

It was a luxury that wasn't destined to last long. She went upstairs for a quick shower. She desperately needed some time to herself, time for her thought processes to be followed through to their natural conclusion, even though the conclusion might not be one she wanted to reach.

She had fallen in love with him. How had that happened? Shouldn't there have been a natural progression of steps to get from A to B? Where was the calm, peaceful contentment she had always associated with falling in love? She had been swept along on a roller coaster ride and now she felt ambushed by an emotion that had crept in without her noticing, without her being able to take the necessary precautions. Whilst she had been racing with the devil and calling it *experience*, a *one-off*, love had been quietly settling like cement and now she felt constricted, unable to move and as fragile as a piece of spun glass.

She went downstairs to find that he had tidied the kitchen, which surely must have been a first for him, and waiting for her with a glass of wine in his hand. His trousers were back on, as was the shirt, although he hadn't bothered to do up the buttons on the shirt which hung rakishly loose, revealing a sliver of bronzed torso.

'Full marks for the appetiser...' Damien sipped some of his wine and regarded her over the rim of the glass. If she had used a shower cap, it hadn't done its job. Damp tendrils clung to her cheeks. She looked clean and rosy and unbelievably sexy, especially with the V-necked striped T-shirt she had put on, which allowed a generous view of her cleavage. It was a constant source of mystery that her appeal hadn't diminished over the course of time. Why was that? Was it because he was fully aware that they came from opposite ends of the pole? That, for a man like him—a man who didn't want commitment—he had found his match in a woman who probably *did* want commitment but not with a man like him? Could that be it?

Violet's eyes skittered away from his beautiful, sinfully sexy face. Every compliment he paid her had to do with sex, with her body, with the physical. She could see now that that had been the start of her downfall. Those husky words of rampant appreciation, delivered with intent, had arrowed in on a part of her that had always been insecure and found their mark. Like a flower coming into bloom, she had opened up and grown in an area of her life that had been stunted and underdeveloped. He had made her feel like a woman, a powerful, beautiful, engaging woman, and she had run with the sensation. She had let him in and, without even realising it, had seen beyond their differences to all the things about him that were strangely endearing.

'Damien...we need to...to talk...'

He continued to smile that crooked little half smile of his but his eyes were suddenly watchful. Women wanting *to talk* was usually synonymous with women *saying things he didn't want to hear.*

'I'm listening.' He strolled across to one of the kitchen chairs and sat down, looking at her carefully as she shuffled to the chair opposite him, so that the width of the table was separating them.

'It's been a while, Damien. Your mother has responded really well to treatment and is out of the danger zone. I agreed to all of this...pretending, the charade...for my sister and then I carried on with it for myself, because I was talked into putting sexual attraction above everything else...'

'Ah. I get it. Are we going to start on a blame game, Violet? With me cast in the role of seducer of innocent girls? If that's the case, then I suggest you have a rethink before you get on your soapbox.'

Violet had forgotten this side to him, the side that could withdraw and grow cold. The fact that it was still there, right beneath the surface, was a timely reminder of why it was so important to begin detaching herself from this relationship, if indeed relationship was what it could be called.

'I wasn't going to do that.'

'No?' Damien drawled. He hadn't been expecting this, not after having had mind-blowing sex, and tension lent a hard, mocking edge to his voice. 'Because no one pointed to a bed and then held a gun to your head while you got undressed.'

'I know that! Why are you being so...so horrible?'

'I'm just waiting to hear what you have to say and reminding you that you were an eager and willing volunteer when it came to sex.' She couldn't meet his eyes. What the hell was going on? How could everything change in a matter of seconds? His confusion angered him because it was yet another niggling reminder that he was not as much in control with this woman as he would have liked to have been.

'I'm saying that I think it would be a good idea if we... we...took a step back...' Violet lowered her eyes and frowned into the glass of wine which had somehow found its way in front of her.

'A step back...'

'Your mother is more than stable enough to deal with our relationship hitting the rocks. She's back to doing stuff with Dominic, can go out in her garden now and again... I feel that the time has come for us to get back to our normal lives...'

'And between us making love in the kitchen and you going to have a shower...you've reached this decision *when...? Exactly...?*'

'I don't have to give you any explanations of when or why I've reached my decision, Damien. It's over. I'm not like you. I can't carry on sleeping with you, knowing that it's something that's not going anywhere.'

'Where do you want it to go?' Damien asked, as quick as a flash.

'I don't want it to go anywhere!'

'And what if I tell you that I don't want what we have to end yet? Doubtless my mother is strong enough to recover from a crash and burn relationship, even if she's unduly fond of you, but it's long ceased to be about my mother, as you well know.' Suddenly restless, he vaulted to his feet, glass in one hand, and began to pace the tiny kitchen. He'd never been dumped by a woman. Pride alone should have had him gathering his jacket and heading for the door. Hadn't he made it his mission to avoid the hassle of the demanding woman? And what was she demanding anyway? She had always made it quite clear that they were poles apart, that he was not the blueprint of the kind of man she would ever consider settling down with.

So...was it money? Underneath all the protestations of not being materialistic, had she become used to the opulence that surrounded him wherever he went? Had she glimpsed a vision of how life could be if she could get access to his? He stifled a sudden feeling of intense disappointment. He was a realist and this was the explanation that made the most sense.

His brain locked into gear. He still wanted her and, whether she admitted it or not, she was still hot for him. So maybe she didn't feel as though she had a stake in their relationship. She made a big song and dance of not wanting to accept anything from him but, in so doing, did she feel that she was utterly disposable? That, despite his offers to buy her no less than he would have bought for any of his lovers, he found her in any way less attractive? If only... Just thinking about the way her breasts spilled heavily out of her bra was enough to engage his mind for a few seconds on a completely different path. If he had felt, in any way, that the sex was beginning to wane, he might have shrugged and taken his leave but he was an expert when it came to gauging responses. He couldn't remember a time when the woman had been the flagging partner and it wasn't the case now. Nor was he about to give up a sex life that was second to none.

'There's something I want you to see.'

Violet was taken aback by a remark that seemed to come from nowhere. 'What is it?'

'Wait here.' In the heat of the moment, he had forgotten the costly item of jewellery nestling in its classy black and gold box. His fait accompli present. Whoever said that the Great One didn't work in mysterious ways?

She was still sitting in the same position in the kitchen when he returned and extended his hand. 'For you,' he informed her solemnly. 'I hear what you're saying and this is just a small measure of what you mean to me...'

Violet took the box but already she could feel her skin beginning to get clammy. *What he meant to her.* How many times had she told him that she didn't want anything from him? She lifted the lid of the box and stared down at an item of jewellery that she knew would have been spectacularly expensive. What she meant to him would never be love, it certainly wasn't durability. She was his willing plaything and her worth could be counted in banknotes. She fought down the stupid urge to cry over a piece of jewellery that would have had any other woman shrieking in delight.

'I don't want it.' She stuck it back in the box, snapped shut the lid and handed it to him.

'What do you mean? I know you've made a big deal about not accepting anything from me, but you want to know what this...what we have...means to me...take it in the spirit with which it was given.' He obviously wasn't about to relieve her of the necklace.

'I think it's time we called this a day, Damien.' It hurt just saying that but say it she knew she had to. In that single gesture he had made her feel sordid and cheap.

'Where the hell is this coming from?'

'I can't be bought for a few weeks or months of sex

until you get tired of me and send me on my way with... with *what*...? Something even bigger and more expensive? A really huge pat on the back, it was nice knowing you goodbye gift?'

Damien wondered how long she had been contemplating the outcome of their relationship and working herself up to wanting more. Was she holding him to ransom or did she genuinely want out and if she did genuinely want out, how was it that she was still on fire for him? No, that made no sense.

But if she wanted more, if she wanted a passport to a lifestyle she could never have attained in a million years, then was it so inconceivable that he give it to her...?

'I don't want to buy you,' he murmured. 'I want to marry you...'

CHAPTER NINE

'SORRY?' THERE WAS a rushing sound in her ears. She thought it might have temporarily impaired her hearing.

'You say you can't be in a relationship if you think it's not going anywhere. Curious considering we embarked on this relationship in the expectation that it wouldn't go anywhere.'

'I didn't think a game of make-believe would…would…' Violet was still grappling with what he had said. Had he actually asked her to marry him? Had she imagined the whole thing? He certainly didn't have the expectant, love struck look of a man who had just voiced a marriage proposal.

'Nor did I. And yet it did and now here we are. Which brings me back to my marriage proposal.'

So, she hadn't been imagining it. And yet nothing in his expression gave any hint that he was talking about anything of import. His eyes were unreadable, his beautiful face coolly speculative. Violet, on the other hand, could feel a burning that began in the pit of her stomach and moved outwards.

Marriage? To Damien Carver? The concept was at once too incredible to believe and yet fiercely seductive. For a few magical seconds, her mind leapfrogged past all the obvious glitches in his wildly unexpected proposal. She was in love with the man who had asked her to marry him! Even when she had been going out with Stu, even though they had occasionally talked about marriage, she had never felt this wonderful surge of pure happiness.

Reality returned and she regretfully left her happy ever after images behind. 'Why would you want to marry me?'

'I'm enjoying what we have. I'm not getting any younger. Yes, at the time we started out on our charade, I had not given a passing thought to settling down, even though I realised that that was what my mother wanted...'

Too hurt by past rejection to go there again...went through Violet's head.

'Now I can see that it makes sense.'

'Makes sense?'

'We get along. You've bonded with my family. They like you. My mother sings your praises. Dominic tells me that you're one of a kind, a gem.' He paused, thought of Annalise with distaste, wondered how he could ever have been so naive as to think that only idiots viewed disability as an unacceptable challenge. He remembered how he had borne the insult delivered to his brother as much as if it had been directly delivered to him. Annalise might have been attractive and clever, but neither of those attributes could have made up for her basic inability to step out of the box. Her neatly laid out future had not included hitches of that nature. Over the years, he had bumped into her, sometimes coincidentally, occasionally at her request. She never mentioned Dominic but she always made a point of informing him how much she had grown up. The fact that Violet naturally and without trying had endeared herself to his mother and his brother counted for a great deal.

'You've asked me to marry you because I get along with your family?'

'Well...that's not the complete story. There's also the

incredible sex...' He scanned her flushed cheeks with lingering appreciation.

'So let me get this straight. You've asked me to marry you because I've been accepted by your family, because we get along and because we're good in bed together. It's not exactly the marriage proposal I dreamed of as a girl.' She kept her voice steady and calm. Inside, her heart was hammering as she absorbed the implications of his proposal. This wasn't about love or a starry-eyed desire to walk off into the sunset with her, holding hands, knowing that they were soulmates, destined to be together for the rest of their lives. This was a marriage proposal of convenience.

'And what when we get tired of one another? I mean, lust doesn't last for ever.' And without love as its foundation, whatever was left when the lust bit disappeared would crumble into dust. When that happened, would he decide that being stuck in a loveless marriage was maybe not quite the sensible option he had gone for? Would his eyes begin to wander? Would he see that other options were available? Of course he would and where would that leave her? Nursing even more heartbreak than if she walked away now with her pride and dignity intact.

'I don't like hypothesising.' Why hadn't she just said yes? He was giving her what any other woman on the planet would want. He knew that without a shred of conceit. He had a lot to offer and he was offering it to her, so what was with the hesitancy and the thousand and one questions? Would he have to fill out an informal questionnaire? To find out if he passed with flying colours?

'I know, but sometimes it's important to look ahead,' Violet persisted stubbornly. In some strange way, this marriage proposal was the nail in the coffin of their relationship. At least as far as she was concerned. She might have wondered aloud where they were going, but she knew, deep down, that she would have been persuaded to carry on, just as she knew that, in carrying on, she would have clung to the belief that her love was returned, that it was just a question of time. She would have allowed hope to propel her forward. But he had proposed what would be a sham of a marriage and she knew, now, exactly where she stood with him.

He liked her well enough but primarily he liked her body. And the added bonus was that she got along with Eleanor and Dominic. When the scales were balanced, he doubtless thought that they weighed in favour of putting a ring on her finger.

'It's not necessary to look ahead,' Damien countered, but sudden unease was stirring a potent mix of anger and bewilderment inside him. 'And I'm not sure where the cross-examination is leading.'

'I can't accept your offer,' Violet said bluntly. 'I'm sorry.'

'Come again?'

'*You* might think we're suited, but I don't.'

'Do we or do we not have amazing sexual chemistry? Do I or do I not turn you on until you're begging me to take you?'

'That's not the point.'

'So you're back to this business of looking for your soulmate. Is that it?'

'There's nothing wrong in thinking that when you settle down you'll do so with the right guy...'

'Do you know the statistics when it comes to divorce? One in three. May even be one in two and a half. For every woman with stars in her eyes and dreams of rocking chairs on verandas with her husband when they're eighty-four with the great-grandchildren running around their feet, I'll show you a hundred who have recently signed their divorce papers and are complaining about the cost of the lawyer's fees. For every child at home with both parents, I'll show you a thousand who have become nomads, travelling between parents and inheriting an assorted family of half-siblings and step-siblings along the way.' He raked impatient, frustrated fingers through his hair. She had made noises about wanting more, and he had blithely assumed that the more she claimed to be wanting was with *him*. It hadn't occurred to him that the more she wanted was with someone else. There was still this amazing, once in a lifetime buzz between them. Was it his fault that he had interpreted that in the only way that seemed possible? And yet here she was, turning him down flat.

'I know that,' Violet said, her mouth stubbornly downturned. Of course, every argument he might use to persuade her that tying the knot was a sensible outcome to their relationship would be based in statistics. In the absence of real emotion, statistics would come in very handy.

She was also aware that sex was only part of the drive behind his proposal. Eleanor's illness had shattered the complacent world he had established around himself and forced him into re-evaluating his relationship with his brother and, by extension, his mother. It had been easy for him to justify his interaction with them and convince himself that there was nothing out of kilter by throwing money in their direction. They had wanted for nothing. Damien had not told her that himself. She had garnered that information via Eleanor, passing remarks, rueful observations... However, as everyone knew, money was not the be-all and end-all when it came to relationships and he had been helped in his fledgling attempts to rebuild what had been lost thanks to her. She knew that without having to be told. She had not entered this peculiar arrangement ever thinking that it would extend beyond the absolutely necessary and yet it had and now all of that had entered the murky mix of logic and rationale that lay behind his proposal.

She didn't want to end up being the convenient other half in a relationship where she would inevitably be taken for granted, nor was it fair on either Eleanor or Dominic for her to slot into their lives where she would eventually pick up the slack, enabling Damien to return to his workaholic life which had no room for anyone, least of all a wife. Even a wife he might temporarily be in lust with.

And yet when she thought of waking up next to him, being able to turn and reach out and touch his warm, responsive body...every morning...

When she half closed her eyes she could recall the feel of his mouth all over her body, kissing and licking and exploring, and a treacherous little voice in her head insisted on telling her that that could be hers. Lust could last a very long time, couldn't it? It could last for ever. It could turn into something else. Couldn't it?

And yet he had approached her the way a person would approach a mathematical equation that needed solving. And that wasn't right. Not when it came to marriage.

But she still had to take a deep breath and steel herself against being sidetracked. Especially when he was sitting right there in front of her, his hands loosely linked, his body leaning towards her, his dark, sinfully beautiful face stirring all sorts of rebellious thoughts inside her.

'But—' she inhaled deeply '—I'm on the side of the minority who actually have working marriages and kids with both parents.' She plucked at her jumper with nerveless fingers. 'And please stop looking at me as though I'm mad. There are some of us out there who prefer to dream rather than just cave in and think that we're never going to be happy...'

'No one's talking about being happy or not being happy...' Damien interrupted impatiently. 'Where did you get that idea from? Did I ask you to marry me with the sub-clause that you shouldn't hold out for happiness?' He wondered why he was continuing to pursue this. She had turned him down and it was time now to take his leave. And yet, although he could feel the sharp teeth of pride kicking in, something was compelling him to stay. Was it because he was keenly aware of how awkward it was going to be breaking the news of their break-up to his mother and Dominic? Made sense. Who liked to be the harbinger of bad news, as he undoubtedly would be? Were it any other woman, he would have left by now. Actually, were it any other woman he would not have proposed in the first place.

'We're not suited. Not in any way that makes sense for a long-term relationship. We might enjoy...you know... the physical side of things...' At this point, she felt faint at that physical side of things no longer being attainable. No more of that breathless excitement. No more melting as their bodies united. But, much more than that, no more heady anticipation knowing that the man she loved was going to be walking through her front door, taking her in his arms... How had she only managed to now work out what should have been obvious from the start? That so much more than just her body looked forward to seeing him? That he had awakened a side to her that she never knew existed and something like that didn't happen in a vacuum? That she just didn't have the sort of personality that could lock away various sides of herself and only bring them out when appropriate?

She had sleep walked herself into loving him and it was a feeling that would never be returned. No amount of persuasive arguments about divorce statistics could change that.

'You're repeating yourself. I don't think there's much point to my remaining here to listen to any more of the same old.' He made to stand and a wave of sickening panic rushed through her at speed, with the force and power of a tsunami.

'But I know you agree with me!' Desperate to keep him with her just a little bit longer, Violet sprang to her feet and placed a restraining hand on his arm.

He looked down at it with withering eyes. 'Our days of touching are over. So...if you don't mind?' He raised one cool eyebrow and Violet removed her hand with alacrity.

'We would end up in a bitter, corrosive relationship if we got married,' she gabbled on, clasping her hands tightly together because she wanted to reach out again and pluck at him to stay. His face was stony. 'I'm sorry I ever said anything about...about... We'd be far better off staying just as we are...' Violet knew that she was backtracking and that there was desperation in that but there was a void opening up in front of her that she knew would be impossible to fill. It was dark and bottomless and terrifying. So what if they just carried on the way they were? Would it be the end of the world? And wouldn't it be better than this? Being a martyr? Hadn't she agreed with him once that martyrdom was cold comfort?

'I don't think so,' Damien said coolly, as he began getting his things together. 'That window's closed, I'm afraid.'

Violet fell back and looked at him in numb silence until he was ready to leave.

'I'll tell my mother this weekend that things didn't work out between us.'

'Let me come with you.' She could feel tears pushing to the back of her eyes.

'What for?'

'I'd like to explain to her myself that...that...'

'There's nothing to explain, Violet. Relationships come and go. Fortunately my mother is in a better place. She'll be able to cope with the disappointment. I wouldn't lose sleep over that if I were you.'

Violet could feel him mentally withdrawing from her at a rate of knots. She hadn't complied and there was no room for anyone in his life who didn't comply.

'Of course I'm going to lose sleep over it! I'm very fond of both Eleanor and Dominic!'

Damien shrugged as though it was of relatively little importance one way or the other. He was moving towards the door. Where was the necklace? No matter. He wanted to tell her that she could consider it a suitable parting gift but he knew he would have to listen to a lecture on all the things money, apparently, couldn't buy. He gritted his teeth at the uncomfortable notion that he would miss those lectures of hers, which had ranged from the ills of money to the misfortune of those who thought they needed it to be happy. She was adept at pointing out all the expensive items that had brought nothing but misery to their owners. She always seemed to have a mental tally at the ready of famous people whose lives had not been improved because they were rich, and had been prone to loftily ignoring him when he pointed out that she should stop reading trashy magazines with celebrity gossip. In between the fantastic sex, which had evolved from their charade in a way that had taken him one hundred per cent by surprise, he was uncomfortably aware that she might have got under his skin in ways he hadn't anticipated.

'In that case,' he returned with supreme indifference, 'I suggest you go see your local friendly doctor and ask him to prescribe you some sleeping pills.'

'How can you be so...so...unsympathetic?' She was traipsing along behind him to the front door. Before she knew it, he was pulling it open, one foot already out as though he couldn't wait to leave her behind.

'There's no point in you having any involvement with me or my family from now on. My mother would be far happier were she spared the tedium of a post-mortem.'

And with that he was gone, slamming the door behind him in a gesture that was as final as the fall of the executioner's axe.

Left on her own, Violet suddenly realised just how lonely the little house was without the promise of his exciting, unsettling presence to bring it to life. She lethargically tidied up the kitchen but her thoughts were exclusively on Damien. She had backed him into a corner and it was no good asking herself whether she had done the right thing or not. You couldn't play around with reality and hope that it might somehow be changed into something else.

But neither could she put thoughts of him behind her as easily as she might have liked. School was no longer gloriously enjoyable because she was busy looking forward to seeing him. There were no little anecdotes saved up for retelling. She spent the following week with the strange sense of having been wrapped up in insulation, something so thick that the outside world seemed to exist around her at a distance. She listened to everyone laughing and chatting but it was all a blur. When Phillipa phoned in a state of high excitement to tell her that she and Andy were getting married at the end of the year, on a beach no less, and would she come over, help her choose a dress or at least a suitably white sarong and bikini, she heard herself saying all the right things but her mind was cloudy, not operating at full whack, as though she had been heavily sedated to the point where her normal reflexes were no longer in proper working order.

Several times she wondered whether she should call Eleanor. But was Damien right? Would his mother be happier to accept their break-up without having to conduct a long conversation about it? Furthermore, what would she say? She had no idea what Damien would have told her. For all she knew, he might have told her that she was entirely to blame, that she had turned into a shrew, a harpy, a gold-digger. It was within his brief to say anything, safe in the knowledge that he wouldn't be contradicted.

And yet she couldn't imagine him being anything other than fair, which, reason told her, was ridiculous, considering the way their relationship had commenced. He had blackmailed her into doing what he wanted. Since when had he turned into a good guy? He had drifted into a sexual relationship for no better reason than she had made a change from the sort of women he usually dated, but he had nothing to offer aside from a consummate ability to make love. So how was it that she had managed to fall in love with him? For every glaring downside in his personality, her rebellious mind insisted on pointing out the good things about him—his wit, his sincere attempts to do what was right for his family, his incredible intellect, which would have made a lesser man sneering and contemptuous of those less gifted than he was, and yet, in Damien's case, did not.

The decision to call Eleanor or not was taken out of her hands when, a week and a half after Damien had walked out of her house, Eleanor called.

She sounded fine. Yes, yes, yes, everything was coming along nicely. The prognosis was good…

'But my son tells me that the two of you have decided to take a break…'

So that was how he had phrased it. Clever in so far as he had left open the possibility that the break might not be permanent. His mother's disappointment would be drip-fed in small stages, protecting her from any dramatic stress their separation might have engendered.

'Um...yes...that's the...er...plan...'

'I confess that I was very surprised indeed when Damien told me...'

'And I'm so sorry I wasn't there to break the news as well, Eleanor.' Violet rushed into apologetic speech. 'I wanted so much to...er...'

'I'd never seen Damien so relaxed and happy.' Eleanor swept past Violet's stammering interruption. 'A different man. I've always worried about the amount of time he devotes to work, but you must have done something wonderful to him, my darling, because he's finally seemed to get his perspective in order... He hasn't just made time for me, but he's made time for his brother...'

'That's...great...'

'Which is why I'm puzzled as to how it is that suddenly you and he are...taking a break...especially when I can see how much the two of you love one another...'

'No! No, no, no... Damien just isn't...he's...we...'

'You're stumbling over your words, my darling,' Eleanor said gently. 'Take your time. You love my son. I know you do. A woman knows these things when it comes to other women...especially an old lady like me...'

Violet lapsed into temporary defeated silence. What could she say to that? Even with Eleanor talking down the end of a phone, she still had the uncanny feeling that the older woman was seeing right into the very heart of her. 'You're not old,' she finally responded. 'And I'm so glad the treatment's going well...'

'Is that your way of changing the conversation?' Eleanor asked tartly. 'Darling, I do wish we could have sat down and talked about this together, woman to woman. Somehow, hearing it from Damien...well, you know what men are like. He can be terribly tight-lipped when it comes to expressing anything emotional…'

'That's true…'

'So why don't you pop over to his place, say this evening…around eight…? We can…chat…'

With unerring ability, Violet realised that Eleanor had found her Achilles heel. She would have thought that Hell might have frozen over before she faced Damien again. She just wanted to somehow try and get him out of her system and paying him a visit was the last thing destined to achieve that goal. But she was very fond of his mother and Eleanor, despite her cheerful optimism about her health, did not deserve to be stressed out.

She was also still in the throes of guilt at not having spoken to the older woman yet.

'You're in London?'

'Flying visit. Check-up… So, darling, I really must dash now. I'll see you shortly, shall I? Can't tell you how much I'm looking forward to that! Don't think that I'm going to allow you to creep out of my life that easily.'

Those two, Eleanor thought with satisfaction as she peered through the window of her chauffeur-driven car on her way back down to Devon, needed to have their heads banged together. Or at least made to sit and really talk because she refused to believe that whatever had taken place between them couldn't be sorted with a heartfelt conversation. And who better to engineer that but herself? If, at the end of it, things were over, then so be it but Damien had been so sketchy in his details, so alarmingly evasive…and men so often didn't recognise what was best for them…

Violet was disconnected before she had time to start thinking on her feet. Was, for instance, Damien going to be present? Would there be an awkward three-way conversation where they both tried desperately to undo what they had so carefully knitted together at the very beginning? She assumed not. She assumed that Eleanor had invited her for a one to one. She had no idea what she would say to the other woman. She would have to be vague. Her fingers itched to dial Damien's mobile and ask him what he had said to his mother but she felt faint just at the thought of hearing that deep, dark, sexy drawl down the end of the line.

Several hours later, standing in front of the imposing Georgian block, some of which had been converted into luxury apartments, others remaining as vast houses, such as his, Violet had to fight down a sickening attack of nerves.

The road where he lived was a statement to the last word in opulence. Gleaming back wrought-iron railings guarded each of the towering white-fronted mansions. The steps to each front door were identical in their scrubbed cleanliness and the front doors were all black with shiny brass knockers for appearance only as a bank of buzzers was located at the side.

She had only been to his place a handful of times but she remembered it clearly. The exquisite hall with its flagstoned floor, the pale walls, the blond wooden flooring that dominated the huge open spaces. Everything within those mega-expensive walls was of the highest standard and state-of-the-art. There was no clutter. She had always found its lack of homeliness off-putting. Now, as she dithered in front of the imposing black door, she had to take some deep breaths to steady her nerves, even though she was nearly a hundred per cent certain that he would not be at home. A cosy chat with Eleanor and she would be on her way. Her uneasy conscience that she hadn't contacted the older woman would be put to rest. They would meet in the future, of course they would, and it would be fine just as long as Damien wasn't around, and maybe, down the line, he could be around because she would have moved on from him.

She pressed the buzzer and settled back to wait because she was certain that Eleanor would not be moving at the speed of light to get to the door, however keen she was to see her.

It had been a lovely day which had mellowed into a cool but pleasant evening. In this expensive part of London, there were few cars and even less foot traffic and she was idly watching a young woman saunter past on the opposite side of the wide, tree-lined road, attempting to infuse a reluctant puppy with enthusiasm for a walk it clearly didn't want, when the door was pulled open behind her.

The greeting died on her lips. For a few seconds her heart seemed to arrest. Damien framed the doorway. He was wearing a pair of faded black jeans that hugged his long, muscular legs and a white T-shirt, close-fitting enough to outline the strong, graceful lines of his body. Memories of touching that body rushed towards her in a tidal wave of hot awareness. In only a matter of a few months, he had guided her down myriad sensual roads never explored before. Her mouth went dry as she thought of a few of them.

'What are you doing here?' she asked inanely.

'It's my house and, funny…I was just about to ask you the same thing.' He half stepped out, pulling the door behind him and blocking out the light from the hall.

'I came to see your mother.' She just wanted to stare and stare and keep on staring. Instead, she looked down at her shoes, some sensible black ballet pumps that worked well with her skinny jeans. She had stopped dressing to hide. It was one of his many lasting legacies to her—the self-confidence to be the person she was.

'And that would be...? Because...?' Damien leant indolently against the doorframe and folded his arms. His fabulous eyes were veiled and watchful as he stared down at her. However, his nerves were taut and he was angry with himself for the seeping away of his self-control. There was nothing left to be said on the subject of their non-relationship. He had offered her marriage. She had thrown his offer back in his face and he was not a man who allowed second bites at the cherry.

He wondered why she had come. Had she had second thoughts? Had she come round to all the advantages marriage to him would provide? His mouth curled with derision. He shifted as his body refused to cooperate and jumped into gear as his eyes unconsciously traced the sexy outline of her breasts underneath the figure-hugging top she was wearing. But hell, she could wear something only seen on someone's maiden aunt and yet have any red-blooded male spinning round in his tracks to stare. He couldn't understand how he could ever have credited her with being anything but sex on legs. He must have been blind and those tight jeans...that jumper. He wanted to pounce and rip them off her so that he could touch what was underneath. Given the circumstances, it was an entirely inappropriate reaction and he was furious with himself for even allowing his mind to travel down those pathways.

'Because your mother phoned and asked me to come here,' Violet muttered. She balled her hands into fists. So he didn't even have the simple courtesy to ask her inside. He would rather conduct a hostile conversation on his doorstep.

'Pull the other one, Violet. My mother left to return to Devon hours ago. So tell me why you imagine she would be waiting here for you? No, don't bother to answer that. I wasn't born yesterday. I *know* what you're doing here.'

Violet's mouth dropped open and she looked at him in bewilderment. At the same time, it was dawning on her that she had been coaxed into coming to his house by Eleanor, who had schemed for...what, exactly? A heartfelt talk where their so-called differences would be ironed out? And a reconciliation might take place? If only she knew the truth of their relationship.

'And you can forget it.'

'Forget what?'

'Any plan you might be concocting to show up here unannounced and resume where we left off.'

'I wasn't doing any such thing!' Violet gasped.

'Expect me to believe that? When you're dressed in the tightest clothes possible? Showing off your assets to maximum advantage?' He pictured her in the unflattering dress she had worn that very first time when she had hesitantly walked into his office and scowled because the image didn't dispel his reaction to her body.

'You're being ridiculous! Your mother asked me over here. She said she wanted to chat and I felt guilty because I should have called her, I should have made contact!'

Damien was fast reaching the same conclusion as Violet had only seconds before. She hadn't come here to try and entice him back into the bedroom. Having recognised that, he had to firmly bank down the fleeting suspicion that he rather enjoyed the notion of her making a pass at him. Naturally, he would have rejected it. But not before he felt immense satisfaction at having her plead with him for a second chance.

'You're impossible!' Violet could scarcely believe the accusations flying at her. Admittedly, there was some small chance that he might have jumped to the wrong conclusions, but how on earth could he think that she had *dressed to impress*? She was suddenly aware of the tightness of her clothes where she hadn't been before. Her breasts were heavy and aching within the constraints of her lacy bra and, as her eyes travelled upwards, doing a reluctant, hateful tour of his impressive body, she could feel herself getting damp between her thighs. She recalled his fingers down there, his mouth sucking and licking until she was writhing for more.

'You have an ego as big as a cruise liner if you imagine that I would come here to…to…make a pass at you! You're the most arrogant man I've ever met!' She longed to inform him, coldly, that she had moved on, but she couldn't bring herself to utter such a whopper.

As she stood there, floundering in front of his assessing eyes, she heard a voice behind him. A woman's voice. Coy and cajoling. For a few seconds she froze and then her eyes widened as the owner of the voice materialised into view.

How on earth could he have dared to accuse her of wearing tight clothes? The leggy brunette with the short, silky bob was clad in white jeans that fitted like a second skin and a small white vest that left very little to the imagination. She was as slender as a reed and Violet could only stare as the brunette sidled up to Damien and slipped her arm through his.

'Aren't you going to introduce us, darling? Though I guess there's no need. You must be Violet…' The pale blue eyes were glacially cold as she stretched out one thin arm in greeting. 'I'm Annalise…'

CHAPTER TEN

IT WAS RAINING by the time Violet made it back to her house. A fine, needle-sharp drizzle that she barely noticed. She took the Tube and bus back to her house on autopilot. She couldn't think straight and her heart was thumping like a steam engine inside her chest, making it uncomfortable to breathe.

She wanted to block out images of Damien with Annalise. She tried hard to tell herself that it didn't matter, that he was a free man who could do whatever he liked with whomever he liked. Unfortunately, no amount of cool logic could paper over the devastation she felt nor could it stop the flood of painful speculation that assailed her, wave upon wave, upon wave until she wanted to pass out.

He was back with his ex, back with the only woman he had never been able to forget, the only woman to whom he had wanted to commit, fully and without reservation or a list of sensible reasons why the match could work out. It certainly hadn't taken him long to reconnect. Was it because her rejection of his proposal had put things into perspective for him? Made him wake up and realise that marriage was more than a list of dos and don'ts? Had that propelled him to seek out Annalise? Had it reminded him that, in his carefully controlled world, there was still one woman who had broken through the boundaries and that he needed to find her and tell her? They certainly had looked very cosy with one another.

And Annalise was much more his style than she, Violet, could ever hope to be. Tall, skinny, beautiful. Nor did she look like a typical bimbo. No, she looked like one of those rare, annoying breeds—a true beauty who also had brains.

She couldn't look at herself in the mirror as she banged about in the bathroom, getting ready for bed. She didn't want to see the comparisons between her and his ex. Thinking about comparisons drained her of all her self-confidence. Had he only really seen her as a novelty? The broad bean versus the runner bean? Had he fallen into bed with her because she had been *there*? Available and eager? Was he any different from any other man in a situation where opportunity was handed to him on a plate? No one could accuse him of being the sort of guy who took relationships seriously, who held out for the right woman. He was a red-blooded male with a rampant libido who took what he wanted. And she had been there for the taking. And then he had proposed because it was convenient. He was never going to fall in love; he had done that with Annalise, so why not hitch up with the woman who had won his family's approval? Noticeably, he had only proposed when he had woken up to the reality that she might walk out on him.

She climbed into bed and tried to read and only realised that she had actually fallen asleep when she was awakened by two things.

The first was the sound of the rain. It had progressed from a persistent drizzle to the wild rapping of rain against her windows. She had left one window slightly ajar and the voile curtain was blowing furiously under the force of the wind. When she went to close it, she realised that the chest of drawers just underneath was splattered in rainwater but she had no intention of doing anything about that just at the moment.

Because, competing with the howling of the wind and the rain, was the thunderous sound of someone banging on her front door.

Outside, dripping water, Damien was cursing the English weather. Between eight, when he had opened his front door to Violet, and midnight, when he had finally managed to get rid of Annalise, the rain had picked up. Now, at a little after three-thirty, the only thing that could be said in favour of his jumping in his car and coming here was the fact that the roads had been traffic-free.

He noticed that one of the lights in the house had now been turned on and breathed a sigh of relief. He really didn't want to remain outside her house for the remainder of the night, although he would have, had she not answered the door.

Violet had stuck on her bathrobe to see who was at the door. Her immediate thought when she had heard the banging was to imagine that it was someone trying to break in but, almost as soon as she thought that, she realised that it was a ridiculous supposition because since when did intruders give advance notice of their intention by banging on doors?

So was it someone who needed help? She knew her neighbours. The old lady living next door was quite frail. Was there something wrong? She tried and failed to imagine small Mrs Wilson, in her late eighties, having the strength to venture out of her house in the early hours of the morning to bang on a door.

As she hurried downstairs, switching on lights in her wake, she could feel her heart pounding because, of course, there was someone else it might be, but, like her scenario involving the polite burglar knocking to warn her of his imminent break-in, the thought that it might be Damien was too far-fetched to be worth consideration.

The safety chain was on and as she opened the door a crack she knew instantly that the one man she had least expected was standing outside. There was a storm raging outside her house, or so it seemed. The wind was sending his trench coat in all directions and the rain was whipping down at a slant. His feet were planted squarely on the ground but, as she pulled the door open a little wider, he placed his hand against the doorframe to look down at her.

He was drenched. Soaked through.

'What do you want?' Violet wrapped the robe tightly around her. 'What are you doing here?'

'Violet, let me in.'

'Where's your girlfriend, Damien? Is she waiting in the car for you?' She could have kicked herself for mentioning Annalise but, at this point, she really didn't care.

'Let me in.'

'I don't know why you've come but I don't want you here.'

'Please.'

That single word stopped Violet in her tracks. She could feel the rain beating down towards her and she stepped back into the house to avoid being soaked.

'I have nothing to say to you.'

'Maybe there are things that *I* need to say to you.'

But, tellingly, he hadn't followed her into the hall. He remained standing on the doorstep, getting drenched. Was he *hesitant*? Violet thought in some confusion. Surely not! Hesitancy was one of those emotions he didn't do. Along with love. And yet he was still standing there, getting wet and looking at her.

'What could you possibly want to say to me, Damien? I just came to see your mother. I didn't come to try and start back what we had! You're out of my life and if I was a little…a little…disconcerted, it was because I hadn't expected to be confronted with your girlfriend! Quick work, Damien!'

'Ex. Ex-girlfriend. Please let me in, Violet. I'm not going to barge my way into your house and if you tell me that you don't want to see me again, then I'll go.'

Tell him to go and she would never see him again. Of course, that would be for the best. They really had nothing to say to one another. Less than nothing. Maybe he had braved the foul weather because he felt badly, because he wanted to explain to her, face to face, how it was that Annalise was back in his life. Perhaps he thought that he might be doing her a favour by playing the good guy and filling her in. And still, painful though that thought was, her mind seized up when she thought of him disappearing back into the driving rain and vanishing out of her life for good, without saying what he had to say.

'It's late.' She stood aside and folded her arms as he dripped his way into her hall and removed the trench coat. His hair was plastered down and he raked his fingers through it, which just scattered the drops of water.

'Perhaps I could have a towel…'

'I suppose so,' Violet muttered a little ungraciously.

She returned a few minutes later to find him in the same spot, standing in the hall. Where was the guy who had never hesitated to make himself at home? Where was the self-assured man who knew the layout of her kitchen, who might be expected to make himself a cup of coffee?

She watched in silence as he roughly dried himself. He made no attempt to remove his jumper, which clung to him, and she bit back the temptation to tell him to take it off because if he didn't he would catch cold.

'I'm sorry you had to find Annalise in my house,' Damien said heavily.

Violet broke eye contact and headed towards the kitchen. He might be comfortable having a conversation neither of them wanted in the middle of her hallway, but she needed to sit down and she needed something to do with her hands. She was aware of him following her. It might be after three in the morning but every sense in her was on red alert.

'It was unexpected, that's all.' She busied herself with the kettle, mugs, spoons, keeping her back to him because she was scared that if he saw her face he would be able to read what was going on in her mind. 'Like I said…'

'I know. My mother got you there on false pretences. I spoke to her. She…thought that a little bit of undercover matchmaking wouldn't go amiss…'

'And did you tell her about Annalise?'

'No. There *is* no Annalise.'

And he didn't know what had possessed him to open the door to her when she had showed up the previous evening. He had opened the door and he had invited her in. She had heard about Violet. Friend of a friend of a friend had seen them together at a restaurant…there were rumours…gossip, even…she was curious…he could talk to *her*…after all, they had a history…they were connected… weren't they…?

At that point, Damien knew that he should have escorted her out. It was quite different bumping into her at a random company affair or even occasionally meeting her in a public place where, like a masochist, he could be reminded of his narrow escape, but letting her into his house had not been a good idea.

And yet hadn't there been a part of him that had *questioned* whether Annalise might not be reintroduced into his life? Violet had walked out and he hadn't known what to do with the chaos of his emotions when she had left. Hadn't a part of him bitterly wondered whether Annalise, who could never wield the sort of crazy control over him that Violet had, might not just be the better bet? He had had his marriage proposal chucked back in his face. Annalise...well, he could buy her and what you could buy, you could control.

He had let her in and the moment of questioning had gone as quickly as it had arrived. But she was in his house and, foolishly, he had prevaricated about throwing her out. Would it have been asking too much of fate to step aside for a while and not steer Violet towards his doorstep?

'What do you mean?' Clasping her cup of coffee between her hands, she stalked out towards the sitting room. She hadn't offered him anything to drink. It was meant as a pointed reminder that she had only allowed him in under duress, but really, if he thought that he could somehow try and come up smelling of roses, then he was mistaken.

She sat down and when she looked up it was to find him hovering by the door.

'You might as well sit down, Damien. But I'm tired and I'm not in the mood for a conversation.'

'I know.' He removed the jumper, which was heavy and wet, and carefully put it over one of the radiators, then he prowled over to the window, parted the curtains a crack and peered outside into the bleak rainy night. 'I didn't invite her,' he offered at last. 'She showed up.'

'It's none of my business anyway.'

'Everything I do should be your business,' Damien muttered, flushing darkly. 'At least, that's what I'd like.' He thought that this must be what it felt like to indulge in a dangerous sport, one where the outcome was a life or death situation. 'And I would understand if you don't believe me, Violet.'

'I don't understand what you're saying.' Violet's voice was wary. She couldn't tear her eyes away from him. He was even more compelling in this strangely vulnerable, puzzling mood. It was a side to him she had never seen before and it threw her. He circled the room, one hand in his trouser pocket, the other playing with his hair, before finally standing directly in front of her so that she was forced to look up at him.

'Would you mind sitting down? I'm getting a crick in my neck looking up at you.'

'I need you to sit next to me,' Damien told her roughly. 'There are things I need...to say to you and I need to have you...next to me when I say them...' He sat on the sofa and patted the spot next to him. 'Please, Violet.' He grinned crookedly and looked away. 'I bet you've never heard me say *please* so many times.'

'I can't do this. Just tell me why you've come. You didn't have to. I know we had...something. You probably feel obliged to explain yourself to me. Well, don't. So we broke up and you've returned to the love of your life.' Violet shrugged. The vacant space on the sofa next to him begged her to fill it but she wasn't going to give in to that dangerous temptation. He had this effect on her...could make her take her eyes off the ball and she wasn't going to fall victim to that now.

'I told you Annalise was my ex and she still is.'

'And this is the ex you've seen on and off over the years?'

'Sometimes it pays to be reminded of your mistakes.'

'I beg your pardon?'

'I can't talk when you're sitting on the other side of the room. It's hard enough...as it is... I don't usually...'

He raked his fingers through his hair and realised that he was shaking.

Reluctantly, Violet went to perch on the sofa. Just closing this small gap between them made her stomach twist in nervous knots.

'Once upon a time,' Damien said heavily, 'I fancied myself in love with Annalise. I was young. She was beautiful, clever…ticked all the boxes. It was a whirlwind romance, just the sort of thing you read about in books, and I proposed to her.'

'You don't need to tell me any of this,' Violet interjected stiffly and yet she wanted to hear every word of it.

'I need to and I want to. You'd be surprised if I told you that I've never felt the slightest inclination to share any of the details of my relationship with Annalise with anyone.'

'I wouldn't be surprised. You keep everything locked up inside.'

'I do.'

'You're agreeing with me. Why?'

'Because you're right. I've always kept everything locked up inside. It's why no one has ever known what Annalise really meant to me.'

And he was about to tell her. Yet the details so far weren't adding up to the love of his life and she fought to subdue the tendril of hope unfurling inside her that there might be another side of the story. Ever since she had met him, her placid life had become a roller coaster ride, hope alternating with despair before rising again to the surface like a terrible virus over which she had no control. Did she want to get back on that ride? Did she want to nurture that tendril of hope until it began growing into something uncontrollable? She could feel tears of frustration and dismay prick the back of her eyes. She curled her fingers in her lap and was shocked when he reached out and slowly uncurled them so that he could abstractedly play with them.

It was just the lightest of touches but it was enough to send her body into wild shock.

'Annalise turned me down because she couldn't cope with the prospect of being saddled, at some point in time, with a disabled brother-in-law.'

'What?' This was not what she had been expecting to hear and she leaned forward to catch what he was saying.

'She met Dominic and I knew instantly that she couldn't cope with his condition. For Annalise, everything was about perfection. Dominic was not perfect. She knew that at some point I would be responsible for him. She had visions of him living with us, her having to incorporate him into the perfect world she was desperate to have.'

'That's...that's awful...' Violet reached out and rested her hand on his arm and felt him shudder.

'From that moment onwards, I knew that never again would I put myself in a position of vulnerability. I enjoyed women but they had their place and I made damn sure that they never overstepped it. And just in case I was ever tempted to forget, I made sure that Annalise was never completely eliminated from my life.'

'And yet she was there tonight. In your...in your house...'

'You turned me down. I asked you to marry me and you turned me down.'

Because you couldn't love me! Despite everything he had said, he still didn't love her. He was just explaining why he couldn't. She would do well to remember that and not get swept away by this strange mood he was in and his haltering confidences.

'When Annalise showed up on my doorstep, I let her in because I was...not myself. No, that doesn't really explain it either. I was going out of my mind. Had been ever since we broke up. I told myself that it was for the best, that you could damn well go your own way and find out first-hand that there was no such thing as the perfect soulmate, but I couldn't think straight, couldn't function... I resented the fact that even when you were no longer around, you were still managing to control my behaviour.'

Violet was finding it impossible to filter the things he was telling her.

'I am ashamed to say that I briefly considered Annalise a known quantity and that maybe the devil you know... Of course, it was just a passing aberration. I got rid of her as fast as I could and then I waited...for normality to return. It didn't.'

'So you came here...to tell me what? Exactly?' She pinned her mouth into a stubborn line but she had broken out in a fine film of nervous perspiration. She tried to ignore the way he was still toying distractedly with her fingers and the way their bodies were leaning urgently towards each other, radiating a fevered heat that made her want to swoon. His familiar scent filled her nostrils. Once, she had found him devastatingly attractive. Having slept with him, knowing the contours of his lean, hard body, the body along which she had run her hands and her mouth so many times, made him horribly, painfully irresistible. Familiarity hadn't bred contempt. The opposite. It had ratcheted up the level of his sexual pull to the extent that she could barely think of anything else as she continued to stare at him, pupils dilated, dreading the way her body was reacting in ways her brain was telling it not to.

'That I proposed to you because...it made sense. I didn't realise...' He withdrew his hand to tousle his dark hair. 'I didn't think that I might have needed you in my life for reasons that didn't make any sense. That you'd climbed under my skin and it wasn't just to do with the good sex.'

'What was it to do with?'

'I'm in love with you. I don't know when that happened or how, but...'

'Say that again?'

'Which bit?'

'The bit about being in love with me.' A feeling of being on top of the world, of pure joy, filled her like life-saving oxygen. She felt heady and giddy and euphoric all at the same time. 'You didn't say,' she told him accusingly, but she was half laughing, half wanting to cry. 'Why didn't you say?'

'I didn't know...until you left...'

She flung herself into his arms and sighed with pure contentment when he wrapped his arms around her and held her close, so close that she could hear the beating of his heart. 'You were so arrogant,' she told him. 'You forced me into an arrangement I hated. You broke all the rules when it came to the sort of guy I could ever be interested in. You didn't want any kind of long-term relationship and I've never approved of men who move from woman to woman. And, as well, I was convinced that you were still wrapped up with Annalise, that you'd never let the memory go, that she was the ex no one had ever been able to live up to. On all fronts you were taboo, and then I met your family and I got sucked in to you...to all of you...and it was like being in quicksand. When you proposed, when you listed all the reasons why marrying me would make sense, I finally woke up to the fact that the one reason why anyone should get married was missing. You didn't love me. I thought you didn't know how and you never would and I couldn't accept your offer, knowing that the power balance would be so uneven. I would forever be the helpless, dependent one, madly in love with you and waiting for the time when you got tired of me physically and the axe fell.'

'And now?'

'And now I'm the happiest person in the world!'

'So if I ask you again to marry me…this time for all the right reasons…'

'Yes! Yes! Yes!'

Damien shuddered with relief. He felt as if he'd been holding his breath ever since he'd walked into the house. His arms tightened around her and he breathed in the fresh floral smell of her hair. 'You've made me the happiest person in the world as well…' Then he gave a low rumble of laughter. 'And I don't think my mother or Dominic will mind too much either…'

EPILOGUE

THEY DIDN'T MIND. Not when Damien and Violet showed up, surprising both Dominic and Eleanor, the following day.

'Of course,' Eleanor said smugly, 'I knew it was just a case of getting you two together so that you could sort out your silly differences. Damien, darling, I love you but you can be stubborn and there was no way that I was going to allow the best thing that ever happened to you to slip through your fingers. Now, let's discuss the wedding plans… Something big and fancy? Or small and cosy…?'

'Fast,' was Damien's response.

They were married six weeks later at the local church close to his mother's house. Dominic was the best man and he performed his duties with a gravity that was incredibly touching and, later, at the small reception which they held at the house, he was cheered on to speak and, bright red, raised his glass to the best brother a man could have.

Phillipa didn't stop teasing her sister that she had managed to beat her down the aisle. 'And you'll probably be preggers by the time I make my vows in my white sarong and crop top!' she wailed, which, as it turned out, was exactly what happened.

On a hot day, watching her sister and her assortment of new-found friends, with the sound of the surf competing with the little band drumming out the wedding march as

Phillipa took her vows, Violet leaned against her husband, hand on the gentle swell of her stomach, and wondered whether it was possible to be happier.

From those inauspicious beginnings, the relationship she never thought would happen had blossomed into something she could not live without, and the man who had fought against becoming involved had turned into the man who frequently told her how much he loved her and how much he hated leaving her side.

'I've come to terms with the value of delegation,' he had confided without a shade of regret, 'and when my son is born...'

'Or daughter...'

'*Or daughter*...I intend to explore its value even more...'

Thinking about what else they explored now brought a hectic flush to her cheeks and, as if reading her mind, Damien leant to whisper in her ear, 'Okay. The ceremony is over. What do you say to us staying for the meal and then heading back to the hotel? I think I need to remind myself of what your nipples taste like... I'm getting withdrawal symptoms...'

Violet blushed and laughed and looked up at him. 'That would be rude...' she said sternly, but already her mind was leaping ahead to the way her developing body fascinated him, the way he lavished attention on her breasts, even more abundant now, and suckled on her nipples, which were bigger and darker and a source of never-ending attention the minute her clothes were off. She felt the heat pool between her legs when she thought of them lying in the air-conditioned splendour of their massive curtained bed, his head on her stomach while he stroked her thighs with his hand, then tickled the swollen, engorged bud of her clitoris, which she would swear was even more sensitive now.

'But I'm sure Phillipa will understand...' she conceded as he planted a fleeting kiss on the corner of her mouth. 'After all, we pregnant ladies can't stay in the heat for too long...'

* * * * *

NOT JUST THE BOSS'S PLAYTHING

CAITLIN CREWS

To the fabulous Sharon Kendrick, who sorted out what was wrong with an early draft of this book on a long, rainy, Irish drive to and from Sligo town (and an atmospheric tour of Yeats country)—both of which amounted to a Master Class in writing Harlequin Presents.

And to Abby Green, Heidi Rice, Fiona Harper and Chantelle Shaw, for our inspiring days in Delphi.

And to all the readers who wrote me to ask for Nikolai's story. This is for you most of all!

CHAPTER ONE

TORTURE WOULD BE preferable to this.

Nikolai Korovin moved through the crowd ruthlessly, with a deep distaste for his surroundings he made no effort to hide. The club was one of London's sleekest and hottest, according to his assistants, and was therefore teeming with the famous, the trendy and the stylish.

All of whom appeared to have turned up tonight. In their slick, hectic glory, such as it was. It meant Veronika, with all her aspirations to grandeur, couldn't be far behind.

"Fancy a drink?" a blank-eyed creature with masses of shiny black hair and plumped-up lips lisped at him, slumping against him in a manner he imagined was designed to entice him. It failed. "Or anything else? Anything at all?"

Nikolai waited impatiently for her to stop that insipid giggling, to look away from his chest and find her way to his face—and when she did, as expected, she paled. As if she'd grabbed hold of the devil himself.

She had.

He didn't have to say a word. She dropped her hold on him immediately, and he forgot her the moment she slunk from his sight.

After a circuit or two around the loud and heaving club, his eyes moving from one person to the next as they propped up the shiny bar or clustered around the leather seating areas, cataloging each and dismissing them, Nikolai stood with his back to one of the giant speakers and simply waited. The music, if it could be called that, blasted out a bass line he could feel reverberate low in his spine as if he was under sustained attack by a series of concussion grenades. He almost wished he was.

He muttered something baleful in his native Russian, but it was swept away in the deep, hard thump and roll of that terrible bass. *Torture.*

Nikolai hated this place, and all the places like it he'd visited since he'd started this tiresome little quest of his. He hated the spectacle. He hated the waste. Veronika, of course, would love it—that she'd be *seen* in such a place, in such company.

Veronika. His ex-wife's name slithered in his head like the snake she'd always been, reminding him why he was subjecting himself to this.

Nikolai wanted the truth, finally. She was the one loose end he had left, and he wanted nothing more than to cut it off, once and for all. Then she could fall from the face of the planet for all he cared.

"I never loved you," Veronika had said, a long cigarette in her hand, her lips painted red like blood and all of her bags already packed. "I've never been faithful to you except by accident." Then she'd smiled, to remind him that she'd always been the same as him, one way or another: a weapon hidden in plain sight. "Needless to say, Stefan isn't yours. What sane woman would have *your* child?"

Nikolai had eventually sobered up and understood that whatever pain he'd felt had come from the surprise of Veronika's departure, not the content of her farewell speech. Because he knew who he was. He knew *what* he was.

And he knew her.

These days, his avaricious ex-wife's tastes ran to lavish

Eurotrash parties wherever they were thrown, from Berlin to Mauritius, and the well-manicured, smooth-handed rich men who attended such events in droves—but Nikolai knew she was in London now. His time in the Russian Special Forces had taught him many things, much of which remained etched deep into that cold, hard stone where his heart had never been, and finding a woman with high ambitions and very low standards like Veronika? Child's play.

It had taken very little effort to discover that she was shacking up with her usual type in what amounted to a fortress in Mayfair: some dissipated son of a too-wealthy sheikh with an extensive and deeply bored security force, the dismantling of which would no doubt be as easy for Nikolai as it was entertaining—but would also, regrettably, cause an international incident.

Because Nikolai wasn't a soldier any longer. He was no longer the Spetsnaz operative who could do whatever it took to achieve his goals—with a deadly accuracy that had won him a healthy respect that bordered on fear from peers and enemies alike. He'd shed those skins, if not what lay beneath them like sinew fused to steel, seven years ago now.

And yet because his life was nothing but an exercise in irony, he'd since become a philanthropist, an internationally renowned wolf in the ill-fitting clothes of a very soft, very fluffy sheep. He ran the Korovin Foundation, the charity he and his brother, Ivan, had begun after Ivan's retirement from Hollywood action films. Nikolai tended to Ivan's fortune and had amassed one of his own thanks to his innate facility with investment strategies. And he was lauded far and near as a man of great compassion and caring, despite the obvious ruthlessness he did nothing to hide.

People believed what they wanted to believe. Nikolai knew that better than most.

He'd grown up hard in post-Soviet Russia, where brutal

oligarchs were thick on the ground and warlords fought over territory like starving dogs—making him particularly good at targeting excessively wealthy men and the corporations they loved more than their own families, then talking them out of their money. He knew them. He understood them. They called it a kind of magic, his ability to wrest huge donations from the most reluctant and wealthiest of donors, but Nikolai saw it as simply one more form of warfare.

And he had always been so very good at war. It was his one true art.

But his regrettably high profile these days meant he was no longer the kind of man who could break into a sheikh's son's London stronghold and expect that to fly beneath the radar. Billionaire philanthropists with celebrity brothers, it turned out, had to follow rules that elite, highly trained soldiers did not. They were expected to use diplomacy and charm.

And if such things were too much of a reach when it concerned an ex-wife rather than a large donation, they were forced to subject themselves to London's gauntlet of "hot spots" and *wait*.

Nikolai checked an impatient sigh, ignoring the squealing trio of underdressed teenagers who leaped up and down in front of him, their eyes dulled with drink, drugs and their own craven self-importance. Lights flashed frenetically, the awful music howled and he monitored the crowd from his strategic position in the shadows of the dance floor.

He simply had to wait for Veronika to show herself, as he knew she would.

Then he would find out how much of what she'd said seven years ago had been spite, designed to hurt him as much as possible, and how much had been truth. Nikolai knew that on some level, he'd never wanted to know. If he never pressed the issue, then it was always possible that Stefan really *was* his, as Veronika had made him believe for the first five years of the boy's life. That somewhere out there, he had a son. That he had done something right, even if it was by accident.

But such fantasies made him weak, he knew, and he could no longer tolerate it. He wanted a DNA test to prove that Stefan wasn't his. Then he would be done with his weaknesses, once and for all.

"You need to go and fix your life," his brother, Ivan, the only person alive that Nikolai still cared about, the only one who knew what they'd suffered at their uncle's hands in those grim years after their parents had died in a factory fire, had told him just over two years ago. Then he'd stared at Nikolai as if he was a stranger and walked away from him as if he was even less than that.

It was the last time they'd spoken in person, or about anything other than the Korovin Foundation.

Nikolai didn't blame his older brother for this betrayal. He'd watched Ivan's slide into his inevitable madness as it happened. He knew that Ivan was sadly deluded—blinded by sex and emotion, desperate to believe in things that didn't exist because it was far better than the grim alternative of reality. How could he blame Ivan for preferring the delusion? Most people did.

Nikolai didn't have that luxury.

Emotions were liabilities. Lies. Nikolai believed in sex and money. No ties, no temptations. No relationships now his brother had turned his back on him. No possibility that any of the women he took to his bed—always nameless, faceless and only permitted near him if they agreed to adhere to a very strict set of requirements—would ever reach him.

In order to be betrayed, one first had to trust.

And the only person Nikolai had trusted in his life was Ivan and even then, only in a very qualified way once that woman had sunk her claws in him.

But ultimately, this was a gift. It freed him, finally, from his last remaining emotional prison. It made everything simple. Because he had never known how to tell Ivan—who had built a life out of playing the hero in the fighting ring and on the screen, who was able to embody those fights he'd won and the roles he'd played with all the self-righteous fury of the untainted, the unbroken, the *good*—that there were some things that couldn't be fixed.

Nikolai wished he was something so simple as *broken*.

He acted like a man, but was never at risk of becoming one. He'd need flesh and blood, heat and heart for that, and those were the things he'd sold off years ago to make himself into the perfect monster. A killing machine.

Nikolai knew exactly what he was: a bright and shining piece of ice with no hope of warmth, frozen too solid for any sun to penetrate the chill. A hard and deadly weapon, honed to lethal perfection beneath his uncle's fists, then sharpened anew in the bloody Spetsnaz brotherhood. To say nothing of the dark war games he'd learned he could make into his own kind of terrible poetry, despite what it took from him in return.

He was empty where it counted, down to his bones. Empty all the way through. It was why he was so good at what he did.

And it was safer, Nikolai thought now, his eyes on the heedless, hedonistic crowd. There was too much to lose should he relinquish that deep freeze, give up that iron control. What he remembered of his drinking years appalled him—the blurred nights, the scraps and pieces of too much frustrated emotion turned too quickly into violence, making him far too much like the brutal uncle he'd so despised.

Never again.

It was better by far to stay empty. Cold. Frozen straight through.

He had never been anything but alone. Nikolai understood that now. The truth was, he preferred it that way. And once he dealt with Veronika, once he confirmed the truth about Stefan's paternity, he would never have to be anything else.

Alicia Teller ran out of patience with a sudden jolt, a wave of exhaustion and irritation nearly taking her from her feet in the midst of the jostling crowd. Or possibly that was the laddish group to her left, all of them obviously deep into the night's drinking and therefore flailing around the dance floor.

I'm much too old for this, she told herself as she moved out of their way for the tenth time, feeling ancient and decrepit at her extraordinarily advanced age of twenty-nine.

She couldn't remember the last time she'd spent a Saturday night anywhere more exciting than a quiet restaurant with friends, much less in a slick, pretentious club that had recently been dubbed *the* place to be seen in London. But then again, she also didn't like to look a gift horse in the mouth—said gift horse, in this case, being her everexuberant best friend and flatmate Rosie, who'd presented the guest passes to this velvet-roped circus with a grand flourish over dinner.

"It's the coolest place in London right now," she'd confidently assured Alicia over plates of *saag paneer* in their favorite Indian restaurant not far from Brick Lane. "Dripping with celebrities and therefore every attractive man in London."

"I am not cool, Rosie," Alicia had reminded her gently. "You've said so yourself for years. Every single time you try to drag me to yet another club you claim will change my life, if memory serves. It might be time for you to accept the possibility that this is who I am."

"Never!" Rosie had cried at once, feigning shock and outrage. "I remember when you were *fun*, Alicia. I've made a solemn vow to corrupt you, no matter how long it takes!"

"I'm incorruptible," Alicia had assured her. Because she also remembered when she'd been *fun*, and she had no desire to repeat those terrible mistakes, thank you, much less that descent into shame and heartache. "I'm also very likely to embarrass you. Can you handle the shame?"

Rosie had rolled her extravagantly mascaraed and shimmery-purple shadowed eyes while tossing the last of the poppadoms into her mouth.

"I can handle it," she'd said. "Anything to remind you that you're in your twenties, not your sixties. I consider it a public service."

"You say that," Alicia had teased her, "but you should be prepared for me to request 'Dancing Queen' as if we're at a wedding disco. From the no doubt world-renowned and tragically hip DJ who will faint dead away at the insult."

"Trust me, Alicia," Rosie had said then, very seriously. "This is going to be the best night of our lives."

Now Alicia watched her best friend shake her hips in a sultry come-on to the investment banker she'd been flirting with all night, and blamed the jet lag. Nothing else could have made her forget for even a moment that sparkly, dramatic still Rosie viewed it as her sacred obligation to pull on a weekend night, the way they both had when they were younger and infinitely wilder, and that meant the exorbitant taxi fare back home from the wilds of this part of East London to the flat they shared on the outskirts of Hammersmith would be Alicia's to cough up. Alone.

"You know what you need?" Rosie had asked on the

chilly trek over from the Tube, right on cue. "Desperately, I might add?"

"I know what *you* think I need, yes," Alicia had replied dryly. "But for some reason, the fantasy of sloppy and unsatisfying sex with some stranger from a club pales in comparison to the idea of getting a good night's sleep all alone in my own bed. Call me crazy. Or, barring that, *a grown-up*."

"You're never going to find anyone, you know," Rosie had told her then, frowning. "Not if you keep this up. What's next, a nunnery?"

But Alicia knew exactly what kind of people it was possible to meet in the clubs Rosie preferred. She'd met too many of them. She'd *been* one of them throughout her university years. And she'd vowed that she would never, ever let herself get so out of control again. It wasn't worth the price—and sooner or later, there was always a price. In her case, all the years it had taken her to get her father to look at her again.

Alicia had been every inch a Daddy's girl until that terrible night the summer she'd been twenty-one. She'd been indulged and spoiled and adored beyond measure, the light of his life, and she'd lost that forever on a single night she still couldn't piece together in her head. But she knew the details almost as if she could remember it herself, because she'd had to sit and listen to her own father tell them to her the next morning while her head had pounded and her stomach had heaved: she'd been so drunk she'd been practically paralytic when she'd come home that night, but at some point she'd apparently wandered out into the back garden—which was where her father had found her, having sex with Mr. Reddick from next door.

Married Mr. Reddick, with three kids Alicia had babysat over the years, who'd been good mates with her dad until that night. The shame of it was still scarlet in her, bright and horrid, all these years later. How could she have done such a vile, despicable thing? She still didn't know.

Afterward, she'd decided that she'd had more than enough *fun* for one lifetime.

"Sorry," Alicia had said to Rosie then, smiling the painful memories away. "Are you talking about love? I was certain we were talking about the particular desperation of a Saturday night shag...."

"I have a radical idea, Saint Alicia," Rosie had said then with another roll of her eyes toward the dark sky above. "Why don't you put the halo aside for the night? It won't kill you, I promise. You might even find you like a little debauchery on a Saturday night the way you used to do."

Because Rosie didn't know, of course. Nobody knew. Alicia had been too embarrassed, too ashamed, too *disgusted* with herself to tell her friend—to tell anyone—why she'd abruptly stopped going out at the weekend, why she'd thrown herself into the job she hadn't taken seriously until then and turned it into a career she took a great deal of pride in now. Even her mother and sisters didn't know why there had been that sudden deep chill between Alicia and her dad, that had now, years later, only marginally improved into a polite distance.

"I'm not wearing my halo tonight, actually," Alicia had replied primly, patting at her riot of curls as if feeling for one anyway. "It clashed with these shoes you made me wear."

"Idiot," Rosie had said fondly, and then she'd brandished those guest passes and swept them past the crowd outside on the pavement, straight into the clutches of London's hottest club of the moment.

And Alicia had enjoyed herself—more than she'd expected she would, in fact. She'd missed dancing. She'd missed the excitement in the air, the buzz of such a big crowd. The particular, sensual seduction of a good beat. But Rosie's version of fun went on long into the night, the way it always had, and Alicia grew tired too easily. Especially when she'd only flown back into the country the day before, and her body still believed it was in another time zone altogether.

And more, when she wasn't sure she could trust herself. She didn't know what had made her do what she'd done that terrible night eight years ago; she couldn't remember much of it. So she'd opted to avoid anything and everything that might lead down that road—which was easier to do when she wasn't standing in the midst of so much cheerful abandon. Because she didn't have a halo—God knows, she'd proved that with her whorish behavior—she only wished she did.

You knew what this would be like, she thought briskly now, not bothering to fight the banker for Rosie's attention when a text from the backseat of a taxi headed home would do, and would furthermore not cause any interruption to Rosie's obvious plans for the evening. *You could have gone straight home after the curry and sorted out your laundry—*

And then she couldn't help but laugh at herself: Miss Misery Guts acting exactly like the bitter old maid Rosie often darkly intimated she was well on her way to becoming. Rosie was right, clearly. Had she really started thinking about her *laundry?* After midnight on a dance floor in a trendy London club while music even she could tell was fantastic swelled all around her?

Still laughing as she imagined the appalled look Rosie would give her when she told her about this, Alicia turned and began fighting her way out of the wild crowd and off the heaving dance floor. She laughed even harder as she was forced to leap out of the way of a particularly energetic couple flinging themselves here and there.

Alicia overbalanced because she was laughing too hard to pay attention to where she was going, and then, moving too fast to stop herself, she slipped in a puddle of spilled drink on the edge of the dance floor—

And crashed into the dark column of a man that she'd thought, before she hurtled into him, was nothing more than an extension of the speaker behind him. A still, watchful shadow.

He wasn't.

He was hard and male, impossibly muscled, sleek and hot. Alicia's first thought, with her face a scant breath from the most stunning male chest she'd ever beheld in real life and her palms actually *touching* it, was that he smelled like winter—fresh and clean and something deliciously smoky beneath.

She was aware of his hands on her upper arms, holding her fast, and only as she absorbed the fact that he *was* holding her did she also fully comprehend the fact that somehow, despite the press of the crowd and the flashing lights and how quickly she'd been on her way toward taking an undignified header into the floor, he'd managed to catch her at all.

She tilted her head back to thank him for his quick reflexes, still smiling—

And everything stopped.

It simply—*disappeared.*

Alicia felt her heart thud, hard enough to bruise. She felt her mouth drop open.

But she saw nothing at all but his eyes.

Blue like no blue she'd ever seen in another pair of eyes before. Blue like the sky on a crystal cold winter day, so bright it almost hurt to look at him. Blue so intense it seemed to fill her up, expanding inside of her, making her feel swollen with it. As if the slightest thing might make her burst wide-open, and some mad part of her wanted that, desperately.

A touch. A smile. Anything at all.

He was beautiful. Dark and forbidding and still, the most beautiful thing she'd ever seen. Something electric sizzled in the air between them as they gazed at each other, charging through her, making her skin prickle. Making her feel heavy and restless, all at once, as if she was a snow globe he'd picked up and shaken hard, and everything inside of her was still floating drowsily in the air, looking for a place to land.

It scared her, down deep inside in a place she hadn't known was there until this moment—and yet she didn't pull away.

He blinked, as if he felt it too, this terrible, impossible, beautiful thing that crackled between them. She was sure that if she could tear her eyes from his she'd be able to see it there in the air, connecting their bodies, arcing between them and around them and through them, the voltage turned high. The faintest hint of a frown etched between his dark brows, and he moved as if to set her away from him, but then he stopped and all he'd done was shift them both even farther back into the shadows.

And still they stood there, caught. Snared. As if the world around them, the raucous club, the pounding music, the wild and crazy dancing, had simply evaporated the moment they'd touched.

At last, Alicia thought, in a rush of chaotic sensation and dizzy emotion she didn't understand at all, all of it falling through her with a certain inevitability, like a heavy stone into a terrifyingly deep well.

"My God," she said, gazing up at him. "You look like a wolf."

Was that a smile? His mouth was lush and grim at once, impossibly fascinating to her, and it tugged in one hard corner. Nothing more, and yet she smiled back at him as if he'd beamed at her.

"Is that why you've dressed in red, like a Shoreditch fairy tale?" he asked, his words touched with the faint, velvet caress of an accent she didn't recognize immediately. "I should warn you, it will end with teeth."

"I think you mean tears." She searched his hard face, looking for more evidence of that smile. "It will end in *tears,* surely."

"That, too." Another small tug in the corner of that mouth. "But the teeth usually come first, and hurt more."

"I'll be very disappointed now if you don't have fangs," she told him, and his hands changed their steely grip on her arms, or perhaps she only then became aware of the heat of his palms and how the way he was holding her was so much like a caress.

Another tug on that austere mouth, and an answering one low in her belly, which should have terrified her, given what she knew about herself and sex. On some level, it did.

But she still didn't move away from him.

"It is, of course, my goal in life to keep strange British women who crash into me in crowded clubs from the jaws of disappointment," he said, a new light in his lovely eyes, and a different, more aware tilt to the way he held his head, the way he angled his big body toward her.

As if he might lean in close and swallow her whole.

Staring back at him then, his strong hands hard and hot on her arms and her palms still pressed flat against his taut chest, Alicia wanted nothing more than for him to do exactly that.

She should have turned away then and bolted for the door. Tried to locate whatever was left of her sanity, wherever she'd misplaced it. But she'd never felt this kind of raw, shimmering excitement before, this blistering heat weighing down her limbs so deliciously, this man so primal and powerful she found it hard to breathe.

"Even if the jaws in question are yours?" she asked, and she didn't recognize that teasing lilt in her voice, the way she tilted her head to look up at him, the liquid sort of feeling that moved in her then.

"Especially if they're mine," he replied, his bright winter gaze on her mouth, though there was a darkness there too, a shadow across his intriguing blade of a face that she nearly got lost in. *Jaws,* she reminded herself. *Fangs. He's telling me what a wolf he is, big and bad.* Surely she should feel more alarmed than she did—surely she shouldn't have the strangest urge to soothe him, instead? "You should know there are none sharper or more dangerous."

"In all of London?" She couldn't seem to keep herself from smiling again, or that sparkling cascade of something like light from rushing in her, making her stomach tighten and her breasts pull tight. *Alive. At last.* "Have you measured them, then? Is there some kind of competition you can enter to prove yours are the longest? The sharpest in all the land?"

Alicia felt completely outside herself. Some part of her wanted to lie down in it, in this mad feeling, in *him*—and exult in it. Bask in it as if it was sunshine. As if *he* was, despite the air of casual menace he wore so easily, like an extra layer of skin. Was that visible to everyone, or only to her? She didn't care. She wanted to roll around in this moment, in him, like it was the first snow of the season and she could make it all into angels.

Her breath caught at the image, and somehow, he heard

it. She felt his reaction in the sudden tension of his powerful frame above her and around her, in the flex of his fingers high on her arms, in the tightening of that connection that wound between them, bright and electric, and made her feel like a stranger in her own body.

His blue eyes lifted to meet hers and gleamed bright. "I don't need to measure them, *solnyshka*." He shifted closer, and his attention returned to her mouth. "I know."

He was an arctic wolf turned man, every inch of him a predator—lean and hard as he stood over her despite the heels Rosie had coerced her into wearing. He wore all black, a tight black T-shirt beneath a perfectly tailored black jacket, dark trousers and boots, and his wide, hard shoulders made her skin feel tight. His dark hair was short and inky black. It made his blue eyes seem like smoke over his sculpted jaw and cheekbones, and yet all of it, all of *him*, was hard and male and so dangerous she could feel it hum beneath her skin, some part of her desperate to fight, to flee. He looked intriguingly uncivilized. Something like feral.

And yet Alicia wasn't afraid, as that still-alarmed, still-vigilant part of her knew she should have been. Not when he was looking at her like that. Not when she followed a half-formed instinct and moved closer to him, pressing her hands flatter against the magnificently formed planes of his chest while his arms went around her to hold her like a lover might. She tilted her head back even farther and watched his eyes turn to arctic fire.

She didn't understand it, but she burned.

This isn't right, a small voice cautioned her in the back of her mind. *This isn't you.*

But he was so beautiful she couldn't seem to keep track of who she was supposed to be, and her heart hurt her where it thundered in her chest. She felt something bright and demanding knot into an insistent ache deep in her belly, and she found she couldn't think of a good reason to step away from him.

In a minute, she promised herself. *I'll walk away in a minute.*

"You should run," he told her then, his voice dark and low, and she could see he was serious. That he meant it. But one of his hands moved to trace a lazy pattern on her cheek as he said it, his palm a rough velvet against her skin, and she shivered. His blue gaze seemed to sharpen. "As far away from me as you can get."

He looked so grim then, so sure, and it hurt her, somehow. She wanted to see him smile with that hard, dangerous mouth. She wanted that with every single part of her and she didn't even know his name.

None of this made any sense.

Alicia had been so good for so long. She'd paid and paid and paid for that single night eight years ago. She'd been so vigilant, so careful, ever since. She was never spontaneous. She was never reckless. And yet this beautiful shadow of a man had the bluest eyes she'd ever seen, and the saddest mouth, and the way he touched her made her shake and burn and glow.

And she thought that maybe this once, for a moment or two, she could let down her guard. Just the smallest, tiniest bit. It didn't have to mean anything she didn't want it to mean. It didn't have to mean anything at all.

So she ignored that voice inside of her, and she ignored his warning, too.

Alicia leaned her face into his hard palm as if it was the easiest thing in the world, and smiled when he pulled in a breath like it was a fire in him, too. Like he felt the same burn.

She stretched up against his hard, tough body and told herself this was about that grim mouth of his, not the wild, impossible things she knew she shouldn't let herself feel or want or, God help her, *do*. And they were in the shadows of a crowded club where nobody could see her and no one would ever know what she did in the dark. It wasn't as if it counted.

She could go back to her regularly scheduled quiet life in a moment.

It would only be a moment. One small moment outside all the rules she'd made for herself, the rules she'd lived by so carefully for so long, and then she would go straight back home to her neat, orderly, virtuous life.

She would. She had to. *She would.*

But first Alicia obeyed that surge of wild demand inside of her, leaned closer and fitted her mouth to his.

CHAPTER TWO

HE TASTED LIKE the night. Better even than she'd imagined.

He paused for the barest instant when Alicia's lips touched his. Half a heartbeat. Less.

A scant second while the taste of him seared through her, deep and dark and wild. She thought that was enough, that small taste of his fascinating mouth. That would do, and now she could go back to her quiet—

But then he angled his head to one side, used the hand at her cheek to guide her mouth where he wanted it and took over.

Devouring her like the wolf she understood he was. *He really was,* and the realization swirled inside of her like heat. His mouth was impossibly carnal, opening over hers to taste her, to claim her.

Dark and deep, hot and sure.

Alicia simply…exploded. It was like a long flash of light, shuddering and bright, searing everything away in the white hot burn of it. It was perfect. It was beautiful.

It was too much.

She shivered against him, overloaded with his bold taste, the scrape of his jaw, his talented fingers moving her mouth where he wanted it in a silent, searing command she was happy to obey. Then his hands were in her hair, buried in her thick curls. Her arms went around his neck of their own volition, and then she was plastered against the tall, hard length of him. It was like pressing into the surface of the sun and still, she couldn't seem to get close enough.

As if there was no *close enough*.

And he kissed her, again and again, with a ruthless intensity that made her feel weak and beautiful all at once, until she was mindless with need. Until she forgot her own name. Until she forgot she didn't know his. Until she forgot how dangerous *forgetting* was for her.

Until she forgot everything but him.

When he pulled back, she didn't understand. He put an inch, maybe two, between them, and then he muttered something harsh and incomprehensible while he stared at her as if he thought she was some kind of ghost.

It took her a long, confused moment to realize that she couldn't understand him because he wasn't speaking in English, not because she'd forgotten her own language, too.

Alicia blinked, the world rushing back as she did. She was still standing in that club. Music still pounded all around them, lights still flashed, well-dressed patrons still shouted over the din, and somewhere out in the middle of the dance floor, Rosie was no doubt still playing her favorite game with her latest conquest.

Everything was as it had been before she'd stumbled into this man, before he'd caught her. Before she'd kissed him.

Before he'd kissed her back.

Everything was exactly the same. Except Alicia.

He was searching her face as if he was looking for something. He shook his head slightly, then reached down and ran a lazy finger over the ridge of her collarbone, as if testing its shape. Even that made her shudder, that simple slide of skin against skin. Even so innocuous a touch seemed directly connected to that pulsing heat between her legs, the heavy ache in her breasts, the hectic spin inside of her.

She didn't have to speak his language to know whatever he muttered then was a curse.

If she were smart, the way she'd tried to be for years now, she would pull her hand away and run. Just as he'd told her she should. Just as she'd promised herself she would. Everything about this was too extreme, too intense, as if he wasn't only a strange man in a club but the kind of drug that usually went with this kind of rolling, wildly out-of-control feeling. As if she was much too close to being high on *him*.

"Last chance," he said then, as if he could read her mind.

He was giving her a warning. Again.

In her head, she listened. She smiled politely and extricated herself. She marched herself to the nearest exit, hailed a taxi, then headed straight home to the comfort of her bloody laundry. Because she knew she couldn't be trusted outside the confines of the rules she'd made for herself. She'd been living the consequences of having no rules for a long, long time.

But here, now, in this loud place surrounded by so many people and all of that pounding music, she didn't feel like the person she'd been when she'd arrived. Everything she knew about herself had twisted inside out. Turned into something else entirely in that electric blue of his challenging gaze.

As if this really was a Shoreditch fairy tale, after all.

"What big eyes you have," she teased him.

His hard mouth curved then, and she felt it like a burst of heat, like sunlight. She couldn't do anything but smile back at him.

"So be it," he said, as if he despaired of them both.

Alicia laughed, then laughed again at the startled look in his eyes.

"The dourness is a lovely touch," she told him. "You must be beating them off with a stick. A very grim stick."

"No stick," he said, in an odd tone. "A look at me is usually sufficient."

"A wolf," she said, and grinned. "Just as I suspected."

He blinked, and again looked at her in that strange way of his, as if she was an apparition he couldn't quite believe was standing there before him.

Then he moved with the same decisiveness he'd used when he'd taken control of that kiss, tucking her into his side as he navigated his way through the dense crowd. She tried not to think about how well she fitted there, under his heavy arm, tight against the powerful length of his torso as he cut through the crowd. She tried not to drift away in the scent of him, the heat and the power, all of it surrounding her and pouring into that ache already inside of her, making it bloom and stretch and grow.

Until it took over everything.

Maybe she was under some kind of spell, Alicia thought with the small part of her that wasn't consumed with the feel of his tall, lean frame as he guided her so protectively through the crowd. It should have been impossible to move through the club so quickly, so confidently. Not in a place like this at the height of a Saturday night. But he did it.

And then they were outside, in the cold and the damp November night, and he was still moving in that same breathtaking way, like quicksilver. Like he knew exactly where they were headed—away from the club and the people still milling about in front of it. He led her down the dark street, deeper into the shadows, and it was then Alicia's sense of self-preservation finally kicked itself into gear.

Better late than never, she thought, annoyed with herself, but it actually *hurt* her to pull away from the magnificent shelter of his body, from all of that intense heat and strength. It felt like she'd ripped her skin off when she stepped away from him, as if they'd been fused together.

He regarded her calmly, making her want to trust him when she knew she shouldn't. She couldn't.

"I'm sorry, but..." She wrapped her arms around her own waist in an attempt to make up for the heat she'd lost when she'd stepped away from him. "I don't know a single thing about you."

"You know several things, I think."

He sounded even more delicious now that they were alone and she could hear him properly. *Russian,* she thought, as pleased as if she'd learned his deepest, darkest secrets.

"Yes," she agreed, thinking of the things she knew. Most of them to do with that insistent ache in her belly, and lower. His mouth. His clever hands. "All lovely things. But none of them worth risking my personal safety for, I'm sure you'll agree."

Something like a smile moved in his eyes, but didn't make it to his hard mouth. Still, it echoed in her, sweet and light, making her feel far more buoyant than she should have on a dark East London street with a strange man even she could see was dangerous, no matter how much she wanted him.

Had she ever wanted anything this much? Had anyone?

"A wolf is never without risk," he told her, that voice of his like whiskey, smooth and scratchy at once, heating her up from the inside out. "That's the point of wolves. Or you'd simply get a dog, pat it on the head." His eyes gleamed. "Teach it tricks."

Alicia wasn't sure she wanted to know the tricks this man had up his sleeve. Or, more to the point, she wasn't sure she'd survive them. She wasn't certain she'd survive this as it was.

"You could be very bad in bed," she said, conversationally, as if she picked up strange men all the time. She hardly recognized her own light, easy, flirtatious tone. She hadn't heard it since before that night in her parents' back garden. "That's a terrible risk to take with any stranger, and awkward besides."

That smile in his eyes intensified, got even bluer. "I'm not."

She believed him.

"You could be the sort who gets very, very drunk and weeps loudly about his broken heart until dawn." She gave a mock shudder. "So tedious, especially if poetry is involved. Or worse, *singing*."

"I don't drink," he countered at once. His dark brows arched over those eyes of his, challenging her. Daring her. "I never sing, I don't write poems and I certainly do not weep." He paused. "More to the point, I don't have a heart."

"Handy, that," she replied easily. She eyed him. "You could be a killer, of course. That would be unfortunate."

She smiled at that. He didn't.

"And if I am?"

"There you go," she said, and nodded sagely. Light, airy. Enchanted, despite herself. "I can't possibly go off into the night with you now, can I?"

But it was terrifying how much she *wanted* to go off with him, wherever he'd take her, and instead of reacting to that as she should, she couldn't stop smiling at him. As if she already knew him, this strange man dressed all in black, his blue eyes the only spot of color on the cold pavement as he stared at her as if she'd stunned him somehow.

"My name is Nikolai," he said, and she had the oddest impression he hadn't meant to speak at all. He shifted, then reached over and traced her lips with his thumb, his expression so fierce, so intent, it made her feel hollowed out inside, everything scraped away except that wild, wondrous heat he stirred in her. "Text someone my name and address. Have them ring every fifteen minutes if you like. Send the police. Whatever you want."

"All those safeguards are very thoughtful," she pointed out, but her eyes felt too wide and her voice sounded insubstantial. Wispy. "Though not exactly wolfish, it has to be said."

His mouth moved into his understated version of a smile

"I want you." His eyes were on fire. Every inch of him that wolf. "What will it take?"

She swayed back into him as if they were magnets and she'd simply succumbed to the pull. And then she had no choice but to put her hand to his abdomen, to feel all that blasting heat right there beneath her palm.

Even that didn't scare her the way it should.

"What big teeth you have," she whispered, too on edge to laugh, too filled with that pulsing ache inside of her to smile.

"The biting part comes later." His eyes gleamed again, with the kind of sheer male confidence that made it difficult to breathe. Alicia stopped trying. "If you ask nicely."

He picked up her hand and lifted it to his mouth, tracing a dark heat over the back of it. He didn't look away.

"If you're sure," she said piously, trying desperately to pretend she wasn't shaking, and that he couldn't feel it. That he didn't know exactly what he was doing to her when she could see full well that he did. "I was promised a wolf, not a dog."

"I eat dogs for breakfast."

She laughed then. "That's not particularly comforting."

"I can't be what I'm not, *solnyshka*." He turned her hand over, then kissed her palm in a way that made her hiss in a sharp breath. His eyes were smiling again, so bright and blue. "But I'm very good at what I am."

And she'd been lost since she'd set eyes on him, hadn't

she? What use was there in pretending otherwise? She wasn't drunk. It wasn't like that terrible night, because she knew what she was doing. Didn't she?

"Note to self," Alicia managed to say, breathless and dizzy and unable to remember why she'd tried to stop this in the first place, when surrendering to it—to him—felt so much like triumph. Like fate. "Never eat breakfast with a wolf. The sausages are likely the family dog."

He shrugged. "Not *your* family dog," he said with that fierce mouth of his, though she was sure his blue eyes laughed. "If that helps."

And this time, when she smiled at him, the negotiation was over.

The address he gave her in his clipped, direct way was in an extraordinarily posh part of town Alicia could hardly afford to visit, much less live in. She dutifully texted it to Rosie, hoping that her friend was far too busy to check it until morning. And then she tucked her phone away and forgot about Rosie altogether.

Because he still moved like magic, tucking her against him again as if there was a crowd he needed to part when there was only the late-night street and what surged between them like heat lightning. As if he liked the way she fitted there as much as she did. And her heart began to pound all over again, excitement and anticipation and a certain astonishment at her own behavior pouring through her with every hard thump.

At the corner, he lifted his free hand almost languidly toward the empty street, and for a second Alicia truly believed that he was so powerful that taxis simply materialized before him at his whim—until a nearby engine turned over and a powerful black SUV slid out of the shadows and pulled to a stop right there before them.

More magic, when she was enchanted already.

Nikolai, she whispered to herself as she climbed inside the SUV, as if the name was a song. Or a spell. *His name is Nikolai.*

He swung in behind her on the soft leather backseat, exchanged a few words in curt Russian with the driver and then pressed a button that raised a privacy shield, secluding them. Then he settled back against the seat, near her but not touching her, stretching out his long, lean body and making the spacious vehicle seem tight. Close.

And then he simply looked at her.

As if he was trying to puzzle her out. Or giving her one last chance to bolt.

But Alicia knew she wasn't going to do that.

"More talk of dogs?" he asked mildly, yet all she heard was the hunger beneath. She could see it in his eyes, his face. She could feel the echo of it in her, new and huge and almost more than she could bear. "More clever little character assessments couched as potential objections?"

"I got in your car," she pointed out, hardly recognizing her own voice. The thick heat in it. "I think I'm done."

He smiled. She was sure of it, though his mouth didn't move. But she could see the stamp of satisfaction on his hard face, the flare of a deep male approval.

"Not yet, *solnyshka,*" he murmured, his voice a low rasp. "Not quite yet."

And she melted. It was a shivery thing, hot and desperate, like she couldn't quite catch her breath against the heat of it.

"Come here," he said.

They were cocooned in the darkness, light spilling here and there as the car sped through the city, and still his blue gaze was brilliant. Compelling. And so knowing—so certain of himself, of her, of what was about to happen—it made her blood run hot in her veins.

Alicia didn't move fast enough and he made a low noise. *A growl*—like the wolf he so resembled. The rough sound made her shake apart and then melt down into nothing but need, alive with that crazy heat she couldn't seem to control any longer.

He simply picked her up and pulled her into his lap, his mouth finding hers and claiming her all over again with an impatience that delighted her. She met him with the same urgency. His hands marveled down the length of her back, explored the shape of her hips, and Alicia's mind blanked out into a red-hot burst of that consuming, impossible fire. Into pure and simple *need*.

It had been so long. *So long,* and yet her body knew exactly what to do, thrilling to the taste of him, the feel of his hard, capable hands first over and then underneath her bright red shirt. His hands on her stomach, her waist, her breasts. So perfect she wanted to die. And not nearly enough.

He leaned back to peel off his jacket and the tight black T-shirt beneath, and her eyes glazed over at the sight of all of that raw male beauty. She pressed herself against the hard planes of his perfect chest, tracing the large, colorful tattoos that stretched over his skin with trembling fingers, with her lips and her tongue, tasting art etched across art.

Intense. Hot. Intoxicating.

And that scent of his—of the darkest winter, smoke and ice—surrounded her. Licked into her. Claimed her as surely as he did.

One moment she was fully clothed, the next her shirt and the bra beneath it were swept away, while his hard mouth took hers again and again until she thought she might die if he stopped. Then he did stop, and she moaned out her distress, her desperation. That needy ache so deep in the core of her. But he only laughed softly, before he fastened his hot mouth to the tight peak of one breast and sucked on it, not quite gently, until she thought she really *had* died.

The noises she heard herself making were impossible. Nothing could really feel this good. This perfect. This wild or this *right*.

Nikolai shifted, lifting her, and Alicia helped him peel her trousers down from her hips, kicking one leg free and not caring what happened to the other. She felt outside herself and yet more fully *in* herself than she had been in as long as she could remember. She explored the expanse of his gorgeous shoulders, the distractingly tender spot behind his ear, the play of his stunning muscles, perfectly honed beneath her.

He twisted them both around, coming down over her on the seat and pulling her legs around his hips with an urgency that made her breath desert her. She hadn't even been aware that he'd undressed. It was more magic—and then he was finally naked against her, the steel length of him a hot brand against her belly.

Alicia shuddered and melted, then melted again, and he moved even closer, one of his hands moving to her bottom and lifting her against him with that devastating skill, that easy mastery, that made her belly tighten.

He was muttering in Russian, that same word he'd used before like a curse or a prayer or even both at once, and the sound of it made her moan again. It was harsh like him, and tender, too. It made her feel as if she might come out of her own skin. He teased her breasts, licking his way from one proud nipple to the other as if he might lose himself there, then moved to her neck, making her shiver against him before he took her mouth again in a hard, deep kiss.

As raw as she was. As undone.

He pulled back slightly to press something into her hand, and she blinked at it, taking much longer than she should have to recognize it was the condom she hadn't thought about for even an instant.

A trickle of unease snaked down the back of her neck, but she pushed it away, too far gone for shame. Not when his blue eyes glittered with sensual intent and his long fingers moved between them, feeling her damp heat and then stroking deep into her molten center, making her clench him hard.

"Hurry," he told her.

"I'm hurrying. You're distracting me."

He played his fingers in and out of her, slick and hot, then pressed the heel of his hand into her neediest part, laughing softly when she bucked against him.

"Concentrate, *solnyshka*."

She ripped open the foil packet, then took her time rolling it down his velvety length, until he cursed beneath his breath.

Alicia liked the evidence of his own pressing need. She liked that she could make his breath catch, too. And then he stopped, braced over her, his face close to hers and the hardest part of him poised at her entrance but not *quite*—

He groaned. He sounded as tortured as she felt. She liked that, too.

"Your name."

She blinked at the short command, so gruff and harsh. His arms were hard around her, his big body pressed her back into the soft leather seat, and she felt delicate and powerful all at once.

"Tell me your name," he said, nipping at her jaw, making her head fall back to give him any access he desired, anything he wanted.

Alive, she thought again. *At last.*

"Alicia," she whispered.

He muttered it like a fierce prayer, and then he thrust

into her—hot and hard and so perfect, so beautiful, that tears spilled from her eyes even as she shattered around him.

"Again," he said.

It was another command, arrogant and darkly certain. Nikolai was hard and dangerous and between her legs, his eyes bright and hot and much too intense on hers. She turned her head away but he caught her mouth with his, taking her over, conquering her.

"I don't think I can—" she tried to say against his mouth, even while the flames still licked through her, even as she still shuddered helplessly around him, aware of the steel length of him inside her, filling her.

Waiting.

That hard smile like a burst of heat inside her. "You will."

And then he started to move.

It was perfect. More than perfect. It was sleek and hot, impossibly good. He simply claimed her, took her, and Alicia met him. She arched into him, lost in the slide and the heat, the glory of it. Of him.

Slick. Wild.

Perfect.

He moved in her, over her, his mouth at her neck and his hands roaming from her bottom to the center of her shuddering need as he set the wild, intense pace. She felt it rage inside her again, this mad fire she'd never felt before and worried would destroy her even as she hungered for more. And more. *And more.*

She met every deep thrust. She gloried in it.

"Say my name," he said, gruff against her ear, his voice washing through her and sending her higher, making her glow. "Now, Alicia. Say it."

When she obeyed he shuddered, then let out another low,

sexy growl that moved over her like a newer, better fire. He reached between them and pressed down hard against the heart of her hunger, hurtling her right over the edge again.

And smiled, she was sure of it, with his warrior's mouth as well as those winter-bright eyes, right before he followed her into bliss.

Nikolai came back to himself with a vicious, jarring thud.

He couldn't move. He wasn't sure he breathed. Alicia quivered sweetly beneath him, his mouth was pressed against the tender junction of her neck and shoulder, and he was still deep inside her lovely body.

What the hell was that?

He shifted her carefully into the seat beside him, ignoring the way her long, inky-black lashes looked against the creamy brown of her skin, the way her perfect, lush mouth was so soft now. He ignored the tiny noise she made in the back of her throat, as if distressed to lose contact with him, which made him grit his teeth. But she didn't open her eyes.

He dealt with the condom swiftly, then he found his trousers in the tangle of clothes on the floor of the car and jerked them on. He had no idea what had happened to his T-shirt, and decided it didn't matter. And then he simply sat there as if he was winded.

He, Nikolai Korovin, *winded*. By a woman.

By *this* woman.

What moved in him then was like a rush of too many colors, brilliant and wild, when he knew the only safety lay in gray. It surged in his veins, it pounded in his temples, it scraped along his sex. He told himself it was temper, but he knew better. It was everything he'd locked away for all these years, and he didn't want it. He wouldn't allow it. It made him feel like an animal again, wrong and violent and insane and drunk....

That was it.

It rang like a bell in him, low and urgent, swelling into everything. Echoing everywhere. No wonder he felt so off-kilter, so dangerously unbalanced. This woman made him feel *drunk*.

Nikolai forced a breath, then another.

Everything that had happened since she'd tripped in front of him flashed through his head, in the same random snatches of color and sound and scent he remembered from a thousand morning-afters. Her laughter, that sounded the way he thought joy must, though he'd no basis for comparison. The way she'd tripped and then fallen, straight into him, and hadn't had the sense to roll herself as he would have done, to break her fall. Her brilliant smile that cracked over her face so easily. Too easily.

No one had ever smiled at him like that. As if he was a real man. Even a good one.

But he knew what he was. He'd always known. His uncle's fists, worse after Ivan had left to fight their way to freedom one championship at a time. The things he'd done in the army. Veronika's calculated deception, even Ivan's more recent betrayal—these had only confirmed what Nikolai had always understood to be true about himself down deep into his core.

To think differently now, when he'd lost everything he had to lose and wanted nothing more than to shut himself off for good, was the worst kind of lie. Damaging. Dangerous. And he knew what happened when he allowed himself to become intoxicated. How many times would he have to prove that to himself? How many people would he hurt?

He was better off blank. Ice cold and gray, all the way through.

The day after Veronika left him, Nikolai had woken bruised and battered from another fight—or *fights*—he couldn't recall. He'd been shaky. Sick from the alcohol and sicker still with himself. Disgusted with the holes in his memory and worse, with all the things he *did* remember. The things that slid without context through his head, oily and barbed.

His fists against flesh. His bellow of rage. The crunch of wood beneath his foot, the shattering of pottery against the stone floor. Faces of strangers on the street, wary. Worried. Then angry. Alarmed.

Blood on a fist—and only some of it his. *Fear in those eyes*—never his. Nikolai was what grown men feared, what they crossed streets to avoid, but he hadn't felt fear himself in years. Not since he'd been a child.

Fear meant there was something left to lose.

That was the last time Nikolai had drunk a drop of alcohol and it was the last time he'd let himself lose control.

Until now.

He didn't understand this. He was not an impulsive man. He didn't pick up women, he *picked* them, carefully—and only when he was certain that whatever else they were, they were obedient and disposable.

When they posed no threat to him at all. Nikolai breathed in, out.

He'd survived wars. This was only a woman.

Nikolai looked at her then, memorizing her, like she was a code he needed to crack, instead of the bomb itself, poised to detonate.

She wore her dark black hair in a cloud of tight curls around her head, a tempting halo around her lovely, clever face, and he didn't want any part of this near-overpowering desire that surged in him, to bury his hands in the heavy thickness of it, to start the wild rush all over again. Her body was lithe and ripe with warm, mouthwatering curves that he'd already touched and tasted, so why did he feel as if it had all been rushed, as if it wasn't nearly enough?

He shouldn't have this longing to take his time, to really explore her. He shouldn't hunger for that lush, full mouth of hers again, or want to taste his way along that elegant neck for the simple pleasure of making her shiver. He shouldn't find it so impossible to look at her without imagining himself tracing lazy patterns across every square inch of the sweet brown perfection of her skin. With his mouth and then his hands, again and again until he *knew* her.

He'd asked her name, as if he'd needed it. He'd wanted her that much, and Nikolai knew better than to want. It could only bring him pain.

Vodka had been his one true love, and it had ruined him. It had let loose that monster in him, let it run amok. It had taken everything that his childhood and the army hadn't already divided between them and picked down to the bone. He'd known it in his sober moments, but he hadn't cared. Because vodka had warmed him, lent color and volume to the dark, silent prison of his life, made him imagine he could be something other than a six-foot-two column of glacial ice.

But he knew better than that now. He knew better than this.

Alicia's eyes fluttered open then, dark brown shot through with amber, almost too pretty to bear. He hated that he noticed, that he couldn't look away. She glanced around as if she'd forgotten where they were. Then she looked at him.

She didn't smile that outrageously beautiful smile of hers, and it made something hitch inside him, like a stitch in his side. As if he'd lost that, too.

She lifted one foot, shaking her head at the trousers that were still attached to her ankle, and the shoe she'd never removed. She reached down, picked up the tangle of her bright red shirt and lacy pink bra from the pile on the floor of the car, and sighed.

And Nikolai relaxed, because he was back on familiar ground.

Now came the demands, the negotiations, he thought cynically. The endless manipulations, which were the reason he'd started making any woman who wanted him agree to his rules before he touched her. Sign the appropriate documents, understand exactly how this would go before it started. Nikolai knew this particular dance well. It was why he normally didn't pick up women, let them into the sleek, muscular SUV that told them too much about his net worth, much less give them his address....

But instead of pouting prettily and pointedly, almost always the first transparent step in these situations, Alicia looked at him, let her head fall back and laughed.

CHAPTER THREE

THAT DAMNED LAUGH.

Nikolai would rather be shot again, he decided in that electric moment as her laughter filled the car. He would rather take another knife or two to the gut. He didn't know what on earth he was supposed to do with laughter like that, when it sparkled in the air all around him and fell indiscriminately here and there, like a thousand unwelcome caresses all over his skin and something worse—much worse—deep beneath it.

He scowled.

"Never let it be said this wasn't classy," Alicia said, her lovely voice wry. "I suppose we'll always have that going for us."

There was no we. There was no *us*. Neither of those words were *disposable*. Alarms shrieked like air raid sirens inside of him, mixing with the aftereffects of that laugh.

"I thought you understood," he said abruptly, at his coldest and most cutting. "I don't—"

"Relax, Tin Man." Laughter still lurked in her voice. She tugged her trousers back up over her hips, then pulled her bra free of her shirt, shooting him a breezy smile that felt not unlike a blade to the stomach as she clipped it back into place. "I heard you the first time. No heart."

And then she ignored him, as if he wasn't vibrating

beside her with all of that darkness and icy intent. As if he wasn't Nikolai Korovin, feared and respected in equal measure all across the planet, in a thousand corporate boardrooms as well as the grim theaters of too many violent conflicts. As if he was the kind of man someone could simply *pick up* in a London club and then dismiss...

Except, of course, he was. Because she had. She'd done exactly that.

He'd let her.

Alicia fussed with her shirt before pulling it over her head, her black curls springing out of the opening in a joyful froth that made him actually ache to touch them. *Her.* He glared down at his hands as if they'd betrayed him.

When she looked at him again, her dark eyes were soft, undoing him as surely as if she really had eviscerated him with a hunting knife. He would have preferred the latter. She made it incalculably worse by reaching over and smoothing her warm hand over his cheek, offering him... comfort?

"You look like you've swallowed broken glass," she said.

Kindly.

Very much as if she cared.

Nikolai didn't want what he couldn't have. It had been beaten out of him long ago. It was a simple, unassailable fact, like gravity. Like air.

Like light.

But he couldn't seem to stop himself from lifting his hand, tracing that tempting mouth of hers once more, watching the heat bloom again in her eyes.

Just one night, he told himself then. He couldn't help it. That smile of hers made him realize he was so tired of the cold, the dark. That he felt haunted by the things he'd lost, the wars he'd won, the battles he'd been fighting all his life. Just once, he *wanted.*

One night to explore this light of hers she shone so indiscriminately, he thought. Just one night to pretend he was something more than ice. A wise man didn't step onto a land mine when he could see it lying there in front of him, waiting to blow. But Nikolai had been through more hells than he could count. He could handle anything for a night. Even this. Even her.

Just one night.

"You should hold on," he heard himself say. He slid his hand around to cup the nape of her neck, and exulted in the shiver that moved over her at even so small a touch. As if she was his. That could never happen, he knew. But he'd allowed himself the night. He had every intention of making it a long one. "I'm only getting started."

If only he really had been a wolf.

Alicia scowled down at the desk in her office on Monday and tried valiantly to think of something—*anything*—other than Nikolai. And failed, as she'd been doing with alarming regularity since she'd sneaked away from his palatial penthouse in South Kensington early on Sunday morning.

If he'd really been a wolf, she'd likely be in hospital right now, recovering from being bitten in a lovely quiet coma or restful medicated haze, which would mean she'd be enjoying a much-needed holiday from the self-recriminating clamor inside her head.

At least I wasn't drunk....

Though if she was honest, some part of her almost wished she had been. *Almost.* As if that would be some kind of excuse when she knew from bitter experience that it wasn't.

The real problem was, she'd been perfectly aware of what she was doing on Saturday. She'd gone ahead and done it precisely *because* she hadn't been drunk. For no other reason than that she'd wanted him.

From her parents' back garden to a stranger in a car. She hadn't learned much of anything in all these years, had she? Given the chance, she'd gleefully act the promiscuous whore—drunk *or* sober.

That turned inside of her like bile, acidic and thick at the back of her throat.

"I think you must be a witch," he'd said at some point in those long, sleepless hours of too much pleasure, too hot and too addicting. He'd been sprawled out next to her, his rough voice no more than a growl in the dark of his cavernous bedroom.

A girl could get lost in a room like that, she'd thought. In a bed so wide. In a man like Nikolai, who had taken her over and over with a skill and a thoroughness and a sheer masculine prowess that made her wonder how she'd ever recover from it. *If* she would. But she hadn't wanted to think those things, not then. Not while it was still dark outside and they were cocooned on those soft sheets together, the world held at bay. There'd be time enough to work on forgetting, she'd thought. When it was over.

When it was morning.

She'd propped herself up on an elbow and looked down at him, his bold, hard face in shadows but those eyes of his as intense as ever.

"I'm not the driving force in this fairy tale," she'd said quietly. Then she'd dropped her gaze lower, past that hard mouth of his she now knew was a terrible, electric torment when he chose, and down to that astonishing torso of his laid out before her like a feast. "Red Riding Hood is a hapless little fool, isn't she? Always in the wrong place at the wrong time."

Alicia had meant that to come out light and breezy, but

it hadn't. It had felt intimate instead, somehow. Darker and deeper, and a different kind of ache inside. Not at all what she'd intended.

She'd felt the blue of his gaze like a touch.

Instead of losing herself there, she'd traced a lazy finger over the steel plates of his harshly honed chest. Devastatingly perfect. She moved from this scar to that tattoo, tracing each pucker of flesh, each white strip of long-ago agony, then smoothing her fingertip over the bright colors and Cyrillic letters that flowed everywhere else. Two kinds of marks, stamped permanently into his flesh. She'd been uncertain if she was fascinated or something else, something that made her mourn for all his body had suffered.

But it wasn't her place to ask.

"Bullet," he'd said quietly, when her fingers moved over a slightly raised and shiny patch of skin below his shoulder, as if she had asked after all. "I was in the army."

"For how long?"

"Too long."

She'd flicked a look at him, but had kept going, finding a long, narrow white scar that slashed across his taut abdomen and following the length of it, back and forth. So much violence boiled down to a thin white line etched into his hard, smooth flesh. It had made her hurt for him, but she still hadn't asked.

"Kitchen knife. My uncle." His voice had been little more than a rasp against the dark. She'd gone still, her fingers splayed across the scar in question. "He took his role as our guardian seriously," Nikolai had said, and his gruff voice had sounded almost amused, as if what he'd said was something other than awful. Alicia had chanced a glance at him, and saw a different truth in that wintry gaze, more vulnerable in the clasp of the dark than she'd imagined he knew. "He didn't like how I'd washed the dishes."

"Nikolai—" she'd begun, not knowing what she could possibly say, but spurred on by that torn look in his eyes.

He'd blinked, then frowned. "It was nothing."

But she'd known he was lying. And the fact that she'd had no choice but to let it pass, that this man wasn't hers to care for no matter how it felt as if he should have been, had rippled through her like actual, physical pain.

Alicia had moved on then to the tattoo of a wild beast rendered in a shocking sweep of bold color and dark black lines that wrapped around the left side of his body, from his shoulder all the way down to an inch or so above his sex. It was fierce and furious, all ferocious teeth and wicked claws, poised there as if ready to devour him.

As if, she'd thought, it already had.

"All of my sins," he'd said then, his voice far darker and rougher than before.

There'd been an almost-guarded look in his winter gaze when she'd glanced up at him, but she'd thought that was that same vulnerability again. And then he'd sucked in a harsh breath when she'd leaned over and pressed a kiss to the fearsome head of this creature that claimed him, as if she could wash away the things that had hurt him—uncles who wielded kitchen knives, whatever battles he'd fought in the army that had got him shot, all those shadows that lay heavy on his hard face. One kiss, then another, and she'd felt the coiling tension in him, the heat.

"Your sins are pretty," she'd whispered.

He'd muttered something ferocious in Russian as he'd hauled her mouth to his, then he'd pulled her astride him and surged into her with a dark fury and a deep hunger that had thrilled her all the way through, and she'd been lost in him all over again.

She was still lost.

"For God's sake, Alicia," she bit out, tired of the endless

cycle of her own thoughts, and her own appalling weakness. Her voice sounded loud in her small office. "You have work to do."

She had to snap out of this. Her desk was piled high after her two weeks abroad, her in-box was overflowing and she had a towering stack of messages indicating calls she needed to return now that she was back in the country. To say nothing of the report on the Latin American offices she'd visited while away that she had yet to put together, that Charlotte, her supervisor, expected her to present to the team later this week.

But she couldn't sink into her work the way she wanted, the way she usually could. There was that deep current of shame that flared inside of her, bright like some kind of cramp, reminding her of the last night she'd abandoned herself so completely....

At least this time, she remembered every last second of what she'd done. What *they'd* done. Surely that counted for something.

Her body still prickled now, here, as if electrified, every time she thought of him—and she couldn't seem to stop. Her nipples went hard and between her legs, she ran so hot it almost hurt, and it was such a deep betrayal of who she'd thought she'd become that it made her feel shaky.

Her thighs were still tender from the scrape of his hard jaw. There was a mark on the underside of one breast that he'd left deliberately, reminding her in that harsh, beautiful voice that *wolves bite, solnyshka*, making her laugh and squirm in reckless delight beneath him on that wide, masculine bed where she'd obviously *lost her mind*. Even her hips held memories of what she'd done, reminding her of her overwhelming response to him every now and again with a low, almost-pleasant ache that made her hate herself more every time she felt it.

She'd been hung over before. Ashamed of herself come the dawn. Sometimes that feeling had lingered for days as she'd promised herself that she'd stop partying so hard, knowing deep down that she wouldn't, and hadn't, until that last night in the back garden. But this wasn't *that*. This was worse.

She felt out of control. Knocked flat. Changed, utterly. A stranger to herself.

Alicia had been so sure the new identity she'd built over these past eight years was a fortress, completely impenetrable, impervious to attack. Hadn't she held Rosie at bay for ages? But one night with Nikolai had showed her that she was nothing but a glass house, precarious and fragile, and a single stone could bring it all crashing down. A single touch.

Not to mention, she hadn't even *thought* about protection that first time. He'd had to *put it in her hand*. Of all her many betrayals of herself that night, she thought that one was by far the most appalling. It made the shame that lived in her that much worse.

The only bright spot in all of this recrimination and regret was that her text to Rosie hadn't gone through. There'd been a big X next to it when she'd looked at her mobile that next morning. And when she'd arrived back at their flat on Sunday morning, Rosie had still been out.

Which meant that no one had any idea what Alicia had done.

"I wish I'd gone home when you did," Rosie had said with a sigh while they sat in their usual Sunday-afternoon café, paging lazily through the Sunday paper and poking at their plates of a traditional full English breakfast. "That place turned *absolutely mental* after hours, and I have to stop getting off with bankers who talk about the flipping property ladder like it's the most thrilling thing on the planet." Then she'd grinned that big grin of hers that meant she didn't regret a single thing, no matter what she said. "Maybe someday I'll actually follow your example."

"What fun would that be?" Alicia had asked lightly, any guilt she'd felt at lying by giant, glaring omission to her best friend drowned out by the sheer relief pouring through her.

Because if Rosie didn't know what she'd done, Alicia could pretend it had never happened.

There would be no discussing Nikolai, that SUV of his or what had happened in it, or that astonishing penthouse that she'd been entirely too gauche not to gape at, openly, when he'd brought her home. There would be no play-by-play description of those things he could do with such ease, that Alicia hadn't known could feel like that. There would certainly be no conversations about all of these confusing and pointless things she felt sloshing around inside of her when she thought about those moments he'd showed her his vulnerable side, as if a man whose last name she didn't know and hadn't asked was something more than a one-night stand.

And if there was no one to talk about it with, all of this urgency, this driving sense of loss, would disappear. *It had to.* Alicia would remain, outwardly, as solid and reliable and predictably boring as she'd become in these past years. An example. The same old Saint Alicia, polishing her halo.

And maybe someday, if she was well-behaved and lucky, she'd believe it again herself.

"Are you ready for the big meeting?"

Her supervisor's dry voice from the open doorway made Alicia jump guiltily in her chair, and it was much harder than it should have been to smile at Charlotte the way she usually did. She was sure what she'd done over her weekend was plastered all over her face. That Charlotte could *see* how filthy she really was, the way her father had. All her sins at a single glance, like that furious creature that bristled on Nikolai's chest.

"Meeting?" she echoed weakly.

"The new celebrity partnership?" Charlotte prompted her. At Alicia's blank look, she laughed. "We all have to show our faces in the conference hall in exactly five minutes, and Daniel delivered a new version of his official presidential lecture on tardiness last week. I wouldn't be late."

"I'll be right along," Alicia promised, and this time, managed a bit of a better smile.

She sighed heavily when Charlotte withdrew, feeling much too fragile. Hollow and raw, as if she was still fighting off that hangover she hadn't had. But she knew it was him. Nikolai. That much fire, that much wild heat, had to have a backlash. She shouldn't be surprised.

This will fade, she told herself, and she should know, shouldn't she? She'd had other things to forget. *It always does, eventually.*

But the current of self-loathing that wound through her then suggested otherwise.

This was not the end of the world. This was no more than a bit of backsliding into shameful behavior, and she wasn't very happy with herself for doing it, but it wouldn't happen again.

No one had walked in on her doing it. No one even knew. Everything was going to be fine.

Alicia blew out a shaky breath, closed down her computer, then made her way toward the big conference hall on the second floor, surprised to find the office already deserted. That could only mean that the celebrity charity in question was a particularly thrilling one. She racked her brain as she climbed the stairs, but she couldn't remember what the last memo had said about it or even if she'd read it.

She hated these meetings, always compulsory and always

about standard-waving, a little bit of morale-building, and most of all, PR. They were a waste of her time. Her duties involved the financial planning and off-site management of the charity's regional offices scattered across Latin America. Partnering with much bigger, much more well-known celebrity charities was more of a fundraising and publicity endeavor, which always made Daniel, their president, ecstatic—but didn't do much for Alicia.

She was glad she was a bit late, she thought as she hurried down the gleaming hallway on the second level. She could slip in, stand at the back, applaud loudly at something to catch Daniel's eye and prove she'd attended, then slip back out again and return to all that work on her messy desk.

Alicia silently eased open the heavy door at the rear of the hall. Down at the front, a man was talking confidently to the quiet, rapt room as she slipped inside.

At first she thought she was imagining it, given where her head had been all day.

And then it hit her. Hard.

She wasn't hearing things.

She knew that voice.

She'd know it anywhere. Her body certainly did.

Rough velvet. Russian. That scratch of whiskey, dark and powerful, commanding and sure.

Nikolai.

Her whole body went numb, nerveless. The door handle slipped from her hand, she jerked her head up to confirm what couldn't possibly be true, couldn't possibly be happening—

The heavy door slammed shut behind her with a terrific crash.

Every single head in the room swiveled toward her, as if she'd made her entrance in the glare of a bright, hot spotlight and to the tune of a boisterous marching band, complete with clashing cymbals.

But she only saw him.

Him. Nikolai. *Here.*

Once again, everything disappeared. There was only the fearsome blue of his beautiful eyes as they nailed her to the door behind her, slamming into her so hard she didn't know how she withstood it, how she wasn't on her knees from the force of it.

He was even more devastating than she'd let herself remember.

Still dressed all in black, today he wore an understated, elegant suit that made his lethal frame look consummately powerful rather than raw and dangerous, a clever distinction. And one that could only be made by expert tailoring to the tune of thousands upon thousands of pounds. The brutal force of him filled the room, filled her, and her body reacted as if they were still naked, still sprawled across his bed in a tangle of sheets and limbs. She felt too hot, almost feverish. His mouth was a harsh line, but she knew how it tasted and what it could do, and there was something dark and predatory in his eyes that made her tremble deep inside.

And remember. Dear God, what she remembered. What he'd done, how she'd screamed, what he'd promised and how he'd delivered, again and again and again....

It took her much too long to recollect where she was *now.*

Not in a club in Shoreditch this time, filled with drunken idiots who wouldn't recall what they did, much less what she did, but *in her office.* Surrounded by every single person she worked with, all of whom were staring at her.

Nikolai's gaze was so blue. So relentlessly, impossibly, mercilessly blue.

"I'm so sorry to interrupt," Alicia managed to murmur, hoping she sounded appropriately embarrassed and apologetic, the way anyone would after slamming that door—and not as utterly rocked to the core, as lit up with shock and horror, as she felt.

It took a superhuman effort to wrench her gaze away from the man who stood there glaring at her—who wasn't a figment of her overheated imagination, who had the same terrifying power over her from across a crowded room as he'd had in his bed, whom she'd never thought she'd see again, *ever*—and slink to an empty seat in the back row.

She would never know how she did it.

Down in the front of the room, a phalanx of assistants behind him and the screen above him announcing who he was in no uncertain terms, NIKOLAI KOROVIN OF THE KOROVIN FOUNDATION, she saw Nikolai blink. Once.

And then he kept talking as if Alicia hadn't interrupted him. As if he hadn't recognized her—as if Saturday night was no more than the product of her feverish imagination.

As if she didn't exist.

She'd never wished so fervently that she didn't. That she could simply disappear into the ether as if she'd never been, or sink into the hole in the ground she was sure his icy glare had dug beneath her.

What had she been thinking, to touch this man? To give herself to him so completely? Had she been drunk after all? Because today, here and now, he looked like nothing so much as a sharpened blade. Gorgeous and mesmerizing, but terrifying. That dark, ruthless power came off him in waves the way it had in the club, even stronger without the commotion of the music and the crowd, and this time, Alicia understood it.

This was who he was.

She *knew* who he was.

He was Nikolai Korovin. His brother was one of the most famous actors on the planet, which made Nikolai famous by virtue of his surname alone. Alicia knew his name like every other person in her field, thanks to his brilliant, inspired management of the Korovin Foundation since its creation two years ago. People whispered he was a harsh and demanding boss, but always fair, and the amount of money he'd already raised for the good causes the Korovin Foundation supported was staggering.

He was *Nikolai Korovin*, and he'd explored every part of her body with that hard, fascinating mouth. He'd held her in his arms and made her feel impossibly beautiful, and then he'd driven into her so hard, so deep, filling her so perfectly and driving her so out of her mind with pleasure, she had to bear down now to keep from reacting to the memory. He'd made her feel so wild with lust, so deliciously addicted to him, that she'd sobbed the last time she'd shattered into pieces all around him. *She knew how he tasted.* His mouth, his neck, the length of his proud sex. That angry, tattooed monster crouched on his chest. She knew what made him groan, fist his hands into her hair.

More than all of that, she knew how those bright eyes looked when he told her things she had the sense he didn't normally speak of to anyone. She knew too much.

He was Nikolai Korovin, and she didn't have to look over at Daniel's beaming face to understand what it meant that he was here. For Daniel as president, for making this happen. For the charity itself. A partnership with the Korovin Foundation was more than a publicity opportunity—it was a coup. It would take their relatively small charity with global ambitions and slam it straight into the big time, once and for all. And it went without saying that Nikolai Korovin, the legendary CEO of the Korovin Foundation and the person responsible for all its business decisions, needed to be kept happy for that to happen.

That look on his face when he'd seen her had been anything but happy.

Alicia had to force herself to sit still as the implications of this washed through her. She had betrayed herself completely and had a tawdry one-night stand. That was bad enough. But it turned out she'd done it with a man who could end her career.

Eight years ago she'd lost her father's respect and her own self-respect in the blur of a long night she couldn't even recall. Now she could lose her job.

Today. At the end of this meeting. Whenever Nikolai liked.

When you decide to mess up your life, you really go for it, she told herself, fighting back the panic, the prick of tears. *No simple messes for Alicia Teller! Better to go with total devastation!*

Alicia sat through the meeting in agony, expecting something to happen the moment it ended—lightning to strike, the world to come crashing to a halt, Nikolai to summon her to the front of the room and demand her termination at once—but nothing did. Nikolai didn't glance in her direction again. He and his many assistants merely swept from the hall like a sleek black cloud, followed by the still-beaming Daniel and all the rest of the upper level directors and managers.

Alicia told herself she was relieved. This had to be relief, this sharp thing in the pit of her stomach that made it hard to breathe, because nothing else made sense. She'd known he was dangerous the moment she'd met him, not that it had stopped her.

Now she knew exactly *how* dangerous.

She was an idiot. A soon-to-be-sacked idiot.

Her colleagues all grimaced in sympathy as they trooped

back downstairs. They thought the fact she'd slammed that door was embarrassing enough. Little did they know.

"Can't imagine having a man like that look at me the way he did you," one said in an undertone. "I think I'd have nightmares!"

"I believe I will," Alicia agreed.

She spent the rest of the afternoon torn between panic and dread. She attacked all the work on her desk, like a drowning woman grasping for something to hold. Every time her phone rang, her heart leaped in her chest. Every time she heard a noise outside her office door, she tensed, thinking she was finished.

Any minute now, she'd be called up to Daniel's office. She could see it spool out before her like a horror film. Daniel's secretary would message the salacious news to half the office even as Alicia walked to her doom. So not only would Alicia be dismissed from her job because of a tawdry one-night stand with a man most people would have recognized and she certainly should have—but everyone she worked with and respected would know it.

It would be as it had been that morning her father had woken her up and told her what he'd seen, what she'd done—but this time, far more people would know what kind of trollop she was. People she'd impressed with her work ethic over the years would now sit about imagining her naked. *Having sex. With Nikolai.* She felt sick even thinking about it.

"I warned you!" Charlotte said as she stuck her head through the doorway, making Alicia jump again. A quick, terrified glance told her that her supervisor looked…sympathetic. Not horribly embarrassed. Not scandalized in the least. "I told Daniel you were on a call that ran a bit long, so no worries there."

"Thank you." Alicia's voice sounded strained, but Charlotte didn't seem to notice.

"Nikolai Korovin is very intense, isn't he?" Charlotte shook her head. "The man has eyes like a laser beam!"

"I expect he doesn't get interrupted very often," Alicia said, fighting for calm. "I don't think he cares for it."

"Clearly not," Charlotte agreed. And then laughed.

And that was it. No request that Alicia pack up her things or don a scarlet letter. No summons to present herself in Daniel's office to be summarily dismissed for her sexually permissive behavior with the fiercely all-business CEO of their new celebrity partner foundation. Not even the faintest hint of a judgmental look.

But Alicia knew it was coming. She'd not only seen the way Nikolai had looked at her, but now that she knew that he was Nikolai *Korovin,* she was afraid she knew exactly what it meant.

He was utterly ruthless. About everything. The entire internet agreed.

It was only a matter of time until all hell broke loose, so she simply put her head down, kept off the internet because it only served to panic her more, and worked. She stayed long after everyone else had left. She stayed until she'd cleared her desk, because that way, when they tittered behind their hands and talked about how they'd never imagined her acting *that way,* at least they wouldn't be able to say she hadn't done her job.

Small comfort, indeed.

It was almost nine o'clock when she finished, and Alicia was completely drained. She shrugged into her coat and wrapped her scarf around her neck, wishing there was a suit of armor she could put on instead, some way to ward off what she was certain was coming. Dread sat heavy in her stomach, leaden and full, and there was nothing she could do about it but wait to see what Nikolai did. Go home, hole up on the couch with a takeaway and Rosie's usual happy chatter, try to ease this terrible anxiety with bad American television and wait to see what he'd do to her. Because he was Nikolai Korovin, and he could do whatever he liked.

And would. Of that, she had no doubt.

Alicia made her way out of the building, deciding the moment she stepped out into the cold, clear night that she should walk home instead of catching the bus. It was only thirty-five minutes or so at a brisk pace, and it might sort out her head. Tire her out. Maybe even allow her to sleep.

She tucked her hands into her pockets and started off, but had only made it down the front stairs to the pavement when she realized that the big black SUV pulled up to the curb wasn't parked there, but was idling.

A whisper of premonition tingled through her as she drew closer, then turned into a tumult when the back door cracked open before her.

Nikolai Korovin appeared from within the way she should have known he would, tall and thunderous and broadcasting that dark, brooding intensity of his. He didn't have to block her path. He simply closed the door behind him and stood there, taking over the whole neighborhood, darker than the sky above, and Alicia was as unable to move as if he'd pinned her to the ground himself.

She was caught securely in his too-knowing, too-blue gaze all over again, as if he held her in his hands, and the shiver of hungry need that teased down the length of her spine only added insult to injury. She despaired of herself.

If she respected herself at all, Alicia knew with that same old kick of shame in her gut, she wouldn't feel even that tiny little spark of something far too much like satisfaction that he was here. That he'd come for her. As if maybe he was as thrown by what had happened between them as she was…

"Hello, Alicia," Nikolai said, a dark lash in that rough voice of his, velvet and warning and so very Russian, smooth power and all of that danger in every taut line of his beautiful body. He looked fierce. Cold and furious. "Obviously, we need to talk."

CHAPTER FOUR

For a moment, Alicia wanted nothing more than to run.

To bolt down the dark street like some desperate animal of prey and hope that this particular predator had better things to do than follow.

Something passed between them then, a shimmer in the dark, and Alicia understood that he knew exactly what she was thinking. That he was picturing the same thing. The chase, the inevitable capture, and *then*...

Nikolai's eyes gleamed dangerously.

Alicia tilted up her chin, settled back on her heels and faced him, calling on every bit of courage and stamina at her disposal. She wasn't going to run. She might have done something she was ashamed of, but she hadn't done it alone. And this time she had to face it—she couldn't skulk off back to university and limit her time back home as she'd done for years until the Reddicks moved to the north.

"Well," she said briskly. "This is awkward."

His cold eyes blazed. He was so different tonight, she thought. A blade of a man gone near incandescent with that icy rage, a far cry from the man she'd thought she'd seen in those quieter moments—the one who had told her things that still lodged in her heart. The change should have terrified her. Instead, perversely, she felt that hunger shiver deeper into her, settling into a hard knot low in her belly, turning into a thick, sweet heat.

"This is not awkward," he replied, his voice deceptively mild. Alicia could see that ferocious look in his eyes, however, and wasn't fooled. "This is a quiet conversation on a deserted street."

"Perhaps the word loses something in translation?" she suggested, perhaps a shade too brightly, as if that was some defense against the chill of him.

"Awkward," he bit out, his accent more pronounced than before and a fascinating pulse of temper in the hinge of his tight jaw, "was looking up in the middle of a business meeting today to see a woman I last laid eyes upon while I was making her come stare right back at me."

Alicia didn't want to think about the last time he'd made her come. She'd thought they were finished after all those long, heated hours. He'd taken that as a challenge. And he'd held her hips between his hands and licked into her with lazy intent, making her writhe against him and sob....

She swallowed, and wished he wasn't watching her. He saw far too much.

"You're looking at me as if I engineered this. I didn't." She eyed him warily, her hands deep in the pockets of her coat and curled into fists, which he couldn't possibly see. Though she had the strangest notion he could. "I thought the point of a one-night stand with no surnames exchanged was that this would never happen."

"Have you had a great many of them, then?"

Alicia pretended that question didn't hit her precisely where she was the most raw, and with a ringing blow.

"If you mean as many as you've had, certainly not." She shrugged when his dark brows rose in a kind of affronted astonishment. "There are no secrets on the internet. Surely you, of all people, must know that. And it's a bit late to tally up our numbers and draw unflattering conclusions, don't you think? The damage is well and truly done."

"That damage," Nikolai said, that rough voice of his too tough, too cold, and that look on his hard face merciless, "is what I'm here to discuss."

Alicia didn't want to lose her job. She didn't want to know what kind of pressure Nikolai was prepared to put on her, what threats he was about to issue. She wanted this to go away again—to be the deep, dark secret that no one ever knew but her.

And it still could be, no matter how pitiless he looked in that moment.

"Why don't we simply blank each other?" she asked, once again a touch too brightly—which she could see didn't fool him at all. If anything, it called attention to her nervousness. "Isn't that the traditional method of handling situations like this?"

He shook his head, his eyes looking smoky in the dark, his mouth a resolute line.

"I do not mix business and pleasure," he said, with a finality that felt like a kick in the stomach. "I do not *mix* at all. The women I sleep with do not infiltrate my life. They appear in carefully orchestrated places of my choosing. They do not ambush me at work. Ever."

Alicia decided that later—much later, when she knew how this ended and could breathe without thinking she might burst into panicked, frustrated tears—she would think about the fact that a man like Nikolai had so many women that he'd developed *policies* to handle them all. *Later.* Right now, she had to fight back, or surrender here and now and lose everything.

"I assure you," she said, as if she had her own set of violated policies and was considering them as she met his gaze, "I feel the same way."

Nikolai shifted, and then suddenly there was no distance between them at all. His hands were on her neck, his thumbs at her jaw, tipping her head back to look up at him. Alicia should have felt attacked, threatened. She should have leaped for safety. Screamed. *Something.*

But instead, everything inside of her went still. And hot.

"I am not here to concern myself with your feelings," he told her in that rough velvet whisper. That fascinating mouth was grim again, but she could almost touch it with hers, if she dared. She didn't. "I am here to eliminate this problem as swiftly and as painlessly as possible."

But his hands were on her. Just as they'd been in the club when he'd told her to run. And she wondered if he was as conflicted as she was, and as deeply. What it would take to see that guarded look on his face again, that vulnerable cast to his beautiful mouth.

"You really are the gift that keeps on giving, Nikolai," she managed to say, retreating to a sarcastic tone, hoping the bite of it might protect her. She even smiled, thinly. "I've never felt happier about my reckless, irresponsible choices."

He let out a short laugh, and whatever expression that was on his hard face then—oddly taut and expectant, dark and hot—was like a flame inside of her. His hands were strong and like brands against her skin. His thumbs moved gently, lazily, as if stroking her jaw of their own accord.

"I don't like sharp women with smart mouths, Alicia," he told her, harsh and low, and every word was a caress against her skin, her sex, as if he was using those long fingers deep in her heat. "I like them sweet. Soft. Yielding and obedient and easily dismissed."

That same electricity crackled between them even here on the cold street, a bright coil that wound tight inside of her, making her feel mad with it. Too close to an explosion she knew she couldn't allow.

"What luck," she said, sharp and smart and nothing like soft at all. "I believe there's a sex shop in the next street, filled with exactly the kind of plastic dolls you prefer. Shall I point you in the right direction?"

He let go of her as if she'd burned him. And she recognized that dark heat in his gaze, the way it changed his expression, the things it did to that mouth.

"Get in the car, Alicia," he ordered her darkly. "I have an aversion to discussing my private life on a public street, deserted or not."

It was her turn to laugh, in disbelief.

"You have to be crazy if you think I'm getting back in that thing," she told him. "I'd rather get down on my hands and knees and crawl across a bed of nails, thank you."

She knew it was a mistake almost before the words left her mouth, and that sudden wolfish look on his face nearly undid her. It was impossible, then, not to picture herself down on her hands and knees, crawling toward that ravenous heat in his winter eyes she could remember too well, and could see right there before her now.

"I wasn't thinking about sex at present," he said coolly, and even though she could see from that fire in his gaze that he'd imagined much the same thing she had, she felt slapped. Shamed anew. "Why? Were you?"

It was time to go, Alicia realized then. It had been time to go the moment she'd seen that SUV idling at the curb. Before this thing got any worse—and she had no doubt at all that it would.

"It was lovely to finally meet you properly, Mr. Korovin," she said crisply. She put a faint emphasis on the word *properly,* and he blinked, looking almost…abashed? But that was impossible. "I'm sure your partnership with the charity will be a huge boost for us, and I'm as grateful as anyone else. And now I'm going home, where I will continue to actively pretend none of this ever happened. I can only hope you'll do the same."

"You didn't tell me you worked for a children's charity."

She didn't know what she'd expected him to say, but it wasn't that, with that sting of accusation. She eyed him warily. "Neither did you."

"Did you know who I was, Alicia?" Nikolai's face was so hard, his gaze so cold. She felt the chill suddenly, cutting into her. "You stumbled into my arms. Then you stumbled into that conference room today. Convenient." His eyes raked over her, as if looking for evidence that she'd planned this nightmare. "Your next stumble had best not involve any tabloid magazines or tell-all interviews. You won't like how I respond."

But she couldn't believe he truly thought that, she realized when the initial shock of it passed. She'd been in that bed with him. She knew better. Which meant he was lashing out, seeing what would hurt her. *Eliminating problems,* as he'd said he would.

"There's no need to draw out this torture," she told him, proud of how calm she sounded. "If you want me sacked, we both know you can do it easily. Daniel would have the entire staff turn cartwheels down the length of the Mall if he thought that would please you. Firing me will be a snap." She squared her shoulders as if she might have to sustain a blow. As if she already had. "If that's what you plan to do, I certainly can't stop you."

He stared at her for a long moment. A car raced past on the street beside them and in the distance she could hear the rush of traffic on the main road. Her breath was coming hard and fast, like she was fighting whole battles in her head while he only stood there, still and watchful.

"You're a distraction, Alicia," he told her then, something like regret in his voice. "I can't pretend otherwise."

"Of course you can," she retorted, fighting to keep calm. "All people do is pretend. I pretended to be the sort of woman—" She didn't want to announce exactly what she'd been pretending for eight years, not to him, so she frowned instead. "Just ignore me and I'll return the favor. It will be easy."

"I am not the actor in the family."

"I didn't ask you to play *King Lear*," she threw at him, panicked and exasperated in equal measure. "I only asked you to ignore me. How difficult can that possibly be? A man like you must have that down to a science."

"What an impression you have of me," Nikolai said after a moment, his voice silken, his eyes narrow. "I treated you very well, Alicia. Have you forgot so soon? You wept out your gratitude, when you weren't screaming my name."

She didn't need the reminder. She didn't need the heat of it, the wild pulse in her chest, between her legs.

"I was referring to your wealth and status," Alicia said, very distinctly. "Your position. The fact you have armies of assistants to make sure no one can approach you without your permission. Not your…"

"Particular talents?" His voice was mild enough as he finished the thought for her. The effect his words had on her, inside her, was not.

But then he leaned back against the side of his car, as if he was perfectly relaxed. Even his face changed, and she went still again, because there was something far more predatory about him in this moment than there had been before. It scraped the air thin.

"I have a better solution," he said, in the confident and commanding tone she recognized from the conference room. "I don't need to fire you, necessarily. It will serve my purposes far better to use this situation to my advantage."

Alicia could only shake her head, looking for clues on

that face of his that gave nothing away. "I don't know what that means."

"It means, Alicia," he said almost softly, a wolf's dangerous smile in those winter eyes if not on that hard mouth, "that I need a date."

He could use this, Nikolai thought, while Alicia stared up at him as if he'd said that last sentence in Russian instead of English. He could use her.

A problem well managed could become a tool. And every tool could be a weapon, in the right hands. Why not Alicia?

He'd expected her to want more than Saturday night—they always did. And the sex they'd had had been...troubling. He'd known it while it was happening. He'd known it in between, when he'd found himself talking of things he never, ever talked about. He'd known it when he'd opened his eyes to watch her tiptoe from his room on Sunday morning, and had discovered he wanted her to stay.

He knew it now, remembering her sweet, hot mouth against his tattoo as if she'd blessed that snarling representation of the monster in him. As if she'd made it sacred, somehow. The moment he'd seen her, he'd expected she would try to leverage that, take it from him somehow. He'd planned to make it clear to her she had to go—before she could try.

But she claimed she wanted to ignore him. He should have been thrilled.

He told himself he was.

"I'm sorry." Her voice was carefully blank when she finally spoke, to match the expression on her face. "Did you say you needed a *date?*"

"I did." It occurred to him that he was enjoying himself, for the first time since he'd looked up and seen her standing in that conference room, in clear violation of all his rules. "There is a Christmas ball in Prague that I must attend in a few weeks, and it will go much more smoothly with a woman on my arm."

These things were always better with a date, it was true. It didn't matter who it was. The presence of any date at his side would repel most of the vulturelike women who always circled him like he was fresh meat laid out in the hot sun, allowing Nikolai to concentrate on business. And in the case of this particular charity ball, on Veronika—who had only this morning confirmed that she and her lover would attend.

Because Nikolai had realized, as he looked at her in the light of the streetlamps and thought strategy instead of containment, that Alicia could very well turn out to be the best weapon yet in his dirty little war.

"I'm certain there are hordes of women who would love nothing more than to fill that opening for you," she said, with none of the deference or courtesy he was used to from his subordinates and dates alike. There was no reason on earth he should find that intriguing. "Perhaps one of your many assistants has a sign-up sheet? A call list? Maybe even an audition process to weed out the lucky winner from the multitudes?"

He'd told her he liked sweet and biddable, and he did. But he liked this, too. He liked the way she talked to him, as if it hadn't occurred to her that she should fear him like everyone else did. It made him want to lick her until all of that tartness melted all over him, and he didn't want to examine that particular urge any closer.

"Something like that," he said. "But it's all very tedious. All I want is a pretty dress, a polite smile. I don't have time for the games."

"Or the person, apparently," she said, her voice dry. "I'm

sure that's very rewarding for whichever pretty dress you choose. But what does this have to do with me?"

Nikolai smiled, adrenaline moving through him the way it always did before a tactical strike. Before another win.

"You want nothing to do with me." His voice was a silken threat in the cold night. "Or so you claim."

"You're right," she said, but her voice caught. "I don't."

"Then it's perfect," he said. "It's only a handful of weeks until the ball. We'll allow ourselves to be photographed on a few dates. The world will think I'm smitten, as I am very rarely seen with the same woman more than once. More specifically, my ex-wife will think the same. And as she has always greatly enjoyed her fantasy that she is the only woman to have any power over me, and has never been one to resist a confrontation, it will put her right where I want her."

She stared at him. "And where is that, exactly?"

"Veronika and I need to have a conversation," Nikolai said with cool dismissal. "Hopefully, our last. The idea that I might have moved on will expedite that, I think."

"How tempting," she said after a moment, her voice as arid as that look in her eyes. "I've always aspired to be cold-bloodedly used to make another woman jealous, of course. It's truly every girl's dream. But I think I'll pass."

"This has nothing to do with jealousy," he said impatiently. "The only thing left between Veronika and me is spite. If that. I'm sure you'll see it yourself at the ball."

"Even more appealing. But still—no."

"Your whole office saw me stare at you today." He shrugged when her eyes narrowed. "They could hardly miss it. How much of a leap will it be for them to imagine that was the beginning of an infatuation?"

"But they won't have to make that leap." Her eyes were

glittering again. "I've declined your lovely offer and we're going to ignore each other."

"I don't think so." He watched her take that in. Knew she didn't like it. Found he didn't much care if she was happy about it, so long as she did it. "I'm going to take an interest in you, Alicia. Didn't you know? Everybody loves a romance."

"They won't believe it." Her voice sounded thick, as if the idea of it horrified her, and he was perverse enough to take that as a challenge. "They won't believe someone like you could get infatuated at all, much less with me."

He smiled. "They will. And more to the point, so will Veronika."

And he could kill two birds with one stone. He could dig into this attraction, the unacceptable intoxication this woman made him feel, and in so doing, strip away its power over him. Make certain he never again felt the need to unburden himself in such a shockingly uncharacteristic manner to a total stranger. At the same time, he could use Veronika's smug certainty about her place in his life against her. It was perfect.

Alicia stared back at him, so hard he thought he could hear her mind racing.

"Why bring any of this into the office at all?" she asked, sounding frustrated. Panicked, even. "If you want me to go to this ball, fine. I'll do it, but I don't see why anyone needs to know about it but us. No unlikely romance necessary."

"And how will that work?" he asked mildly. "When pictures of us at that ball show up in all the papers, and they will, it will look as if we were keeping our relationship a secret. As if we were hiding something. Think of the gossip then."

"You said you're not an actor," she said. "Yet this seems like a very elaborate bit of theater."

"I told you, you're a distraction," he replied, almost gently. He wanted to show her what he meant. To bury his face in that crook of her neck. To make her quiver for him the way he knew he could. Only the fact he wanted it too much kept him from it. "I don't allow distractions, Alicia. I neutralize them or I use them for my own ends."

"I don't want to be in any papers." Her voice was low, her eyes intense on his. It took him a moment to realize she was panicked. A better man might not have enjoyed that. "I don't want *pictures* of me out there, and certainly not with you."

"There's a certain liberty in having no choices, Alicia," he told her, not sure why it bothered him that she was so opposed to a picture *with him*. It made his voice harsher. "It makes life very simple. Do what I tell you to do, or look for a new job."

Nikolai didn't think that was the first moment it had occurred to her that he held all the power here, but it was no doubt when she realized he had every intention of using it as he pleased. He saw it on her face. In her remarkable eyes.

And he couldn't help but touch her again then, sliding his hand over her cheek as he'd done before. He felt the sweet heat of her where his fingertips touched her hairline, the chill of her soft skin beneath his palm. And that wild heat that was only theirs, sparking wild, charging through him.

Making him almost wish he was a different man.

She wore a thick black coat against the cold, a bright red scarf looped around her elegant neck. Her ink-black curls were pulled back from her face with a scrap of brightly patterned fabric, and he knew that beneath it she was dressed in even more colors, bright colors. Emerald greens and chocolate browns. She was so bright it made his head spin, even here in the dark. It made him achingly hard.

She is nothing more than an instrument, he told himself.

Another weapon for your arsenal. And soon enough, this intoxication will fade into nothing.

"Please," she whispered, and he wished he were the kind of man who could care. Who could soothe her. But he wasn't, no matter what he told her in the dark. "You don't understand. I don't want to lose my job, but I can't do this."

"You can," Nikolai told her. "And you will." He felt more in control than he had since she'd slammed into him at the edge of that dance floor, and he refused to give that up again. He wouldn't. "I'll be the one infatuated, Alicia. You need only surrender."

She shook her head, but she didn't pull her face from his grasp, and he knew what that meant even if she didn't. He knew what surrender looked like, and he smiled.

"Feel free to refuse me at first," he told Alicia then, his voice the only soft thing about him, as if he was a sweet and gentle lover and these words were the poetry he'd told her he didn't write. As if he was someone else. Maybe it would help her to think so. "Resist me, if you can. That will only make it look better."

"I won't do it," Alicia told him, hearing how unsteady her voice was and hating that he heard it, too. Hating all of this. "I won't play along."

"You will," he said in that implacable way that made something inside her turn over and shiver, while that half smile played with the corner of his hard mouth as if he knew something she didn't. "Or I'll have you sacked so fast it will make your head spin. And don't mistake sexual attraction for mercy, Alicia. I don't have any."

"Of course not," she bit out, as afraid that she would burst into tears right there as she was that she would nestle further into his hand, both impulses terrible and overwhelming at once. "You're the big, bad wolf. Fangs and teeth. I get the picture. I still won't do it."

She wrenched herself away from the terrible beguilement of his touch then, and ran down the street the way she should have at the start, panic biting at her heels as if she thought he might chase her.

He didn't—but then, he didn't have to chase her personally. His words did that for him. They haunted her as she tossed and turned in her sleepless bed that night. They moved over her like an itch she couldn't scratch. Like a lash against her skin, leaving the kind of scars he wore in their wake. Kitchen knives and bullets.

Do what I tell you to do.

Alicia was appalled at herself. He could say terrible things, propose to use her in some sick battle with his ex-wife, and still, she wanted him. He was mean and surly and perfectly happy to threaten her—and she wanted him. She lay awake in her bed and shivered when she thought about that last, simple touch, his hand hot despite the chill of the night air, holding her face so gently, making everything inside her run together and turn into honey.

Because that fool inside of her wanted that touch to mean something more. Wanted this attraction between them to have more to do with that vulnerability he'd shown her than the sex they'd had.

Wanted Saturday night to be different from that terrible night eight years ago.

He wants to use you, nothing more, she reminded herself for the millionth time, punching at her pillow in exhausted despair. *It means nothing more than that.*

But Alicia couldn't have pictures of herself in the tabloids. Not at all, and certainly not in the company of a man who might have been called a playboy, had he been less formidable. Not that it mattered what they called him—her father would know exactly what he was. Too wealthy, too hard. Too obvious. A man like that wanted women for one thing only, and her father would know it.

He would think she was back to old tricks. She knew he would.

Alicia shuddered, her face pressed into her pillow. She could *see* that awful look on her father's face that hideous morning as if he stood in front of her the way he'd done then.

"He is a *married man*. You know his wife, his children," her father had whispered, looking as deeply horrified as Alicia had felt.

"Dad," she'd managed to say, though her head had pounded and her mouth had been like sand. "Dad, I don't know what happened.... It's all—I don't remember—"

"I know what happened," he'd retorted, disgust plain in his voice and all across his face. "I saw you, spread-eagled on the grass with a *married man,* our *neighbor*—"

"Dad—" she'd tried again, tears in her voice and her eyes, afraid she might be sick.

"The way you dress, the way you flaunt yourself." He'd shaken his head, condemnation and that deep disgust written all over him. "I knew you dressed like a common whore, Alicia, but I never thought you'd *act* like one."

She couldn't go through that again, she thought then, staring in mute despair at her ceiling. She wouldn't go through it again, no matter how *infatuated* Nikolai pretended he was. No matter what.

He was going to have to fire her, she decided. She would call his bluff.

"No," she said, very firmly, when a coworker ran up to her the following day as she fixed herself a midmorning cup of tea and breathlessly asked if she'd *heard*. "Heard what?"

But she had a terrible suspicion she could guess. Ruthless and efficient, that was Nikolai.

"Nikolai Korovin *expressly* asked after you at the meeting this morning!" the excitable Melanie from the PR team whispered in that way of hers that alerted the entire office and most of the surrounding neighborhood, her eyes wide and pale cheeks red with the thrill of it all. "He *grilled* the team about you! Do you think that means he…?"

She couldn't finish that sentence, Alicia noted darkly. It was too much for Melanie. The very idea of Nikolai Korovin's interest—his *infatuation*—made the girl practically crumple into a shivering heap at Alicia's feet.

"I imagine he's the kind of man who keeps an annotated enemies list within arm's reach and several elaborate revenge plots at the ready," Alicia said as calmly as possible, dumping as much cold water on this fire of his as she could, even though she suspected it wouldn't do any good. "He certainly doesn't *like* me, Melanie."

The other woman didn't looked particularly convinced, no doubt because Alicia's explanation flew in the face of the grand romance she'd already concocted in her head. Just as Nikolai had predicted.

"No, thank you," Alicia told the emissary from his army of assistants two days after that, who walked up to Alicia as she stood in the open plan part of the office with every eye trained on her and asked if she might want to join them all for a meal after work?

"Mr. Korovin wanted me to tell you that it's a restaurant in Soho he thinks you'd quite enjoy," the woman persisted, her smile never dropping from her lips. "One of his favorites in London. And his treat, of course."

Alicia's heart hammered in her chest so hard she wondered for a panicked moment if she was having some kind of heart attack. Then she remembered how many people were watching her, much too avidly, and forced a polite smile in return.

"I'm still catching up from my trip," she lied. "I'll have to work late again, I'm afraid. But please do thank Mr. Korovin for thinking of me."

Somehow, that last part didn't choke her.

By the end of that week, the fact that ruthless and somewhat terrifying billionaire Nikolai Korovin had *taken an interest* in Alicia was the only thing anyone in the office seemed able to talk about, and he'd accomplished it without lowering himself to speak to her directly. She felt hunted, trapped, and she hadn't even seen him since that night on the street.

He was diabolical.

"I believe Nikolai Korovin wants to *date* you, Alicia," Charlotte said as they sat in her office on Friday morning, going over the presentation for their team meeting later that afternoon. She grinned widely when Alicia looked at her. "I don't know whether to be excited or a bit overwhelmed at the idea of someone like him dating a normal person."

"This is so embarrassing," Alicia said weakly, which was perhaps the first honest thing she'd said on the topic all week. "I honestly don't know why he's doing this."

"Love works in mysterious ways," Charlotte singsonged, making Alicia groan.

Everybody loves a romance, he'd said in that cold, cynical voice of his. Damn him.

"This is a man who could date anyone in the world, and has done," Alicia said, trying to sound lighter, breezier, than she felt. "Why on earth should a man like that want to date *me?*"

"You didn't drop at his feet on command, obviously," Charlotte said with a shrug. Only because he hadn't issued that particular command that night, Alicia thought sourly, fighting to keep her expression neutral. "Men like Nikolai Korovin are used to having anything they desire the moment they desire it. Ergo, they desire most what they can't have."

Alicia hadn't been so happy to see the end of a work week in years. She hated him, she told herself that weekend, again and again and again, until she could almost pretend that she really did. That it was that simple.

"I hate him," she told Rosie, taking out her feelings on the sad little boil-in-the-bag chicken curry they'd made for Sunday dinner with a violent jab of her fork. It had been two blessed Nikolai-free days. She couldn't bear the thought of what tomorrow might bring. "He's incredibly unprofessional. He's made the whole office into a circus! Nothing but gossip about him and me, all day every day!"

Rosie eyed Alicia from her side of the sofa, her knees pulled up beneath her and her blond hair piled haphazardly on her head.

"Maybe he likes you."

"No. He does not. This is some kind of sick game he's playing for his own amusement. That's the kind of man he is."

"No kind of man goes to all that trouble," her friend said slowly. "Not for a game. He really could simply like you, Alicia. In his own terrifyingly wealthy sort of way, I mean."

"He doesn't like *me,* Rosie," Alicia retorted, with too much heat, but she couldn't stop it. "The women he likes come with their own *Vogue* covers."

But she could see that Rosie was conjuring up Cinderella stories in her head, like everyone else, as Nikolai had known they would. Alicia felt so furious, so desperate and so trapped, that she shook with it. She felt his manipulation like a touch, like he was sitting right there next to her, that big body of his deceptively lazy, running his amused fingers up and down her spine.

You wish you were anything as uncomplicated as furious, a little voice taunted her, deep inside.

"Maybe you should play along," Rosie said then, and she grinned wide. "It's not going to be a drink down at the pub on a date with the likes of him, is it? He's the sort who has *mistresses,* not *girlfriends.* He could fly you to Paris for dinner. He could whisk you off to some private island. Or one of those great hulking yachts they always have."

"He could ruin my reputation," Alicia countered, and yet despite herself, wondered what being Nikolai's *mistress* would entail—what sort of lover he would be, what kind of sensual demands he would make if he had more than one night to make them. All of that lethal heat and all the time in the world... How could anyone survive it? She shoved the treacherous thoughts aside. "He could make things very difficult for me at work."

"Only because they'll all be seething with jealousy," Rosie said with a dismissive sniff. "And your reputation could use a little ruining."

Because she couldn't imagine what it was like to *actually* be ruined, Alicia knew. To have gone and ruined herself so carelessly, so irrevocably. She couldn't know what it was like to see that disgust in her own father's eyes whenever he looked at her. To feel it in her own gut, like a cancer.

Rosie smiled again, wickedly. "And I think Nikolai Korovin sounds like the kind of man who knows his way around a ruining."

Alicia only stabbed her chicken again. Harder. And then scowled at the television as if she saw anything at all but Nikolai, wherever she looked.

CHAPTER FIVE

ALICIA WAS RUNNING a file up to Charlotte's office the following week when she finally ran into him, larger than life, sauntering down the stairs in the otherwise-empty stairwell as if he hadn't a care in the world.

The shock of it—the force and clamor that was Nikolai—hit her as hard as it had at the club. As it had outside the office building that night. Making her feel restless in her own skin. Electric.

Furious, she told herself sternly.

He saw her instantly and smiled, that tug in the corner of his hard mouth that made her insides turn to water no matter how much she wished it didn't. No matter how much she wanted to be immune to it. To him.

Because whatever she was, whatever this *thing* was that made her so aware of him, she certainly wasn't immune.

And Nikolai knew it.

He moved like water, smooth and inexorable. He seemed bigger than he actually was, as if he was so powerful he couldn't be contained and so expanded to fit—and to effortlessly dominate—any and all available space. Even an ordinary stairwell. Today he wore another absurdly well-fitting suit in his usual black, this one a rapturous love letter to his lean, muscled, dangerous form. He looked sinfully handsome, ruthless and cool, wealthy beyond imagining, and it infuriated her. So deeply it hurt.

Alicia told herself that was all it did.

"This is harassment," she informed him as she marched up the stairs, her heels clicking hard against each step, her tone as brisk as her spine was straight.

"No," he said, his gaze on hers. "It isn't."

Alicia stopped moving only when she'd reached the step above him, enjoying the fact it put her on eye level with him, for once. Even if those eyes were far too blue, bright and laughing at her, that winter cold moving in her, heating her from within.

She hated him.

God, how she wished she could hate him.

"It most certainly is," she corrected him with a bit of his own frostiness. "And I hate to break this to you when you've gone ahead and made your pretend infatuation so public, but it's actually quite easy to resist you."

"Is it?" He shouldn't sound so amused. So indulgent.

She would have scowled at him, but thought he would read that as weakness. Instead, she tilted up her chin and tried to project the kind of tough, cool competence she wished she felt as she called his bluff to his face.

"I'm not going to take part in your little bit of revenge theater no matter how much time you spend feeding the office gossip mill," she told him. Tough. Calm. Cool. "If you want to have me fired because you took me home from a club of your own free will, go right ahead." She let that sit there for a moment, then angled her head ever so slightly closer to his, for emphasis. "I didn't do anything wrong, I'm not afraid of you and I'd advise you try to communicate with your ex-wife through more traditional channels."

Nikolai simply…shifted position.

He moved with a primal grace that robbed her of speech,

pivoting without seeming to do so much as breathe. All Alicia knew was that she was facing him one moment and the next her back was up against the wall. As if he'd *willed* her to let him cage her there, his hands flat against the smooth wall on either side of her face.

He hadn't laid so much as a single finger upon her. He didn't now. He leaned in.

Much too close, and her body reacted as if he'd plugged her into the nearest socket. The white-hot light of this shocking heat between them pulsed through her, making her gasp. Her body betrayed her in a shivering flush, sensation scraping through her, making her skin pull taut, her breasts feel suddenly full and that wet, hot hunger punch its way into her belly before settling down between her legs. Where it stayed, a wild and greedy need, and all of it his. *His.*

As if she was, too.

"What the hell are you doing?" But it was no more than a whisper, and it gave her away as surely as that treacherous ache inside of her that Alicia was sure he could sense, somehow.

"I am a man possessed," Nikolai murmured, his mouth so close to hers she felt the pull of it, the ache, roll through her like a flash of pain, despite the hint of laughter she could hear in his voice. "Infatuated. Just as I promised you."

"I can see why your brother is the famous actor while you storm about, growling at other rich men and demanding their money." But her voice was little more than a breath, completely insubstantial, and she had to dig her fingers into the folder she carried to keep from touching that glorious chest that was right there in front of her, taunting her. "Because you're not terribly convincing, and by the way, I'm fairly certain this counts as stalking."

"Those are very strong words, Alicia." He didn't sound

concerned. Nikolai rested his considerable, sleek weight on his hands and surrounded her. Hemmed her in. Let his body remind her of all those things she wanted to forget. *Needed* to forget. "Harassment. Stalking."

"Strong, yes." She could feel her pulse in her throat, a frantic staccato. "And also accurate."

Alicia felt more than heard his small laugh against the tender skin of her neck, and she knew he saw the goose bumps that prickled there when he lifted that knowing gaze to hers.

"This is the first time I've seen you inside this office since you walked into the conference hall." Nikolai didn't move back. He gave her no room to breathe. If she tried to twist away, to escape him the way she wanted to do, she would have to brush up against him—and she didn't dare do that. She couldn't trust herself. Not when he smelled like winter. Not when she had the alarming urge to bury her face in his chest. "I haven't followed you around making suggestive comments. I extended a single invitation to you, Alicia. I didn't even do it myself. And you declined it without any repercussions at all."

"Says the man who has me pinned up against a wall."

"I'm not touching you," Nikolai pointed out, that dangerously lazy gleam in his bright gaze. "I'm not restraining you in any way. I could, of course." That gleam grew hotter, making her toes curl inside her shoes, making that need inside her rage into a wildfire. Making her despair of herself. "All you have to do is ask."

"I want you to stop this," she managed to get out, desperate to fight off the maelstrom he'd unleashed in her, the images carnal and tempting that chased through her head and made her much too aware of how weak she was.

How perilously close to compounding the error she'd already made with this man, right here in her office. In the *stairwell*. Every inch of her the whore her father had called her.

"Which *this?*" He sounded impossibly male, then. Insufferably smug, as if he knew exactly how close she was to capitulation. "Be specific."

She shifted then, and it was agonizing. He was *right there,* and she knew she couldn't allow herself to touch him, not even by accident—but she was terribly afraid she wasn't going to be able to help herself. How could she fight herself *and* him?

"I'd rather be sacked right now than have to put up with this," she whispered fiercely.

He laughed again then, and she wished that sound didn't get to her. She wished she could simply ignore it and him along with it. But it made him that much more beautiful, like a perfect sunset over a rugged mountain, and it made something inside of her ignite no matter how much she wished it didn't.

"You and I both know I could prove you a liar." He dropped his head slightly, and inhaled, as if pulling the scent of her skin deep into his lungs, and that fire in her began to pulse, greedy and insistent. Her nipples pressed against the soft fabric of her dress, and she was terrified he'd see it. Terrified he'd *know.* "How long do you think it would take, *solnyshka?* One second? Two? How long before you wrap yourself around me and beg?"

Of course he knew. Hadn't that long night with him taught her anything?

Alicia stiffened, panic like a drumbeat inside of her, but it only seemed to make that fire in her burn hotter. Nikolai moved even closer, somehow, though that shouldn't have been possible, and he was so big, so powerful, that it was as if nothing existed except the breadth of his shoulders. He surrounded her, and there was a part of her way down deep that wasn't at all conflicted. That simply exulted in it. In him.

But that was the part that had started all this. The part that had looked up into his face in that dark club and surrendered, there and then. She couldn't succumb to his version of dark magic again. She had too much to lose.

"You don't understand," she said hurriedly, almost desperately. "This is—you are—" She pulled in a breath. "I'm afraid—"

But she couldn't tell Nikolai Korovin the things she feared. She couldn't say them out loud, and anyway, this was only a bitter little game to him. The ways she hated herself, the ways she'd let herself down, the way she'd destroyed her relationship with her father—he didn't need to know about any of that.

She couldn't understand why she had the strange urge to tell him anyway, when she'd never told a soul.

It seemed to take him a very long time to pull his head back far enough to look her in the eyes, to study her too-hot face. Even through her agitation, she could see him grow somber as he watched her. Darker. He pushed back from the wall, letting his hands drop to his sides, and Alicia told herself that was exactly what she'd wanted.

"Good," he said quietly, an expression she couldn't read on his hard face. "You should be afraid of me. You should have been afraid that night."

She scowled at him, not caring anymore what he read into it.

"For God's sake," she snapped, not liking that look on his face and not at all sure why it bothered her so much and so deeply. "I'm not afraid of *you*."

That sat there between them, telling him things she should have kept to herself, and the expression on his face made her think of that moment in his bed, suddenly. When he'd talked of kitchen knives and sins and she'd kissed his tattoo, as if she could kiss it all away. As if he was wounded.

"I thought you liked the fact that I *don't* want you," she said after a moment, when all he did was stare at her, in a manner she might have called haunted if it was someone other than Nikolai. "Why are you so determined to prove otherwise?"

"You mistake me." His voice was silky then, but there was a dark kick beneath it, and it shivered over her skin like a caress. "I know you want me. I still want you. I told you this was a distraction." He stuck his hands in his pockets, shifting back on his heels, and his expression grew cooler. More distant. Assessing her. "It's your disinterest in having any kind of connection to me, your horror at the very idea, that makes the rest of this possible."

"And by that do you mean keeping my job?" she asked, ignoring his talk of who wanted who, because she didn't dare let herself think about it. She couldn't go there, or who knew what would become of her? "Or the twisted game you feel you need to play with your ex-wife?"

Nikolai only stared back at her, his face a study in ice. Impassive and cool.

"Let me guess," she said tightly. "You only want what you can't have."

"But you don't qualify, Alicia," he said, in that dangerously soft way of his that was like a seismic event inside of her, and she had to fight to hide the aftershocks. "I've already had you."

"That was a mistake," she retorted, and she wanted to play it down. Laugh, smile. But his eyes flashed and she knew she'd sounded too dark. Too close to *hurt*. "There won't be a repeat."

"You don't want to challenge me to prove you wrong."

His winter eyes probed hers, moved over her face, saw things she didn't want to share. "Or perhaps you do."

That last was a low growl. Wolf again, not man, and she wasn't sure she could survive it without imploding. Without betraying herself all over again, and there was no *wild night* to lose herself in, not here in this chilly stairwell. No pounding music, no shouting crowd. She felt the danger in him, the profound sensual threat, like heat all around her, seducing her without a single word or touch. She could smell that scent that was only his, the faint smoke and crisp slap of winter. She felt the strength of him, that lethal power, and her fingers ached to explore it again, every last lean muscle, until he groaned beneath her hands.

And she *wanted*.

Suddenly, and with every last cell in her body, Alicia wanted to be someone else. Someone free of her past, free to throw herself heedlessly into all of this wondrous fire and not care if it swallowed her whole. Someone who could do what she liked with this man without bringing her whole world down around her all over again.

Someone very much like the person she'd seemed to think she was the night she'd met him.

But she couldn't. And Nikolai still didn't touch her, which almost made it worse.

"It's time to move into the public phase of this arrangement," he told her in that distant way again, as if this was a planned meeting in the stairwell to calmly discuss the calendar of events that would lead to her downfall. "We'll start with dinner tomorrow night. There are things we need to discuss."

"What a lovely invitation—"

"It's not a request."

She studied him for a moment, all that ice and steel. "I'm otherwise engaged."

"Cancel."

"And if I refuse?"

Nikolai's smile turned dangerous. Her stomach contracted hard at the sight, and the ache of it sank low, turning molten and making her despair of herself anew.

It was that easy. *She* was that easy.

"You can try to run from me if you like." He looked intrigued at the prospect, and something dark and sensual twisted through her, leaving marks. "But I should give you fair warning—I'll find you. And you might not like the mood I'm in when I do."

"Fine," she made herself say, because she couldn't think of an alternate plan, certainly not while he stood there in front of her with a look on his face that told her he'd love to spend more time convincing her. She couldn't have that. And she certainly didn't want him to pursue her through the streets of London, to run her to ground like some mutinous fox, which she had no doubt he would do.... Did she? "Tomorrow night we'll suffer through the date from hell. That sounds delightful. Where do you want me to meet you?"

He reached out then and she braced herself, but he only wrapped a sprig of her curls around his finger, gave them a tug that was very nearly gentle, then let his hand drop, an odd cast to his fierce, proud mouth as he did it.

There was no reason at all that should pierce her heart.

"Don't try to top from the bottom, Alicia," he said, laughter in his brilliant gaze for a moment before it chilled into something much harder. More ruthless. "I'll let you know what I want tomorrow. And you'll do it. Because I really will have you fired if you don't, and despite this entertaining display of bravado, I think you know it."

And there it was.

She didn't want to lose her job—which meant she'd have to figure out how to survive losing her father all over again, once there were pictures to prove once more that she was nothing but a whore. And if there was a tiny spark inside of her, because some foolish part of her wished this wasn't all a game, that it wasn't all for show, that she was the kind of person men didn't use, she did her best to ignore it.

"I don't want to do this." Her voice was small, but still firm, and she thought she'd be proud, later, that she kept her head high. Even in defeat. "Any of it."

"I know you don't," Nikolai said, whole winters in his voice, in his beautiful eyes, so blue she wanted to cry. And there was a flash of something there, bright for a moment and then gone, as if this was more of a struggle for him than it seemed. It scared her, how much she wanted to believe that. "But you will."

Alicia sat where Nikolai had put her, at the corner of the dark wood table that stretched across a significant length of the great two-story room that was the center of his apartment, all low-slung modern couches and soaring windows. Nikolai could read her stiff tension in the way she sat, the way she held her lips too tight, the precise, angry movements of her hands.

His staff had served a five-star dinner that she'd barely touched. Nikolai hadn't spoken a word, and she hadn't broken the silence. Now she was pushing her dessert around on her plate, and he was well aware that her agitation level had skyrocketed even higher than before.

Bastard that he was, that amused him. He lounged in his seat, at the head of the table with her at his right, and studied her. He would figure her out. He would solve the mystery of this woman and when he did, lose interest in her. It was inevitable.

But he hadn't anticipated he would enjoy the process quite this much.

"You're a terrible date," he told her, and her dark eyes flashed when they met his. Then, after a moment, she rolled them. *At* him.

No one else would dare.

"Thank you," she said in that dry way that made him want her beneath him, right there on the table. He had to yank himself back under control, and it was significantly harder than it should have been. *Focus,* he ordered himself. "I can see why you're considered such a catch."

"This is an excellent opportunity to discuss my expectations," Nikolai said, as if her fearless defiance didn't make him want to lick his way into the heat of her, to make her writhe and sob in his hands. And he would, he promised himself, as soon as they came to an understanding. "Dating me comes with a number of requirements, Alicia. Making appropriate dinner conversation is only one of them."

"You're perfectly capable of making conversation," she pointed out in the same dry tone. "In fact, you're doing it right now, though I don't know if it qualifies as 'appropriate.'" She considered him for a moment, a small smile that he didn't like, yet found he wanted to taste, flirting with her full lips. "I suspected there must be some kind of application process and I'm delighted I'm right, but I'm not dating you. This isn't real." Her gaze turned hard on his. "This is blackmail."

"Call it whatever you like," he said, with a careless shrug. "The result is the same."

"Blackmail," she repeated, very distinctly. "I think you'll find that's what it's called when you force someone into doing something they don't want to do by holding something else over their head."

Nikolai could see all of that temper in her dark gaze, the flash of it when she couldn't hide her feelings. She wore a sleeveless wool top tonight in a deep aubergine shade, with a neck that drooped down low and left her smooth, toned arms on display, looking soft and sweet in the candlelight. But most important, he could see every time she tensed, every time she forced herself to relax, written up and down the lean, elegant shape of those arms and all across her slender frame. Like now, when she forced her shoulders back and down, then smiled at him as if she wasn't agitated at all.

She didn't know, yet, that he could read her body the way others read words on a page. But she would learn, and he would greatly enjoy teaching her. First, though, they had business to take care of. If it alarmed him that he had to remind himself of business before pleasure for the first time in living memory, he ignored it.

"There is a confidentiality agreement that you'll need to sign," he told her, dismissing her talk of blackmail, which he could see she didn't like. "Beyond that, I have only standard expectations. Don't venture out into public unless you're prepared to be photographed, as terrible pictures of you could lead to negative coverage of me, which is unacceptable. I'll let you know what pleases me—"

"If you mention a single thing about altering my appearance to suit your tastes, whatever those might be," she said almost conversationally, though there was murder in her eyes, "I will stab you with this fork. I'm not dating you, Nikolai. I'm acquiescing to your bizarre demands because I want to keep my job, but we're not reenacting some sick little version *My Fair Lady*. I don't care about pleasing you."

Nikolai was definitely enjoying himself. Especially when he saw that little shiver move through her, and knew they were both thinking about all the ways she could please him. All the ways she had. He smiled slightly.

"Is that a passive-aggressive demand that I compliment your looks?" he asked silkily. "I had no idea you were so insecure, Alicia. I'd have thought the fact that I had my mouth on every inch of that gorgeous body of yours would have told you my feelings on that topic in no uncertain terms. Though I'm happy to repeat myself."

"I may stab you with this fork anyway." She met his gaze then and smiled. But he could see that her breathing had quickened. He knew arousal when he saw it. When he'd already tasted it. All of that heat and need, sweet against her dark skin. "Fair warning."

"You can always try."

She considered that for a moment, then sat back against her chair, inclining her head slightly as if she held the power here and was granting him permission to carry on.

"Don't ever keep me waiting," Nikolai said, continuing as if she hadn't interrupted him. "Anywhere. For any reason. My time is more valuable than yours."

Her eyes narrowed at that, but she didn't speak. Perhaps she was learning, he thought—but he hoped not. He really hoped not. He wanted her conquered, not coerced. He wanted to do it himself, step by delectable step.

"Don't challenge my authority. In your case, I'll allow some leeway because I find that smart mouth of yours amusing, but only a little leeway, Alicia, and never in public. Your role is as an ornament. I won't tolerate disrespect or disobedience. And I will tell you what you are to me, explicitly—never imagine yourself anything else. I can't stress that enough."

The silence between them then felt tighter. Hotter. Breathless, as if the great room had shrunk down until there was nothing but the two of them and the gently flickering candles. And her eyes were big and dark and he realized he could no longer read the way she looked at him.

"You're aware that this is a conversation about dating you *for show,* not working for you as one of your many interchangeable subordinates at the Korovin Foundation," she said after a moment. "Aren't you?"

"The roles aren't dissimilar."

He stretched his legs out in front of him and lounged even lower in the chair.

"Is this your usual first date checklist, then?"

Her gaze swept over him, and he had no idea what she saw. It surprised him how much he wanted to know.

He nodded, never taking his gaze from hers. "More or less."

"You actually ask a woman to dinner and then present her with this list." She sounded dubious, and something else he wasn't sure he recognized. "Before or after you order starters? And what if she says no? Do you stand up and walk out? Leave her with the bill for her temerity?"

"No one has ever said no." He felt that fire between them reach higher, pull tighter. He could see it on her face. "And I don't take women to dinner without a signed confidentiality agreement. Or anywhere else."

Alicia tapped a finger against her lips for a moment, and he wanted to suck that finger into his own mouth almost more than he wanted his next breath. Need raked through him, raw and hungry.

"You brought me here that night," she pointed out, her tone light, as if there was no tension between them at all. "I certainly didn't sign anything."

Nikolai almost smiled. "You are an anomaly."

"Lucky me," she murmured, faint and dry, and there was no reason that should have worked through him like a match against flint. He didn't like anomalies. He shouldn't have to keep telling himself that.

"If you've absorbed the initial requirements," he said, watching her intently now, "we can move on."

"There are more? The mind boggles."

She was mocking him, he was sure of it. He could see the light of it bright in her eyes and in that wicked twist of her lips, and for some reason, he didn't mind it.

"Sex," he said, and liked the way she froze, for the slightest instant, before concealing her reaction. He had to shift in his seat to hide his.

"You don't really have rules for sex with your girlfriends, Nikolai," she said softly. Imploring him. "Please tell me you're joking."

"I think of this as setting clear boundaries," he told her, leaning forward and smiling when she shivered and sat back. "It prevents undue confusion down the line."

"Undue confusion is what relationships are all about," Alicia said, shaking her head. Her dark eyes searched his, then dropped to her lap. "I rather think that might be the whole point."

"I don't have relationships." He waited until her eyes were on him again, until that tension between them pulled taut and that electric charge was on high, humming through them both. "I have sex. A lot of it. I'll make you come so many times your head will spin, which you already know is no idle boast, but in return, I require two things."

Nikolai watched her swallow almost convulsively, but she didn't look away. She didn't even blink. And he didn't quite know why he felt that like a victory.

"Access and obedience," he said, very distinctly, and was rewarded with the faintest tremor across those lips, down that slender frame. "When I want you, I want you—I don't want a negotiation. Just do what I tell you to do."

He could hear every shift in her breathing. The catch, the slow release. It took every bit of self-control he possessed to wait. To keep his distance. To let her look away for a moment and collect herself, then turn that dark gaze back on him.

"I want to be very clear." She leaned forward, putting her elbows on the table and keeping her eyes trained on him. "What you're telling me, Nikolai, is that every woman pictured on your arm in every single photograph of you online has agreed to all of these *requirements*. All of them."

He wanted to taste her, a violent cut of need, but he didn't. He waited.

"Of course," he said.

And Alicia laughed.

Silvery and musical, just as he remembered. It poured out of her and deep into him, and for a moment he was stunned by it. As if everything disappeared into the sound of it, the way she tipped back her head and let it light up the room. As if she'd hit him from behind and taken him down to the ground without his feeling a single blow.

That laughter rolled into places frozen so solid he'd forgotten they existed at all. It pierced him straight through to a core he hadn't known he had. And it was worse now than it had been that first night. It cut deeper. He was terribly afraid it had made him bleed.

"Laugh as much as you like," he said stiffly when she subsided, and was sitting back in her chair, wiping at her too-bright eyes. "But none of this is negotiable."

"Nikolai," she said, and that clutched at him too, because he'd never heard anyone speak his name like that. So warm, with all of that laughter still moving through her voice. It was almost as if she spoke to someone else entirely, as if it wasn't his name at all—but she looked directly at him, those dark eyes dancing, and he felt as if she'd shot him. He wished she had. He knew how to handle a bullet wound. "I'll play this game of yours. But I'm not going to do any of that."

He was so tense he thought he might simply snap into pieces, but he couldn't seem to move. Her laughter sneaked inside him, messing him up and making even his breathing feel impossibly changed. He hated it.

So he couldn't imagine why he wanted to hear it again, with an intensity that very nearly hurt.

"That's not one of your options," he told her, his voice the roughest he'd ever heard it.

But she was smiling at him, gently, and looked wholly uncowed by his tone.

"If I were you, Nikolai," she said, "I'd start asking myself why I'm so incapable of interacting with other people that I come up with ridiculous rules and regulations to govern things that are supposed to come naturally. That are *better* when they do."

"Because I am a monster," he said. He didn't plan it. It simply came out of his mouth and he did nothing to prevent it. She stopped smiling. Even the brightness in her eyes dimmed. "I've never been anything else. These rules and regulations aren't ridiculous, Alicia. They're necessary."

"Do they make you feel safe?" she asked with a certain quiet kindness he found deeply alarming, as if she knew things she couldn't possibly guess at, much less *know*.

But this was familiar ground even so. He'd had this same conversation with his brother, time and again. He recognized the happy, delusional world she'd come from that let her ask a question like that, and he knew the real world, cynical and bleak. He recognized himself again.

It was a relief, cold and sharp.

"Safety is a delusion," he told her curtly, "and not one I've ever shared. Some of us live our whole lives without succumbing to that particular opiate."

She frowned at him. "Surely when you were a child—"

"I was never a child." He pushed back from the table and rose to his feet. "Not in the way you mean."

She only watched him, still frowning, as he crossed his

arms over his chest, and she didn't move so much as a muscle when he glared down at her. She didn't shrink back the way she should. She looked at him as if he didn't scare her at all, and it ate at him. It made him want to show her how bad he really was—but he couldn't start down that road. He had no idea where it would lead.

"Why do you think my uncle tried to keep me in line with a kitchen knife? It wasn't an accident. He knew what I was."

"Your parents—"

"Died in a fire with seventy others when I was barely five years old," he told her coldly. "I don't remember them. But I doubt they would have liked what I've become. This isn't a bid for sympathy." He shrugged. "It's a truth I accepted a long time ago. Even my own brother believes it, and this after years of being the only one alive who thought I could be any different. I can't." He couldn't look away from her dark eyes, that frown, from the odd and wholly novel notion that she wanted to fight *for* him that opened up a hollow in his chest. "I won't."

"Your brother is an idiot." Her voice was fierce, as if she was prepared to defend him against Ivan—and even against himself, and he had no idea what to do with that. "Because while families always have some kind of tension, Nikolai, monsters do not exist. No matter what an uncle who holds a knife on a child tells you. No matter what we like to tell ourselves."

"I'm glad you think so." Nikolai wasn't sure he could handle the way she looked at him then, as if she hurt for him. He wasn't sure he knew how. "Soft, breakable creatures like you *should* believe there's nothing terrible out there in the dark. But I know better."

CHAPTER SIX

THAT WAS *PAIN* on his face.

In those searing eyes of his. In the rough scrape of his voice. It was like a dark stain that spilled out from deep inside of him, as if he was torn apart far beneath his strong, icy surface. *Ravaged*, it dawned on her, as surely as if that ferocious thing on his chest rent him to pieces where he stood.

Alicia felt it claw at her, too.

"I'm neither soft nor breakable, Nikolai." She kept her voice steady and her gaze on his, because she thought he needed to see that he hadn't rocked her with that heartbreakingly stark confession, even if he had. "Or as naive as you seem to believe."

"There are four or five ways I could kill you from here." His voice was like gravel. "With my thumb."

Alicia believed him, the way she'd believed he'd be good in bed when he'd told her he was, with a very similar matter-of-fact certainty. It occurred to her that there were any number of ways a man could be talented with his body—with his clever hands for pleasure, with his thumb for something more violent—and Nikolai Korovin clearly knew every one of them. She thought she ought to be frightened by that.

What was wrong with her that she wasn't?

"Please don't," she said briskly, as if she couldn't feel the sting of those claws, as if she didn't see that thick blackness all around him.

Nikolai stared at her. He stood so still, as if he expected he might need to bolt in any direction, and he held himself as if he expected an attack at any moment. As if he expected *she* might be the attacker.

Alicia thought of his coldness tonight, that bone-deep chill that should have hurt, so much harsher than the gruff, darkly amusing man she'd taken by surprise in that club. Who'd surprised her in return. She thought about what little he'd told her of his uncle meant for the boy he must have been—what he must have had to live through. She thought about a man who believed his own brother thought so little of him, and who accepted it as his due. She thought of his lists of rules that he obviously took very seriously indeed, designed to keep even the most intimate people in his life at bay.

I am a monster, he'd said, and she could see that he believed it.

But she didn't. She couldn't.

She ached for him. In a way she was very much afraid—with that little thrill of dark foreboding that prodded at her no matter how she tried to ignore it—would be the end of her. But she couldn't seem to make it stop.

"Nikolai," she said when she couldn't stand it any longer—when she wanted to reach over and touch him, soothe him, and knew she couldn't let herself do that, that *he* wouldn't let her do that anyway, "if you were truly a monster, you would simply *be* one. You wouldn't announce it. You wouldn't know how."

A different expression moved across his face then, the way it had once before in the dark, and tonight it broke her heart. That flash of a vulnerability so deep, so intense. And then she watched him pack it away, cover it in ice, turn it hard and cold.

"There are other things I could do with my thumb," he said, his voice the rough velvet she knew best. Seductive. Demanding. "That wouldn't kill you, necessarily, though you might beg for it before I was done."

But she knew what he was doing. She understood it, and it made her chest hurt.

"Sex is easier to accept than comfort," she said quietly, watching his face as she said it. He looked glacial. Remote. And yet that heat inside of him burned, she could feel it. "You can pretend it's not comfort at all. Just sex."

"I like sex, Alicia." His voice was a harsh lash through the room, so vicious she almost flinched. "I thought I made that clear our first night together. Over and over again."

He wanted to prove he was the monster he said he was. He wanted to prove that he was exactly as bad, as terrifying, as he claimed he was. Capable of killing with nothing more than his thumb. She looked at that cold, set face of his and she could see that he believed it. More—that he simply accepted that this was who he was.

And she found that so terribly sad it almost crippled her.

She got up and went to him without consciously deciding to move. He didn't appear to react, and yet she had the impression he steeled himself at her approach, as if she was as dangerous to him as he was to her. But she couldn't let herself think about that stunning possibility.

Nikolai watched her draw near, his expression even colder. Harder. Alicia tilted her head back and looked into his extraordinary eyes, darker now than usual as he stared back at her with a kind of defiance, as if he was prepared to fight her until she saw him as he saw himself.

Until she called him a monster, too.

"Do you want to know what I think?" she asked.

"I'm certain I don't."

It was a rough scrape of sound, grim and low, but she thought she saw a kind of hunger in his eyes that had nothing to do with his sexual prowess and everything to do with that flash of vulnerability she almost thought she'd imagined, and she kept going.

"I think you hide behind all these rules and boundaries, Nikolai." She felt the air in the room go electric, but she couldn't seem to stop herself. "If you tell yourself you're a monster, if you insist upon it and act upon it, you make it true. It's a self-fulfilling prophecy."

And she would know all about that, wouldn't she? Hadn't she spent eight long years doing exactly that herself? That unexpected insight was like a kick in the stomach, but she ignored it, pushing it aside to look at later.

"Believe me," she said then, more fiercely than she'd intended. "I know."

His hands shot out and took her by the shoulders, then pulled her toward him, toward his hard face that was even more lethal, even more fierce than usual. His touch against her bare arms burned, and made her want nothing more than to melt into him. It was too hot. Too dark.

And he was close then, so powerful and furious. *So close.* Winter and need, fire and longing. The air was thick with it. It made her lungs ache.

"Why don't you have the good sense to be afraid of me?" he said in an undertone, as if the words were torn from that deep, black part of him. "What is the matter with you? Why do you *laugh* when anyone else would cry?"

"I don't see any monsters when I look at you, Nikolai," she replied, winning the fight to keep her tone light, her gaze on his, no matter how ravaged he looked. How undone. Or how churned up she felt inside. "I only see a man. I see you."

His hands tightened around her shoulders for a brief

instant, and then he let her go. Abruptly, as if he'd wanted to do the opposite.

As if he couldn't trust himself any more than she could.

"You don't want to play with this particular fire," he warned her, his expression fierce and dark, his gaze drilling holes into her. "It won't simply burn you—it will swallow you whole. That's not a self-fulfilling prophecy. It's an inevitability."

Alicia didn't know what seared through her then, shocking and dark, thrilling to the idea of it. Of truly losing herself in him, in that fire neither one of them could control, despite the fact there was still that panicked part of her— that part of her that wished she'd gone home and done her laundry that night and never met him—that wanted anything but that. And he saw it. All of it.

She had no idea what was happening to her, or how to stop it, or why she had the breathless sense that it was already much too late.

"Get your coat," he growled at her. "I'll take you home."

Alicia blinked, surprised to find that she was unsteady on her own feet. And Nikolai was dark and menacing, watching her as if no detail was too small to escape his notice. As if he could see all those things inside of her, the fire and the need. That dark urge to demand he throw whatever he had at her, that she could take it, that she understood him—

Of course you don't understand him, she chided herself. *How could you?*

"That's unnecessary," she said into the tense silence, stiffly, and had to clear the roughness from her voice with a cough.

She straightened her top, smoothed her hands down the sides of her trousers, then stopped when she realized she was fidgeting and he'd no doubt read the anxiety that betrayed the way he did everything else.

"You don't have to take me home," she said when he didn't respond. When he only watched her, his expression brooding and his blue eyes cold. She frowned at him. "This night has been intense enough, I think. I'll get a taxi."

The ride across London—in the backseat of Nikolai's SUV with him taking up too much of the seat beside her because he'd informed her a taxi was not an option—was much like sitting on simmering coals, waiting for the fire to burst free.

Not exactly comfortable, Alicia thought crossly. And as the fever of what had happened between them in his penthouse faded with every mile they traveled, she realized he'd been right to warn her.

She felt scorched through. Blackened around the edges and much too close to simply going up in flames herself, until she very much feared there'd be nothing left of her. A few ashes, scattered here and there.

Had she really stood there thinking she wanted more of this? Anything he had to give, in fact? What *was* the matter with her?

But then she thought of that bleak look in his beautiful eyes, that terrible certainty in his voice when he'd told her what a monster he was, and she was afraid she knew all too well what was wrong with her.

"You can go," she told him, not bothering to hide the tension in her voice as they stood outside the door that led into her building in a narrow alcove stuck between two darkened shops.

Nikolai had walked her to the door without a word, that winter fire roaring all around them both, and now stood close beside her in the chilly December night. Too close beside her. Alicia needed to get inside, lock her doors, take a very long soak in the bath—*something* to sort her head out before she lost whatever remained of her sanity, if not something far worse than that. *She needed him to go.* She dug for her keys in her bag without looking at him, not trusting herself to look away again if she did.

"I'm fine from here. I don't need an escort."

He didn't respond. He plucked the keys from her hand when she pulled them out, and then opened the door with no hesitation whatsoever, waving her inside with a hint of edgy impatience.

It would not be wise to let him in. That was perfectly clear to her.

"Nikolai," she began, and his gaze slammed into her, making her gulp down whatever she might have said.

"I understand that you need to fight me on everything," he said, his accent thicker than usual. "If I wanted to psychoanalyze you the way you did me, I'd say I suspect it makes you feel powerful to poke at me. But I wouldn't get too comfortable with that if I were you."

"I wasn't psychoanalyzing you!" she cried, but he brushed it off as if she hadn't spoken.

"But you should ask yourself something." He put his hand on her arm and hauled her into the building, sent the door slamming shut with the back of his shoulder and then held her there in the narrow hall. "Exactly what do you think might happen if you get what you seem to want and I lose control?"

"I don't want—"

"There are reasons men control themselves," he told her, his face in hers, and she should have been intimidated. She should have been terrified. And instead, all she felt was that greedy pulse of need roll through her. That impossible kick of this jagged-edged joy he brought out in her no matter what she thought she *ought* to feel. "Especially men like me, who stand like wolves in the dark corners of more than just London clubs. You should think about what those reasons are. There are far worse things than a list of demands."

"Like your attempts to intimidate me?" she countered, trying to find her footing when she was so off balance she suspected she might have toppled over without him there to hold her up.

"Why don't you laugh it off?" he asked softly, more a taunt than a question, and she had the wild thought that this might be Nikolai at his most dangerous. Soft and deadly and much too close. His gaze brushed over her face, leaving ice and fire wherever it touched. "No? Is this not funny anymore?"

"Nikolai." His name felt unwieldy against her tongue, or perhaps that was the look in his eyes, spelling out her sure doom in all of that ferocious blue. "I'm not trying to make you lose control."

"Oh, I think you are." He smiled, though it was almost feral and it scraped over her, through her. "But you should make very, very sure that you're prepared to handle the consequences if you succeed. Do you think you are? Right here in this hallway, with a draft under the door and the street a step away? Do you think you're ready for that?"

"Stop threatening me," she bit out at him, but it was a ragged whisper, and he could see into her too easily.

"I don't make threats, Alicia." He leaned in closer and nipped at her neck, shocking her. Making her go up in flames. And flinch—or was that simply an electric charge? "You should think of that, too."

And then he stepped away and jerked his head in an unspoken demand that she lead him up the stairs. And Alicia was so unsteady, so chaotic inside, so unable to process all the things that had happened tonight—what he'd said, what she'd felt, that deep ache inside of her, that fire that never did anything but burn hotter—that she simply marched up the stairs to the flat she shared with Rosie on the top floor without a word of protest.

He didn't ask if she wanted him inside when they reached her door, he simply strode in behind her as if he owned the place, and the insanity of it—of *Nikolai Korovin* standing there *in her home*—was so excruciating it was like pain.

"I don't want you here," she told him as he shut her door behind him, the sound of the latch engaging and locking him inside with her too loud in her ears. "I didn't invite you in."

"I didn't ask."

He was still dressed in black, and that very darkness made him seem bigger and more lethal as he walked inside, his cold gaze moving over the cheerful clutter that was everywhere. Bright paperbacks shoved haphazardly onto groaning shelves, photographs in colorful frames littering every surface, walls painted happy colors and filled with framed prints of famous art from around the world. Alicia tensed, expecting Rosie to pad into view at any moment, but the continuing stretch of silence suggested she was out. *Thank God.*

"It's messy," she said, aware she sounded defensive. "We never quite get around to cleaning it as we should. Of course, we also don't have a household staff."

"It looks like real people live here," he replied, frowning at one of Rosie's abandoned knitting projects, and it took her a moment to understand that this, too, was a terribly sad thing to say.

That ache in her deepened. Expanded. Hurt.

Alicia tossed her keys on the table in the hall, her coat over the chair, and then followed Nikolai warily as he melted in and out of the rooms of the flat like a shadow.

"What are you looking for?" she asked after a few minutes of this.

"There must be a reason you're suicidally incapable of recognizing your own peril when you see it," he said, his eyes moving from place to place, object to object, taking everything in. Cataloging it, she thought. Examining every photograph the way he did every dish left in the sink, every pair of shoes kicked aside in the hall, and the spine of every book piled on the overstuffed bookshelves. "Perhaps there are environmental factors at play."

He moved past the kitchen off to the right and stood at the far end of the hall that cut down the middle of the flat, where the bedrooms were.

"And what would those be, do you think?" she asked, her voice tart—which felt like a vast improvement. Or was perhaps a response to what had sounded like the faintest hint of that dark humor of his. It was absurd how much she craved more of it. "Fearlessness tucked away in the walls like asbestos?"

Nikolai didn't answer her, he only sent one of those simmering looks arrowing her way down the hallway, as effective from a few feet away as it was up close. And almost as devastating.

Alicia blew out a breath when he opened the door to her bedroom, the aftershocks of that winter-blue look shifting into something else again. A kind of nervous anticipation. He looked inside for a long moment, and her heart raced. She wished, suddenly, that she'd had the presence of mind to prevent this. She didn't like the fact that he knew, now, that she favored all those silly, self-indulgent throw pillows, piled so high on her bed, shouting out how soft and breakable she really was. They felt like proof, somehow—and when he looked back at her it was hard to stand still. To keep from offering some kind of explanation.

"A four-poster bed." It could have been an innocent comment. An observation. But the way he looked at her made her knees feel weak. "Intriguing."

Alicia thought she understood then, and somehow, that eased the relentless pulse of panic inside.

"Let me guess." She leaned her hip against the wall and watched him. "The faster you puzzle me out, the less you think you'll have to worry about losing this control of yours."

"I don't like mysteries."

"Will it make you feel safe to solve whatever mystery you think I am, Nikolai? Is that what this is?"

The look he gave her then did more than simply *hurt*. It ripped straight down into the center of her, tearing everything she was in two, and there was nothing she could do but stand there and take it.

"I'm not the one who believes in safety, Alicia," he said softly. "It's nothing more than a fairy tale to me. I never had it. I wouldn't recognize it." His expression was hard and bleak. Almost challenging. "The next time you tally up my scars, keep a special count of those I got when I was under the age of twelve. That knife was only one among many that drew my blood. My uncle used the back of his hand if I was lucky." His beautiful mouth twisted, and her heart dropped to her feet. "But I was never very lucky."

He stood taller then. Almost defiant. And it tore at her. She felt her eyes heat in a way that spelled imminent tears and knew she couldn't let herself cry for this hard, damaged man. Not where he could see it. She knew somehow that he would never forgive her.

"Don't waste your pity on me." His voice was cold, telling her she'd been right. No sympathy allowed. No compassion. He sounded almost insulted when he continued, as if whatever he saw on her face was a slap. "Eventually,

I learned how to fight back, and I became more of a monster than my uncle ever could have been."

"We're all monsters," she told him, her voice harsh because she knew he wouldn't accept anything softer. Hoping against hope he'd never know about that great tear inside of her that she could feel with every breath she took, rending her further and further apart. "Some of us actually behave like monsters, in fact, rather than suffer through the monstrous actions of others. No one escapes their past unscathed."

"What would you know about it, Alicia?" His gaze was cold, his tone a stinging lash. "What past misdeeds could possibly haunt you while you're tucked up in your virginal little bedroom, laughing your way through your cheery, happy life? What blood do you imagine is on your hands?"

And so she told him.

Alicia had never told a soul before, and yet she told Nikolai as easily as if she'd shared the story a thousand times. Every detail she could remember and all the ones she couldn't, that her father had filled in for her that awful morning. All of her shame, her despicable actions, her unforgivable behavior, without garnishment or pretense. As if that tear in her turned her inside out, splayed there before him.

And when she was finished, she was so light-headed she thought she might sag straight down to the floor, or double over where she stood.

"Everyone has ghosts," she managed to say, crossing her arms over her chest to keep herself upright.

Nikolai turned away from her bedroom door and moved toward her, thrusting his hands into the pockets of his trousers as he did. It made him look more dangerous, not less. It drew her attention to the wide strength of his shoulders, the long, lethal lines of his powerful frame. It made her wonder how anyone could have hurt him so badly when he'd been small that he'd felt he needed to transform himself into so sharp, so deadly a weapon. It made her feel bruised to the core that he'd no doubt look at her now the way her father had....

His eyes burned as they bored into hers, and he let out one of those low laughs that made her stomach tense.

"That doesn't sound like any ghost," he said, his voice dark and sure. "It sounds like an older man who took advantage of a young girl too drunk to fight him off."

Alicia jolted cold, then flashed hot, as he turned her entire life on end that easily. She swayed where she stood.

"No," she said, feeling desperate, as some great wave of terror or emotion or *something* rolled toward her. "My father said—"

"Your father should have known better than to speak to you like that." Nikolai scowled at her. "News flash, Alicia. Men who aren't predators prefer to have sex with women who are capable of participating."

Her head was spinning. Her stomach twisted, and for a panicked moment she thought she might be sick. She felt his words—so matter-of-fact, as if there could be no other interpretation of that night, much less the one that she'd held so close all these years—wash through her, like a quiet and devastating tsunami right there in her own hallway.

"What's his name?" Nikolai asked, in that soft, lethal way of his that lifted the hairs at the back of her neck. "The man who did these things to you? Does he still live next door to your parents?"

He was the first person she'd told. And the only one to defend her.

Alicia couldn't understand how she was still standing upright.

"That doesn't sound like a question a monster would ask," she whispered.

"You don't know what I'd do to him," he replied, that dark gleam in his gaze.

And he looked at her like she was important, not filthy. Not a whore. Like what had happened had been done to *her,* and hadn't been something *she'd* done.

Like it wasn't her fault after all.

She couldn't breathe.

His gaze shifted from hers to a spot down at the other end of the flat behind her, and she heard the jingling of keys in the hall outside. She felt as if she moved through sticky syrup, as if her body didn't understand what to do any longer, and turned around just as Rosie pushed her way inside.

Rosie sang out her usual hello, slinging her bags to the floor. Nikolai stepped closer to Alicia's back, then reached around to flatten his hand against the waistband of her trousers before pulling her into his bold heat. Holding her to his chest as if they were lovers. Claiming her.

"What…?" Alicia whispered, the sizzle of that unexpected touch combining with the hard punch of the revolution he'd caused inside of her, making her knees feel weak.

"I told you we were taking this public," he replied, his voice a low rumble pitched only to her that made her shiver helplessly against him. "Now we have."

Rosie's head snapped up at the sound of his voice. Her mouth made a perfect, round O as if the devil himself stood there behind Alicia in the hall, no doubt staring her down with those cold winter eyes of his. And then she dropped the bottle of wine she'd been holding in her free hand, smashing it into a thousand pieces all over the hall floor.

Which was precisely how Alicia felt.

Nikolai stared out at the wet and blustery London night on the other side of his penthouse's windows while he waited for the video conference with Los Angeles to begin. His office was reflected in the glass, done in imposing blacks and burgundies, every part of it carefully calculated to trumpet his wealth and power without him having to say a word to whoever walked in. The expensive view out of all the windows said it for him. The modern masterpieces on the walls repeated it, even louder.

It was the sort of thing he'd used to take such pleasure in. The application of his wealth and power to the most innocuous of interactions, the leverage it always afforded him. War games without a body count. It had been his favorite sport for years.

But now he thought only of the one person who seemed as unimpressed with these trappings of wealth and fame as she did with the danger he was well aware he represented. Hell, *exuded*. And instead of regaining his equilibrium the more time he spent with Alicia, instead of losing this intense and distracting interest in her the more he learned about her, he was getting worse.

Much worse. Incomprehensibly worse. And Nikolai knew too well what it felt like to spiral. He knew what obsession tasted like. *He knew.*

She was a latter-day version of his favorite drink, sharp and deadly. And he was still nothing but a drunk where she was concerned.

He'd ordered himself not to hunt down the man who had violated her, though he knew it would be easy. Too easy. The work of a single phone call, an internet search.

You are not her protector, he told himself over and over. *This is not your vengeance to take.*

He'd sparred for hours with his security team in his private gym, throwing them to the floor one after the next, punching and kicking and flipping. He'd swum endless laps in his pool. He'd run through the streets of London in the darkest hours of the night, the slap of the December weather harsh against his face, until his lungs burned and his legs shook.

Nothing made the slightest bit of difference. Nothing helped.

She'd all but pushed him out her front door that night, past her gaping flatmate and the wine soaking into her floorboards, her eyes stormy and dark, and he'd let her.

"Rosie calls me *Saint Alicia* and I *like* it," she'd whispered fiercely to him, shoving him into the narrow hall outside her flat. She'd been scolding him, he'd realized. He wasn't sure he'd ever experienced it before. His uncle had preferred to use his belt. "It's better than some other things I've been called. But you looming around the flat will be the end of that."

"Why?" he'd asked lazily, those broken, jagged things moving around inside of him, making him want things he couldn't name. Making him want to hurt anyone who'd dared hurt her, like she was his. "I like saints. I'm Russian."

"Please," she'd scoffed. "You have 'corruptor of innocents' written all over you."

"Then we are both lucky, are we not, that neither one of us is innocent," he'd said, and had enjoyed the heat that had flashed through her eyes, chasing out the dark.

But by the next morning, she'd built her walls back up, and higher than before. He hadn't liked that at all, though he'd told himself it didn't matter. It shouldn't matter. He told himself that again, now.

It was the end result he needed to focus on: Veronika. The truth about Stefan at long last, and the loose thread she represented snipped off for good. Whatever he suffered on the way to that goal would be worth it, and in any case, Alicia would soon be nothing but a memory. One more instrument he'd use as he needed, then set aside.

He needed to remember that. There was only a week left

before the ball. Nikolai could handle anything for one last week, surely. He'd certainly handled worse.

But she was under his skin, he knew, no matter how many times he told himself otherwise. No matter how fervently he pretended she wasn't.

And she kept clawing her way deeper, like a wound that wouldn't scar over and become one more thing he'd survived.

He'd picked her up to take her to the Tate Modern on the opening night of some desperately chic exhibit, which he'd known would be teeming with London's snooty art world devotees and their assorted parasites and photographers. It wasn't the kind of place a man took a woman he kept around only for sex. Taking a woman to a highly intellectual and conceptual art exhibit suggested he might actually have an interest in her thoughts.

It was a perfect place for them to be "accidentally spotted," in other words. Nikolai hadn't wanted to dig too deeply into his actual level of interest in what went on inside her head. He hadn't wanted to confront himself.

Alicia had swung open the door to her flat and taken his breath that easily. She'd worn a skimpy red dress that showed off her perfect breasts and clung to her curves in mouthwatering ways he would have enjoyed on any woman, and deeply appreciated on her—and yet he'd had the foreign urge to demand she hide all of her lush beauty away from the undeserving public. That she keep it for him alone. He'd been so startled—and appalled—at his line of thought that he'd merely stood there, silent and grim, and stared at her as if she'd gone for his jugular with one of her wickedly high shoes.

Alicia had taken in the black sweater with the high collar he wore over dark trousers that, he'd been aware, made him look more like a commando than an appropriately urbane date to a highly anticipated London art exhibit.

Not that commandos wore cashmere, in his experience.

"Have you become some kind of spy?" she'd asked him, in that dry way that might as well have been her hands on his sex. His body hadn't been at all conflicted about how he should figure her out. It had known exactly what it wanted.

When it came to Alicia, he'd realized, it always did.

"You must be confusing me for the character my brother plays in movies," he'd told her dismissively, and had fought to keep himself from simply leaning forward and pressing his mouth to that tempting hollow between her breasts, then licking his way over each creamy brown swell until he'd made them both delirious and hot. He'd almost been able to taste her from where he stood in the doorway.

Alicia had pulled on her coat from the nearby chair and swept her bag into her hand. She hadn't even been looking at him as she stepped out into the hall and turned to lock her door behind her.

"Your brother plays you in his Jonas Dark films," she'd replied in that crisp way of hers that made his skin feel tight against his bones. "A disaffected kind of James Bond character, stretched too thin on the edge of what's left of his humanity, yet called to act the hero despite himself."

Nikolai had stared at her when she'd turned to face him, and she'd stared back, that awareness and a wary need moving across her expressive face, no doubt reflecting his own. Making him wish—

But he'd known he had to stop. He'd known better from the first with her, hadn't he? He should have let her fall to the floor in that club. He'd known it even as he'd caught her.

"I'm no hero, Alicia," he'd said, sounding like sandpaper and furious that she'd pushed him off balance again. Hadn't he warned her what would happen? Was that what she wanted? She didn't know what she was asking—but he did. "Surely you know this better than anyone."

She'd looked at him for a long moment, her dark gaze shrewd, seeing things he'd always wanted nothing more than to hide.

"Maybe not," she'd said. "But what do you think would happen if you found out you were wrong?"

And then she'd turned and started down the stairs toward the street, as if she hadn't left the shell of him behind her, hollow and unsettled.

Again.

Nikolai saw his own reflection in his office windows now, and it was like he was someone else. He was losing control and he couldn't seem to stop it. He was as edgy and paranoid and dark as he'd been in those brutal days after he'd quit drinking. Worse, perhaps.

Because these things that raged in him, massive and uncontrollable and hot like acid, were symptoms of a great thaw he knew he couldn't allow. A thaw she was making hotter by the day, risking everything. Oceans rose when glaciers melted; mountains fell.

He'd destroy her, he knew. It was only a matter of time.

If he was the man she seemed to think he was, the man he sometimes wished he was when she looked at him with all of those things he couldn't name in her lovely dark eyes, he'd leave her alone. Play the hero she'd suggested he could be and put her out of harm's way.

But Nikolai knew he'd never been any kind of hero. Not even by mistake.

CHAPTER SEVEN

NIKOLAI HADN'T HEARD his family nickname in such a long time that when he did, he assumed he'd imagined it.

He frowned at the sleek and oversize computer display in front of him, realizing that he'd barely paid attention to the video conference, which was unlike him. Stranger still, no one remained on his screen but his brother.

Nikolai wasn't sure which was more troubling, his inattention during a business meeting or the fact he'd imagined he'd heard Ivan speak his—

"Kolya?"

That time there was no mistaking it. Ivan was the only person alive who had ever used that name, very rarely at that, and Nikolai was looking right at him as he said it from the comfort of his Malibu house a world away.

It was the first time he'd spoken directly to Nikolai in more than two years.

Nikolai stared. Ivan was still Ivan. Dark eyes narrowed beneath the dark hair they shared, the battered face he'd earned in all of those mixed martial arts rings, clothes that quietly proclaimed him Hollywood royalty, every inch of him the action hero at his ease.

Nikolai would have preferred it if Ivan had fallen into obvious disrepair after turning his back on his only brother so cavalierly. Instead, it appeared that betrayal and delusion suited him.

That, Nikolai reflected darkly, and the woman who'd caused this rift between them in the first place, no doubt.

"What's the matter with you?" Ivan asked in Russian, frowning into his camera. "You've been staring off into space for the past fifteen minutes."

Nikolai chose not to investigate the things that churned in him, dark and heavy, at the way Ivan managed to convey the worry, the disappointment and that particular wariness that had always characterized the way he looked at Nikolai, talked to him, in two simple sentences after so much silence. And yet there was a part of him that wanted nothing more than to simply take this as a gift, take his brother back in whatever way Ivan was offering himself....

But he couldn't let himself go there. Ivan's silence had been a favor to him, surely. He knew where it led, and he wanted nothing to do with that particular prison any longer.

"I'm reeling from shock," he said. "The mighty Ivan Korovin has condescended to address me directly. I imagine I ought to feel festive on such a momentous occasion." He eyed Ivan coolly, and without the faintest hint of *festive*. "I appreciate the show of concern, of course."

Nikolai could have modified his tone, the sardonic slap of it. Instead, he kept his face expressionless, his gaze trained on his brother through the screen. *Your brother is an idiot,* Alicia had said, so emphatically. It felt like encouragement, like her kind hand against his cheek even when she wasn't in the room.

But he didn't want to think about Alicia. She didn't know what he'd done to deserve the things his brother thought of him. And unlike her confession of the sins of others, Nikolai really had done each and every thing Ivan thought he had.

Ivan's mouth flattened and his dark eyes flashed with his familiar temper.

"Two years," he said in that gruff way of his, his long-suffering older brother voice, "and that's what you have to say to me, Nikolai? Why am I not surprised that you've learned nothing in all this time?"

"That's an excellent question," Nikolai replied, his voice so cold he could feel the chill of it in his own chest. "If you wanted me to learn something you should have provided some kind of lesson plan. Picked out the appropriate hair shirts for me to wear, outlined the confessions you expected me to make and at what intervals. But you chose instead to disappear, the way you always do." He shrugged, only spurred on by the flash of guilt and fury he knew too well on his brother's face. "Forgive me if I am not weeping with joy that you've remembered I exist, with as much warning as when you decided to forget it." He paused, then if possible, got icier. *"Brother."*

"Nikolai—"

"You come and you go, Vanya," he said then, giving that darkness in him free rein. Letting it take him over. Not caring that it wasn't fair—what was *fair?* What had ever been *fair?* "You make a thousand promises and you break them all. I stopped depending on you when I was a child. Talk to me or don't talk to me. What is it to me?"

Ivan's face was dark with that same complicated fury—his guilt that he'd left Nikolai years before to fight, his frustrated anger that Nikolai had turned out so relentlessly feral despite the fact he'd rescued him, eventually; even his sadness that this was who they were, these two hard and dangerous men—and Nikolai was still enough his younger brother to read every nuance of that. And to take a kind of pleasure in the fact that despite the passage of all this time, Ivan was not indifferent.

Which, he was aware, meant he wasn't, either.

"One of these days, little brother, we're going to fight this out," Ivan warned him, shoving his hands through his dark hair the way he'd no doubt like to shove them around Nikolai's neck and would have, had this conversation taken place in person. Nikolai felt himself shift into high alert, readying for battle automatically. "No holds barred, the way we should have done two years ago. And when I crush you into the ground, and I will, this conversation will be one of the many things you'll apologize for."

"Is that another promise?" Nikolai asked pointedly, and was rewarded when Ivan winced. "I understand this is your pet fantasy and always has been. And you could no doubt win a fight in any ring, to entertain a crowd. But outside the ring? In real life with real stakes?" Nikolai shook his head. "You'd be lucky to stay alive long enough to beg for mercy."

"Why don't you fly to California and test that theory?" Ivan suggested, his expression turning thunderous. "Or is it easier to say these things when there are computer screens and whole continents to hide behind?"

"You would follow the rules, Vanya," Nikolai said with a certain grim impatience. "You would fight fair, show mercy. This is who you are." He shrugged, everything inside of him feeling too sharp, too jagged. "It will be your downfall."

"Mercy isn't weakness," Ivan growled.

"Only good men, decent men, have the luxury of dispensing it," Nikolai retorted, ignoring the way his brother stared at him. "I wouldn't make that kind of mistake. You might put me on the ground, but I'd sink a knife in you on my way back up. You should remember that while you're issuing threats. I don't fight fair. I fight to survive."

They stared at each other for an uncomfortable moment. Ivan settled back in his chair, crossing his strong arms over his massive chest, and Nikolai sat still and watchful, like the sentry he'd once been.

"Is this about your new woman?" Ivan asked. Nikolai didn't betray his surprise by so much as a twitch of his eyelid, much less a reply. Ivan sighed. "I've seen the papers."

"So I gather."

Ivan studied him for another moment. "She's not your usual type."

"By which you mean vapid and/or mercenary, I presume," Nikolai said coldly. He almost laughed. "No, she's not. But you of all people should know better than to believe the things you read."

Ivan's gaze on his became curiously intent.

"Tabloid games don't always lead where you think they will, brother. You know that."

It was Nikolai's turn to sigh. "And how is your favorite tabloid game gone wrong?" he asked. "Your wife now, if I'm not mistaken. Or so I read in the company newsletter."

"Miranda is fine," Ivan said shortly, and then looked uncomfortable, that guilty look flashing through his dark eyes again. "It was a very private ceremony. No one but the man who married us."

"I understand completely," Nikolai murmured smoothly. "It might have been awkward to have to explain why your only living family member, the acting CEO of your foundation, was not invited to a larger wedding. It might have tarnished your image, which, of course, would cost us all money. Can't have that."

"She's my family, Kolya." Ivan's voice was a hard rumble, his jaw set in that belligerent way of his that meant he was ready to fight. Here and now.

And that really shouldn't have felt like one of his brother's trademark punches, a sledgehammer to the side of the head. It shouldn't have surprised him that Ivan considered that woman his family when he'd so easily turned his back on his only actual blood relation. Or that he was prepared to fight Nikolai—again—to defend her.

And yet he felt leveled. Laid out flat, no air in his lungs.

"Congratulations," he ground out. Dark and bitter. Painful. "I hope your new family proves less disappointing than the original version you were so happy to discard."

Ivan wasn't the only one who could land a blow.

Nikolai watched him look away from the screen, and rub one of his big hands over his hard face. He even heard the breath that Ivan took, then blew out, and knew his brother was struggling to remain calm. That should have felt like a victory.

"I know you feel that I abandoned you," Ivan said after a moment, in his own, painful way. "That everyone did, but in my case, over and over, when you were the most vulnerable. I will always wish I could change that."

Nikolai couldn't take any more of this. Ice floes were cracking apart inside of him, turning into so much water and flooding him, drowning him—and he couldn't allow this to happen. He didn't know where it was heading, or what would be left of him when he melted completely. He only knew it wouldn't be pretty. For anyone. He'd always known that. The closest he'd ever been to *melted* was drunk, and that had only ever ended in blood and regret.

"It's only been two years, Ivan." He tried to pull himself back together, to remember who he was, or at least pretend well enough to end this conversation. "I haven't suddenly developed a host of tender emotions you need to concern yourself with trampling."

"You have emotions, Nikolai. You just can't handle them," Ivan corrected him curtly, a knife sliding in neat and hard. Deep enough to hit bone. His eyes were black and intense, and they slammed into Nikolai from across the globe with all of his considerable power. "You never learned how to have them, much less process them, so your first response when you feel something is to attack. Always."

"Apparently things *have* changed," Nikolai shot back with icy fury. "I wasn't aware you'd followed your wife's example and become no better than a tabloid reporter, making up little fantasies and selling them as fact. I hope the tips of the trade you get in bed are worth the loss of self-respect."

"Yes, Nikolai," Ivan bit out, short and hard. "Exactly like that."

Nikolai muttered dark things under his breath, fighting to keep that flood inside of him under control. Not wanting to think about what his brother had said, or why it seemed to echo in him, louder and louder. Why he had Alicia's voice in his head again, talking about sex and comfort in that maddeningly intuitive way of hers, as if she knew, too, the ways he reacted when he didn't know how to feel.

Did he ever know how to feel?

And Ivan only settled back in his chair, crossing his arms over his chest, and watched Nikolai fall apart.

"I'm the thing that goes bump in the night," Nikolai said through his teeth after a moment or two. "You know this. I've never pretended to be anything else."

"Because our uncle told you so?" Ivan scoffed. "Surely you must realize by now that he was in love with our mother in his own sick way. He hated us both for representing the choice she made, but you—" He shook his head. "Your only sin was in resembling her more than I did."

Nikolai couldn't let that in. He couldn't let it land. Because it was nothing but misdirection and psychological inference when he knew the truth. He'd learned it the hard way, hadn't he?

"I know what I am," he gritted out.

"You like it." Ivan's gaze was hard. No traces of any guilt now. "I think it comforts you to imagine you're an irredeemable monster, unfit for any kind of decent life."

You make it true, Alicia had told him, her dark eyes filled with soft, clear things he hadn't known how to define. *It's a self-fulfilling prophecy.*

"You think it yourself," Nikolai reminded Ivan tightly. "Or did I misunderstand your parting words two years ago?"

"If I thought that," Ivan rumbled at him, "I wouldn't think you could do better than this, would I? But you don't want to accept that, Nikolai, because if you did, you'd have to take responsibility for your actions." He held Nikolai's gaze. "Like a man."

I only see a man, Alicia had told him, her dark gaze serious. *I see you.*

But that wasn't what Nikolai saw. Not in the mirror, not in Alicia's pretty eyes, not in his brother's face now. He saw the past.

He saw the truth.

He'd been nine years old. Ivan had been off winning martial arts tournaments already, and Nikolai had borne the brunt of one of his uncle's drunken rages, as usual.

He'd been lucky the teeth he'd lost were only the last of his milk teeth.

"I can see it in you," his uncle had shouted at him, over and over again, fists flying. "It looks out of your eyes."

He'd towered over Nikolai's bed, Nikolai's blood on his hands and splattered across his graying white shirt. That was the part Nikolai always remembered so vividly, even now—that spray of red that air and time had turned brown, set deep in the grungy shirt that his uncle had never bothered to throw out. That he'd worn for years afterward, like a promise.

His uncle had always kept his promises. Every last one, every time, until his nephews grew big enough to make a few of their own.

"Soon there'll be nothing left," his uncle had warned him, his blue eyes, so much like Nikolai's, glittering. "That thing in you will be all you are."

Ivan hadn't come home for days. Nikolai had thought that his uncle had finally succeeded in killing him, that he'd been dying. By the time Ivan returned and had quietly, furiously, cleaned him up, Nikolai had changed.

He'd understood.

There was nothing good in him. If there had been, his uncle wouldn't have had to beat him so viciously, so consistently, the way he had since Nikolai had come to live with him at five years old.

It was his fault his uncle had no choice but to beat the bad things out.

It was his fault, or someone would have rescued him.

It was his fault, or it would stop. But it wouldn't stop, because that thing inside of him was a monster and eventually, he'd understood then, it would take him over. Wholly and completely.

And it had.

"Nikolai."

Maybe Ivan had been right to sever this connection, he thought now. What did they have between them besides terrible memories of those dark, bloody years? Of course Ivan hadn't protected him, no matter how Nikolai had prayed he might—he'd barely managed to protect himself.

And now he'd made himself a real family, without these shadows. Without all of that blood between them.

"Kolya—"

"I can't tell you how much I appreciate this brotherly talk," Nikolai said, his tone arctic. Because it was the only way he knew to protect Ivan. And if Nikolai could give that to him, he would, for every bruise and cut and broken bone that Ivan had stoically tended to across the years. "I've missed this. Truly."

And then he reached out and cut off the video connection before his brother could say another word. But not before he saw that same, familiar sadness in Ivan's eyes. He'd seen it all his life.

He knew it hurt Ivan that this was who Nikolai was. That nothing had changed, and nothing ever would.

Ivan was wrong. Nikolai *was* changing, and it wasn't for the better. It was a terrible thing, that flood inside him swelling and rising by the second, making all of that ice he'd wrapped himself in melt down much too quickly.

He was changing far more than he should.

Far more than was safe for anyone.

He knew he needed to stop it, he knew how, and yet he couldn't bring himself to do it. At his core, he was nothing but that twisted, evil thing who had earned his uncle's fists.

Because he wasn't ready to give her up. He had a week left, a week of that marvelous smile and the way she frowned at him without a scrap of fear, a week of that wild heat he needed to sample one more time before he went without it forever. He wanted every last second of it.

Even if it damned them both.

Alicia stood in a stunning hotel suite high above the city of Prague, watching it glow in the last of the late-December afternoon, a storybook kingdom brought to life before her. Snow covered the picturesque red rooftops and clung to the spires atop churches and castles, while the ancient River Vltava curved like a sweet silver ribbon through the heart of it. She listened as bells tolled out joyful melodies from every side, and reminded herself—again—that she wasn't the princess in this particular fairy tale, despite appearances to the contrary.

That Nikolai had told her the night he'd met her that it would end in teeth. And tears.

The charity Christmas ball was the following night, where he would have that conversation with his ex-wife at last, and after that it wouldn't matter how perfect Prague looked, how achingly lovely its cobbled streets or its famous bridges bristling with Gothic saints. It didn't matter how golden it seemed in the winter sunset, how fanciful, as if it belonged on a gilded page in an ancient manuscript. She would leave this city as she'd found it, and this agonizing charade would end. Nikolai would get what he wanted and she would get her life back.

She should want that, she knew. She should be thrilled.

If she stuck her head out her door she could hear the low rumble of Nikolai's voice from somewhere else in the great, ornate hotel suite he'd chosen, all golds and reds and plush Bohemian extravagance. He was on a call, taking care of business in that ruthless way of his. Because he didn't allow distractions—he'd told her so himself.

Not foreign cities that looked too enchanted to be real. Certainly not her.

And Alicia was in a room that was twice the size of her flat and a hundred times more lush, one deep breath away from losing herself completely to the things she was still afraid to let herself feel lest she simply explode across the floor like that bottle of wine, practicing her prettiest smile against the coming dark.

None of this was real, she reminded herself, tracing her finger across the cold glass of the window. None of this was hers.

In the end, none of it would matter.

The only thing that would remain of these strange

weeks were the pictures in the tabloids, stuck on the internet forever like her very own scarlet letter. There would be no record of the way she ached for him. There would be no evidence that she'd ever felt her heart tear open, or that long after he'd left that night, she'd cried into her mountain of frilly pillows for a scared little boy with bright blue eyes who'd never been lucky or safe. And for the girl she'd been eight years ago, who only Nikolai had ever tried to defend from an attack she couldn't even remember. No one would know if she healed or not, because no one would know she'd been hurt.

There would only be those pictures and the nonexistent relationship Nikolai had made sure they showed to the world, that she'd decided she no longer cared if her father knew about.

Let him think what he likes, she'd thought.

Alicia had taken the train out for his birthday dinner the previous week, and had sat with her sisters around the table in his favorite local restaurant, pretending everything was all right. The way she always pretended it was.

But not because she'd still been racked with shame, as she'd been for all those years. Instead, she'd realized as she'd watched her father *not* look at her and *not* acknowledge her and she understood at last what had actually happened to her, she'd been a great deal closer to furious.

"Will you have another drink, love?" her mother had asked her innocuously enough, but Alicia had been watching her father. She'd seen him wince at the very idea, as if another glass of wine would have Alicia doffing her clothes in the middle of the King's Arms. And all of that fury and pain and all of those terrible years fused inside of her. She'd been as unable to keep quiet as she'd been when she'd told Nikolai about this mess in the first place.

"No need to worry, Dad," she'd said brusquely. "I haven't

been anywhere close to drunk in years. Eight years to be precise. And would you like to know why?"

He'd stared at her, then looked around at the rest of the family, all of them gaping from him to Alicia and back.

"No need," he'd said sharply. "I'm already aware."

"I was so drunk I couldn't walk," she'd told him, finally. "I take full responsibility for that. My friends poured me into a taxi and it took me ages to make it up to the house from the lane. I didn't want to wake anyone, so I went into the garden and lay down to sleep beneath the stars."

"For God's sake, Alicia!" her father had rumbled. "This isn't the time or place to bring up this kind of—"

"I passed out," she'd retorted, and she'd been perfectly calm. Focused. "I can't remember a single thing about it because I was *unconscious*. And yet when you saw Mr. Reddick helping himself to your comatose daughter, the conclusion you reached was that I was a whore."

There'd been a long, highly charged silence.

"He tried it on with me, too," her older sister had declared at last, thumping her drink down on the tabletop. "Vile pervert."

"I always thought he wasn't right," her other sister had chimed in at almost the same moment. "Always staring up at our windows, peering through the hedge."

"I had no idea," her mother had said urgently then, reaching over and taking hold of Alicia's hand, squeezing it tightly in hers. Then she'd frowned at her husband. "Bernard, you should be ashamed of yourself! Douglas Reddick was a menace to every woman in the village!"

And much later, after they'd all talked themselves blue and teary while her father had sat there quietly, and Douglas Reddick's sins had been thoroughly documented, her father had hugged her goodbye for the first time in nearly a decade. His form of an apology, she supposed.

And much as she'd wanted to rail at him further, she hadn't. Alicia had felt that great big knot she'd carried around inside of her begin to loosen, and she'd let it, because she'd wanted her father back more than she'd wanted to be angry.

She'd have that to carry with her out of her fake relationship. And surely that was something. Only she would know who had helped her stand up for herself eight years later. Only she would remember the things he'd changed in her when this was over. When the smoke cleared.

That was, if the smoke didn't choke her first.

"It's not even real," Alicia had blurted out one night, after a quarter hour of listening to Rosie rhapsodize about what a wedding to a man like Nikolai Korovin might entail, all while sitting on the couch surrounded by her favorite romance novels and the remains of a box of chocolates.

"What do you mean?"

"I mean, it's not real, Rosie. It's for show."

Alicia had regretted that she'd said anything the instant she'd said it. There'd been an odd, twisting thing inside of her that wanted to keep the sordid facts to herself. That hadn't wanted anyone else to know that when it came down to it, Nikolai Korovin needed an ulterior motive and a list of requirements to consider taking her out on a fake date.

Not that she was bitter.

"You're so cynical," Rosie had said with a sigh. "But I'll have you know I'm optimistic enough for the both of us." She'd handed Alicia a particularly well-worn romance novel, with a pointed look. "I know you sneak this off my shelf all the time. I also know that this tough, skeptical little shell of yours is an act."

"It's not an act," Alicia had retorted.

But she'd also taken the book.

If she'd stayed up too late some nights, crouched over

her laptop with her door locked tight, looking through all the photos of the two of them together online, she'd never admit it. If she'd paused to marvel over the way the tabloids managed to find pictures that told outright lies—that showed Nikolai gazing down at her with something that looked like his own, rusty version of affection, for example, or showed him scowling with what looked like bristling protectiveness at a photographer who ventured too close, she'd kept that to herself, too. Because if she'd dared speak of it, she might betray herself—she might show how very much she preferred the tabloid romance she read about to what she knew to be the reality.

And then there was Nikolai.

"Kiss me," he'd ordered her a few days before they'd had to leave for Prague, in that commanding tone better suited to tense corporate negotiations than a bright little café in his posh neighborhood on a Tuesday morning. She'd frowned at him and he'd stared back at her, ruthless and severe. "It will set the scene."

He'd been different these past few days, she'd thought as she'd looked at him over their coffees. Less approachable than he'd been before, which beggared belief, given his usual level of aloofness. He'd been much tenser. Darker. The fact that she'd been capable of discerning the differences between the various gradations of his glacial cold might have worried her, if she'd had any further to fall where this man was concerned.

"What scene?" she'd asked calmly, as if the idea of kissing him hadn't made her whole body tremble with that ever-present longing, that thrill of heat and flame. "There's a wall between us and the street. No one can see us, much less photograph us."

"We live in a digital age, Alicia," he'd said icily. "There are mobile phones everywhere."

Alicia had looked very pointedly at the people at the two other tables in their hidden nook, neither of whom had been wielding a mobile. Then she'd returned her attention to her steaming latte and sipped at it, pretending not to notice that Nikolai had continued to stare at her in that brooding, almost-fierce way.

"They took pictures of us walking here," she'd pointed out when the silence stretched too thin, his gaze was burning into her like hot coals and she'd worried she might break, into too many pieces to repair. "Mission accomplished."

Because nothing screamed *contented domesticity* like an early-morning stroll to a coffee place from Nikolai's penthouse, presumably after another long and intimate night. That was the story the tabloids would run with, he'd informed her in his clipped, matter-of-fact way, and it was guaranteed to drive his ex-wife crazy. Most of Nikolai's women, it went without saying—though her coworkers lined up to say the like daily—were there to pose silently beside him at events and disappear afterward, not stroll anywhere with him as if he *liked* them.

She'd been surprised to discover she was scowling. And then again when he'd stood up abruptly, smoothing down his suit jacket despite the fact it was far too well made to require smoothing of any kind. He'd stared at her, hard, then jerked his head toward the front of the café in a clear and peremptory command before storming that way himself.

Alicia had hated herself for it, but she'd smiled sheepishly at the other patrons in the tiny alcove, who'd eyed Nikolai's little display askance, and then she'd followed him.

He stood in the biting cold outside, muttering darkly into his mobile. Alicia had walked to stand next to him, wondering if she'd lost her spine when she'd felt that giant ripping thing move through her in her flat that night, as if she'd traded it for some clarity about what had happened to her eight years ago. Because she certainly hadn't used it since. She hadn't been using it that morning, certainly. The old, spined Alicia would have let Nikolai storm off as he chose, while she'd sat and merrily finished her latte.

Or so she'd wanted to believe.

Nikolai had slid his phone into a pocket and then turned that winter gaze on her, and Alicia had done her best to show him the effortlessly polite—if tough and slightly cynical—mask she'd tried so hard to wear during what he'd called *the public phase of this arrangement*. Yet something in the way he'd stared down at her that gray morning, that grim mouth of his a flat line, had made it impossible.

"Nikolai..." But she hadn't known what she'd meant to say.

He'd reached over to take her chin in his leather-gloved hand, and she'd shivered though she wasn't cold at all.

"There are paparazzi halfway down the block," he'd muttered. "We must bait the trap, *solnyshka*."

And then he'd leaned down and pressed a very hard, very serious, shockingly swift kiss against her lips.

Bold and hot. As devastating as it was a clear and deliberate brand of his ownership. His possession.

It had blown her up. Made a mockery of any attempts she'd thought she'd been making toward politeness, because that kiss had been anything but, surging through her like lightning. Burning her into nothing but smoldering need, right there on the street in the cold.

She'd have fallen down, had he not had those hard fingers on her chin. He'd looked at her for a long moment that had felt far too intimate for a public street so early in the morning, and then he'd released her.

And she'd had the sinking feeling that he knew exactly

what he'd done to her. Exactly how she felt. That this was all a part of his game. His plan.

"Let me guess what that word means," she'd said after a moment, trying to sound tough but failing, miserably. She'd been stripped down to nothing, achingly vulnerable, and she'd heard it clear as day in her voice. There'd been every reason to suppose he'd read it as easily on her face. "Is it Russian for gullible little fool, quick to leap into bed with a convenient stranger and happy to sell out her principles and her self-respect for any old photo opportunity—"

"Little sun," he'd bit out, his own gaze haunted. Tormented. He'd stared at her so hard she'd been afraid she'd bear the marks of it. She'd only been distantly aware that she trembled, that it had nothing to do with the temperature. He'd raised his hand again, brushed his fingers across her lips, and she'd had to bite back something she'd been terribly afraid was a sob. "Your smile could light up this city like a nuclear reactor. It's a weapon. And yet you throw it around as if it's nothing more dangerous than candy."

Here, now, staring out at the loveliest city she'd ever seen, as night fell and the lights blazed golden against the dark, Alicia could still feel those words as if he'd seared them into her skin.

And she knew it would be one more thing that she'd carry with her on the other side of this. One more thing only she would ever know had happened. Had been real. Had mattered, it seemed, if only for a moment.

She blinked back that prickly heat behind her eyes, and when they cleared, saw Nikolai in the entrance to her room. No more than a dark shape behind her in the window's reflection. As if he, too, was already disappearing, turning into another memory right before her eyes.

She didn't turn. She didn't dare. She didn't know what she'd do.

"We leave in an hour," he said.

Alicia didn't trust herself to speak, and so merely nodded.

And she could feel that harshly beautiful kiss against her mouth again, like all the things she couldn't allow herself to say, all the things she knew she'd never forget as long as she lived.

Nikolai hesitated in the doorway, and she held her breath, but then he simply turned and melted away, gone as silently as he'd come.

She dressed efficiently and quickly in a sleek sheath made of a shimmery green that made her feel like a mermaid. It was strapless with a V between her breasts, slicked down to her waist, then ended in a breezy swell at her knees. It had been hanging in her room when she'd arrived, next to a floor-length sweep of sequined royal blue that was clearly for the more formal ball tomorrow night. And accessories for both laid out on a nearby bureau. She slid her feet into the appropriate shoes, each one a delicate, sensual triumph. Then she picked up the cunning little evening bag, the green of the dress with blues mixed in.

He's bought and paid for you, hasn't he? she asked herself as she walked down the long hall toward the suite's main room, trying to summon her temper. Her sense of outrage. Any of that motivating almost-hate she'd tried to feel for him back in the beginning. *There are words to describe arrangements like this, aren't there? Especially if you're foolish enough to sleep with him....*

But she knew that the sad truth was that she was going to do this, whether she managed to work herself into a state or not. She was going to wear the fine clothes he'd bought her and dance to his tune, quite literally, because she no longer had the strength to fight it. To fight him.

To fight her own traitorous heart.

And time was running out. By Monday it would be as if she'd dreamed all of this. She imagined that in two months' time or so, when she was living her normal life and was done sorting out whatever Nikolai fallout there might be, she'd feel as if she had.

A thought that should have made her happy and instead was like a huge, black hole inside of her, yawning and deep. She ignored it, because she didn't know what else to do as she walked into the lounge. Nikolai stood in front of the flat-screen television, frowning at the financial report, but turned almost before she cleared the entryway, as if he'd sensed her.

She told herself she hardly noticed anymore how beautiful he was. How gorgeously lethal in another fine suit.

Nikolai roamed toward her, his long strides eating up the luxurious carpet beneath his feet, the tall, dark, brooding perfection of him bold and elegant in the middle of so much overstated opulence. Columns wrapped in gold. Frescoed ceilings. And his gaze was as bright as the winter sky, as if he made it daylight again when he looked at her.

There was no possibility that she would survive this in anything like one piece. None at all.

You can fall to pieces next week, she told herself firmly. It would be Christmas. She'd hole up in her parents' house as planned, stuff herself with holiday treats and too much mulled wine, and pretend none of this had ever happened. That *he* hadn't happened to her.

That she hadn't done this to herself.

"Are you ready?" he asked.

"Define ready." She tried to keep her voice light. Amused. Because anything else would lead them to places she didn't want to go, because she doubted she'd come back from them intact. "Ready to attend your exciting whirl of corporate events? Certainly. Ready to be used in my capacity as weapon of choice, aimed directly at your ex-wife's face?" She even smiled then, and it felt almost like the real thing. "I find I'm as ready for *that* as I ever was."

"Then I suppose we should both be grateful that there will be no need for weaponry tonight," he said, in that way of his that insinuated itself down the length of her back, like a sliver of ice. The rest of her body heated at once, inside and out, his brand of winter like a fire in her, still. "This is only a tedious dinner. An opportunity to make the donors feel especially appreciated before we ask them for more money tomorrow."

When he drew close, he reached over to a nearby incidental table and picked up a long, flat box. He held it out to her without a word, his expression serious. She stared at it until he grew impatient, and then he simply cracked open the box himself and pulled out a shimmering necklace. It was asymmetrical and bold, featuring unusually shaped clusters of blue and green gems set in a thick rope that nonetheless managed to appear light. Fun. As fanciful, in its way, as this golden city they stood in.

The very things this man was not.

"I would have taken you for the black diamond sort," Alicia said, her eyes on the necklace instead of him, because it was the prettiest thing she'd seen and yet she knew it would pale next to his stark beauty. "Or other very, very dark jewels. Heavy chunks of hematite. Brooding rubies the color of burgundy wine."

"That would be predictable," he said, a reproving note in his low voice, the hint of that dark humor mixed in with it, making her wish. *Want.*

He slid the necklace into place, cool against her heated skin, his fingers like naked flame. She couldn't help the sigh that escaped her lips, and her eyes flew to his, finally, to find him watching her with that lazy, knowing intensity in his gaze that had been her undoing from the start.

He reached around to the nape of her neck, taking his time fastening the necklace, letting his fingertips dance and tease her skin beneath the cloud of her curls, then smoothing over her collarbone. He adjusted it on her neck, making sure it fell as he wanted it, one end stretched down toward the upper swell of one breast.

Alicia didn't know if he was teasing her or tearing her apart. She could no longer tell the difference.

When he caught her gaze again, neither one of them was breathing normally, and the room around them felt hot and close.

"Come," he said, and she could hear it in his voice. That fire. That need. That tornado that spiraled between them, more and more out of control the longer this went on, and more likely to wreck them both with every second.

And it would, she thought. *Soon.*

Just as he'd warned her.

CHAPTER EIGHT

A GOLD-MIRRORED LIFT delivered them with hushed and elegant efficiency into the brightly lit foyer of the presidential suite in one of Prague's finest hotels, filled with the kind of people who were not required to announce their wealth and consequence because everything they did, said and wore did it for them. Emphatically.

These were Nikolai's people. Alicia kept her polite smile at the ready as Nikolai steered her through the crowd. This was his world, no matter how he looked at her when they were in private. No matter what stories she'd told herself, she was no more than a tourist, due to turn straight back into a pumpkin the moment the weekend was over. And then stay that way, this strange interlude nothing more than a gilt-edged memory.

She could almost feel the heavy stalk beginning to form, like a brand-new knot in her stomach.

Nikolai pulled her aside after they'd made a slow circuit through the monied clusters of guests, into a small seating area near the farthest windows. Outside, in the dark, she could see the magnificence of Prague Castle, thrusting bright and proud against the night. And inside, Nikolai looked down at her, unsmiling, in that way of his that made everything inside of her squeeze tight, then melt.

"I told you this would be remarkably boring, did I not?"

"Perhaps for you," she replied, smiling. "I keep wondering if the American cattle baron is going to break into song at the piano, and if so, if that very angry-looking German banker will haul off and hit him."

His blue eyes gleamed, and she felt the warmth of it all over, even deep inside where that knot curled tight in her gut, a warning she couldn't seem to heed.

"These are not the sort of people who fight with their hands," Nikolai said, the suggestion of laughter in his gaze, on his mouth, lurking in that rough velvet voice of his. "They prefer to go to war with their checkbooks."

"That sounds a bit dry." She pressed her wineglass to her lips and sipped, but was aware of nothing but Nikolai. "Surely throwing a few punches is more exciting than writing checks?"

"Not at all." His lips tugged in one corner. "A fistfight can only be so satisfying. Bruises heal. Fight with money, and whole companies can be leveled, thousands of lives ruined, entire fortunes destroyed in the course of an afternoon." That smile deepened, became slightly mocking. "This also requires a much longer recovery period than a couple of bruises."

Alicia searched his face, wondering if she was seeing what she wanted to see—or if there really was a softening there, a kind of warmth, that made that wide rip in her feel like a vast canyon and her heart beat hard like a drum.

He reached over and traced one of the clever shapes that made up the necklace he'd given her, almost lazily, but Alicia felt the burn of it as if he was touching her directly. His gaze found hers, and she knew they both wished he was.

It swelled between them, bright and hot and more complicated now, that electric connection that had shocked her in that club. It was so much deeper tonight. It poured into every part of her, changing her as it went, making her realize she didn't care what the consequences were any longer. They'd be worth it. Anything would be worth it if it meant she could touch him again.

She couldn't find the words to tell him that, so she smiled instead, letting it all flow out of her. Like a weapon, he'd said. Like candy.

Like love.

Nikolai jerked almost imperceptibly, as if he saw what she thought, what she felt, written all over her. As if she'd said it out loud when she hardly dared think it.

"Alicia—" he began, his tone deeper than usual, urgent and thick, and all of her confusion and wariness rolled into the place where she'd torn in two, then swelled into that ache, making it bloom, making her realize she finally knew what it was....

But then the energy in the suite all around them shifted. Dramatically. There was a moment of shocked silence, then an excited buzz of whispering.

Nikolai's gaze left hers and cut to the entryway, and then, without seeming to move at all, he froze solid. She watched him do it, saw him turn from flesh and blood to ice in a single breath.

It was the first time he'd scared her.

Alicia turned to see the crowd parting before a graceful woman in a deceptively simple black dress, flanked by two security guards. She was cool and aristocratic as she walked into the room, smiling and exchanging greetings with the people she passed. Her dark red hair was swept back into an elegant chignon, she wore no adornment besides a hint of diamonds at her ears and the sparkle of the ring on her hand, and still, she captivated the room.

And had turned Nikolai to stone.

Alicia recognized her at once, of course.

"Isn't that...?"

"My brother's wife. Yes."

Nikolai's tone was brutal. Alicia flicked a worried glance at him, then looked back to the party.

Miranda Sweet, wife of the legendary Ivan Korovin and easily identifiable to anyone with access to Rosie's unapologetic subscription to celebrity magazines, swept through the assembled collection of donors with ease. She said a word or two here, laughed there and only faltered when her gaze fell on Nikolai. But she recovered almost instantly, squaring her shoulders and waving off her security detail, and made her way toward him.

She stopped when she was a few feet away. Keeping a safe distance, Alicia thought, her eyes narrowing. Miranda Sweet was prettier in person, and taller, and the way she looked at Nikolai was painful.

While Nikolai might as well have been a glacier.

Alicia could have choked on the thick, black tension that rose between the two of them, so harsh it made her ears ring. So intense she glanced around to see if anyone else had noticed, but Miranda's security guards had blocked them off from prying eyes.

When she looked back, Nikolai and his brother's wife were still locked in their silent battle. Alicia moved closer to Nikolai's side, battling the urge to step in front of him and protect him from this threat, however unlikely the source.

Then, very deliberately, Nikolai dropped his gaze. Alicia followed it to the small swell of Miranda's belly, almost entirely concealed by her dress. Alicia never would have seen it. She doubted anyone was supposed to see it.

When Nikolai raised his gaze to his sister-in-law's again, his eyes were raw and cold. Alicia saw Miranda swallow. Hard. Nervously, even.

Another terrible moment passed.

Then Miranda inclined her head slightly. "Nikolai."

"Miranda," he replied, in the same tone, so crisp and hard and civil it hurt.

Miranda glanced at Alicia, then back at Nikolai, and something moved across her face.

Fear, Alicia thought, confused. *She's afraid of him.*

Miranda hid it almost immediately, though her hand moved to brush against her belly, her ring catching the light. She dropped her hand when she saw Nikolai glance at it.

"He misses you," she said after a moment, obvious conflict and a deep sadness Alicia didn't understand in her voice. "You broke his heart."

"Are you his emissary?"

"Hardly." Miranda looked at Nikolai as if she expected a reply, but he was nothing but ice. "He would never admit that. He'd hate that I said anything."

"Then why did you?" Cold and hard, and Alicia thought it must hurt him to sound like that. To be that terribly frigid.

Miranda nodded again, a sharp jerk of her head. Her gaze moved to Alicia for a moment, as if she wanted to say something, but thought better of it. And then she turned and walked away without another word, her smile in place as if it had never left her.

While Alicia stood next to Nikolai and hurt for him, hard and deep, and all the things he didn't—couldn't—say.

"I take it you weren't expecting her," she said after a while, still watching Miranda Sweet work the party, marveling at how carefree she looked when she'd left a wind chill and subzero temperatures in her wake.

"I should have." Nikolai's gaze was trained on the crowd, dark and stormy. "She often makes appearances at high-level donor events when Ivan is held up somewhere else. It helps bring that little bit of Hollywood sparkle."

He sounded as if he was reporting on something he'd read a long time ago, distant and emotionless, but Alicia knew better. She felt the waves of that bitter chill coming off him, like arctic winds. This was Nikolai in pain. She could feel it inside her own chest, like a vise.

"A bit of a chilly reunion, I couldn't help but notice."

Nikolai shifted. "She believes I tried to ruin her relationship with Ivan."

Alicia frowned up at him. "Why would she think that?"

It took Nikolai a breath to look down, to meet her eyes. When he did, his gaze was the coldest she'd ever seen it, and her heart lurched in her chest.

"Because I did."

She blinked, but didn't otherwise move. "Why?"

A great black shadow fell over him then, leaving him hollow at the eyes and that hard mouth of his too grim. *Grief,* she thought. And something very much like shame, only sharper. Colder.

"Why do I do anything?" he asked softly. Terribly. "Because happiness looks like the enemy to me. When I see it I try to kill it."

Alicia only stared at him, stricken. Nikolai's mouth tugged in one corner, a self-deprecating almost smile that this time was nothing but dark and painful. Total devastation in that one small curve.

"You should be afraid of me, Alicia," he said, and the bleak finality in his voice broke her in two. "I keep warning you."

He turned back to the crowd.

And Alicia followed an instinct she didn't fully understand, that had something to do with that deep ache, that wide-open canyon in her chest she didn't think would ever go away, and the proud, still way he stood next to her, ruthlessly rigid and straight, as if bracing himself for another blow.

Like that brave boy he must have been a lifetime ago, who was never safe. Or lucky. Who had given up all hope.

She couldn't bear it.

Alicia reached over and slid her hand into his, as if it belonged there. As if they fitted together like a puzzle, and she was clicking the last piece into place.

She felt him flinch, but then, slowly—almost cautiously—his long fingers closed over hers.

And then she held on to him with all of her might.

Nikolai hadn't expected Alicia to be quite so good at this, to fill her role so seamlessly tonight, as if she'd been born to play the part of his hostess. As if she belonged right there at his side, the limb he hadn't realized he'd been missing all along, instead of merely the tool he'd planned to use and then discard.

He stood across the room, watching from a distance as she charmed the two men she'd thought might break into a fight earlier. She was like a brilliant sunbeam in the middle of this dark and cold winter's night, outshining his wealthiest donors in all their finery even here, in a luxurious hotel suite in a city renowned for its gleaming, golden, incomparable light.

Nikolai had never seen her equal. He never would again.

She'd held on to his hand. *To him*. Almost ferociously, as if she'd sensed how close he'd been to disappearing right where he stood and had been determined to stand as his anchor. And so she had.

Nikolai couldn't concentrate on his duties tonight the way he usually did, with that single-minded focus that was his trademark. He couldn't think too much about the fact that Ivan had a child on the way, no matter the vows they'd made as angry young men that they would never inflict the uncertain Korovin temper on more innocent children.

He couldn't think of anything but that press of Alicia's palm against his, the tangling of their fingers as if they belonged fused together like that, the surprising strength of her grip.

As if they were a united front no matter the approaching threat—Miranda, the pregnancy Ivan had failed to mention, the donors who wanted to be celebrated and catered to no matter what quiet heartbreaks might occur in their midst, even the ravaged wastes of his own frigid remains of a soul.

She'd held his hand as if she was ready to fight at his side however she could and that simple gesture had humbled him so profoundly that he didn't know how he'd remained upright. How he hadn't sunk to his knees and promised her anything she wanted, anything at all, if she would only do that again.

If she would choose him, support him. Defend him. Protect him.

If she would treat him like a man, not a wild animal in need of a cage. If she would keep treating him like that. Like he really could be redeemed.

As if she hadn't the smallest doubt.

Because if he wasn't the irredeemable monster he'd always believed—if both she and Ivan had been right all along—then he could choose. He could choose the press of her slender fingers against his, a shining bright light to cut through a lifetime of dark. Warmth instead of cold. Sun instead of ice. *He could choose.*

Nikolai had never imagined that was possible. He'd stopped wanting what he couldn't have. He'd stopped *wanting.*

Alicia made him believe he could be the man he might have been, if only for a moment. She made him regret, more deeply than he ever had before, that he was so empty. That he couldn't give her anything in return.

Except, a voice inside him whispered, *her freedom from this.*

From him. From this dirty little war he'd forced her to fight.

Nikolai nearly shuddered where he stood. He kept his eyes trained on Alicia, who looked over her shoulder as if she felt the weight of his stare and then smiled at him as if he really was that man.

As if she'd never seen anything else.

That swift taste of her on a gray and frigid London street had led only to cold showers and a gnawing need inside of him these past few days, much too close to pain. Nikolai didn't care anymore that he hardly recognized himself. That he was drowning in this flood she'd let loose in him. That he was almost thawed through and beyond control, the very thing he'd feared the most for the whole of his life.

He wanted Alicia more. There was only this one last weekend before everything went back to normal. Before he had his answer from Veronika. And then there was absolutely no rational reason he should ever spend another moment in her company.

He'd intended to have her here, in every way he could. To glut himself on her as if that could take the place of all her mysteries he'd failed to solve, the sweet intoxication that was Alicia that he'd never quite sobered up from. He'd intended to make this weekend count.

But she'd let him imagine that he was a better man, or could be. He'd glimpsed himself as she saw him for a brief, brilliant moment, and that changed everything.

You have to let her go, that voice told him, more forcefully. *Now, before it's too late.*

He imagined that was his conscience talking. No wonder he didn't recognize it.

Nikolai took her back to their hotel when the dinner

finally ground to a halt not long after midnight. They stood outside her bedroom and he studied her lovely face, committing it to memory.

Letting her go.

"Nikolai?" Even her voice was pretty. Husky and sweet. "What's the matter?"

He kissed her softly, once, on that very hand that had held his with such surprising strength and incapacitating kindness. It wasn't what he wanted. It wasn't enough. But it would be something to take with him, like a single match against the night.

"You don't need to be here," he said quietly, quickly, because he wasn't sure he'd do it at all if he didn't do it fast. "Veronika will seek me out whether you're with me or not. I'll have the plane ready for you in the morning."

"What are you talking about?" Her voice was small. It shook. "I thought we had a very specific plan. Didn't we?"

"You're free, Alicia." He ground out the words. "Of this game, this blackmail. Of me."

"But—" She reached out to him, but he caught her hand before she could touch him, because he couldn't trust himself. Not with her. "What if I don't particularly want to be free?"

Under any other circumstances, he wouldn't have hesitated. But this was Alicia. She'd comforted him, protected him, when anyone else would have walked away.

When everyone else had.

It wasn't a small gesture to him, the way she'd held his hand like that. It was everything. He had to honor that, if nothing else.

"I know you don't," Nikolai said. He released her hand, and she curled it into a fist. Fierce and fearless until the end. That was his Alicia. "But you deserve it. You deserve better."

And then he'd left her there outside her room without another word, because a good man never would have put her in this position in the first place, blackmailed her and threatened her, forced her into this charade for his own sordid ends.

Because he knew it was the right thing to do, and for her, he'd make himself do it, no matter how little he liked it.

"But I love you," Alicia whispered, knowing he was already gone.

That he'd already melted into the shadows, disappeared down the hall, and that chances were, he wouldn't want to hear that anyway.

She stood there in that hall for a long time, outside the door to her bedroom in a mermaid dress and lovely, precarious heels he'd chosen for her, and told herself she wasn't falling apart.

She was fine.

She was in love with a man who had walked away from her, leaving her with nothing but a teasing hint of heat on the back of her hand and that awful finality in his rough, dark voice, but Alicia told herself she was absolutely, perfectly *fine*.

Eventually, she moved inside her room and dutifully shut the door. She pulled off the dress he'd chosen for her and the necklace he'd put around her neck himself, taking extra care with both of them as she put them back with the rest of the things she'd leave behind her here.

And maybe her heart along with them.

She tried not to think about that stunned, almost-shattered look in his beautiful eyes when she'd grabbed his hand. The way his strong fingers had wrapped around hers, then held her tight, as if he'd never wanted to let her go. She tried not to torture herself with the way he'd looked at her across the dinner table afterward, over the sounds of merriment and too much wine, that faint smile in the corner of his austere mouth.

But she couldn't think of anything else.

Alicia changed into the old T-shirt she wore to sleep in, washed soft and cozy over the years, and then she methodically washed her face and cleaned her teeth. She climbed into the palatial bed set high on a dais that made her feel she was perched on a stage, and then she glared fiercely at that book Rosie had given her without seeing a single well-loved sentence.

The truth was, she'd fallen in love when she'd fallen into him at that club.

It had been that sudden, that irrevocable. That deeply, utterly mad. The long, hot, darkly exciting and surprisingly emotional night that had followed had only cemented it. And when he'd let her see those glimpses of his vulnerable side, even hidden away in all that ice and bitter snow, she'd felt it like a deep tear inside of her because she hadn't wanted to accept what she already knew somewhere inside.

Alicia let out a sigh and tossed the paperback aside, sinking back against the soft feather pillows and scowling at the billowing canopy far above her.

She wasn't the too-drunk girl she'd been at twenty-one any longer—and in fact, she'd never been the shameful creature she'd thought she was. Had she tripped and fallen into any other man on that dance floor that night, she would have offered him her embarrassed apologies and then gone straight home to sort out her laundry and carry on living her quiet little life.

But it had been Nikolai.

The fact was, she'd kicked and screamed and moaned about the way he'd forced her into this—but he hadn't. She could have complained. Daniel was a CEO with grand plans for the charity, but he wasn't an ogre. He wouldn't have simply let her go without a discussion; he might not have let her go at all. And when it came down to it, she hadn't even fought too hard against this mad little plan of Nikolai's, had she?

On some level, she'd wanted all of those tabloid pictures with their suggestive captions, because her fascination with him outweighed her shame. And more, because they proved it was real. That the night no one knew about, that she'd tried so hard to make disappear, had really, truly happened.

She'd tasted him in that shiny black SUV, and she'd loved every moment of his bold possession. She'd explored every inch of his beautiful body in that wide bed of his. She'd kissed his scars and even the monster he wore on his chest like a warning. And he'd made her sob and moan and surge against him as if she'd never get enough of him, and then they'd collapsed against each other to sleep in a great tangle, as if they weren't two separate people at all.

All of that had happened. All of it was real.

All of this is real, she thought.

Alicia picked up the paperback romance again, flipping through the well-worn pages to her favorite scene, which she'd read so many times before she was sure she could quote it. She scanned it again now.

Love can't hinge on an outcome. If it does, it isn't love at all, the heroine said directly to the man she loved when all was lost. When he had already given up, and she loved him too much to let him. When she was willing to fight for him in the only way she could, even if that meant she had to fight every last demon in his head herself. *Love is risk and hope and a terrible vulnerability. And it's worth it. I promise.*

"You either love him or you don't, Alicia," she told herself then, a hushed whisper in her quiet room.

And she did.

Then she took a deep breath to gather her courage, swung out of the high bed and went to prove it.

Nikolai sat by the fire in the crimson master bedroom that dominated the far corner of the hotel suite, staring at the flames as they crackled and danced along the grate.

He wished this wasn't the longest night of the year, with all of that extra darkness to lead him into temptation, like one more cosmic joke at his expense. He wished he could take some kind of pride in the uncharacteristic decision he'd made instead of sitting here like he needed to act as his own guard, as if a single moment of inattention would have him clawing at her door like an animal.

He wished most of all that this terrible thaw inside of him wasn't an open invitation for his demons to crawl out and fill every extra, elongated hour with their same old familiar poison.

He shifted in the plush velvet armchair and let the heat of the fire play over his skin, wishing it could warm him inside, where too many dark things lurked tonight, with their sharp teeth and too many scenes from his past.

He hated Prague, happy little jewel of a city that it was, filled to the top of every last spire with all the joyful promises of a better life even the Iron Curtain had failed to stamp out. Anywhere east of Zurich he began to feel the bitter chill of Mother Russia breathing down his neck, her snow-covered nails digging into his back as if she might drag him back home at any moment.

It was far too easy to imagine himself there, struggling to make it through another vicious winter with no end, dreamless and broken and half-mad. Feral to the bone. In his uncle's bleak home in Nizhny Novgorod. In corrupt, polluted, snowbound Moscow with the equally corrupt and polluted Veronika, when he'd been in the military and had thought, for a time, it might save him from himself.

Or, even sadder in retrospect, that Veronika might.

Being in Prague was too much like being back there. Nikolai was too close to the raw and out-of-control creature he'd been then, careening between the intense extremes that were all he'd ever known. Either losing himself in violence or numbing himself however he could. One or the other, since the age of five.

He could feel that old version of him right beneath his skin, making him restless. On edge.

Then again, perhaps it wasn't Prague at all. Perhaps it was the woman on the other side of this hotel suite even now, with her dark eyes that saw more of him than anyone else ever had and that carnal distraction of a mouth.

He was in trouble. He knew it.

This was the kind of night that called for a bottle of something deliberately incapacitating, but he couldn't allow himself the escape. He couldn't numb this away. He couldn't slam it into oblivion. He had to sit in it and wait for morning.

Nikolai scowled at the fire while his demons danced on, bold and sickening and much too close, tugging him back into his dirty past as if he'd never left it behind.

As if he never would.

A scant second before Alicia appeared in his door, he sensed her approach, his gaze snapping to meet hers as she paused on the threshold.

He almost thought she was another one of his demons, but even as it crossed his mind, he knew better. Alicia was too alive, that light of hers beaming into his room as if she'd switched on the lamps, sending all of those things that tortured him in the dark diving for the shadows.

She'd changed out of her formal attire and was standing

there in nothing but an oversized wide-necked T-shirt—a pink color, of course—that slid down her arm to bare her shoulder and the upper slope of one breast. Her curls stood around her head in abandon, and her feet were bare.

Nikolai's throat went dry. The rest of him went hard.

"It's below zero tonight," he barked at her, rude and belligerent. *Desperate*. "You shouldn't be walking around like that unless you've decided to court your own death, in which case, I can tell you that there are far quicker ways to go."

The last time he'd used a tone like that on a woman, she'd turned and run from him, sobbing. But this was Alicia. His strong, fearless Alicia, and she only laughed that laugh of hers that made him want to believe in magic.

When he looked at her, he thought he might.

"I've come to your room wearing almost nothing and your first reaction is to talk about the weather and death," she said in that dry way of hers, and God help him, this woman was worse than all his demons put together. More powerful by far. "Very romantic, indeed. My heart is aglow."

Nikolai stood up then, as if that would ward her off. He didn't know which was worse. That she was standing there with so much of her lush brown skin on display, her lithe and supple legs, that shoulder, even the hint of her thighs—naked and smooth and far too tempting. Or that teasing tone she used, so dry and amused, that set off brushfires inside him.

His body felt as if it was someone else's, unwieldy and strange. He wished he hadn't stripped down to no more than his exercise trousers, low on his hips, the better to while away a sleepless night at war with himself.

There was too much bare flesh in the room now. Too many possibilities. He could only deny himself so much....

He scowled at her, and she laughed again.

"Relax," she said, in that calm, easy way that simultaneously soothed and inflamed him. "*I'm* seducing *you*, Nikolai. You don't have to do anything but surrender."

"You are not seducing me," he told her, all cold command, and she ignored it completely and started toward him as if he hadn't spoken. As if he hadn't said something similar to her what seemed like a lifetime ago. "And I am certainly not surrendering."

"Not yet, no," she agreed, smiling. "But the night is young."

"Alicia." He didn't back away when she roamed even closer, not even when he could see her nipples poking against the thin material of her shirt and had to fight to keep himself from leaning down and sucking them into his mouth, right then and there. "This is the first time in my life I've ever done the right thing deliberately. Some respect, I beg you."

Her smile changed, making his chest feel tight though he didn't know what it meant.

"Tell me what the right thing is," she said softly, not teasing him any longer, and she was within arm's reach now. Warm and soft. *Right there.* "Because I think you and I are using different definitions."

"It's leaving you alone," he said, feeling the stirrings of a kind of panic he thought he'd excised from himself when he was still a child. "The way I should have done from the start."

She eased closer, her scent teasing his nose, cocoa butter and a hint of sugar, sweet and rich and *Alicia*. He was so hard it bordered on agony, and the way she looked up at him made his heart begin to hit at him, erratic and intense, like it wanted to knock him down. Like it wouldn't take much to succeed.

"You vowed you didn't want to sleep with me again," he reminded her, almost savagely. "Repeatedly."

"I'm a woman possessed," she told him, her voice husky and low, washing over him and into him. "Infatuated, even."

He remembered when he'd said those same words to her in that far-off stairwell, when her scent had had much the same effect on him. Her dark eyes had been so wide and anxious, and yet all of that heat had been there behind it, electric and captivating. Impossible to ignore. Just as she was.

Tonight, there was only heat, so much of it he burned at the sight. And he wanted her so badly he was afraid he shook with it. So badly he cared less and less with every passing second if he did.

"I've never had the slightest inclination to behave the way a good man might," he began, throwing the words at her.

"That simply isn't true."

"Of course it is. I keep telling you, I—"

"You've dedicated your life to doing good, Nikolai," she said, cutting him off, her voice firm. "You run a foundation that funds a tremendous amount of charity work. Specifically, children's charities."

"I'm certain bands of activists would occupy me personally if they could pin me down to a single residence or office." He glared at her, his voice so derisive it almost hurt, but he knew he wasn't talking to her so much as the demons in all the corners of the room, dancing there in his peripheral vision. "I take money from the rich and make it into more money. I am the problem."

"Like Robin Hood, then? Who was, as everyone knows, a great villain. Evil to the very core."

"If Robin Hood were a soulless venture capitalist, perhaps," Nikolai retorted, but there was that brilliant heat inside of him, that terrible thaw, and he was on the verge of something he didn't want to face. He wasn't sure he could.

Alicia shook her head, frowning at him as if he was hurting her. He didn't understand that—this was him *not* hurting her. This was him *trying*. Why was he not surprised that he couldn't do that right, either?

"You help people," she said in that same firm, deliberate way, her gaze holding his. "The things you do and the choices you make *help people*. Nikolai, you do the right thing *every single day*."

He didn't know what that iron band was that crushed his chest, holding him tight, making everything seem to contract around him.

"You say that," he growled at her, or possibly it was even a howl, torn from that heart he'd abandoned years ago, "but there is blood on my hands, Alicia. More blood than you can possibly imagine."

She stepped even closer, then picked up his much larger hands in hers. He felt a kind of rumbling, a far-off quake, and even though he knew there was nothing but disaster heading toward him, even though he suspected it would destroy him and her and possibly the whole of the city they stood in, the world, the stars above, he let her.

And he watched, fascinated beyond measure and something like terrified, that tight, hard circle around him pulling tighter and tighter, as she turned each hand over, one by one, and pressed a kiss into the center of each.

The way she'd done for the creature on his chest, that she'd called *pretty*.

She looked up at him again, and her dark eyes were different. Warm in a way he'd never seen before. Sweet and something like admiring. Filled with that light that made him feel simultaneously scraped hollow and carved new.

Shining as if whatever she saw was beautiful.

"I don't see any blood," she said, distinct and direct, her gaze fast to his. "I only see you. I've never seen anything but you."

And everything simply...ended.

Nikolai shattered. He broke. All of that ice, every last glacier, swept away in the flood, the heat, the roaring inferno stretching high into the night, until he was nothing but raw and wild and *that look* she gave him took up the world.

And replaced it with fire. Fire and heat and all of the things he'd locked away for all those bleak and terrible reasons. Color and light, flesh and blood. Rage and need and all of that hunger, all of that pain, all of that sorrow and grief, loss and tragedy. His parents, taken so young. His brother, who should never have had to fight so hard. The uncle who should have cared for them. The army that had broken him down and then built him into his own worst nightmare. Veronika's lies and Stefan's sweet, infant body cradled in his arms, like hope. Every emotion he'd vowed he didn't have, roaring back into him, filling him up, tearing him into something new and unrecognizable.

"You have to stop this," he said, but when it left his mouth it was near to a shout, furious and loud and she didn't even flinch. "You can't be *kind* to a man like me! You don't know what you've done!"

"Nikolai," she said, without looking away from him, without hiding from the catastrophic storm that was happening right there in front of her, without letting go of his hands for an instant or dropping her warm gaze, "I can't be anything else. That's what *you* deserve."

And he surrendered.

For the first time in his life, Nikolai Korovin stopped fighting.

CHAPTER NINE

Nikolai dropped to his knees, right there in front of her

For a moment he looked ravaged. Untethered and lost, and then he slid his arms around her hips, making Alicia's heart fall out of her chest, her breath deserting her in a rush. She could feel the storm all around them, pouring out of him, enveloping them both. His hard face became stark, sensual. Fierce.

It all led here. Now. To that look in his beautiful eyes that made her own fill with tears. A fledging kind of joy, pale and fragile.

Hope.

And she loved him. She thought she understood him. So when that light in his eyes turned to need, she was with him. It roared in her too, setting them both alight.

He pulled up the hem of her T-shirt with a strong, urgent hand that shook slightly, baring her to his view, making her quiver in return. And that fire that was always in her, always his, turned molten and rolled through her, making her heavy and needy and almost scared by the intensity of this. Of him. Of these things she felt, storming inside of her.

Her legs shook, and he kissed her once, high on her thigh. She could feel the curve of his lips, that rare smile, and it went through her like a lightning bolt, burning her straight down to the soles of her feet where they pressed into the thick carpet.

And then slowly, so slowly, he peeled her panties down her legs, then tossed them aside.

Alicia heard a harsh sort of panting, and realized it was her.

"Solnyshka," he said, in that marvelous voice of his, darker and harsher than ever, and it thrilled her, making her feel like the sun he thought she was, too bright and hot to bear. "I think you'd better hold on."

He wrapped one strong arm around her bottom and the back of her thighs, and then, using his shoulder to knock her leg up and out of his way, he leaned forward and pressed his mouth against her heat.

And then he licked into her.

It was white-hot ecstasy. Carnal lightning. It seared through her, almost like pain, making her shudder against him and cry out his name. She fisted her hands in his hair, his arms were tight around her to keep her from falling, and she simply went limp against his mouth.

His wicked, fascinating, demanding mouth.

She detonated. Her licked her straight over the edge, and she thought she screamed, lost in a searingly hot, shuddering place where there was nothing left but him and these things he did to her, this wild magic that was only his. *Theirs.*

"Too fast," he rumbled, from far away, but everything was dizzy, confused, and it took her a long breath, then another, to remember who she was. And where.

And then another to understand that he'd flipped them around to spread her out on the deep rug in front of the fire.

"Nikolai," she said, or thought she did, but she lost whatever half-formed thought that might have been, because he was taking up where he'd left off.

He used his mouth again, and his hands. He stroked deep into her core, throwing her straight back into that inferno as if she'd never found release. Soon she was writhing against him, exulting in how he held her so easily, with such confident mastery, and used his tongue, his teeth, even that smile again, like sensual weapons.

Alicia arched up against him, into him. Her hands dug at the carpet below her, and his mouth was an impossible fire, driving her wild all over again, driving her higher and higher, until he sucked hard on the very center of her heat and she exploded all around him once again.

When she came back to herself this time, he was helping her up, letting her stumble against him and laughing as he pulled her T-shirt over her head, then muttering something as he took her breasts in his hands. He tested their weight, groaned out his approval, and then pulled each hard, dark nipple into his mouth.

Lighting the fire in her all over again. Making her burn.

He picked her up and carried her to the bed, following her down and stretching out beside her, sleek and powerful, tattooed and dangerous. He'd rid himself of his trousers at some point and there was nothing between them then.

Only skin and heat. Only the two of them, at last.

For a while, it was enough. They explored each other as if this was the first time, this taut delight, this delicious heat. Alicia traced the bright-colored shapes and lines that made up his monster with her tongue, pressed kisses over his heart, hearing it thunder beneath her. Nikolai stroked his big hands down the length of her back, testing each and every one of her curves as he worshipped every part of her equally.

He didn't speak. And Alicia kissed him, again and again, as if that could say it for her, the word she dared not say, but could show him. With her mouth, her hands. Her kiss, her smile.

They teased the flames, built them slowly, making up for all those lost weeks since the last time they'd touched like this. Until suddenly, it was too much. They were both out of breath and the fire had turned into something darker, more desperate. Hotter by far.

Nikolai reached for the table near his bed and then rolled a condom down his hard length, his eyes glittering on hers, and Alicia almost felt as if he was stroking her that way, so determined and sure. She could feel his touch inside of her, stoking those flames. Making her wild with smoke and heat and need.

Alicia couldn't wait, as desperate to have him inside her again as if she hadn't already found her own pleasure, twice. As if this was new.

Because it felt that way, she thought. It felt completely different from what had gone before, and she knew why. She might have fallen hard for him the night she met him, but she loved the man she knew. The man who had saved her from a prison of shame. This man, who looked at her as if she was a miracle. This man, who she believed might be one himself.

"Kiss me," she ordered him, straddling his lap, pressing herself against his delicious hardness, torturing them both.

He took her face in his hands and then her mouth with a dark, thrilling kiss, making her moan against him. He tasted like the winter night and a little bit like her, and the kick of it rocketed through her, sensations building and burning and boiling her down until she was nothing but his.

His.

The world was his powerful body, his masterful kiss, his strong arms around her that anchored her to him. And she loved him. She loved him with every kiss, every taste. She couldn't get close enough. She knew she never would.

He lifted her higher, up on her knees so she knelt astride him, then held her there. He took her nipple into his mouth again, the sharp pull of it like an electric charge directly into her sex, while his wicked fingers played with the other. Alicia shuddered uncontrollably in his arms, but he held her still, taking his time.

And all the while the hardest part of him was just beneath her, just out of reach.

"Please..." she whispered frantically. "Nikolai, *please*..."

"Unlike you," he said in a voice she hardly recognized, it was so thick with desire, with need, with this mighty storm that had taken hold of them both, "I occasionally obey."

He shifted then, taking her hips in his hands, and then he thrust up into her in a single deep stroke, possessive and sure.

At last.

And for a moment, they simply stared at each other. Marveling in that slick, sweet, perfect fit. Nikolai smiled, and she'd never seen his blue eyes so clear. So warm.

Alicia moved her hips, and his breath hissed out into a curse. And then she simply pleased them both.

She moved on him sinuously, sweetly. She bent forward to taste the strong line of his neck, salt and fire. She made love to him with every part of her, worshipping him with everything she had. She couldn't say the words, not to a man like Nikolai, not yet, but she could show him.

And she did.

Until they were both shuddering and desperate.

Until he'd stopped speaking English.

Until he rolled her over and drove into her with all of his dark intensity, all of that battle-charged skill and precision. She exulted beneath him, meeting every thrust, filled with that ache, that wide-open rift he'd torn into her, that only this—only he—could ever soothe.

And when he sent her spinning off into that wild magic for the third time, he came with her, holding her as if he loved her too, that miraculous smile all over his beautiful face.

At last, she thought.

"You're in love with him, aren't you?"

Alicia had been so lost in her own head, in Nikolai, that she hadn't heard the door to the women's lounge open. It took her a moment to realize that the woman standing next to her at the long counter was speaking to her.

And another moment for what she'd said to penetrate.

Veronika.

The moment stretched out, silent and tense.

Alicia could hear the sounds of the ball, muffled through the lounge's walls. The music from the band and the dull roar of all those well-dressed, elegant people, dancing and eating and making merry in their polite way. She'd almost forgotten that *this* was the reason she was here at all. This woman watching her with that calculating gleam in her eyes, as if she knew things about Alicia that Alicia did not.

There was nothing hard or evil-looking about Veronika, as Alicia had half expected from what little Nikolai had said of her. Her hair cascaded down her back in a tumble of platinum waves. She wore a copper gown that made her slender figure look lithe and supple. Aside from the way she looked at Alicia, she was the picture of a certain kind of smooth, curated, very nearly ageless beauty. The kind that, amongst other things, cost a tremendous amount to maintain and was therefore an advertising campaign in itself.

Alicia told herself there was no need for anxiety. She was wearing that bold, gorgeous blue dress, alive with sequins, that had been waiting for her in her room. It clung to her from the top of one shoulder to the floor, highlighting all of her curves, sparkling with every breath, and until this moment she'd felt beautiful in it. Nikolai had smiled that sexy wolf's smile when he saw her in it, and they'd been late coming here tonight. Very late.

Standing with him in this castle-turned-hotel, dressed for a ball in a gorgeous gown with the man she loved, she'd felt as if she might be the princess in their odd little fairy tale after all.

She'd let herself forget.

"Tell me that you're not so foolish," Veronika said then, breaking the uncomfortable silence. She sounded almost... sympathetic? It put Alicia's teeth on edge. "Tell me you're smart enough to see his little games for what they are."

It was amazing how closely this woman's voice resembled the ones in her head, Alicia thought then. It was almost funny, though she was terribly afraid that if she tried to laugh, she'd sob instead. She was still too raw from last night's intensity. A bit too fragile from a day spent in the aftermath of such a great storm.

She wasn't ready for this—whatever this was.

"If you want to speak to Nikolai," she said when she was certain her tone would be perfectly even, almost blandly polite, "he's in the ballroom. Would you like me to show you?"

"You must have asked yourself why he chose you," Veronika said conversationally, as if this was a chat between friends. She leaned closer to the mirror to inspect her lipstick, then turned to face Alicia. "Look at you. So wholesome. So *real*. A charity worker, of all things. Not his usual type, are you?"

She didn't actually *tell* Alicia to compare the two of them. She didn't have to, as Alicia was well aware that all of Nikolai's previous women had been some version of the one who stood in front of her now. Slender like whippets, ruthlessly so. Immaculately and almost uniformly manicured in precisely the same way, from their perfect hair to their tiny bodies and their extremely expensive clothes. The kind of women rich men always had on their arms, like interchangeable trophies, which was precisely how Nikolai treated them.

Hadn't Alicia told him no one would believe he was interested in her after that kind of parade?

"I can't say I have the slightest idea what his 'type' is," she lied to Veronika. "I've never paid it as much attention as you've seemed to do."

Veronika sighed, as if Alicia made her sad. "He's using you to tell a very specific story in the tabloids. You must know this."

Alicia told herself she didn't feel a chill trickle down her spine, that something raw didn't bloom deep within at that neat little synopsis of the past few weeks of her life. She told herself that while Veronika was partly right, she couldn't know about the rest of it. She couldn't have any idea about the things that truly mattered. The things that were only theirs.

"Or," she said, trying desperately not to sound defensive, not to give any of herself away, "Nikolai is a famous man, and the tabloids take pictures of him wherever he goes. No great conspiracy, no 'story.' I'm sorry to disappoint you."

But she was lying, of course, and Veronika shook her head.

"Who do you think was the mastermind behind Ivan Korovin's numerous career changes—from fighter to Hollywood leading man to philanthropist?" she asked, a razor's edge beneath her seemingly casual tone, the trace of Russian in her voice not nearly as appealing as Nikolai's. "What about Nikolai himself? A soldier, then a security specialist, now a CEO—how do you think he manages to sell these new versions of himself, one after the next?"

"I don't see—"

"Nikolai is a very talented manipulator," Veronika said, with that sympathetic note in her voice that grated more each time Alicia heard it. "He can make you believe anything he wants you to believe." Her gaze moved over Alicia, and then she smiled. Sadly. "He can make you fall in love, if that's what he needs from you."

Alicia stared back at her, at this woman who *smiled* as she listed off all of Alicia's worst fears, and knew that she should have walked away from this conversation the moment it started. The moment she'd realized who Veronika was. Nothing good could come of this. She could already feel that dark hopelessness curling inside of her, ready to suck her in....

But her pride wouldn't let her leave without putting up some kind of fight—without making it clear, somehow, that Veronika hadn't got to her. Even if she had.

"You'll forgive me," she said, holding the other woman's gaze, "if I don't rush to take your advice to heart. I'm afraid the spiteful ex makes for a bit of a questionable source, don't you think?"

She was congratulating herself as she turned for the door. What mattered was that she loved Nikolai, and what she'd seen in him last night and today. What she knew to be true. Not the doubts and fears and possible outright lies this woman—

"Do you even know what this is about?"

Alicia told herself not to turn back around. Not to cede her tiny little bit of higher ground—

But her feet wouldn't listen. They stopped moving of their own accord. She stood there, her hand on the door, and ordered herself to walk through it.

Instead, like a fool, she turned around.

"I try not to involve myself in other people's relationships, past or present," she said pointedly, as if the fact she hadn't left wasn't evidence of surrender. As if the other woman wasn't aware of it. "As it's none of my affair."

"He didn't tell you."

Veronika was enjoying herself now, clearly. She'd dropped the sympathy routine and was now watching Alicia the way a cobra might, when it was poised to strike.

Leave, Alicia ordered herself desperately. *Now.*

Because she knew that whatever Veronika was about to say, she didn't want to hear it.

"Of course he didn't tell you." Veronika picked up her jeweled clutch and sauntered toward Alicia. "I told you, he's very manipulative. This is how he operates."

Alicia felt much too hot, her pulse was so frantic it was almost distracting, and there was a weight in her stomach that felt like concrete, pinning her to the ground where she stood. Making it impossible to move, to run, to escape whatever blow she could feel coming.

She could only stare at Veronika, and wait.

The other woman drew close, never taking her intent gaze from Alicia's.

"Nikolai wants to know if my son is his," she said.

It was like the ground had been taken out from under her, Alicia thought. Like she'd been dropped into a deep, black hole. She almost couldn't grasp all the things that swirled in her then, each more painful than the next.

Not here, she thought, fighting to keep her reaction to herself, and failing, if that malicious gleam in Veronika's eyes was any indication. *You can't deal with this here!*

She would have given anything not to ask the next question, not to give this woman that satisfaction, but she couldn't help herself. She couldn't stop. None of this had ever been real, and she needed to accept that, once and for all. None of this had ever been—nor ever would be—hers.

No matter how badly she wished otherwise. No matter how deeply, how terribly, how irrevocably she loved him.

"Is he?" she asked, hating herself. Betraying herself. "Is your son Nikolai's?"

And Veronika smiled.

Nikolai saw Alicia from the other side of the ballroom, a flash of shimmering blue and that particular walk of hers that he would know across whole cities.

He felt it like a touch. Like she could reach him simply by entering the same room.

Mine, he thought, and that band around his chest clutched hard, but he was almost used to it now. It meant this woman and her smile were his. It meant that odd sensation, almost a dizziness, that he found he didn't mind at all when he looked at her.

It meant this strange new springtime inside of him, this odd thaw.

At some point last night, it had occurred to him that he might survive this, after all.

Nikolai had lost track of how many times they'd come together in the night, the storm in him howling itself out with each touch, each taste of her impossible sweetness. All of her light, his. To bathe in as he pleased.

And in the morning, she'd still been there. He couldn't remember the last time any woman had slept in his bed, and he remembered too well that the first time, Alicia had sneaked away with the dawn.

Daylight was a different animal. Hushed, he thought. Something like sacred. He'd washed every inch of her delectable body in the steamy shower, learning her with his eyes as well as his greedy hands. Then he'd slowly lost his mind when she'd knelt before him on the thick rug outside the glass enclosure, taking him into her mouth until he'd groaned out his pleasure to the fogged-up mirrors.

He didn't think he'd ever get enough of her.

She curled her feet beneath her when she sat on the sofa beside him. Her favorite television program was so embarrassing, she'd claimed, that she refused to name it. She was addicted to cinnamon and licked up every last bit of it from the pastries they'd had at breakfast, surreptitiously wetting her fingertip and pressing it against the crumbs until they were gone. She read a great many books, preferred tea first thing in the morning but coffee later, and could talk, at length, about architecture and why she thought that if she had it to do over again, she might study it at university.

And that was only today. One day of learning her, and he'd barely scratched the surface. Nikolai thought that maybe, this time, he wouldn't have to settle for what he could get. This time, he might let himself want…everything. Especially the things he'd thought for so long he couldn't have, that she handed him so sweetly, so unreservedly, as if they were already his.

Mine, he thought again, in a kind of astonishment that it might be true. That it was even possible. *She's mine.*

Alicia disappeared in the jostling crowd, and when she reappeared she'd almost reached him. Nikolai frowned. She was holding herself strangely, and there was a certain fullness in her eyes, as if she were about—

But then he saw the woman who walked behind her, that vicious little smile on her cold lips and victory in her gaze, and his blood ran cold.

Like ice in his veins and this time, it hurt. It burned as he froze.

"*Privyet,* Nikolai," Veronika purred triumphantly when the two of them finally reached him. As sure of herself as she'd ever been. And as callous. "Look who I discovered. Such a coincidence, no?"

This, he thought, was why he had no business anywhere near a bright creature like Alicia. He'd destroy her without even meaning to do it. He'd already started.

This is who you are, he reminded himself bitterly, and it was worse because he'd let himself believe otherwise. He'd fallen for the lie that he could ever be anything but the monster he was. It only took a glance at Veronika, that emblem of the bad choices he'd made and with whom, to make him see that painful truth.

"Alicia. Look at me."

And when she did, when she finally raised her gaze to his, he understood. It went off inside him like a grenade, shredding him into strips, and that was only the tiniest fraction of the pain, the torment, he saw in Alicia's lovely brown eyes.

Dulled with the pain of whatever Veronika had said to her.

He'd done this. He'd put her in harm's way. He was responsible.

Nikolai had been tested last night. He'd had the opportunity to do the right thing, to imagine himself a good man and then act like one, and he'd failed. Utterly.

All of his demons were right.

Nikolai moved swiftly then, a cold clarity sweeping through him like a wind. He ordered Veronika to make herself scarce, told her he'd come find her later and that she'd better have the answer he wanted, and he did it in Russian so Alicia wouldn't hear the particularly descriptive words he used to get his point across.

"No need," Veronika said, also in Russian, looking satisfied and cruel. He wanted to wring her neck. "I had the test done long ago. You're not the father. Do you want to know who is?" She'd smiled at Nikolai's frigid glare. "I'll have the paperwork sent to your attorney."

"Do that," Nikolai growled, and if there was a flash of pain at another small hope snuffed out, he ignored it. He'd see to it that Stefan was taken care of no matter what, and right now, he had other things to worry about.

He forgot Veronika the moment he looked away. He took Alicia's arm and he led her toward the door, amazed that she let him touch her. When they got to the great foyer, he let her go so he could pull his mobile from his tuxedo jacket and send a quick, terse text to his personal assistant.

"Whatever you're about to say, don't," he told her when she started to speak, not sure he could keep the riot of self-hatred at bay just then. She pressed her lips together and scowled fiercely at the floor, and his self-loathing turned black.

Your first response when you feel something is to attack, Ivan had said. But Nikolai had no idea how to stop. And for the first time since he was a boy, he realized that that sinking feeling in him was fear.

He slipped his mobile back in his pocket, and guided her toward the front of the hotel, not stopping until they'd reached the glass doors that led out through the colonnaded entrance into the December night. Above them, the palatial stairs soared toward the former palace's grand facade, but this entranceway was more private. And it was where his people would meet them and take her away from him. Take her somewhere—anywhere she was safe.

Finally, he let himself look at her again.

She was hugging herself, her arms bare and tight over her body. There was misery in her dark eyes, her full lips trembled, and he'd done this. He'd hurt her. Veronika had hurt *him,* and he'd been well nigh indestructible. Why had he imagined she wouldn't do her damage to something as bright and clean as Alicia, simply to prove she could? She'd probably been sharpening her talons since the first picture hit the tabloids.

This was entirely his fault.

"Your ex-wife is an interesting woman," Alicia said.

"She's malicious and cruel, and those are her better qualities," Nikolai bit out. "What did she say to you?"

"It doesn't matter what she said." There was a torn, thick sound in her voice, and she tilted back her chin as if she was trying to be brave. He hated himself. "Everyone has secrets. God knows, I kept mine for long enough."

"Alicia—"

"I know what it's like to disappoint people, Nikolai," she said fiercely. "I know what it's like to become someone the people you love won't look at anymore, whether you've earned it or not."

He almost laughed. "You can't possibly understand the kind of life I've led. I dreamed about a father who would care about me at all, even one who shunned me for imagined sins."

"Congratulations," she threw at him. "Your pain wins. But a secret is still a—"

"Secrets?" He frowned at her, but then he understood, and the sound he let out then was far too painful to be a laugh. "She told you about Stefan."

And it killed him that Alicia smiled then, for all it was a pale shadow of her usual brightness. That she gave him that kind of gift when he could see how much she hurt.

"Is that his name?"

"He's not mine," he said harshly. "That's what she told me back there. And it's not a surprise. I wanted to be sure."

"But you wanted him to be yours," Alicia said, reading him as she always did, and he felt that band around his chest pull so tight it hurt to breathe, nearly cutting him in half.

"You want to make me a better man than I am," he told her then, losing his grip on that darkness inside of him. "And I want to believe it more than you can imagine. But it's a lie."

"Nikolai—"

"The truth is, even if Stefan was my son, he'd be better off without me." It was almost as if he was angry—as if this was his temper. But he knew it was worse than that. It was that twisted, charred, leftover thing she'd coaxed out of its cave. It was what remained of his heart, and she had to *see*. She had to *know*. "I was drunk most of the five years I thought I was his father. And now I'm—" He shook his head. *"This."*

"You're what?" Her dark eyes were glassy. "Sober?"

He felt that hard and low, like a kick to the gut. He didn't know what was happening to him, what she'd done. He only knew he had to remove her from this—get her to a minimum safe distance where he could never hurt her again, not even by mistake.

"Seeing Veronika made things perfectly clear to me," he told her. "All I will ever do is drag you down until I've stolen everything. Until I've ruined you. I can promise you that." He wanted to touch her, but he wouldn't. He couldn't risk it. "I would rather be without you than subject you to this—this sick, twisted horror show."

He was too close to her, so close he could hear that quick, indrawn breath, so close he could smell that scent of hers that drove him wild, even now.

He was no better than an animal.

Alicia looked at him for a long moment. "Are you still in love with her?" she asked.

"Do I *love* her?" Nikolai echoed in disbelief. "What the hell is *love*, Alicia?"

His voice was too loud. He heard it bouncing back at

him from the polished marble floors, saw Alicia straighten her back as if she needed to stand tall against it. He hated public scenes and yet he couldn't stop. He rubbed his hands over his face to keep himself from punching the hard stone wall. It would only be pain, and it would fade. And he would still be right here. He would still be him.

"Veronika made me feel numb," he said instead, not realizing the truth of it until he said it out loud. Something seemed to break open in him then, some kind of painful knotted box he'd been holding on to for much too long. "She was an anesthetic. And I thought that was better than being alone." He glared at her. "And she didn't love me either, if that's your next question. I was her way out of a dead-end life, and she took it."

"I think that however she's capable of it, she does love you," Alicia argued softly. "Or she wouldn't want so badly to hurt you."

"Yes," he said, his voice grim. "Exactly. That is the kind of love I inspire. A vile loathing that time only exacerbates. A hatred so great she needed to hunt you down and take it out on you. Such are my gifts." He prowled toward Alicia then, not even knowing what he did until she'd backed up against one of the marble columns.

But he didn't stop. He couldn't stop.

"I was told I loved my parents," he said, the words flooding from him, as dark and harsh as the place they'd lived inside him all this time. "But I can't remember them, so how would I know? And I love my brother, if that's what it's called." He looked around, but he didn't see anything but the past. And the demons who jeered at him from all of those old, familiar shadows. "Ivan feels a sense of guilt and obligation to me because he got out first, and I let him feel it because I envy him for escaping so quickly while

I stayed there and rotted. And then I made it my singular goal to ruin the only happiness he'd ever known."

He'd thought he was empty before, but now he knew. This was even worse. This was unbearable, and yet he had no choice but to bear it.

"That's a great brotherly love, isn't it?"

"Nikolai," she said thickly, and she'd lost the battle with her tears. They streaked down her pretty face, each one an accusation, each one another knife in his side. "You aren't responsible for what happened to you as a child. With all the work you do, you can't truly believe otherwise. You *survived*, Nikolai. That's what matters."

And once again, he wanted to believe her. He wanted to be that man she was called to defend. He wanted to be anything other than *this*.

"I've never felt anything like these things I feel for you," he told her then, raw and harsh, so harsh it hurt him, too, and then she started to shake, and that hurt him even more. "That light of yours. The way you look at me—the way you *see* me." He reached out as if to touch her face, but dropped his hand back to his side. "I knew it that first night. I was *happy* when you walked into that conference room, and it terrified me, because do you know what I do with *happy*?"

"You do not kill it," she told him fiercely. "You try, and you fail. Happiness isn't an enemy, Nikolai. You can't beat it up. It won't fight back, and eventually, if you let it, it wins."

"I will suck you dry, tear you down, take everything until nothing remains." He moved closer, so outside himself that he was almost glad that he was so loud, that he was acting like this so she could see with her own eyes what kind of man he was. "Do I love you, Alicia? Is that what this is? This charred and twisted thing that will only bring you pain?"

"I love you," she said quietly. Clearly and distinctly, her

eyes on his. Without a single quaver in her voice. Without so much as a blink. Then she shifted, moved closer. "I love you, Nikolai."

Nikolai stilled. Inside and out. And those words hung in him like stained glass, that light of hers making them glow and shine in a cascade of colors he'd never known existed before.

He thought he almost hated her for that. He told himself he'd rather not know.

He leaned in until her mouth was close enough to kiss, and his voice dropped low. Savage. "Why would you do something so appallingly self-destructive?"

"Because, you idiot," she said calmly, not backing away from him, not looking even slightly intimidated. "*I love you.* There's always a risk when you give someone your heart. They might crush it. But that's no reason not to do it."

He felt as if he was falling, though he wasn't. He only wished he was. He leaned toward her, propping his hands on either side of her head as he had once before, then lowering his forehead until he rested it against hers.

And for a moment he simply breathed her in, letting his eyes fall shut, letting her scent and her warmth surround him.

He felt her hands come up to hold on to him, digging in at his hips with that strong grip that had already undone him once before, and he felt a long shudder work through him.

"This is the part where you run for cover, Alicia," he whispered fiercely. "I told you why I couldn't lose control. Now you know."

He heard her sigh. She tipped back her head, then lifted her hands up to take his face between them. When he opened his eyes, what he saw in her gaze made him shake.

"This is where you save yourself," he ground out at her.

She smiled at him, though more tears spilled from her eyes. She held him as if she had no intention of letting him go. She looked at him as if he was precious. Even now. "And then who saves you?"

CHAPTER TEN

Nikolai's hands slipped from the marble column behind her, his arms came around her, and he held her so tightly, so closely, that Alicia wasn't sure she could breathe.

And she didn't care.

He held her like that for a long time.

A member of the hotel staff came over to quietly inquire if all was well, and she waved him away. A trio of black-suited people who could only be part of Nikolai's pack of assistants appeared, and she frowned at them until they backed off.

And outside, in the courtyard of the former palace, it began to snow.

Nikolai let out a long, shaky breath and lifted his head. He kissed her, so soft and so sweet it made her smile.

"If I had a heart, I would give it to you," he said then, very seriously. "But I don't."

She shook her head at him, and kissed him back, losing herself in that for a long time. His eyes were haunted, and she loved him so much she didn't know if she wanted to laugh or cry or scream—it seemed too big to contain.

And he loved her, too. He'd as much as said so. He just didn't know what that meant.

So Alicia would have to show him. Step by step, smile by smile, laugh by laugh, until he got it. Starting now.

"You have a heart, Nikolai," she told him gently, smiling up at that beautifully hard face, that perfectly austere mouth, her would-be Tin Man. "It's just been broken into so many pieces, and so long ago, you never learned how to use it properly."

"You're the only one who thinks so," he said softly.

She reached out and laid her hand on his chest, never looking away from him.

"I can feel it. It's right here. I promise."

"And I suppose you happen to know how one goes about putting back together a critically underused heart, no doubt fallen into disrepair after all these years," he muttered, but his hands were moving slow and sweet up her back and then down her arms to take her hands in his.

"I have a few ideas," she agreed. "And your heart is not a junked-out car left by the side of a road somewhere, Nikolai. It's real and it's beating and you've been using it all along."

He looked over his shoulder then, as if he'd only then remembered where they were. One of his assistants appeared from around the corner as if she'd been watching all along, and he nodded at her, but didn't move. Then he looked out the glass doors, at the snow falling into the golden-lit courtyard and starting to gather on the ground.

"I hate snow," he said.

"Merry Christmas to you, too, Ebenezer Scrooge," Alicia said dryly. She slid an arm around his waist and looked outside. "It's beautiful. A fairy tale," she said, smiling at him, "just as you promised me in the beginning."

"I think you're confused." But she saw that smile of his.

It started in his eyes, made them gleam. "I promised you fangs. And tears. Both of which I've delivered, in spades."

"There are no wolves in a story involving ball gowns, Nikolai. I believe that's a rule."

"Which fairy tale is this again? The ones I remember involved very few ball gowns, and far more darkness." His mouth moved into that crooked curve she adored, but his eyes were serious when they met hers. "I don't know how to be a normal man, Alicia. Much less a good one." His smile faded. "And I certainly don't know how to be anything like good for you."

Alicia smiled at him again, wondering how she'd never known that the point of a heart was to break. Because only then could it grow. And swell big enough to hold the things she felt for Nikolai.

"Let's start with normal and work from there," she managed to say. "Come to Christmas at my parents' house. Sit down. Eat a huge Christmas dinner. Make small talk with my family." She grinned. "I think you'll do fine."

He looked at her, that fine mouth of his close again to grim.

"I don't know if I can be what you want," he said. "I don't know—"

"I want you," she said. She shook her head when he started to speak. "And all you have to do is love me. As best you can, Nikolai. For as long as you're able. And I'll promise to do the same."

It was like a vow. It hung there between them, hushed and huge, with only the falling snow and the dark Prague night as witness.

He looked at her for a long time, and then he leaned down and kissed her the way he had on that London street. Hard and demanding, hot and sure, making her his.

"I can do that," he said, when he lifted his head, a thousand brand-new promises in his eyes, and she believed every one. "I can try."

Nikolai stood facing his brother on a deep blue July afternoon. The California sky arched above them, cloudless and clear, while out beyond them the Pacific Ocean rolled smooth and gleaming all the way to the horizon.

"Are you ready?" Ivan barked in gruff Russian. He wore his game face, the one he'd used in the ring, fierce and focused and meant to be terrifying.

Nikolai only smiled.

"Is this the intimidating trash talk portion of the afternoon?" he asked coolly. "Because I didn't sign up to be bored to death, Vanya. I thought this was a fight."

Ivan eyed him.

"You insist on writing checks you can't cash, little brother," he said. "And sadly for you, I am the bank."

They both crouched down into position, studying each other, looking for tells—

Until a sharp wail cut through the air, and Ivan broke his stance to look back toward his Malibu house and the figures who'd walked out from the great glass doors and were heading their way.

Nikolai did a leg sweep without pausing to think about it, and had the great satisfaction of taking Ivan down to the ground.

"You must never break your concentration, brother," he drawled, patronizingly, while Ivan lay sprawled out before him. "Surely, as an undefeated world champion, you should know this."

Ivan's dark eyes promised retribution even as he jackknifed up and onto his feet.

"Enjoy that, Kolya. It will be your last and only victory."

And then he grinned and slapped Nikolai on the back, throwing an arm over his shoulders as they started toward the house and the two women who walked to meet them.

Nikolai watched Alicia, that smile of hers brighter even than a California summer and her lovely voice on the wind, that kick of laughter and cleverness audible even when he couldn't hear the words.

"You owe him an apology," she'd told him. It had been January, and they'd been tucked up in that frilly pink bedroom of hers that he found equal parts absurd and endearing. Though he did enjoy her four-poster bed. "He's your brother. Miranda is afraid of you, and she still risked telling you how hurt he was."

He'd taken her advice, stilted and uncertain.

And now, Nikolai thought as he drew close to her with his brother at his side, he was learning how to build things, not destroy them. He was learning how to trust.

The baby in Miranda's arm wailed again, and both women immediately made a cooing sort of sound that Nikolai had never heard Alicia make before his plane had landed in Los Angeles. Beside him, Ivan shook his head. And then reached over to pluck the baby from his wife's arms.

"Naturally, Ivan has the magic touch," Miranda said to Alicia with a roll of her eyes, as the crying miraculously stopped.

"How annoying," Alicia replied, her lips twitching.

Nikolai stared down at the tiny pink thing that looked even smaller and more delicate in Ivan's big grip.

"Another generation of Korovins," he said. He caught Miranda looking at him as he spoke, and thought her smile was slightly warmer than the last time. Progress. He returned his attention to Ivan and the baby. "I don't think you thought this through, brother."

"It's terrible, I know," Ivan agreed. He leaned close and

kissed his daughter's soft forehead, contentment radiating from him. "A disaster waiting to happen."

Nikolai smiled. "Only if she fights like you."

Later, after he and Ivan spent a happy few hours throwing each other around and each claiming victory, he found Alicia out on the balcony that wrapped around their suite of rooms. He walked up behind her silently, watching the breeze dance through the cloud of her black curls, admiring the short and flirty dress she wore in a bright shade of canary yellow, showing off all of those toned brown limbs he wanted wrapped around him.

Now. Always.

She gasped when he picked her up, but she was already smiling when he turned her in his arms. As if she could read his mind—and he often believed she could—she hooked her legs around his waist and let him hold her there, both of them smiling at the immediate burst of heat. The fire that only grew higher and hotter between them.

"Move in with me," he said, and her smile widened. "Live with me."

"Here in Malibu in this stunning house?" she asked, teasing him. "I accept. I've always wanted to be a Hollywood star. Or at least adjacent to one."

"The offer is for rain and cold, London and me," he said. He shifted her higher, held her closer.

"This is a very difficult decision," she said, but her eyes were dancing. "Are you sure you don't want to come live with me and Rosie instead? She's stopped shrieking and dropping things when you walk in rooms. And she did predict that the night we met would be momentous. She's a prophet, really."

"Move in with me," he said again, and nipped at her neck, her perfect mouth. He thought of that look on his brother's face, that deep pleasure, that peace. "Marry me, someday. When it's right. Make babies with me. I want to live this life of yours, where everything is multicolored and happiness wins."

And then he said the words, because he finally knew what they meant. She'd promised him he had a heart, and she'd taught it how to beat. He could feel it now, pounding hard.

"I love you, Alicia."

She smiled at him then as if he'd given her the world, when Nikolai knew it was the other way around. She'd lit him up, set him free. She'd given him back his brother, broke him out of that cold, dark prison that had been his life. She was so bright she'd nearly blinded him, all those beautiful colors and all of them his to share, if he liked. If he let her.

"Is that a yes?" He pulled back to look at her. "It's okay if you don't—"

"Yes," she said through her smile. "Yes to everything. Always yes."

She'd loved him when he was nothing more than a monster, and she'd made him a man.

Love hardly covered it. But it was a start.

"Look at you," she whispered, her dark eyes shining. She smoothed her hands over his shoulder, plucking at the T-shirt she'd bought him and made him wear. He'd enjoyed the negotiation. "Put the man in a blue shirt and he changes his whole life."

She laughed, and as ever, it stopped the world.

"No, *solnyshka*," Nikolai murmured, his mouth against hers so he could feel that smile, taste the magic of her laughter, the miracle of the heart she'd made beat again in him, hot and alive and real. "That was you."

* * * * *

LET'S TALK
Romance

For exclusive extracts, competitions
and special offers, find us online:

- facebook.com/millsandboon
- @MillsandBoon
- @MillsandBoonUK

Get in touch on 01413 063232

For all the latest titles coming soon, visit
millsandboon.co.uk/nextmonth

WANT EVEN MORE ROMANCE?

SUBSCRIBE AND SAVE TODAY!

'Mills & Boon books, the perfect way to escape for an hour or so.'

MISS W. DYER

'Excellent service, promptly delivered and very good subscription choices.'

MISS A. PEARSON

'You get fantastic special offers and the chance to get books before they hit the shops.'

MRS V. HALL

Visit millsandboon.co.uk/Subscribe and save on brand new books.

MILLS & BOON
A ROMANCE FOR EVERY READER

- **FREE** delivery direct to your door
- **EXCLUSIVE** offers every month
- **SAVE** up to 25% on pre-paid subscriptions

SUBSCRIBE AND SAVE

millsandboon.co.uk/Subscribe

MILLS & BOON

THE HEART OF ROMANCE

A ROMANCE FOR EVERY KIND OF READER

MODERN — Prepare to be swept off your feet by sophisticated, sexy and seductive heroes, in some of the world's most glamourous and romantic locations, where power and passion collide.
8 stories per month.

HISTORICAL — Escape with historical heroes from time gone by. Whether your passion is for wicked Regency Rakes, muscled Vikings or rugge[d] Highlanders, awaken the romance of the past.
6 stories per month.

MEDICAL — Set your pulse racing with dedicated, delectable doctors in the high-pressure world of medicine, where emotions run high an[d] passion, comfort and love are the best medicine.
6 stories per month.

True Love — Celebrate true love with tender stories of heartfelt romance, fr[om] the rush of falling in love to the joy a new baby can bring, and focus on the emotional heart of a relationship.
8 stories per month.

Desire — Indulge in secrets and scandal, intense drama and plenty of siz[zling] hot action with powerful and passionate heroes who have it all: wealth, status, good looks…everything but the right woman.
6 stories per month.

HEROES — Experience all the excitement of a gripping thriller, with an int[ense] romance at its heart. Resourceful, true-to-life women and stron[g,] fearless men face danger and desire - a killer combination!
8 stories per month.

DARE — Sensual love stories featuring smart, sassy heroines you'd want a[s a] best friend, and compelling intense heroes who are worthy of t[hem.]
4 stories per month.

To see which titles are coming soon, please visit

millsandboon.co.uk/nextmonth

JOIN US ON SOCIAL MEDIA!

Stay up to date with our latest releases, author news and gossip, special offers and discounts, and all the behind-the-scenes action from Mills & Boon...

millsandboon

millsandboonuk

millsandboon

It might just be true love...

GET YOUR ROMANCE FIX!

MILLS & BOON
— *blog* —

Get the latest romance news, exclusive author interviews, story extracts and much more!

blog.millsandboon.co.uk